Ernst Wicher

The Green Gate. A Romance

Ernst Wichert

The Green Gate. A Romance

Reprint of the original, first published in 1875.

1st Edition 2024 | ISBN: 978-3-38538-726-3

Verlag (Publisher): Outlook Verlag GmbH, Zeilweg 44, 60439 Frankfurt, Deutschland
Vertretungsberechtigt (Authorized to represent): E. Roepke, Zeilweg 44, 60439 Frankfurt, Deutschland
Druck (Print): Books on Demand GmbH, In de Tarpen 42, 22848 Norderstedt, Deutschland

THE GREEN GATE.

POPULAR WORKS

AFTER THE GERMAN.

BY MRS. A. L. WISTER.

THE SECOND WIFE. After the German of E. MARLITT. By Mrs. A. L. WISTER. 12mo. Fine cloth.

THE OLD MAM'SELLE'S SECRET. After the German of E. MARLITT. By Mrs. A. L. WISTER. 12mo. Fine cloth. $1.50.

"A more charming story, and one which, having once commenced, it seemed more difficult to leave, we have not met with for many a day."—*The Round Table.*

GOLD ELSIE. After the German of E. MARLITT. By Mrs. A. L. WISTER. 12mo. Fine cloth. $1.50.

"A charming story charmingly told."—*Baltimore Gazette.*

COUNTESS GISELA. After the German of E. MARLITT. By Mrs. A. L. WISTER. 12mo. Fine cloth. $1.50.

" There is more dramatic power in this than in any of the stories by the same author that we have read."—*New Orleans Times.*

THE LITTLE MOORLAND PRINCESS. After the German of E. MARLITT. By Mrs. A. L. WISTER. 12mo. Fine cloth. $1.75.

" By far the best foreign romance of the season."—*Philadelphia Press.*

ONLY A GIRL. After the German of WILHELMINE VON HILLERN. By Mrs. A. L. WISTER. 12mo. Fine cloth. $2.00.

" This is a charming work, charmingly written, and no one who reads it can lay it down without feeling impressed with the superior talent of its gifted author."—*Pittsburg Dispatch.*

ENCHANTING AND ENCHANTED; or, FAIRY SPELLS. From the German of HACKLÄNDER. By Mrs. A. L. WISTER. Illustrated. 12mo. Fine cloth. $1.50.

"A charming book in the best style of German romance, pure in sentiment and elegant in diction, with a nameless artlessness, which gives tone to the language of the heart."—*Christian Intelligencer.*

WHY DID HE NOT DIE? After the German of AD. VON VOLCKHAUSEN. By Mrs. A. L. WISTER. 12mo. Fine cloth. $1.75.

" From the beginning to the end the interest never flags, and the characters and scenes are drawn with great warmth and power."—*New York Herald.*

HULDA; or, THE DELIVERER. After the German of F. LEWALD. By Mrs. A. L. WISTER. 12mo. Fine cloth. $1.75.

⁎ For sale by all Booksellers, or will be sent by mail, postage paid, upon receipt of price by

J. B. LIPPINCOTT & CO., Publishers, Philadelphia.

THE

GREEN GATE.

A ROMANCE.

BY

ERNST WICHERT.

TRANSLATED FROM THE GERMAN

By MRS. A. L. WISTER,

TRANSLATOR OF "THE SECOND WIFE," "HULDA," "THE OLD MAM'SELLE'S SECRET,"
"ONLY A GIRL," ETC.

PHILADELPHIA:

J. B. LIPPINCOTT & CO.

1875.

THE GREEN GATE.

CHAPTER I.

THE train was rushing through one of the many tunnels on the road across the Apennines from Bologna to Florence.

In a second-class carriage the flame of the dim oil lamp in the roof was just dying out. It flashed up fitfully now and then, as if to look after matters in the carriage; and at each revival a fat, middle-aged Italian woman, leaning back against the black cushions in a corner, opened her sleepy eyes, only to close them immediately. By her sat a puny little man, the end of a cigar held loosely between the fingers of the hand that hung down at his side, his hat upon the back of his head,—evidently, judging from the tone of the conversation lately carried on between himself and the lady, her husband. In another corner crouched a Frenchman, his knees drawn up almost to his chin, his feet cased in embroidered slippers; the travelling-bag hanging above him proclaimed him a commercial traveller. The third corner was occupied by a man who had entered the carriage at Poretta, and had transferred a number of stones from his various pockets to a small wallet which he carried, already near'y full of such treasures. From the colour of his hair and beard, indeed, from the entire character of his face and figure, he would have passed for Italian, and he exchanged several fluent remarks in that tongue with the guard before the train left the station at Poretta. Immediately afterwards, however, he had addressed a young man sitting opposite him in German, receiving from him several curt answers in the same tongue, which provoked the smiling observation, " I was not mistaken, then, in supposing you a countryman of mine? Only a German could cast such keen and longing glances from the carriage-window during the short delay at the station. Confess that the frequent tunnels that have snatched from your gaze and plunged into blackest night so much of the romantic scenery of the Apennines have fairly disgusted you, and that you are ready to cross the mountains on foot that you may see something of the country and its inhabitants." The stranger admitted that it was so, except that his slight knowledge of Italian made any departure from the beaten track of travel impossible for him, while really one was indemnified now and then for the sudden subterranean night by exquisite glimpses of mountain and valley, their beauty certainly enhanced by force of contrast. Never had the time flown so quickly, he thought, as during these last few hours. " We are a contented race," the other responded, " and we are never at a loss to find reasons for enjoyment." And there the conversation halted for awhile.

The traveller who had shown such readiness to be pleased maintained during the remainder of the journey his eager attitude at the open window, determined to lose no glimpse, however fleeting, of picturesque beauty. He sat, leaning forward upon his elbow, immovable, even while the train passed through the longest tunnels, gazing out upon the black walls of rock, dotted here and there with sparks from the locomotive, patiently waiting for the first glimmer of daylight to dawn upon the blackness, heralding a return to blue, sunny skies, lovelier than ever after the moments of " shades forlorn." Evidently his mind was so absorbed in thus waiting and enjoying that he had no time for conversation : as if fearful of losing some instant view if he allowed his attention to stray even momentarily, he returned monosyllabic answers to questions addressed to him, scarcely turning his head as he spoke. Nevertheless, his more vivacious neighbor opposite contrived to learn that he was a merchant, or the son of a merchant, and from a commercial city in Northern Germany, that he had never been in Italy before, and hoped to travel as far as Palermo. It was best, he thought, to plan as extensive a journey as possible, since there was no knowing when he should be able to leave his native place again. This was his most lengthy remark, made in the pitchy darkness of a seemingly interminable tunnel.

And now they had just entered the last. " Be prepared now," said the other, " to enjoy something really worth seeing, as I remember it upon my last visit to Italy, when I was obliged from lack of time to make use of the railway. I usually prefer the old road across Lojano and Pietramala. We are about to leave all these rocks, and at our feet we shall have the lovely valley of the Arno. The sun is just low enough to give it to us in its most beautiful aspect. See, the light is beginning to gleam on the damp stone—there !"

He was right; the view was enchanting. Around, the gray, rugged rocks were still keeping sentinel. Far below lay the pretty town of Pistoja; around it the broad valley, dotted with villas, and, in the distance, the spires and turrets of Florence. Even the Italians cast satisfied glances through their window, and the Frenchman stretched his neck curiously. An " ah !" escaped the parted lips of the North German, but he gave no further expression to his admiration. There was but little time for enjoyment of the distant view as the train pursued its winding way down the mountain-side.

It is a charming ride of about an hour from Pistoja to Florence, through gardens of olives and fruit, past charming villas, with glimpses of the valley bounded by the spurs of the Apennines, •r, on the other side, of the fruitful plains of the

Arno. The North German seemed never to weary of all this magnificence. It was quite late when he took out his guide-book, looked for Florence in the index, and buried himself in descriptions of hotels and rates of droschky hire.

The train, once arrived at the "Station Centrale," was soon emptied. Those who had been for so long shut up together in the narrow space of the same compartment scarcely bowed in token of adieu; each one was busied about his or her own individual interests. At the top of the steps leading up and out from the depot into the public square were stationed the agents of the various hotels, each bawling out the title of his special caravansary,—" Gran Bretagna," "Italia," "Porta Rossa," "Bonciani," "Nuova York, ponte alla Carraja," "Roma, Roma!" The carriages were ranged in line beside the narrow sidewalk, their doors all wide open.

The traveller, who had hitherto been so easily content, now seemed suddenly to become fastidious; or was it a simple fit of indecision that prompted him to walk slowly to and fro past the open doors of the carriages, reading and re-reading their titles, but apparently forgetting to enter any one of them? As he was turning at the end of the long row, he perceived his fellow-traveller slowly approaching him, and his face bright-ened at the sight. "I will see where he stops," he evidently said to himself, "and follow his example."

"Well, signor," his former companion began, "has your Baedecker left you in the lurch? In truth, choice here is no easy matter. All these gorgeous vehicles appear to have just come brand-new from the same manufactory,—they are equally bright with varnish and gilding,—and I cannot decide whether crimson or green plush cushions are the more attractive. They tell nothing of the quality of the various hotels to which they severally consign their prisoners. Once place your foot within them, and there is no escape. Well, can you not make up your mind?"

" I should like to select an inn," the other replied, " where they speak German and I could have German cooking."

" Ah, there is no way of telling anything about that from these vehicles; and, besides, in Italy an Italian *ménage* is sure to be the best. Follow the customs of the country, is my motto."

" You seem to be familiar with the place, sir; perhaps you can——"

" Familiar! This is not, to be sure, my first sight of 'Firenze la bella,' but my stay here has always been very short, and I have the poorest memory for the names of hotels. Roma, Italia, Gran Bretagna,—in all these Italian towns really there seems to be no specific difference between them. I suppose it is of small consequence which we choose. Suppose we leave it to chance?—always a sure refuge for travellers."

" I agree," the other at once assented, evidently glad to be taken in charge.

" Name some number, then."

" A number?"

" Any number you choose."

" Twelve."

" Agreed! To the right or the left?"

" To the right."

" To the right be it, then. One—two—three—" and he counted on until he came to the twelfth vehicle in the row. " This is the one. Admirable! Gray plush, mirrors at the end, and wonderfully clean. Pray get in; I have hopes that we have drawn a prize." He threw his travelling-bag—with a loud rattle of the stones inside—upon the seat, and helped his companion to enter. " Have you any luggage? Of course you have. Give me your ticket. How many pieces?"

The conductor now made his appearance and took matters in hand. In a few moments the trunks were all tumbled up upon the roof of the carriage, the porter had been paid,

A*

and the vehicle was jolting along across the Piazza Santa Maria Novella to the old part of the city, past the Palazzo Strozzi, and into one of the side-streets off the Via Condotta. There it drew up before an antique structure with a spacious entrance and a huge portico. With its dingy stone abutments, and its small square windows in the lower story, protected by rusty iron gratings, it looked more like a prison than a resting-place for travellers in search of entertainment. He who had so recklessly invoked chance to aid, looked at his companion with a sly smile, but the latter exclaimed, with a beaming countenance, "We could not have done better. I delight in these old places, and live in just such another in my own home. Oh, the houses in my part of Germany still preserve the memory of the times when a man did well to build his dwelling like a small fortress. Here in Italy the architecture——"

He would probably have continued to discourse fluently upon the difference between the mediæval architecture of Northern Germany and of Italy, but his mentor was already out of the carriage, and, as he entered beneath the portico, called over his shoulder, "So much the better, so much the better. Shall I order an apartment for you?"

"If you will have the great kindness to do so," was the reply, as the speaker slowly entered the house, glancing approvingly at the façade and examining with interest the two figures of stone at the entrance, each of which held in its hands a winged wheel. Gravely following his guide, who was conversing with great vivacity in Italian, he reached the inner court, around which ran galleries, while a little fountain gaily bubbled and leaped in one corner, whence a broad flight of steps, much worn in the lower portion, led upwards.

The preliminary discussion soon came to an end; the luggage was carried up-stairs, and the stranger, as he took his protégé's arm and followed to his room, remarked, "The prices are not too high, although, for such a smoky old dungeon——

But it will be better inside. The present host, they say, is an enterprising fellow, and has determined to make a first-class modern hotel out of this mediæval albergo. Signor Uccello* is, you will be glad to hear, a German by birth; with us he would be 'Herr Vogel.' He will do himself the honour to wait upon us at dinner. You will dine? Dinner will be served shortly."

Meanwhile, they had passed along a gallery lined with faded frescoes and through an archway lighted by gas. "Here," said the waiter, pointing to a marble doorway with broad folding-doors, " is the dining-hall, where dinner will await the signori in a few moments. A magnificent apartment! only a few months ago restored at great expense. The rooms of the signori are here," and he threw open two doors, and, entering, drew aside the window-curtains. "The signori will be charmed with the views,—not very extensive, but so interesting. By leaning out a little, one can plainly see the tower of the Palazzo Vecchio. Oh, it is a most central situation,—the very middle of the town."

While the experienced traveller, without paying any attention to the man's praises of the house, was testing the comfort of the beds and lounges, the other was examining the elaborate carving of the wainscot blackened by age. "This must be German work," he said; "I have seen similar patterns in Nuremberg, only they are much finer in this olive-wood." The waiter, not understanding a word he said, assured the signori that in the course of a year Signor Uccello would have all that old trash removed; all the rooms were to be "restored" and papered suitably, but such alterations took time.

"Is it possible that so barbarous a work of destruction can be permitted in Italy?" cried the stranger, in dismay. "I should be only too happy to pass my life in such a room as this!"

---

* " Uccello " is the German " Vogel " and the English " Bird."

" Aha, you are a lover of antiquities !" remarked his fellow-traveller, who was just inspecting the washing-apparatus. " If that is the case, you have certainly come to the right place, for, unless I greatly err, we are in the palazzo of some extinct noble Florentine family, whose very name is probably not known to more than ten living men. Has this house been a hotel for many years ?" he asked of the waiter.

" Very many," the man replied ; " but it was formerly in bad hands, and has been left to go to ruin. An old palazzo, signor."

" What family did it belong to ?"

The man shrugged his shoulders. " No one can tell you that, signor. There are many hotels here that once belonged to Italian nobles. But no one cares to know their history, except now and then some learned professor."

" You hear," his questioner observed to his companion. " The builder of this palace could hardly have foreseen that it would one day be converted into an inn for the accommodation of strangers, ignorant even of his name. *Tempora mutantur.*"

Some minutes later the two men were seated at table in the dining-hall, which, although it scarcely justified the waiter's enthusiastic praise, was nevertheless a noble room. The boasted "restoration" had here, fortunately, effected nothing more than a papering over of some old frescoes on the walls, and a sweeping and scrubbing of the marble floor. Although the beautiful ceiling plainly showed traces of decay, nothing had been attempted in the way of repairing it. The young antiquary bestowed far more attention upon it than upon the table before him.

His neighbor touched him to attract his notice to some dish that was passing. " Do you know," he said, with a laugh, " that I am tempted to explore Florence with you ?"

" You are very kind. But are you not familiar with it ?"

"I mean mediæval Florence. I know the modern city pretty thoroughly, and might be a tolerable guide for you, but I have but small knowledge of mediæval Florence."

"I thought that was what every one came to see."

"Oh, the place has a multitude of attractions. I think life here may be very delightful even if one does not visit the Uffizi daily. And hitherto it has been to me only a stopping-place upon my various journeys. If ever I make a wedding-tour, I shall come here and explore the place."

"You enjoy nature, it seems, more than art?"

"Hm! What interests me in nature can hardly be enjoyed in your acceptation of the word. I am a student of natural history, and of course I must explore the mountains."

"That, then, is the reason why your travelling-bag was filled——"

"With stones? Yes; I must draw water everywhere for my mill. You understand why I gave a week to Poretta, with its remarkable sulphur springs, and intended to pass only a single night at Florence. Now, as I said, I am tempted to stay a day longer."

His companion took from his pocket-book a card and handed it to him. "Allow me to introduce myself," he said.

He of the dark beard bowed, with a smile. "Philip Amberger," he read, half aloud, "and no designation. I suspected a secret associate in you, I admit, for that you were a merchant, as you hinted in the railway-carriage——"

"I may perhaps be called a merchant," Amberger interrupted him. "The calling has been an inheritance in our family for centuries, and my late father wished that both his sons should take an interest in commerce. My inclinations were early opposed to trade."

"You have a brother?"

"Moritz Amberger. He is a genuine merchant, and we each accord all freedom to the other. My father, it is true, hoped we should work together—— Oh, thank you!" This exclamation had reference to the card that his neighbor handed to him at that moment: "'Dr. Xaver Schönrade, Professor,'—ah, Professor: I thought so."

They shook hands. "Our dessert will have a better relish," the Professor said, kindly. "What do you say to a walk through the town afterwards?"

Amberger agreed. "It is bright moonlight," he said; "nothing could be more delightful."

Signor Uccello presented himself to the two gentlemen as a compatriot. His German name had been "Vogelstein," but some twenty years previously, when he came to Italy to found a home in a new country, he had, for the sake of brevity, dropped the "stein," and upon the occasion of his marriage translated "Vogel" into "Uccello." "The reverse was my own case," the Professor remarked. "To be sure, I had no 'stein' to throw aside, and I am not married, but my name I translated into German from Italian, much to my mother's disgust, although she, as well as myself, was born on the other side of the Alps."

Amberger made numerous inquiries with regard to the old palazzo, which greatly interested him. Its present possessor could tell him nothing concerning it, except that the family to whom it had formerly belonged had either become extinct at the close of the previous century, or had been exiled after the confiscation of their estate in revolutionary times. "We constantly find," he continued, "in Italy, no less than in Germany, trade usurping the former habitations of the nobility, now falling to decay. I myself was born in one of those old dens, half castle, half fortress, that had been deserted by its former masters. It was just sufficiently preserved to afford a shelter to my father, a simple gardener. Thereby hangs a long story."

No curiosity was expressed with regard to the host's "long

story." Amberger remarked that, in his opinion, trade should show more reverence for antiquity and art, and mentioned with admiration the wainscoting in his bedroom. The host replied that few travellers could find pleasure in such dark, gloomy walls, and that one must cater for the popular taste. " But if you would like to see more of this queer old carving, gentlemen," he continued, "I should be proud to show you my own private apartments. Nothing has yet been restored there; my wife says we must think last of ourselves, and my daughter imagines that she really likes the old rubbish, and has even had her room furnished with old rickety furniture that we found in the attics. Perhaps you may like to see it."

Amberger accepted his invitation with thanks. The daughter pleased him even before he had seen her.

CHAPTER II.

THE moon was high in the deep-blue heaven when the two men began their after-dinner ramble. The Professor conducted the young man, towards whom he felt a most friendly inclination, along the beautiful Via Calzaioli, where every outline stood out clear and soft in the lovely moonlight, to the Baptistery, then through narrow streets to the Piazza della Signoria, where Amberger stood amazed at the moon-illumined mass of the Palazzo Vecchio, and then beneath the gleaming arcades of the Uffizi to the silvery waters of the Arno. They sauntered on for awhile, watching the gliding river, and then took shelter beneath the awning before a confectioner's shop, to enjoy an ice. Here Amberger again showed himself ready for conversation.

"When you entered the compartment of the railway carriage," he said, "I took you for a child of this lovely land, and your remark at dinner awhile ago convinced me that I was not entirely mistaken. You said, did you not, that you had translated your name?"

"My mother's name—yes," replied the Professor, taking out his cigar-case.

Amberger laid his hand upon it. "Try these," he said, offering him several cigars of his own. "I have contrived to smuggle a few in my trunks."

The Professor accepted them as frankly as they were offered. "Never despise the gifts the gods provide you," he said. "These are indeed a rare enjoyment here."

"Your mother's name—did you say?"

"I did. That most excellent lady, whom I revere as well as love, has seen fit persistently to withhold from me. the name of my father, although I am thoroughly convinced that she has no reason to be ashamed of it. In my own estimation a mere name is of small consequence, and I attach as much value to my mother's as to my father's. Beyond even the possibility of doubt I know my mother to have been married, and then divorced from her husband. Did I say she withheld his name from me? That was scarcely a fair statement of the fact. She never alludes to any circumstance of her married, life, all memory of which is evidently most painful to her, and I never question her regarding it. As far back as I can recollect, she was an opera-singer,—oh, I assure you, quite a celebrity in her time,—and now for some years she has been living upon the income resulting from the property purchased with the smaller part of her savings, and from the investment which she made in me of the larger portion, in giving me the best education that Europe could afford. Indeed, I owe to her everything that I am, and why should she not claim the right to bestow upon me her name also,—a name which has been

held in high honour in the musical world? She is called
'Camilla Bellarota.'"*

"Ah, and that you translate by——"

"The German 'Schönrade,' which you read upon my card.
My schoolmates translated my name for me when I was a boy
at school, and the translation was preferable to the distor-
tions of the Italian name that boyish fun or malice suggested.
When I published my first book in Germany, in the German
tongue, the change of name seemed to me but natural, and
then it became a fixed fact. And if my name is known to
science, I now surely have a right to say that I made it
myself."

"The best right in the world!"

"It was difficult for my mother to accustom herself to it.
She is by no means free from family pride, and boasts that the
Bellarotas were of noble blood. Small as her knowledge of them
is, she likes to speak of it. She was only ten years old when
her father, who had spent most of his life in Germany, died.
He was attached as a singer and actor to the court of a German prince, but always maintained that he was of noble birth,
and married the descendant of one of our old decayed noble
families. His wife died at the birth of their first child, and
shortly afterwards he himself, already advanced in years, lost
his voice, and with it of course his position. He then appears
to have dragged out ten years more of life, travelling from place
to place with his little daughter, needy and forlorn, until his
death occurred in the hospital of a town in Northern Germany
where he had in his youth reaped golden harvests as a favourite
tenor. Carlo Bellarota left no papers behind him to throw
any light upon his birth or history; all that was known of him

---

* "Bellarota" is the German "Schönrade," and the English "Fair-
wheel," as the German "Schönberg" is the French "Belmont," and the
English "Fairhill" or "Fairmount."

was that he had borne that name ever since his stay in Germany, which dated from the beginning of the present century. My mother has often declared, without indeed explaining her words, that the want of her father's baptismal certificate had been the great misfortune of her life. According to a few sentences written on the fly-leaf of an old missal, the owner of the book was a certain Pietro Bellarota, whose only son Carlo was. Carlo himself has added a few sentences, stating that his father died in prison, whither he was sent for political offences, having endeavoured to restore to his country the republican form of government under which it had once been so great and prosperous. In the attempt he had lost not only his liberty, but the remains of what had once been great wealth, and his son was forced to live an exile among strangers, his only inheritance, apparently, this missal, which had been the companion of his father's captivity. He never mentions the name of the town where the family had once been rich and great, but states that a branch of the name in Rome, and another in Naples, had been advanced by papal protection and royal patronage, and that his father's fate would have been a happier one had it not been for his faith in the possibility of an Italian republic, to which he was always true and loyal."

"And have you never made any further search into your family history during your frequent sojourns in Italy?" asked Amberger, with great interest.

"Only very superficially," the Professor replied. "I must confess I take very little interest in such matters, and that I think my time can be far more profitably employed than in prying into a pedigree to which I am quite indifferent. My grandmother and my father were Germans, and, independently of that, I myself belong, both in mind and education, to your nation. Why, then, should I seek to gratify an idle curiosity? For my good mother's sake I instituted a few inquiries in Rome and Naples, and found our name here and there in old official registers; but it would have cost an immense amount of time to pursue these investigations to any result. And what would it have availed me even if I had come across this very Pietro Bellarota? His son Carlo's baptismal certificate is lost; it was once, I understand, searched for fruitlessly. I am quite willing to leave the illumination of the darkness here to chance; and if it should never be illumined, I shall most certainly die as calmly as the bourgeois Professor Schönrade as though I were sure of a resting-place for my bones in the Bellarota family vault. However, I am none the less fond of Italy, and, in proof of my affection, frequently pursue my scientific researches within its borders. That is all I can do for the land of my grandfather."

He beckoned to a waiter, and paid the reckoning. It was late when they slowly walked back to the hotel, where, before entering, Amberger inspected from all sides the stone figures that graced the doorway. Silently and thoughtfully he then followed the Professor, who ran up-stairs two steps at a time, whistling an opera-air. In his own apartment, before going to bed, Amberger spent some time in examining the carved wainscot, copying a few of the most remarkable arabesques into his sketch-book. In the next room the Professor made a great rattling with his bits of stone, but was soon quietly asleep.

The next morning they did not meet at breakfast. The Professor, as he passed Amberger's door on his way to the dining-hall, knocked gently; but, finding that the young man still slept, he drank his coffee alone and went out, leaving word with the porter that he had a couple of business visits to pay, and would return in an hour or two. Philip Amberger had an abundance of time, therefore, to wander about and examine the different stories and galleries of the old palazzo, to admire the faded frescoes, and to linger in the court-yard, allowing the water of the little fountain to trickle over his hands, already tanned by the Italian sun. Here he was soon joined by Signor Uccello, who, af.er inquiring how he had slept, had a couple of chairs placed in the cool shade, and began a lively description of all that was worth seeing in Florence. The most superficial observer could hardly think of leaving it for three or four weeks at the least. He really did not speak as a host from interested motives. He had not yet seen Florence thoroughly himself, but then, to be sure, he was greatly confined by his business. His daughter Lucia, however,—than whom there could be no better cicerone for all that was interesting in Florence,—assured him that she had never exhausted the interest of the place. Travellers were too much in the habit of merely passing through Florence on their way to Rome. Amberger made inquiries as to the dealers in antique objects of interest, remarking that he was a collector The host mentioned two or three names, but promised to ask his daughter for further particulars,—she was much interested in such matters. Amberger hereupon reminded him of his yesterday's promise to show him his own dwelling-rooms, and was immediately conducted thither, Signor Uccello, as he led the way, remarking that it would be better that his guest should hear what Lucia had to say about Florentine antiquities.

Signora Uccello, a rather stout dame, in a morning-wrapper, was profuse in excuses for her husband, "who imagined that there could be anything in such gloomy, shabby old rooms to interest a traveller of distinction." She bewailed the want of air and light in her apartments, declaring that she should die if her husband did not rebuild them thoroughly; indeed, she would rather be buried in San Miniato than live in such a dreary prison. Her husband shrugged his shoulders and smiled diplomatically. Evidently she had rung the changes upon this theme until he knew them all by heart. When she was called away, he observed, "Women would be miserable without something to complain of. She hardly looks, I think, as if she had been deprived of light and air." Then he knocked at a door almost black with age,—the carving of which had already attracted Amberger's attention,—and called out, " Lucia, Lucia, may we come in ?"

The door opened heavily, but without noise, and the slender figure of a girl appeared upon the threshold. The room behind her was lighted from the side opposite the door, and was already streaked with the morning sunlight, making a golden background for the figure, which, enclosed in the heavy door-frame, stood out against it like some old picture. The sunlight played over the dark carving of the wainscot and the carved backs of some curious old leather-covered chairs. The floor of light-blue and yellowish marble seemed translucent, and the high Venetian glasses on the chimney-piece against the mirror in its faded frame were like air-blown bubbles. Lucia wore a dark-blue dress, with a short-sleeved, low-necked bodice over a white under-dress, gathered to the throat, with full puffed sleeves. At her girdle, which was fastened by a silver buckle, hung a small bag of antique fashion and workmanship, and the ruffle at her neck was confined by a coral necklace as by a red ribbon. She had her mother's black hair and her father's blue eyes. Philip Amberger thought he had never seen so lovely a picture, and was not sorry that his guide's lengthy explanation as to the purpose of their visit gave him time to admire its grace and beauty.

Lucia turned her large, quiet eyes upon the stranger, as her father spoke, and then, with a gentle smile, stood aside and allowed him to enter. She had been working before an easel in the deep recess of a window, painting a copy of an old picture of a Madonna. The room was furnished entirely in the style of the sixteenth century,—furniture, carpets, pictures, and tapestry all genuinely old. Lucia took a lute from a lounge that filled one corner, and prayed the signori to be seated. She

herself took possession of an arm-chair that she drew forth
from behind the easel. Signor Uccello excused himself on the
plea of business, and the young people were left alone.

Philip Amberger seemed to himself to be living in dream-
land. His knowledge of Italian was but small, and now he
could not remember a word of it. Lucia assured him that
she perfectly understood German, although she could hardly
venture to speak that tongue, and her replies could be made
in her own language. He availed himself of her permission
to speak German, and the conversation soon flowed easily
enough. Lucia displayed her little store of antique treasures
with much pride, and was pleased to find in him the enthusiasm of a genuine connoisseur, especially when he admired the
carved wainscot of her room, worm-eaten although it certainly
was here and there. "This room shall not be touched," she
cried, "however the rest of the dear old house may be spoiled
to suit modern taste, or rather want of taste." He applauded
her resolution, and noted particularly a figure that was continually repeated in the wood-work of all the rooms,—that of
a graceful, elaborate circlet. "Yes," she rejoined, "you will
find this symbol, whatever it may mean, everywhere through
the house, with such variation as the skill and ingenuity of
the carver have been able to effect. And you will observe that
the two marble figures at the entrance also bear this same
ornamented ring in their hands. And on the ceiling of the
dining-hall the same figure—which must have been a favourite
with the former possessor of the mansion—occurs continually."

"Perhaps," Philip suggested, "it may have formed part of
the escutcheon of the former lords of the mansion; I have
seen similar heraldic devices in old German houses."

She led the conversation to Germany. "I should like to
cross the Alps," she said, "and see my father's old home.
But it must be in the depth of winter. We have cold weather,
and even snow now and then here in December and January;

but I want to see such a winter as my father describes,—where the rivers are frozen over, icicles hang from the trees, and the frost makes flowers upon the window-panes."

"The unknown always attracts us," he replied, smiling. "We Germans come here to look for skies that are always blue, and warm sunshine, and you want to shiver in the blasts of our Northern winter. Shall you not be able to carry out your wishes?"

"Hardly, signor, hardly."

"You should come to us. My mother, who worthily maintains her position as a merchant's wife of the old German school, would welcome any one who could genuinely enjoy our German winter; and my study is quite such another room as this, only not so charming. I invite you now."

She laughed merrily. "A charming plan! I wonder what my father would say. That my German blood makes me restless, I think. But a girl, you see, signor——"

A knock at the door interrupted her, and Professor Schönrade appeared, to carry away his companion. He paid very little attention to the curious furniture and objects of antique art still scattered upon the chairs and tables, and seemed to regard Lucia as only one of a class,—a young girl with whom a few words might very pleasantly be exchanged now and then. This vexed Philip, who had no mind to be carried off thus peremptorily. But the Professor never noticed his reluctance to leave, and all that the young man could do was to ask and obtain permission to repeat his visit shortly.

"A pretty face," the Professor remarked, as they reached the street.

Amberger made no reply. Pretty, indeed!

They visited the Cathedral. The Professor paid but scant attention to what Philip thought points of great interest, and, when they had made the rounds, merely remarked, "'Tis a pity that we must continue our walk, it is so delightfully cool here."

An unsympathetic silence was Philip's only reply ; he could
have stood for hours in the blazing sun with pleasure before
some of these treasures of art.

Schönrade hailed a fiacre.   " To San Marco !   That is the
place for you," he cried, as they entered the vehicle.   " Haunted
by memories of Savonarola.   Pictures so old that you can't
distinguish their subjects at all.   Convent cells—oh, everything fascinating !   I shall gloat over your enthusiasm, if you
will only enjoy less egotistically than in the Cathedral."

" I am apt to be very quiet in the presence of great beauty
and antiquity," Amberger remarked.

" Not a good habit, my dear fellow-countryman on the
paternal side," laughed the Professor ; " our enthusiasm ought
not to live in a snail-shell, and should even be able to endure
a poor joke now and then."

They grew more and more at ease with each other.   Amberger became less reserved, and Schönrade more sympathetic.
Their breakfast in a birraria was greatly relished.   The Professor proposed a visit to a mosaic-factory, and here each could
thoroughly enjoy—Amberger the artistic workmanship, and
Schönrade the rare kinds of stone.   Thus the time passed
quickly enough before they returned to dine at the hotel.

The first thing that Amberger did after they were seated at
table was to look up at the ceiling.   Perhaps he imagined that
from the medallion in the centre a girlish face like Lucia's
might look down upon him.   At any rate, she was quite right
about the figure to be found there,—the circlet ornamented
with a graceful tracery of leaves was here in the frame enclosing the frescoed centre of the ceiling.   And, upon a closer
examination, the ring was surely a——

" What in the name of Heaven are you doing, my dear
fellow ?" cried the Professor ; " you will give yourself a stiff
neck.   Is the old ceiling really worth letting your soup get
cold for ?"

Amberger gazed absently at him. " An idea has suddenly occurred to me, Herr Professor," he said, mysteriously.

" Ideas are sure to occur suddenly," the other said, drily. " Well, may I share it ?"

" Good heavens, 'tis a very important one for you !"

" Indeed ? I am quite curious."

" The Bellarota family, of whom you told me yesterday——"

" Ah, pray don't disturb your dinner on their account."

" No, no, I am really in earnest. They belonged to Florence."

" Perhaps they did."

" They did ! they did ! and we are now in the Palazzo Bellarota."

The Professor pushed back his chair and gazed at the young man, as if slightly doubtful of his sanity.

But Amberger was no whit abashed by the gaze. " Look up," he continued. " What do you see there ? A circlet enwreathed with flowers; in fact, nothing more or less than an ornamented wheel. Look attentively, and you will see the hub in the centre, and the spokes radiating from it. It is a wheel,—a beautiful wheel,—bella rota. It is repeated everywhere through the house, over windows and doors and upon the floors; the two stone figures at the entrance bear it winged in their hands. There is no doubt of it at all."

The Professor laughed aloud. " Take your ease, I pray you, in the palace of my forefathers," he said, with a gracious wave of his hand, " and regard honest Signor Uccello simply as my major-domo, at your service. Although, for the present, circumstances over which I have no control compel me to endure the sight within my ancestral halls of this motley assemblage,—chiefly vagabonds from the North, who conceive that the payment of a certain amount of filthy lucre gives them a right to strut and swagger here,—yet I confidently hope that in a short time my geological investigations will place me in possession of a deposit of gold sufficient to redeem my family estate. You, however, my dear fellow, to whom I owe the discovery that will reinstate the lawful owner in his rights, must consent to be my guest for this day at least. Signor Uccello, a bottle of your best, if you please."

Amberger was half vexed, and yet could not help smiling. " But look, am I not right?" he persisted; " and is it not worth the trouble to follow out this evident clue? If I were in your place, I would never rest——"

" Until your thirst for knowledge were appeased, anti-quary that you are! Is it of any possible consequence to the development of the human race that we should know whether a certain Dr. Schönrade from Berlin be the lineal descendant of the noble Bellarotas of Florence, or whether his grand-father found it best to invent a pretty name for the opera-bills, that the world—' *mundus vult decipi*,' you know—might believe in his genuine Italian tenor? Solve me this problem !"

" But you cannot be indifferent——"

" I am, utterly. If, to be sure, an advertisement were to appear in the public journals announcing that a large treasure had been discovered indubitably the property of a genuine scion of the Bellarotas, I might——But I am thoroughly convinced that the noble race was impoverished before the doors of the family vault closed upon it, and it is far more to my liking to regard myself as a *homo novus*, who is to found a new dynasty,—a wife, 'tis true, is wanting as yet. And, by the way, an exalted idea occurs to me. What if I regained the palace of my fathers by—marriage? That charming little Uccello with whom I found you to-day——"

But here Philip Amberger was seized with a sudden fit of coughing, and was obliged to leave the table.

Before retiring for the night, the Professor paid him a visit in his room, and found him writing. "Dutiful man that you are," he cried, "is there a future bride at home, who must be thus remembered daily?"

"Not at all," the young man explained. "I am writing to my sister."

"You have a sister, then? Tell her that you have encountered an insufferable man here, but that, fortunately, he is obliged to set off to-morrow for the mountains."

"What! are you going so soon?"

"You recognize the portrait, then? So much the better,—write it down."

"But, my dear Herr Professor, if you would only read this letter——"

Schönrade held out his hand and looked kindly into the frank eyes that met his own. "I don't know why it is," he said, "but I feel sure we are not saying good-bye forever. I believe in animal magnetism, and in the sympathetic attraction caused by it. For the present, farewell!"

Amberger shook him cordially by the hand. He had perhaps been somewhat vexed by him, and had cherished a secret wish that he might not see all of Florence in his society; but that was forgotten now, and something really like sadness took possession of him as the door closed and he was left alone.

He wrote to his sister that he should probably remain "a long time in Florence, to become entirely familiar with the treasures of art that it contained." He did not add that in the process he relied upon Lucia's support and assistance. In fact, there was no allusion to her in the entire letter.

CHAPTER III.

Councillor-of-Commerce Wiesel, a portly, middle-aged gentleman, with a round, smoothly-shaven face, straight, fair hair, and a snowy-white cravat, was seated in the Moorish pavillion belonging to his mansion in the Thiergarten Strasse, deliberately eating an ice from a pretty little pink-glass saucer.

Opposite him, by a Japanese table, in a rocking-chair, his head thrown back, his eyes fixed upon a Chinese lantern hanging from the ceiling, and a cigar between his thin lips, sat a somewhat younger man, with a sallow face, in which no amount of repose or absence of expression could obliterate the deep wrinkles around the corners of the mouth. Herr Otto Feinberg was certainly taking great pains to appear intensely comfortable, as if, in his easy rocking-chair and smoking the best cigars, nothing in the world had much power to interest him, least of all, perhaps, the subject of which he was speaking. In fact, he hardly spoke at all: merely throwing, as it were, a word or two now and then up to the ceiling, and then pausing to note if haply it might fall near the Councillor and be caught by him in its descent. Thus the discourse was pursued,—its subject was a new railway enterprise.

Behind them, nearer the bow-window that looked out upon a beautiful group of palms and other tropical plants, the Councillor's wife, very much dressed, reclined upon a Turkish divan. She had an open book in her hand,—from a circulating library, as its cover proclaimed; but more than half of her attention was given to a cockatoo with a yellow crest, who upon his stand, at a little distance, was playing all kinds of antics. She numbered, perhaps, rather nearer forty than thirty years, and in her youth must have been pretty. But now all freshness of colour had faded from her face, and her eyes had a weary look in them, betokening either physical suffering or perpetual ennui.

Upon the trim gravelled walk, outside in the garden, two young girls were sauntering arm-in-arm. One might have been a couple of years younger than the other, and both were pretty, very pretty, although they were very unlike. The younger, tall and slender, with a delicate oval face, resembled the Councillor's wife; the other was shorter, more vivacious, with teeth like pearls, dimples in cheeks and chin, and masses of fair hair. A tall young man, dressed after the latest fashion, with an unimpeachable cravat and lemon-coloured gloves, was walking with them, trying at every turn of the path to keep his place by the side of the younger girl.

The elder talked the most. "Do you often go to the theatre, Mr. Fairfax?" she asked.

"Not very often," he replied, with an English accent. "I do not like the German drama."

"What is your objection to it?"

"Oh, it is stupid. Every one is so possessed with the idea of being natural that it grows tiresome."

"I thought the greatest praise that could be bestowed upon an actor was to call him natural. Did not you, Lilli?"

The younger girl, whom she addressed, did not seem to have been attending to the conversation. "Oh—I——" she stammered, looking appealingly at Mr. Fairfax, as if to summon him to her aid.

"You Germans," he said, "are so ready to be pleased, to make up for any deficiencies, to see more than is really visible. I, for my part, when I go to the theatre, must have my attention riveted by the force and power of the acting."

They were approaching the pavilion. The lady at the window arose and beckoned to Mr. Fairfax. The young girls continued their promenade.

"Tell me something to amuse me," the Councillor's wife said to the young man as he entered, and she motioned him to a seat beside her. "My book has tired me so."

"A German novel, is it not? German novels are always very tiresome."

"We ought to have gone to some watering-place long ago, but my husband really cannot leave his business. Would you go with us to Wiesbaden, Mr. Fairfax?"

"I am entirely at your service, my dear madame. You know that I have nothing more nearly at heart than to become intimately known to you all."

"Do you not find our dear Lilli still very much of a child?"

"I could not desire to see her otherwise. Were her character entirely formed, I could scarcely hope to produce the lasting impression which I now trust to be able to make upon her pure, child-like nature."

The lady extended her hand to him. "You are not disappointed, then?"

He imprinted a kiss upon it. "Should I be here now if I were? Let me confess that I have passively submitted to the arrangement made long since by our respective fathers, only because I was fully resolved that, when we met, all right of decision should be accorded to our hearts alone."

"I was sure of it, and we too——"

"I never could have denied the heart its rights; although at the same time I admit that, as a practical man, the union of our two houses was anything but a matter of indifference to me. Nothing would so insure the stability and success of our great business undertakings as an alliance of this close nature between the English and German firms."

"I never understand anything of the kind," said the lady, casting down here yes; "but my husband agrees with you, and he loves Lilli most fondly. What do you think of my daughter's friend,—Katrine Amberger?"

" Oh, a very pretty, lively girl."

" Do you know I was half undecided whether to invite her here just at this time? I was afraid she would quite throw my Lilli into the shade."

" Surely, dear madame, you cannot be serious? Fräulein Lilli can only be a gainer by the contrast."

" Do you think so?"

The conversation halted here. In a few moments the Englishman began again, without any apparent connection with the previous topic:

" Moritz Amberger seems to me rather a rash speculator. I scarcely know the resources of his house, however. Fräulein Katharina's property, I suppose, is secured to her?"

" I really do not know; probably it is," the lady answered, carelessly. " Herr Otto Feinberg there—a prudent man, I am told—is a suitor of hers, and her brother, I understand, favours the alliance."

Their talk was then pursued almost in a whisper, for the subject of it was near at hand. Herr Otto Feinberg was still puffing forth rings of cigar-smoke, lolling back in his rocking-chair. Quite a cloud of it had collected about the Chinese lantern hanging from the ceiling. " There can be no doubt, my dear Councillor," he drawled, in his affectedly indifferent monotone, " that the projected road will in a few years be a source of immense profit. There are so few difficulties to overcome along the entire line,—for freight-trains will inevitably prefer this shorter and more convenient route to the great business marts,—and the advantage that must accrue to the projectors is evident." He paused an instant, and, without altering his attitude, slightly turned his head and cast a keen side-glance at the Councillor, who was just transferring the last spoonful of ice from the saucer to his mouth. As no syllable either of assent or of dissent was uttered, there was nothing for it but the direct question, " Well, what do you say to it? Will you join us? Will you recommend it to your English associates, and under what conditions?"

Then for the first time the Councillor appeared to take the matter into consideration. That is to say, a wavy line made its appearance upon his smooth forehead, and he inclined his head slightly to one side. A minute elapsed, nevertheless, before he decided to open his mouth, and he then remarked, as if casually, "Is Amberger to be with you?"

Feinberg shrugged his shoulders. "I should let him suppose that we could do without him, at least until I am quite sure of him. Moritz is, as you know, betrothed to my niece Sidonie, but my niece Sidonie is capricious, and my brother Ignaz is very weak in that direction. Moritz has promised me his influence with his sister Katharina, but then he is in great measure dependent upon his brother Philip, and Philip is not to be relied upon. You see, we have some need of caution; but if you really desire——"

"My wish need not be taken into consideration at all," said the Councillor, with a deprecatory wave of his hand. "Admirable as your project is, there are two objections to it which would have to be removed before I could hope to gain for it the confidence of my English friends."

Feinberg sat upright in his chair. "Two objections?"

"Two objections. If the road is what it ought to be, it must traverse the boundary-line. You will have to do with two different governments, and you will hardly reconcile their separate interests."

Feinberg smiled. "Oh, as to that, we shall enlist several large firms beyond our borders, who will find it for their own interest to use their influence for us. All that has been thought of."

The Councillor deliberately lighted a cigar, and, smoking it slowly for a moment, inhaled its fragrance with an air of great content. "My dear friend," he then said, "depend upon it, those people will require to be well paid, and what they gain you will lose."

" Who will lose ? The public must pay for all these unavoidable expenses."

" If they can be estimated beforehand. But perhaps it is so. You have probably considered it well, and find there is enough profit insured to make the project sufficiently attractive. Will not our own government, however, give you some trouble ?"

" Hardly. Why should it ?"

" Then I am better informed than you are. It will give you trouble. If I understand you correctly, you rely upon the enlargement and co-occupation of the present depot."

" Of course, of course !"

" Let me inform you that your proposals on this point will be emphatically rejected—emphatically !"

Feinberg tilted his chair forward and leaned both arms upon the table. " But for what earthly reason ?"

" What reason ? A very palpable reason, my dear fellow. Your town was built in old Hanseatic times, when there was more thought of defence against sudden attack than of easy communication. Consequently, the central streets leading to and from the railroad depot scarcely afford a passage for the traffic of to-day, accidents, more or less grave, are continually occurring, freight-wagons are so often blocked up that all the exertions of the police are necessary to preserve order. Under no circumstances will the government allow of any farther obstruction to traffic there."

" Oh, you exaggerate matters."

" That may be ; but I happen to know, through a confidential friend, that this view of mine is the one at present entertained by the ministry. The erection of a new depot on the other side of the town will certainly be made one condition of your success, and then the question arises whether the site for

B*

it can be purchased, and, what is far more important, whether such site will seem to the government sufficiently accessible from all parts of the town, in view of the increase of traffic which the new road should produce. As far as my own knowledge of your town goes, narrow gateways here and there connect the central streets with the old fosse, and in some of these streets two wagons could hardly pass each other. Whole rows of ancient mansions would have to be pulled down to allow of free passage-way. I doubt whether you and your brother have thought of this."

Feinberg knocked the ashes from his cigar. "Who would have thought of it?" he said, with irritation. "We must see the burgomaster, we must—the deuce!"

The Councillor arose, and pulled down his waistcoat. "At any rate, my dear fellow," he said, composedly, "the plan is not yet so mature that we need come to any decision. Suppose we walk a little."

His guest also arose, and with him descended the steps into the garden, bestowing but small attention upon the palmettos and large-leaved plants on either side of the path.

Meanwhile, the two girls had been engaged in what, to judge from their air and gestures, was a very serious and interesting conversation. Lilli was no longer so mute as in Mr. Fairfax's presence. When he was first called away by her mother, he was for awhile the subject of conversation. Lilli asked what Katrine thought of him and of his conduct to her, and Katrine replied, smiling, that his aim was easily discovered. This seemed to terrify Lilli, who then confessed that she had suspected him of paying her particular attention, and that she also thought she could see that her parents favoured him.

"What do you think of him yourself?" Katrine asked.

Lilli could not say. Mr. Fairfax seemed very amiable, and certainly was extremely handsome, but she could not bear the idea of any previous arrangement between their parents, such as she suspected; and then—oh, there was something else. Naturally, her friend begged to know what this something was, but for some time Lilli could not be prevailed upon to reveal its nature, glad though she evidently would have been to disburden herself of her secret. At last she extorted a promise of the deepest secrecy from Katrine, and then confessed, blushing crimson the while, that the previous winter she had been one of a class of young girls who had met weekly at the houses of their several parents to enjoy the instruction imparted in a series of lectures given by a certain distinguished Professor; and this Professor—he might not be so regularly handsome as Mr. Fairfax, but he was quite young, and so interesting—had been invited to many entertainments at which she also had been present, and had called upon her mother; and for her he was—oh, he was the only man worth thinking of in the world! Unfortunately, several others of his youthful hearers shared her sentiments; some decided coolnesses had arisen among them in consequence. Since then, to be sure, Emma Finkenstein and Theodora Hellmann had been betrothed to two officers, and Melinda Vanderbeeren, who was the most enthusiastic of all, was as good as engaged to her cousin; for her own part, she could not understand such fickleness,—her heart was constant. Thus far she had got in her revelations, when Katrine asked, in astonishment, "Has any promise passed between you?"

"Heavens, no!" Lilli replied. "That would have been impossible. But I have vowed to myself that none but he——" She stopped, and turned away her face.

"Has he by word or sign given you to understand——"

Lilli shook her head.

"Has he so distinguished you from the rest that you must believe——"

"Oh, how could he? Mamma was always by, and of

course he talked with her. But he was very kind to me, and often looked at me during the lecture; he must have felt——"

"The matter has gone no farther, then," said Fräulein Amberger. "Does he continue his visits?"

"He did until late in the spring, when he went on a journey somewhere. That was the time that Mr. Fairfax first began to come every day, and—it was very wrong of me, but I had really almost forgotten the Professor as entirely as his lectures, when——"

"When?"

"When we met him yesterday as we were out driving. He touched his hat so kindly, it went to my very heart. Mr. Fairfax, who sat opposite me, noticed how pale I grew, and I really felt ill. Katrine, if he comes again—and he will—I know it——" She pressed her friend's arm close to her side.

"But I can see nothing to distress you in such a prospect. If he really loves you——"

"Ah, that would be terrible!"

"How terrible?"

"My father and mother would never consent. Think! a Professor, and with no money! If he only had rank!"

"But if you love him, Lilli——"

"Yes, but how can I be sure of that? And if I do, I would not for the world let him know it; and I never should have the courage to disobey my father and mother. Oh, how unhappy I am!"

Lilli spoke in accents of despair, and pressed Katrine's soft little hand. Her friend was silent for awhile, and then said, gently and gravely, "But you really do not dislike Mr. Fairfax?"

"How could I?" asked Lilli. "But I owe it to my heart——"

"Do your heart no violence," Katrine counselled, with a laugh, "and listen to me. If the Professor makes his appearance, I will see whether it is not worth while to fall in love with him myself, out of pure friendship, my dear."

" It is no jesting matter," Lilli replied, with an air of gentle reproach. The two gentlemen just then passed them ; as they did so, the Councillor good-humouredly patted his daughter on the cheek, and Feinberg handed to Katharina a rose-bud which he had just plucked in no amiable mood. " Is mamma right," Lilli whispered, when they had pursued their opposite paths, " in saying that Herr Feinberg makes sure of winning you ?"

Katrine waved to and fro in the air the rose-bud, which she held by the extreme end of the stem. " Is that what 'mamma says ? Very likely there may have been some fine business arrangements agreed upon among the higher powers. I, however, fortunately reserve for myself——"

At that moment Lilli's arm twitched her own so perceptibly that the rose-bud fell to the ground. " What is the matter ?" she asked, in surprise, without stooping to pick it up.

" The Professor !" Lilli tremblingly whispered in her ear.

Katharina looked up. A gentleman had entered the garden, and was just taking off his hat to the Councillor, revealing a broad brow, a face tanned by the sun, and masses of close black curls. " I have just returned from my Italian journey," he said, in a mellow, melodious voice, "and hasten to pay my respects to you all."

Wiesel greeted him cordially, and presented him to Feinberg as " Professor Schönrade, one of the most distinguished scholars of our capital, and my daughter's instructor in—in—- What was it that you taught her, my dear Professor? these things slip one's memory so easily !" The Professor took no notice of the question, but turned towards the pavilion, where he observed the Councillor's wife. She rose, and came towards him, and, after he had kissed her hand, presented " Mr. Fairfax, of the great firm of Fairfax & King, in London." The Englishman greeted the guest rather formally, and the Professor deigned the merchant no other notice than an easy bow. The cockatoo grew uneasy on his perch, and lifted his yellow crest with a shrill cry. "Aha! there you are, old friend!" cried the Professor, as he stepped up to the bird and stroked down its ruffled feathers.

The two girls now ascended the pavilion steps. Schönrade bowed to Lilli, and looked rather curiously at her fair companion, who was, on her part, certainly interested to observe the man who had turned so many heads. Two pairs of very fine eyes gazed for an instant into each other, and were apparently well pleased with what they saw. The Councillor's wife drew her daughter towards her, and presented " Fräulein Katharina Amberger, the sister of a valued friend of my husband's, and one of Lilli's very dear companions."

Katrine gently inclined her head and cast down her eyes, but the Professor was evidently interested. " Amberger?" he asked. " Did I understand the name aright?"

The Councillor's wife assented, and to her inquiry as to what interested him, he replied, " Oh, the strangest chance. You have a brother Philip, Fräulein Amberger?"

" I have. At present absent from home, in Italy."

" Yes, in Italy. Do you know, I had the pleasure of making his acquaintance a few days ago in Florence, and even of lodging with him in the palace of my ancestors?"

Katharina laughed: " In the palace of your ancestors?"

" Oh, it is too long a story to rehearse at present, but perhaps at some future time—— It must be the fact, for Herr Philip Amberger vouches for its truth, and I have the greatest respect for his archæological wisdom."

" He is riding his hobby in Italy, then?" his sister observed. " How did you leave him?"

" Apparently in the best of health, after a whole day of irritation at my defective comprehension of art and antiquity. I really should not wonder if he had the entire palace where

he now is packed up in boxes and transported across the Alps,
together with Signor Uccello, the host, and his pretty daughter,
who is wonderfully well versed in a knowledge of the contents
of every rubbish-shop in Florence."

"Yes, he squanders an immense quantity of money that
were better employed in business—with those tastes of his,"
Feinberg here interposed.

Katrine gave him a withering glance. "I think Moritz's
stud more expensive than these hobbies of Philip's," she said,
carelessly.

"And there must be such queer fellows," Wiesel here
struck in, affably. "For my part, I like to buy pictures. All
modern, though: they are the only ones to hang up in our
houses. None of your old masters; thank Heaven, there are
churches and museums enough for them. We people of to-
day want fresh, bright colours,—eh, Herr Professor?"

"I am hardly a competent judge," Schönrade replied. "You
would find my principal tastes and occupations queerer still, I
am afraid; since I would with pleasure pay more for the fossil
impression of some fish that was alive and swimming mil-
lions of years ago—yes, even for a single fish-scale—than for
your finest champagne breakfast, my dear Councillor."

Wiesel laughed good-humouredly. "You wise ones are queer
fellows," said he. "Every one to his liking, say I!"

The Professor turned to Lilli: "And you, lady fair, have
you been pursuing your researches into prehistoric times with
enthusiasm since we met?"

Lilli blushed to the roots of her hair. "To tell the truth,
Herr Professor——" she stammered.

"You have not even opened the horrid book that I recommended to you, and have entirely forgotten all that I had the
honour of communicating to you in my lectures," he interrupted her, with a bright smile. "That is quite as it should
be. Such matters rarely do more than awaken a short-lived

curiosity in young ladies, and I disapprove of overloading their memories."

"Oh, I remember a great deal," said Lilli. "Only the other day I had a dispute with Mr. Fairfax about——"

"What? a dispute?" her mother asked, playfully shaking her finger at her.

"About chalk,—and I was victorious."

"Fräulein Lilli took notes of your lectures," the Englishman added, "and swears by their correctness."

"Rather rash on her part, I think," said Katrine, with a look at which her friend blushed still more deeply.

"Oh, no penalty attaches to scientific perjury," said the Professor. "And really very little importance is attached to chalk nowadays. In a short time no one will know what is meant by the phrase to 'chalk up a score.' Such a simple style of book-keeping will be entirely buried in oblivion."

The conversation continued merrily enough, Schönrade taking the lead, involuntarily appealing most frequently to Katharina Amberger. He stayed until after supper, and was entreated by his host and hostess to repeat his visit shortly. His promise to do so was most conscientiously kept.

Wiesel could hardly have been the cause of his visits; Feinberg had left the city; and although Mr. Fairfax, upon a nearer acquaintance, proved to be a man of culture, rather agreeable than otherwise to the Professor, the Councillor's wife did not for one moment suppose him to be the attraction. Scarcely a day passed that did not bring him, if only for a few minutes, "just because he was passing." "I really hardly understand myself," he said, "why, as soon as I shut up my books and go out for my daily walk, I am sure to find myself before long at this house. I really cannot pass by without coming in."

"And why should you wish to pass us by, my dear Professor?" the lady inquired, with an encouraging smile.

"Because I ought not to be so weak as to be unable to resist the enchantment of this garden," he replied. " My feet are stayed as by magic, my hand is forced to lift the latch of the gate, and, before I know it, here I am, not even attempting to stammer out an excuse for my presence."

" As if it needed any ! We so enjoy our evenings in your society !" she declared, casting down her eyes. " Do we not, Mr. Fairfax ? Am I not right, young ladies ?"

The Englishman hastened to confirm her words, Lilli grew crimson and nodded to Katrine instead of to her mother, while Katrine gave an odd little laugh and shot one glance from beneath her long lashes at the Professor, who could not take his eyes from her.

" Very well, then," he said ; " I will come until you are really tired of me, and I trust to your friendship to tell me when it is so."

And thus he came regularly every evening. Even the rainy weather, which, although it was the middle of summer, set in and lasted a week, did not delay his visits in the least. He himself laughed at his own punctuality, for which he did not seem at all dependent upon his watch.

To tell the truth, the Councillor's wife was greatly inclined to ascribe to herself that power of attraction which the Professor had described as so magical.

She would have been virtuously indignant if her most confidential friend had believed her capable of unfaithfulness to her husband, towards whom, although she had never felt any enthusiasm of affection, she had always, and, in her younger days, in spite of various temptations, preserved that mixture of respect and esteem which her relations with him required. Surely he had good cause to be as free from jealousy or mistrust of her as he certainly was. It had assuredly never yet occurred to her to cherish any actual sentiment for the interesting Professor that could be in any way offensive to her husband ; but in order to pass away the time that hung so heavily

on her hands, she read such a quantity of novels that her head
was filled with all sorts of sentimental nonsense, and it entertained her to give her foolish fancy free play, and imagine herself a heroine of romance, who might have sentimental trials
if she chose. To be sure, it was rather an unpleasant reflection that, although she was still so young as not to have outgrown those needs of the heart which her rather phlegmatic
but very worthy husband was ill fitted to satisfy, she had
a grown-up daughter on the probable eve of marriage. Re-
clining upon her luxurious lounge, with a book in her hand
that condoned so amiably all small deviations from the right
and brought matters to a crisis so entertainingly, extricating
the heroine so deftly from her delicate distresses, it was easy
to fancy to herself many an exciting and thrilling scene, wherein
she always played the principal part, and which she could lead
to a tragic or a cheerful conclusion according to her mood of
the moment. To the Professor was assigned the part of·the
ami de la maison, concealing beneath the quiet mask of friendship the most dangerous qualities. Suppose he should find
her alone here some day, and, throwing himself at her feet,
declare his passion, and then suppose that, before she had time
to recall him to himself, Wiesel, or her daughter, or even the
housemaid, should come in and surprise them. Here were
three startling contingencies. Without any fault of her own,
her husband might insult her by most unworthy suspicions,
and his jealousy once aroused might transform him to a
blood-thirsty tiger; or Lilli herself might cherish a secret
passion for the Professor, and distressing scenes would then
ensue between the mother and the daughter, in which, naturally enough, Mr. Fairfax would come to play a part; or the
housemaid, in possession of such a secret, might prove her
tyrant and tormentor, embittering her existence, until matters
should be made smooth once more by an open confession and
a touching scene of forgiveness. All these situations were fre-

quent in books, why should they not exist in reality? She did
not actually believe that they would come to pass, but the con-
templation of their possible occurrence had for her an inex-
haustible charm. And her romance was not, after all, quite
air-spun; there must be some reason for the Professor's constant visits. It was so good of him to bestow upon her so
much of his time; why should she not be grateful, without,
of course, allowing him to perceive how much more she gave
to him? why should her hand not tremble slightly when he
kissed it as he took leave of her? why should not her fingers
contract in a slight pressure? why should not her pale cheek
flush beneath his gaze, her weary eye brighten? It was all a
device, to be sure, to relieve the tedium of her existence. So
long as he retained his attitude of respectful deference, why
should not she encourage his advances, since she could repel
them when she chose?

It was a pity that no one was more entirely unconscious of
all her coquettish manœuvres than Schönrade himself. The
Councillor's wife, with her languishing airs, her irritable nerves,
her idleness, and her want of culture, had never attracted him
in the least, although, of course, he was courtesy itself towards
her, indebted to her hospitality as he was. It never entered
his mind that she could attribute the duration and frequency
of his visits to her own charms, but he felt too sensibly the
value of her good will to neglect any opportunity of paying
friendly court to her, and perhaps sometimes he was even
more courteous than the occasion demanded. Wiesel himself
thought the Professor a great favourite, but he had entire
confidence in his better half, and was glad to profit by the
improvement that was evident in her daily temper of mind.
She did not talk nearly so much of her nerves or of visiting
some watering-place.

Lilli accounted after her own fashion for the Professor's
increased attentions to her mother, from whom she seemed to

have inherited the capacity for inventing startling situations.
Every day she saw more clearly that Schönrade had perceived
her preference, and was now doing all that he could to ingratiate
himself with her mother, that her sympathies might be enlisted
upon his side when the decisive moment should arrive. She
knew well that he could never hope for success in his suit; but
when she trembled at this thought it was not in the anticipa
tion of a conflict with her parents or with a sense that life was
empty without him, but with pity for the poor man of whose
misery she should be the cause. In a frank self-examination
she was obliged to admit that she did not really care for him.
He had impressed her greatly by his learning, his judgment,
and his manly maturity of thought, but in the familiar home-
circle his image lost the misty charm with which distance had
invested it: he was altogether too real; he was older than she
had supposed, and not nearly so handsome; she was never at
her ease with him; in fact, he was far better suited to be her
mother's companion than hers. She turned with relief to the
young Englishman, although he was not half so interesting.
And the poor child was distressed to see that the Professor
never suspected danger in Mr. Fairfax, but treated him with
all the courtesy and kindness possible, as if he were too sure
of the future to be affected by the presence of a rival. She
would have liked to warn him that his hopes were vain, if she
had only known how to begin; at all events, she could treat
him with increasing coolness, while she was amiability itself to
the Englishman. She took it quite ill of Katharina that she
had not kept her promise. "You said," she complained, "that
you would make the Professor fall in love with you, that I
might be absolved from my promise to myself, and you have
done nothing, nothing at all for me, although I have told you
everything. Do you call that friendship?"

Katrine kissed her, and whispered, soothingly, "Wait awhile;
all may yet be well. I can't help his taking no notice of me."

But she knew better. Schönrade's visits were all on the fair Katharina's account, and he was at as great pains to convince her privately of this as to conceal his preference for her from the rest of the household. Every one was so self-occupied that he succeeded admirably. True, minutes, sometimes only seconds, of time were all that were vouchsafed to him in which he could approach her unobserved; but he made the best use of them, and, when he ventured to hope that he was understood, love quickened his inventive faculty, and he resorted to a hundred devices for showing her his preference unobserved by the others. And Katrine understood him. There seemed to have existed a mutual understanding between them from that first evening when these two people, until then entire strangers, had first gazed in each other's eyes.

The Professor belonged to an order of men hitherto unknown to Katharina, and she could not but wonder to find herself so entirely at ease in his society. At home, those composing her social circle were chiefly her brother's business friends, or elderly scholars, who were invited to the house upon the occasion of any festivity. Now, for the first time in her life, she had the opportunity of daily intercourse with a man still young who belonged to the first rank of social and mental culture,— accomplished, learned, and yet evidently taking the greatest delight in her society, scarcely more than a school-girl though she were. He knew so much, and yet made no pretension; his views of life were so cheerful, and yet so profound. It was delightful to converse with him, feeling that, so far from looking down upon her, he enjoyed her gay replies to his own brilliant remarks. And he did indeed enjoy them. How musically she laughed! and what magnificent masses of fair hair she had! and then her eyes!

His eyes, too! Katrine thought them entirely different from all other eyes in the world. They fairly spoke, and she believed she could understand what they said. And if he handed her a flower, and their hands met for an instant, it was something to remember all day long.

Each day brought some fresh proof of mutual understanding, and each parting glance carried with it the hope of the next meeting.

Who could wonder that the Professor found the Councillor very agreeable, his wife very interesting, Lilli most amiable, and even the young Englishman quite entertaining?

One afternoon, upon presenting himself at the villa at the usual time, he learned to his great regret, from the servant, that the family were from home and would not return before night. He left his regards for them, and with downcast looks sauntered slowly through the garden towards the gate. As he passed by a rose-bush he stopped to admire a full-blown rose which he and Katrine had noticed for its beauty as a bud on the previous evening. He could not resist taking it in his hand and carrying it to his lips; not for the sake of inhaling its fragrance—no,—he kissed it, and then, as if by that act he had made it his own, he broke it from its stem. Suddenly he heard a well-known voice exclaim, " Oho! I call that robbery !"

He looked round, startled, and saw Katharina Amberger in the pavilion. She was sitting at a small table, with her writing-materials before her, and shaking her pen at him with an air of playful menace. He could almost have shouted for joy.

" Are you really at home?" he cried, going directly towards the pavilion.

" If you are sure this is not my ghost."

" I can hardly make up my mind upon that point yet."

" Oh, you don't believe in ghosts?"

" Don't I? I believe with all my heart in good spirits."

" And how can you tell, Herr Professor, that a spirit is a good spirit?"

" Good spirits never vanish. I simply repeat the old formula, 'All good spirits praise the Lord!'" He raised his
hands like Doctor Faust. " You are there still ?"

" I have not yet quite learned to fly through the air on a
broomstick."

" Then you must allow me to believe you the very best
spirit ever veiled in a mortal form. May I come in ?"

She extended her arms across the space between the slender
pillars. " No ; 'twill not do. I have a headache."

He was standing on the lowest step, his hat in his hand,
and there was a look of entreaty in his fine eyes. " Ah, you
have a headache !" he said, with compassionate credulity.

" And so I stayed at home," she continued, letting her
arms drop ; " for indeed I must write letters. Mamma expects one, and Philip——"

" Oh, he can wait," he interrupted her. " You have no
idea how shadowy one's home becomes in Italy."

" Was that your case ?"

" Oh, I had nothing to become shadowy but a mother, and
she has always been most indulgent." And he ascended
another step.

" Mothers are not always indulgent," she observed, and her
forehead contracted into a slight frown, as she rested the end
of her silver pen-holder against her chin.

" She won't mind my staying a minute."

" I'm not sure of that."

He hesitated. " May I offer you this exquisite rose ?" And
as he spoke he mounted the last step and stood beside her.

" To make me your accomplice in theft," she said, retreat-
ing to the table.

" It is the same that we admired yesterday in the bud," he
said ; " to-morrow it would have faded." And then, more
seriously, " I pray you, do not refuse this rose."

Her face, too, suddenly grew grave. She stretched out her

hand and took the flower, saying nothing, but, with downcast eyes fixed upon it, seeming to wait for him to take leave of her.

He felt that he ought not to remain any longer, and yet he could not stir from the spot. When would such another moment be his? Perhaps never again. Katrine alone!— Good heavens! what mortal man could make his bow and carry away his.heart full to overflowing from such a presence? Such a one would deserve to fail. This moment was his own: he would not lose it. His heart throbbed almost painfully; he sought Katrine's eyes, but her long lashes were not raised.

"Fräulein Katharina," he said, in a low voice, "may I ask one question of fate?"

"It will not answer," she replied, in as low a tone.

"*You* are my fate," he rejoined, with a hurried earnestness that evidently startled her, "and you can answer if you will."

He waited a moment, listening for some word from her; but none came, and she grew very pale. Then she slowly raised the rose in her hand to her lips, and held it there.

He thrilled with delight. Had he not kissed it too?

"You must know already what I would say to you," he continued. "I love you. But the consciousness that you know it does not content me. I must ask you——"

The rose in her hand trembled violently. "No, no!" she begged, "do not ask—not now—not here—oh, do not ask!"

"And should I obey you, what should I carry from your presence? A restless heart. And what should I leave here? A restless heart. No, we must understand each other now, now that we stand here face to face. Do not fear lest too much happiness should cause me to forget that you are not in your own home,—that others who are to be consulted are

far from here. But answer me, I entreat you, as you would
answer your own heart. Can you, will you, give your happiness into my keeping?"

She clasped her hands about the flower, and, looking full in
his face with eyes in which joy and pain were strangely blended,
said, "I will."

For one instant it seemed to him that the impulse to throw
himself at her feet, to clasp her to his heart, was irresistible.
But he retained his self-control; his eyes alone, flashing with
exultation and glowing with love, betrayed the ecstasy of happiness that he felt. Thus they stood for a minute gazing into
the depths of each other's souls, and then he said, gently, "My
eyes kiss you, Katrine."

A burning blush suffused her cheeks, and she whispered,
"Go, go! I cannot bear this. We must not meet again thus."

"No, not thus," he cried; "you are right. To-morrow
morning I shall start for your home, present myself to your
mother and brother, and ask your hand from them."

Her look grew timorous and startled. "And if they
refuse?"

"Oh, how can they?" he interrupted her. "How could
they destroy our happiness? With the knowledge that you
love me, I fear nothing. Surely there is no reason why I may
not woo and win you."

Katrine smiled gratefully upon him, but her look was still
troubled. "You do not know—you cannot imagine how all
the habits of an ancient merchant race—— My father's will
gives my brothers great power over me; and my mother——"

"She shall know that her child's affection is given to a man
of honour, in whom she can trust."

"But she has prejudices and opinions that you do not
dream of. She never will comprehend—— Oh, heavens!
how could I without first obtaining her consent——"

"Do you repent, Katrine?"

C   5

" No, no, no !"

" Then let us hope for the best. And if we fearlessly cling to each other, who can separate our hearts ?"

He held out his hand to her, and she placed her own within it. Then he turned hastily away, and, with a gay "*Au revoir,*" hurried down the pavilion steps and towards the garden-gate.

Katrine looked after him. Once he turned, and their gaze met, and then he vanished among the trees.

She wrote no letters that day.

CHAPTER IV.

THE Professor turned into the first cross-street leading to the Thiergarten, and pursued his way for a time, scarcely knowing whither he was going. Suddenly he hailed a passing droschky, and gave directions to be driven to a house in the Charlottenstrasse. His mother lived there.

From old Hanna, who occupied a position between servant and friend,—in former times she had been first chorus-singer, and then dresser,—he learned that her mistress had gone to the theatre. " Would he not await her return ?" she asked, opening the door into the pretty little drawing-room. But he was too restless to spend half an hour here quietly waiting. He would return in a little while, if it were not too late, and he walked slowly along towards the Lindens and the opera-house, thinking that he would wait for his mother there.

He could hardly tell why he was so determined to see her before he slept, but so it was. He had nothing especial to say to her, for he could not yet tell her of what at present filled his heart and mind. But he could not bear to be alone, and no one in the world was so near to him as his mother. He reproached himself with having rather neglected her of late, and wished to atone for such short-comings. And thus he walked to and fro before the opera-house, waiting until the performance should be over.

He wondered whether his mother had ordered a carriage. He knew that she preferred driving to walking, but living in Berlin was expensive, and she avoided all unnecessary outlay. The opera was, however, one of the necessities of her life,—she could economize elsewhere; he knew that her supper would be a frugal one, and that he could hardly hope to be invited to share it. The noble Signora Camilla Bellarota had some very German traits, and her son, in whose veins there was a still larger admixture of German blood, was sometimes greatly amused by them, although he respectfully concealed such amusement. But to-day he longed to give her some special proof of his affection. He had no cause to resort to philosophical reasoning, he knew instinctively that the affec tion with which his heart was overflowing, unlike other treas ures, increased the more it was bestowed. If there was any loser by this new love of his, it was his mother, who had hitherto had no rival in his heart.

He was not afraid of missing her in the crowd. She took a child-like delight, not perhaps in striking attire, but in bright colors, and usually wore at night a scarlet wrap, that was easily distinguished. She was taller, too, than most women, and treading the boards of the stage had given her an unmistakable stateliness of carriage. Her son would have recognized her among thousands without seeing her face. He looked this evening for the scarlet wrap, and soon found her whom he sought, and for whom he had selected the best of the long row of fiacres drawn up against the sidewalk.

Camilla smiled brightly as she recognized her son's noble

figure standing hat in hand among the crowd outside of the house, and waved her hand, in which she still held her fan and opera-glass. He addressed her in her paternal tongue, and offered her his arm to conduct her to the carriage. She took it with a grace that was all her own, making no remark upon his filial attention, to which she was indeed accustomed.

"Why did you not tell me," he asked, "that you were going to the opera to-night? I thought that now that our principal prime donne have gone, and the season is over——"

"But I love this opera," she interrupted him, quickly. "I used to sing in it very often, and then I like to hear those of our singers who, although they are not stars, have still sufficient voice and culture to give great pleasure. I know from experience how much they suffer in being deposed from the front rank to give place to some favourite voice whose reputation may not, after all, be genuine. And the *ensemble* to-night was excellent. I have been greatly entertained."

While she was speaking, he had put her into the carriage and seated himself beside her. "You know," he said, in a tone of gentle reproach, "that I am always at your service as an escort, although my means, unfortunately, do not allow of my keeping a carriage for you." She leaned lightly upon his shoulder, tapped his hand gently with her fan, and said, with a laugh, "All in good time. You have been fairly buried in your books since your return. Confess, now, that you are glad not to have me interrupt you."

If there had been light enough in the carriage, Camilla would have seen him blush; and the jolting of the vehicle accounted for the stammer with which he muttered some excuse for the infrequency of his visits. His conscience pricked him, and he could hardly understand such a state of affairs; a few short weeks previously he would have affirmed that there could be no secrets between his mother and himself, on his

side. Surely what had thus changed him was most incomprehensible.

The carriage stopped. The Professor handed his mother
out, and she took his hand as if in farewell. " When will you
come again ?" she asked.

He thought he knew why she was so ready to dismiss him,
but determined to pay no heed. " Haven't you a little time
for me now ?" he inquired. " You cannot sleep immediately
after the opera."

" Certainly, certainly," she said ; " but if you have had no
supper——" touching upon the point she would have avoided
if possible.

" Oh, I have had quite enough," he hastened to assure her,
and with perfect truth, although his food had not been of the
" meat that perisheth."

" At this season of the year I take nothing after the theatre
but a glass of lemonade and a biscuit," she remarked, thus
making all due explanation of her frugal meal.

As they went up-stairs, she gave orders to have the two large
lamps in the little drawing-room lighted. The Professor listened
with a smile ; he knew how his mother liked to have her room
brilliantly lighted for her guests, and that he was the most honoured among them. She herself lighted the candles upon the
piano, and, sitting down for an instant, ran her fingers lightly
over the keys in a reminiscence of the opera she had just heard.

As we know, the Professor really had nothing of importance
to say to his mother ; he only wanted to be with her for awhile
And so he leaned comfortably back in an arm-chair, smoking,
by special permission, a cigarette, while Camilla sat upon a
lounge, preparing her lemonade. They talked easily and gayly
upon all manner of indifferent subjects. The still beautiful
woman, with masses of black, slightly waving hair, and large,
fine eyes, was an adept in this kind of conversation, which her
stage career had given her abundant opportunity of cultivating.

The Professor could have no better relaxation after a day of
hard work than in listening to her gay talk.   She seemed to
wear her heart upon her sleeve, but it was no easy task to discover its depths.

He was more absent-minded than was his wont, and, like an
unskilful steersman, allowed the conversation to drift too near
what he wished to avoid.   After his return from Italy he had
told her of his meeting with a young man in Florence who
had " discovered the palace of his ancestors," without, however,
mentioning Philip's name, then a matter of indifference to him.
Now he referred to the story again, and she reminded him that
he had told her all about it.

" But to my surprise," he said, " there is a sequel to it.   I
met at Councillor Wiesel's, the other day, a young girl, a sister
of Philip Amberger's."

" Amberger ?" she repeated, in a tone of inquiry.

" Does the name interest you ?" he asked, pleased that she
should pursue the subject.

" I knew a family of that name," she said, with some hesitation, " but it is long since."

He mentioned the town to which they belonged, and she
nodded thoughtfully, without replying.   " A very charming
young person," he remarked, and then was vexed with himself
for saying anything so commonplace about Katharina Amberger.   Camilla replied merely by an indifferent " Indeed ?" and
then changed the subject of conversation.

Again he steered his craft in among the shoals.   He was
thinking, he observed, of taking another journey.   This interested her, and she asked whither he was going and how long
he should be gone.   He named the town where Katharina
lived, and, to divert any suspicion of the real purport of his
journey, laid great stress upon the fact that it had always
been a member of the Hanseatic League, and must certainly
contain many interesting relics and architectural curiosities

from those old times, well worthy of study. Then, just as he directed towards her what was intended for an indifferent glance, he saw that she had grown very pale and was looking at him anxiously.

"How came you to think of that?" she stammered. All cheerfulness had vanished from her face, which wore a hard, stern expression.

"I told you——" he replied; and, without venturing to repeat his former pretext, broke off, and said, "It seems to affect you strangely."

She hastily assented. "It does, it certainly does. Do not go there, my son."

"But why not? Do you know the town?"

Her dark eyes suddenly glistened with tears. She arose and went to her writing-table, and took from it a little bronze easel upon which was a picture in a medallion-frame, at which she looked for a moment and then returned it to its place. The Professor let his cigar go out and regarded her with amazement.

"The name of this town seems to awaken recollections that agitate you," he began, after awhile. "Will you tell me——"

"No, no!" she cried, resuming her seat; "it is nothing!"

"Nothing, mother?"

"It has long been nothing, and never shall be anything again. Only this,—your grandfather, Carlo Bellarota, died there."

"There?"

"In the public hospital, poor and homeless. He, great singer that he was! I have talked with those who heard him in his best days; they spoke of him with enthusiasm. And, only a few years before his death, he had had a perfect ovation in that very town; laurel-wreaths were thrown upon the stage at his feet. And when he lost his voice,—his sole possession, —what was he? A beggar, left to die in a hospital. He, of so ancient a race! Was it not enough that he was forced to leave his country and seek his fortune as a wandering exile? How hard to see his wife die in giving me birth, and to leave me with no means of support! In those days there were none of these premiums, these benefits, that enrich even mediocre talent; and he so hated mèdiocrity. He was a singer by the grace of God and of art. Oh, his like would be hard to find! And so he died poor. But that among all those who had fèted and caressed him not one was found to hold it an honour to offer the poor broken man an asylum in his house,—not one,—not even that Amberger who prided himself upon never missing an opera,—is an insult that I never can forget, Xaver, that I never will forget, and that you never should forget when you enter the gate of that town whose best-born citizens are such sordid tradesmen."

"Were, mother,—were," he corrected her. "You are speaking of more than forty years ago. Everything is changed since then. And you were a child, with no judgment; you could not know——"

"But I could see, I could see," she said, coming to his side and raising her clear voice. "Did I not see him lying in his rough coffin, my father, Carlo? And when, years afterwards, I wished to erect a cross upon his grave, did I not have to search for it among the resting-places of the nameless dead? Even the one who—— But do not say a word in excuse of such miserable neglect,—those who live there now are of the same race."

The signora's cheeks glowed, her dark eyes flashed: she raised her right hand in menace; there was perhaps something theatric in her air and manner, but they were, nevertheless, full of grace and dignity. Her passionate outbreak did not surprise the Professor, who well knew her filial reverence for her father's memory, and who had often heard her indulge in similar complaints. She usually, however, studiously avoided mentioning names, and he thus learned now for the first time the name of the town where Carlo Bellarota had ended his career. Here, then, was where his mother's early youth had been passed. Had the Amberger family any associations with that past of hers? It terrified him to hear her utter the name of Katrine's father or grandfather.

He made no reply, but sat, with downcast eyes, sunk in his own thoughts, as Camilla walked to and fro in an agitated manner in the apartment, finally seating herself, and drinking her glass of lemonade. The more he thought, the more unlikely did it seem to him that her aversion to the place spoken of was the simple result of the unmerited neglect that her father had experienced there. She must be thinking of experiences of her own; all that she had hitherto carefully concealed from him must now be present to her thoughts. What was it? And could it have any possible influence upon his own wishes and hopes?

After a few minutes he felt her hand upon his arm. "Do not go there," she said, calmly and gently; "give up this journey, Xaver!"

He bent over and kissed her hand. "Carlo Bellarota sleeps as peacefully beneath the green sod as under a marble monument," he replied, gravely. "His best memorial is in his child's heart. Why, you yourself,—think of the thousands whom you have enchanted by your voice! And do you look for any reward from them? Must I hate the thankless public that has forgotten you? The tide of life obliterates us all. Let us submit with composure."

"It is not only that," she said, as if speaking to herself and not for his ear,—"it is not only that: I have other reasons for wishing you not to go near that place."

"And these other reasons,—will you tell me what they are, mother?"

She compressed her lips, and thoughtfully leaned her chin upon her hand. "No," she said, at last, sternly; "no, Xaver,

c*

I vowed I would be silent, and I will be silent. You never shall learn what I suffered before I became what you have always known me,—the singer, Camilla Bellarota. You will not love your mother the less, I hope?"

He gave her a loving smile. "You know me well," he said. "I have always respected your secret, and it is sacred to me now. Let me ask you one question only, mother, and answer it with a simple yes or no. That Amberger of whom you spoke,—have you any cause of complaint against him or his family in reference to your affairs?"

She shook her head. "Neither against him nor against any one else."

"Then I shall go to-morrow," he said, rising. "I too have good reasons for acting as I do, and I beg you to trust me without any explanation on my part."

Camilla sighed sadly, but made no farther attempt to induce him to resign his purpose; she seemed convinced that it would be fruitless. The conversation was not renewed again, the Professor only remarking, as he took his leave, "No one will suspect Professor Schönrade of being the son of the prima donna Camilla Bellarota."

"No one there would know the singer Camilla Bellarota," she said, shaking her head, as she dismissed her son with a kiss.

The Professor did not go home immediately. The day had been a most important one, marking a turning-point in his life. Fair as the road which he had hitherto travelled lay behind him, he could not borrow from retrospect any certainty as to the path upon which he had now entered. He knew his mother's passionate temperament, and that she often ascribed undue weight to unimportant matters when they affected her personally; yet he could not but feel that he had just stirred within her memories relating to the gravest and most important interests of her life, and, perhaps, of his own. For the first time, the veil in which she had so carefully shrouded the ten years ensuing upon her father's death irritated him. During that time he had been born. Now he no longer belonged solely to himself; others would have a right to inquire into circumstances and antecedents that were a mystery to him. What could have happened? what accidental discoveries might prove obstacles to his hopes and wishes? He began to regret that he had not made his mother his confidante. Perhaps his confidence would have begotten confidence on her part. But it was too late now : affairs must take their course.

CHAPTER V.

EARLY the next morning Schönrade left Berlin upon his proposed expedition.

The nearer he drew to his journey's end, the more restless and uneasy he became; and indeed he had cause for wonderment in the changed aspect of his life and of himself. He had reached the age of thirty without having been once seriously attracted by any woman; he had been given over entirely to scientific studies, and had gradually come to believe that men of his stamp were never destined to be bound in rosy chains. And suddenly he had fallen blindly in love, like some boy of twenty, with a charming child of eighteen, and was captive to a pair of beautiful eyes, to masses of fair hair, and to roguish dimples in cheek and chin. He had known nothing but that she enchanted him,—he, a professor who had written and published thick books upon the most abstruse subjects, and who believed he had left all youthful follies far behind him. He had seemed to himself older than he really was, because he had achieved results that usually belong to older years, and because so many of his colleagues were gray-haired men :

but he had suddenly awakened to the consciousness that he was a young man, with the best right in the world to be only a young man ; and he was confused and dismayed by the discovery. He had not been without a certain self-esteem,—it certainly was not vanity,—the consequence of his consciousness that he was widely known and valued. But his latest triumph had been achieved entirely without the assistance of his scientific attainments, nor could they have any share in making this triumph a practical gain to him. It was certainly embarrassing to present himself among people who had most probably never heard either of him or of his investigations, and from whom he wished to demand a treasure which they had carefully guarded, and which they apparently desired to intrust to far other hands. Like Philip Amberger, he looked constantly out of the window, not to admire the country, however, but to divert his troubled thoughts.

He laughed to himself as he followed on foot into the town the porter who took his small trunk in charge. It would hardly have been thought that his errand was the wooing of a wealthy merchant's daughter.

The porter, who evidently knew not what to make of him, asked, " To what hotel ?" and received, somewhat to his astonishment, the reply, " To the best, of course." He then turned into a street lined with stately old mansions, " Lange Strasse," as the signs at the corners proclaimed. Towards the middle of it it widened to a little market-place, on one side of which stood the Rathhaus, a curious old building, with deep arcades on the ground-floor, irregular gothic windows, and a huge pointed roof. A fountain built of piles of hewn stones, surmounted by a gigantic Neptune, was but scantily supplied with water ; several slender streams trickling through metal pipes, peeping out here and there, into the empty basin. The opposite building, also very ancient, was, as the porter explained, the Arsenal. But there were no longer any cannon there, he added, as in "olden times;" the lower rooms were occupied as a market, and the upper story as a museum. Not far beyond this little square a large building of modern construction stood, conspicuous among its gabled brethren,— the "Hotel Europa," the man said, "and the best in the town, mein Herr."

Again our Professor laughed to himself, as he refused to be directed to an upper story by the host, but took possession of two apartments on the first floor, where "he could receive visits without a blush," and where he soon completed his toilette standing before the long mirror in its faded gilt frame. He judged it best to proceed immediately to pay the important visit that was the purpose of his journey.

He was conscious of a kind of desperate inclination to make a jest of the whole affair, and, when the servant came in answer to his bell, gravely asked whether he did not look like a millionaire, enjoying the fellow's embarrassed glance at his small trunk, reposing upon the stand that had evidently been intended for a nobler freight. The man was reassured, however, by his inquiry as to where the Messrs. Amberger resided. "The Messrs. Amberger?" he repeated, with a bow, hurrying to the window and opening the shutters wide. "You cannot possibly miss the way, sir. If you will kindly look from this window,—that is the way to their house, one of the oldest in the town,—built in old Hanseatic times. Very wealthy they are, although——"

"Although?"

"Oh, the Messrs. Amberger are the very first people in the place, but they do say that most of their money was made by old Peter Amberger, grandfather of the present gentleman —and a very different man. He had a great deal to do with grain; he built many storehouses, and supplied quantities of lading-vessels for foreign traffic. The present gentlemen have nearly entirely given up that business; they are bankers,—

Herr Moritz is, I mean, for Herr Philip Amberger cares nothing for any business, and Frau Barbara Amberger doesn't count."

"Why doesn't Frau Barbara count?"

"Oh, so they say. Yes, whenever she is mentioned, they say, 'She doesn't count,' although——"

"Another although?"

"She is stout and strong enough,—it would not be easy to thrust her aside,—when she drives out in her landau she takes up all the back seat."

"And the house,—the house, my good fellow?"

"Oh, yes. You go up the 'Lange Strasse' to the turn, and then to the left through the Bremer Gate, and you will see upon the hill the old Cathedral with the big and little tower; there, just by the hill, is the Amberger mansion."

"By the hill? That is why they are called *Amberger*,* then?"

The man looked completely puzzled. "Oh, 'tis their family name, sir."

The Professor hurried away in the best of humours, his courage quite restored.

The Amberger mansion had not escaped restoration. Plate-glass windows had been inserted in the side looking towards the street, and the massive old stone portico had been provided with a flight of steps far too ornamental and airy for its solid proportions, while an accumulation of scaffolding and ladders in a narrow side-street indicated that the front, weather-stained and gray with age, was to be renovated. Schönrade was no great enthusiast for architectural antiquities, but as he looked up at the venerable building he shook his head and muttered, "A pity! a pity!"

The thought occurred to him that Philip's absence was

---

* "Am Berge," the German for "by the hill."

taken advantage of in a way that would not prepare for him
a very joyful return. As he ascended the steps, he learned
by the signs on either hand that the Messrs. Amberger were
agents and general agents for all sorts of insurance companies
and grand lotteries, directors also of a steamboat company, and
negotiators of bills of exchange.

The lower story of the house seemed to be entirely ap-
propria.ed to business purposes. Although it was quite late
in the afternoon, men were hurrying hither and thither, and
the chink of money was heard uninterruptedly from the rooms
on either side of the great hall. One of the doors standing
open revealed a long row of desks, at which clerks were busily
writing.

He had no bills to exchange, no insurance to purchase.
For a moment he thought of buying a lottery-ticket that
would be sure to win if his love were unsuccessful; but this
was but a grim jest, and he ascended the staircase to the second
story, where were the dwelling-rooms of the family. A servant
in livery took his card from him, and, ushering him into a
drawing-room, assured him that madame would receive him
immediately.

Self-possessed as he usually was, his heart beat a little faster
than was its wont. Everything about him produced the impression of solid and ancient wealth,—the English carpets, the
heavy curtains, the pictures on the walls, the ponderous chan-
deliers, all of the costliest and best. " You are no better than
a beggar in the estimation of these people," he said to himself two or three times.

A servant drew aside the portière, and Frau Barbara Amberger appeared upon the threshold, short and stout, unmis-
takably like her daughter, although not so much of a blonde.
Her thick black silk fitted her plump figure without a wrinkle,
a small cap of fine lace rested lightly upon her gray hair, a
heavy gold chain was passed several times around her neck

and shoulders, and the fingers of her small white hands were covered with rings. She cast a searching glance at the Professor, who was standing in the middle of the room, and who involuntarily bowed unusually low. Perhaps she suspected a commonplace petitioner in him, for she did not immediately ask him to sit down, but inquired, with an air of cold dignity, "Is your business with me, sir, or with my son? In the latter case, his rooms are on the lower story."

"I have requested the honour of an interview with yourself, madame," he answered, advancing a step and bowing again. "I arrived only an hour ago from Berlin, and hastened hither."

This threw no light for the lady of the mansion upon the object of his coming. She scanned him afresh, and said, slowly, "Herr Professor Schönrade, your card says, I believe."

"Professor Schönrade, madame. I must pray you to excuse——"

"Not at all, not at all," she interrupted him; "I am quite at your service. Something with regard to lectures, I suppose. The present season, to be sure——"

"I have no intention of making any such demand upon your patience, madame," he observed, with a smile; "but pray accept my thanks for your readiness to render me assistance, —an assistance of which I stand greatly in need in another direction; and in the first place let me give you the latest news from your daughter, whose acquaintance I have had the great pleasure of making at Councillor Wiesel's."

"Ah, my daughter! Indeed?" exclaimed Frau Amberger, and a gleam like April sunshine passed across her face. "But pray sit down, Herr Professor. Oh, yes, yes,—at Councillor Wiesel's. Katrine is there on a visit, learning something of life in a large city. My son has had business relations with that house—a very solid and excellent one—for a long time, and the girls became acquainted with each other at Wiesbaden last summer. At their age friendships ripen fast. Lilli, to be sure, is a little younger, but very well brought up, well taught, perhaps a trifle too learned. But her mother likes that. Were you her tutor?"

There was a change in these last words from the easy conversational tone of the first sentences, and they were accompanied by a look that said plainly that the speaker was still puzzled with regard to her visitor's presence, the object of which she should be glad to learn.

The Professor understood the look perfectly. "I have never occupied a position as tutor, madame," he said, with a gentle shake of the head, "but as soon as the doctorate was accorded to my rather youthful ambition, I betook myself to travel, in pursuance of the practical part of my studies. I then gave private instruction at one of our universities, and a year ago I was called to Berlin to occupy the chair of Professor of Natural Science."

It seemed strange enough to him to be thus declaring his title and dignities to an entire stranger, but he apprehended the necessity of establishing his position before proceeding farther. His information did not entirely fail to produce the desired impression, but it was too meagre to satisfy Frau Amberger's desire for enlightenment. She felt that she must still treat him with a certain prudent reserve, the needful gauge for his importance being yet wanting. The mention of his travels was some satisfaction; no one could travel without means; he must have some private fortune. This, therefore, was the topic to pursue, and she inquired what countries he had visited.

Schönrade was not very well pleased to find the conversation thus diverted from Katharina, but he could do no less than follow Frau Amberger's lead. "I have, in following the path of sulphur, madame," he said, "devoted myself principally to volcanic regions. The most remote points of my expeditions have been Iceland and Mexico. My work upon extinct craters

has found favour with men of science, but it can scarcely recommend itself as a favourite in a lady's drawing-room."

Frau Barbara Amberger cleared her throat slightly, "dallied
with her golden chain," and looked up at him in some embarrassment. After awhile she observed, "A few days ago I
read something about volcanoes in an illustrated magazine;
perhaps you wrote that? It was very amusing."

The Professor regretted that his publications could scarcely
be called amusing, and mentioned that he had, during the previous winter, given a short course of popular lectures in the
circle of which Frau Wiesel and her daughter were members.

"Then I was not entirely wrong in regarding you as Lilli's
instructor," the lady declared, with a self-satisfied air.

"Oh, I assure you I am very proud of my lady pupils," he
replied, gallantly.

A pause ensued in the conversation. Frau Amberger had
exhausted her inquiries, and seemed to think that the visit had
lasted long enough. The Professor was pondering the continuance of his campaign. He was forced to admit that he
had, as yet, made no approach to the fortress. As he did not
rise to take leave, she remarked, in a meditative tone, "It is a
pity that my son Philip is not at home; he is thought something of a scholar, and he could have shown you his curious
collections."

Here was a topic of mutual interest. Schönrade told of his
accidental meeting with Philip in Florence, and was listened
to with interest.

"He must have been greatly pleased with Florence," said
his mother. "He stayed there several weeks, and now writes
us from Rome that he shall go no farther south, but probably
return thither for a second visit."

The Professor smiled diplomatically. "He has made the
acquaintance in Florence," he observed, "of a young person
who is quite an authority upon those matters of art in which

he is so much interested, but whether she can be transported across the Alps, like one of his favourite Etruscan vases, is, of course, doubtful as yet."

Either she did not, or did not choose to, understand his jest. " He is a dear, good fellow," she said, " but entirely spoiled for business. My late husband might have yielded to his wishes, and allowed him to study as he pleased ; he will hardly be forced to play the schoolmaster for his living."

This last observation so plainly indicated her own point of view, that her guest began to doubt whether he should be thought quite right in his mind if he touched upon his own aspirations, and he could not regret that the visit was here interrupted by the entrance of a young man whom he rightly divined to be the chief of the house of Amberger. Frau Barbara presented the two men to each other, and the Professor rose to go.

Moritz was very unlike his brother in appearance. He had a round, smooth face, quick, lively eyes, carefully-parted hair, and altogether the air of a man who was no stranger to the joys of good living. He held a little riding-stick in one hand, and had a trick of inserting the thumb of the other in the armhole of his waistcoat and drumming upon his chest with his fingers. As he spoke, there was now and then a slight contraction of his left eyelid, which seemed to say, " Listen, and you will learn something worth hearing." Perhaps this habit had been acquired in his counting-room in his character of man of business. He announced that he had taken advantage of the fine weather to arrange an expedition for the afternoon with the Feinbergs. He and Sidonie were to ride with a couple of young officers, and he had ordered the carriage for Madame Feinberg and her husband and brother-in-law. But if Frau Barbara, as he hoped, would join them, Otto Feinberg should be her escort. They were to go out to Seehausen and take supper. Orders had been sent out, and they would have excellent fish; the wine he meant to supply from his own cellar.

"I am surprised to hear of it first at this late date," said his mother, with some pique. "Why did you not tell me of it at dinner?"

He kissed her hand. "Because I only heard of it myself a little while ago. This morning a sail in our new boat had been decided upon, but at dinner Sidonie laid a wager with Herr von Otten that her mare would leap like a bird a ditch which his brown gelding refused yesterday, and it must be decided. You know that when Sidonie once gets an idea into her head——"

She sighed. "Yes, yes, she often gets such ideas into her head. You ought to get them out again, Moritz."

He looked at her in amazement. "I?" he asked, and it sounded as if he thought himself the last to be able to effect such a change. His mother went on, without heeding his exclamation, in a tone of disapproval: "What a wager! Sidonie will break an arm or a leg some day in these wild rides of hers. And then to race with an officer for a wager!"

"I shall be with her, mother," he reminded her.

She shook her head. "It does not please me. I saw you from the window the other day—you rode meekly behind her like her groom."

"Only in your eyes, mother," he said, tossing his head. "It would be ridiculous for me to be always close at her elbow. May I order your phaeton? They thought it odd at the Feinbergs' the other day that you so often pleaded an engagement."

"They thought it odd?" she asked, stiffly. "I should suppose that Madame Feinberg knew——" Moritz stopped her by a glance towards their guest.

The Professor now took leave, Moritz having taken but small notice of him, seeming quite absorbed by the proposed expedition. Frau Barbara thanked him for his visit, but made no inquiries as to the length of his stay in town. A longer delay was impossible; even before he clearly appreciated that he had not advanced one step towards his aim, he found himself descending the steps. The great hall-door was closed and secured behind him with iron bolts; just such a door seemed to close between himself and all that he hoped to attain.

As he walked slowly along the street, he had never seemed to himself so stupid, so devoid of expedient. He would have liked to take the next train for Berlin, but how could he face his Katrine? He must await some fortunate chance which might bring him into closer association with her family; something must happen,—something should happen. But how to dispose of his time until the next day in this strange place, without books or occupation of any kind?

The assiduous waiter made civil inquiries as to whether he had found the house, and it suddenly occurred to the Professor to ask, why he knew not, how far it was to Seehausen.

"About a mile, or a mile and a half," the man replied. "A delightful road,—impossible to miss it,—through the Krämer-gate and the Neustadt and the English garden, by the broad alley, to the ferry; then along the right side of the river, through a fine forest of firs, to a small lake. Beyond it lies Castle Seehausen, belonging to one of our princes,—he comes there to hunt now and then; to the left is the mill, and the miller keeps the inn; very well kept it is too,—our first people patronize it. Shall I order a carriage for you, sir?"

"Is it too far to walk?"

"No, not too far," the man replied, "but it is more convenient——"

A sudden thought occurred to the Professor. "Can you let me have a riding-horse, my man?"

"A riding-horse? That, sir, you will find at the livery-stable."

"Get me a good riding-horse, and you shall be well paid, —but it must be a good one, remember, and at the door in half an hour."

The man looked rather puzzled, but bowed, and vanished obediently.

Twenty minutes afterwards, a groom was walking a powerful gray horse to and fro before the door of the hotel, awaiting the Professor's pleasure.

Schönrade was a practised rider,—his seat was excellent, his horsemanship perfect, and as he rode through the town many a passer-by turned to look, wondering who the graceful stranger might be. He rode by the Amberger mansion, and said to himself, as he saw a phaeton waiting before it, "Frau Barbara is going, then." After a rapid trot to the English garden, he let his horse walk slowly along the shady alley, thinking it likely that the riding-party would overtake him.

And so it turned out. In a few moments he heard behind him the noise of horses' feet; he did not turn his head, but calmly pursued his way, and soon four horses' heads appeared side by side. Nearest to him rode an officer, then a young lady in a blue riding-habit, then another officer, and lastly a gentleman in civilian's dress. They gradually distanced the Professor, who did not increase his horse's speed, and in passing each honoured him with a scrutinizing glance, followed, on the part of the gentleman in civilian's dress, by a slight bow, and a lifting of his hat. Moritz Amberger recognized him, and apparently thought him much more worthy of notice on horseback than as a guest in his mother's drawing-room. Schönrade could see that the others addressed some inquiry to him, to which he laughingly replied. A hundred steps further on, the fair rider turned her head and inspected both steed and horseman, after which she gave her mare the spur, and the gentlemen followed fast behind her.

By the ferry the road turned aside into the forest. As soon

as the riders were hidden by the trees, Schönrade permitted his steed more liberty. Through the winding wood-path he rode, among high fir-trees and scanty brushwood, until the forest opened upon an extensive marshy meadow traversed by deep and broad draining-ditches. The principal ditch cut the road at right angles, and was bridged across. Near this bridge, in the middle of the meadow, the riders had halted. Moritz Amberger's horse stood parallel with the bridge,—its master was evidently to enact the part of spectator. One of the officers retreated to the border of the forest, then, turning, rode back and put his horse at the ditch, but it refused the leap. The other officer made a like attempt, with equal ill success. At this moment the young lady observed the Professor, and, seeming to think it a favourable time for displaying her prowess, gathered up her bridle, backed her mare, whose delicate hoofs sank deep in the marshy ground, and then suddenly struck her sharply with the whip and gave utterance to the peculiar cry with which the amazons of the circus encourage their steeds. The mare reared, and the saddle-girth snapped; then she planted her forefeet upon the bank of the ditch, evidently not liking the water, and, as her rider continued to ply her with the whip, reared again wildly, and the saddle began to turn. The fair rider's hat, with its floating blue veil, threatened to fall off her high hair; she put up her hand to keep it on, and lost her stirrup. Fortunately, she retained sufficient presence of mind to clasp the neck of her mare, that turned and rushed wildly through the meadow towards a recent clearing, thickly strewn with stumps half hidden in tall ferns. The young merchant and the two officers galloped after her, but their pursuit only terrified still more the already frightened animal.

Schönrade appreciated the danger instantly, and lost no time in averting it. He motioned to her pursuers to fall back, and, directing his course to that part of the field whither the mare was rushing, met her there, rode neck and neck with her for a few minutes, during which time he gathered up the hanging bridle, and successfully assisted the rider to regain her seat, and to soothe her mare, who was soon reduced to order and brought to a pause.

"I thank you, sir," said Sidonie, arranging her hat upon her dishevelled locks, with affected composure. "There was no danger, indeed, but the situation might have become—disagreeable, and—I thank you." Then she patted her mare's neck, and regarded the Professor with a look that was half curiosity, half approval. "I still insist that my mare can easily take the ditch," she continued, "but the other horses refused it, and a bad example is catching. But you know nothing of our wager. Here comes Herr von Otten most gallantly. Do not exult too soon, Herr von Otten, you are not yet out of the woods. You shall see with your own eyes that I am right."

.Moritz Amberger held out his hand to her. "Thank God," he said, "you are safe! I was in terror for you. You never ought to——"

She laughed loudly. "What was there to be afraid of? The mare would soon have come to her senses, and if the worst had come to the worst I could have thrown myself off. It is all the fault of my groom, who did not. see to her girth carefully enough. I think it can yet be made all right." She turned and beckoned to a man who was tending some cattle on the border of the forest.

Meanwhile, Schönrade had made acquaintance with the officers. The second was presented to him as a Herr von Oschersdorf. He declared that the livery-stable Almansor was hardly to be recognized under his present rider. "Why, really," exclaimed Herr von Otten, slightly through his nose, "I did not know him at all. He is still a fine creature. Where in the world did you get such an excellent seat?"

Schönrade's face was perfectly impassive. "I have ridden a great deal in Mexico," he quietly remarked, "where one does not hire horses from a livery-stable." Involuntarily the hands of the two officers sought their caps, as if for a military salute, and Amberger regarded his new acquaintance with more respect.

In the mean time the herdsman had approached, and by Sidonie's directions, which she gave without getting off her mare, the girth was arranged so as to serve its purpose for the present. While he was busy with it, she talked with the gentlemen, perfectly at her ease, accepting and lighting a cigarette which Herr von Otten offered her.

"All the women smoke in Mexico, I believe?" she said, addressing herself to Schönrade.

"The bad practice of smoking is almost universal there," he replied.

"But you smoke yourself, Herr Professor," she remarked, in some surprise at his temerity.

"That gives me the right to criticise the habit," he rejoined, courteously.

The herdsman's task was ended. Sidonie threw him a piece of money, and turned her mare off to the meadow again.

"What are you going to do, Sidonie?" Amberger exclaimed.

"To try the ditch again, of course," she replied, with great composure. He rode up to her and whispered a few words in her ear. "Don't trouble yourself," she replied, aloud. "I know perfectly well what to do, and what not to do."

"But, Sidonie, I pray——"

She gave her mare the spur. "Better not pray at all, Moritz; my mind is made up. There is the bridge, built on purpose for those who are afraid to leap the ditch."

"Give it up, Fräulein Sidonie! give it up!" both the officers called out to her; "the bank on either side of the ditch is too soft." She paid them no heed, but continued to urge on her mare, who tossed her head wildly at every fresh stroke of the whip.

" Your horses are both young, gentlemen," observed the Professor, following the lady; " you can. do nothing by attempting to force them. They break, and refuse the ditch because they are unaccustomed to leaping, but they will readily follow when they see there is no danger. My respectable Almansor, although he is no longer one of the strongest upon his forefeet, will make a very fair bell-wether. Let them follow him : there is not the slightest danger." As he spoke the words he passed Sidonie, touched his horse lightly with the spur, and cleared the ditch with perfect ease. Sidonie followed close upon his heels, and the two officers immediately after her. Amberger's steed still refused to leap, and he crossed by the bridge, whereat his betrothed railed loudly.

" Herr von Otten admits that I have won my wager," she added. " It would as certainly have been won if the Herr Professor had waited a moment longer ; do you not think so, gentlemen?" What could the gentlemen do but assent eagerly? Amberger was vexed at his failure, and declared that he should sell his horse and buy an animal that could be trusted.

" I'll lay another wager, Moritz," Sidonie called out to him, "that if you change horses with the Herr Professor you will immediately find out that Almansor is too weak in the knees to make that leap, but that your horse can take it easily. Every horse has as much courage as its rider, and no more."

The young merchant showed no inclination to accept this wager. " Rather a bold assertion," he muttered, in a tone of irritation, and then fell silent. When, soon after, the equipages arrived, he devoted himself to Madame Feinberg, who appeared *en grande toilette* beside her husband, a little man almost buried in a huge coat.

Naturally enough, Professor Schönrade was one of the party.

Sidonie, in especial, appeared to take great pleasure in his society, retaining him by her side, keeping up a steady conversation with him, and asking him all sorts of questions with regard to himself. The officers hovered around her, being only now and then allowed to pick up some crumb of her favour. Of her betrothed she took not the slightest notice.

When they arrived at the mill, romantically situated by the lake, Moritz dismounted and helped the ladies to descend from their vehicles. Madame Feinberg and Frau Barbara Amberger greeted each other with great formality. Herr Ignaz Feinberg, small, round-shouldered, with a sly face, little twinkling gray eyes, and a wide, thin-lipped mouth, walked to and fro, with his hands in his coat-pockets. Otto Feinberg offered his arm to Frau Amberger, and conducted her to a seat by a table beneath a huge linden-tree. She greeted the Professor after her own measured fashion, manifesting no surprise at finding him one of the party.

The fat miller, who was also inn-keeper at Seehausen, showed great respect for his guests. He was all servility and desire to please. Several bottles of wine were produced from the boxes of the carriages, and ice was required to cool them. It was brought in a bucket, the host lamenting the while that, although he had ordered a wine-cooler some months previously, it had not yet arrived. "No matter," cried Herr von Otten, "rustic fashions are good fashions. Eh, madame?"

Madame Feinberg, to whom his remark was addressed, an elderly lady with remarkably fine teeth, tossed back over her shoulder the curl that hung from her huge chignon, and remarked, in a soft, lisping tone, "I do indeed love pure unadulterated nature." Frau Amberger smiled to herself,—she had already taken her knitting out of a pretty little workbasket, and to Herr von Oschersdorf's sprightly entreaty that this "divine evening might not be profaned by labour," simply replied that she "greatly disliked being idle."

Moritz Amberger, who seemed to have forgotten his irritation, and to wish to make others forget it, paid great attention to
his betrothed, without eliciting from her much notice in return.
She had thrown herself negligently into an arm-chair, in which
some carriage-cushions had first been placed, and now drank
glass after glass of wine, jesting meanwhile with the two officers, whose replies were not always of the choicest. It seemed
to annoy her that the Professor confined his attentions to Frau
Amberger and paid not the slightest homage to herself; she
mingled in the conversation whenever she could, and tried to
attract his notice. Frau Feinberg regarded her daughter with
great admiration across the table, now and then exclaiming
to Herr von Otto, behind her hand, but quite audibly, "Isn't
she charming? Isn't she lovely and brilliant to-day?" He
was lavish in his praises; but Frau Amberger, to whom her
remarks were addressed on her other side, did not assent so
enthusiastically, but gravely continued to knit. Herr Ignaz
Feinberg found the evening to be growing much cooler,
and the air from the lake almost too fresh, in view of which
he had his paletôt brought him from the carriage. In one of
its pockets he found a newspaper, and he was soon buried in
the prices of stocks.

The sun was setting. Part of the forest was in shadow,
but the red roof and the high white chimneys of Castle Seehausen glowed in the parting light. Schönrade called attention
to the beautiful sight. "Ah, heavens, what nature!" cried
Frau Feinberg, with enthusiasm, waving her hand in its straw-
colored glove towards the horizon. Her husband's eyes never
left his paper. Herr von Oschersdorf obligingly thought the
sky, and particularly the "*ensemble*," magnificent, while Herr
von Otten emptied a glass to the departing sun, with a wish
that "no sadder tear might fall upon its disappearance."

Sidonie suddenly grew sentimental. "When the last sun-
set comes——" she sighed.

'You have no cause for any foreboding, Fräulein Sidonie," the Professor reassured her. "As long as our earth turns upon its axis we shall enjoy our beautiful sunrises and sunsets, —the sunsets at least, for I fear that few of this honourable company appreciate the beauty of a sunrise."

Sidonie leaned her head upon her hand and looked with an air of melancholy at the speaker. "You jest," she said; "but why should not all this splendour fall to decay in a single night? Would it be an impossibility?"

"Oh, not at all," Schönrade rejoined, with great gravity. "May not this earth be neither more nor less than a huge bombshell filled with all sorts of stones and having a mine of fulminating matter in its centre? The volcanoes may be nothing more than the fuse, as Herr von Oschersdorf can explain to you far better than I,—they are filled with combustible material, and their fire is fanned by the outer air. Let it once communicate with the centre, and instead of our beautiful earth a hundred little planets will go careering around the sun, to the wonder of astronomers in Jupiter."

"Don't joke so horribly," said Madame Feinberg. "All that would be so very unnatural."

Sidonie arose, and observed, with great unction, "This hour, at least, is ours to enjoy!" She walked to the shore of the lake and untied the miller's boat from its mooring. The gentlemen looked after her curiously, and immediately followed her.

She would probably have been allowed to do as she pleased had not just at this moment the inn-door opened and various servants appeared bearing smoking dishes,—the preparations for a good supper being at length completed. Moritz Amberger remonstrated with her. "Do you wish to go upon the lake now, Sidonie?" he asked. "The air is quite cool, and the mists are rising. You have no shawl. Do not leave the party thus."

She drew the boat by its loosened chain up on the sandy shore. "I do not require that you should accompany me," she replied, composedly; "do not come if you dislike the mists, which are the chief charm to me of a sail in the cool twilight. My nature craves such refreshment, but that imposes no obligations upon you."

Moritz went up to her side and tried to take the chain from her, saying, in a low tone, "You know how my mother disapproves of such extravagances. Pay her, I beg of you, the respect I have a right——"

"Do not spoil the evening for me, Moritz," she interrupted him, as, laying her hand on his shoulder, she sprang into the boat.

"But, Fräulein Sidonie," exclaimed Herr von Otten, with a degree of excitement that was comical, "I pray you look,— see what a splendid fish they have just put upon the table!"

"And Herr Otto Feinberg says there is a wonderfully fine dish of asparagus to come," added Herr von Oschersdorf; "*magnifique,* he tells me." He smacked his lips. "Can we leave all these delights to row about the lake in that gray mist, while the dishes grow cold and the wine grows warm? Another time, another time, Fräulein Sidonie."

Sidonie took up an oar and leaned upon it. "What is to hinder you, gentlemen," she called out to them, "from resigning yourselves entirely to the pleasures of the table? I propose for once to live upon air. Herr Professor, is your nature so gross that you prefer fish and asparagus to a lovely row on the lake? Pray do it no violence on my account." She prepared to push off from the shore, but did not immediately succeed in doing so.

"I am the only unaccredited guest at that Lucullan banquet," said Schönrade, "and I have not yet ordered my own supper."

"Oh," Moritz Amberger interrupted him, "surely you cannot need a formal invitation? Of course you are our guest."

"A little exercise, then, will season the feast," said the Professor, offering him his hand. "Return to the table; I will bring you back your lady fair safe and sound. We cannot let her go entirely alone," he added, in a low tone.

Amberger hesitated. "I am willing to go," he muttered; but the Professor was already in the boat, and had pushed off from the shore.

'Pray hand me the oar, Fräulein Feinberg," he said, holding out his hand for it.

"No, no! I will row myself," she exclaimed; "it is my great delight. I thank you for coming with me. Pray be quite at your ease,—light a cigar, and take no trouble. Is it not an entertaining change to be rowed about by a lady, instead of having to play the courtier? Thank Heaven, neither Herr von Otten nor Von Oschersdorf came: they would have made such a fuss about having the oars,—very likely nearly capsized the boat. There would have been no danger for me, however: I swim very well."

"You swim, too?"

"Oh, yes. I am an only child, and have been allowed to learn everything I wished to. Where shall we row?"

"Towards the middle of the lake, I think, so that they may keep us in view from beneath the linden."

"For that very reason I should prefer to sail behind that projecting cape of forest. I do not like to be observed."

"But Herr Amberger will be anxious about you."

"Oh,—Moritz? He must learn to accustom himself to that, or we shall never get along together."

Schönrade perfectly agreed with her, but, of course, made no reply.

He leaned over the side of the boat and let his hand dip into the water, making a little furrow in its mirror-like surface. Sidonie rested upon her oars and looked at him.

"Is there a moon to-night?" she asked.

"Too late for us to see it, Fräulein Feinberg."

"Why?"

"If I do not mistake, it does not rise before eleven."

"Let the rest go home without us; we can find the way to town alone."

The words were quietly spoken, but they startled Schönrade. He could not regard them as the naïve remark of a young girl ready to rave about moonlight, and careless of propriety. He already suspected her sentimentality. "You are floating in-shore, Fräulein Feinberg," he said, grasping a handful of rushes.

She looked hastily over her shoulder. "True!" she exclaimed. "I kept too much to the right."

One or two vigorous strokes of her oar brought the light skiff into clear water again. The wooded point lay just before them, the trees rising as it were out of their mirrored presentments in the clear lake, and sharply defined against the crimson-and-yellow horizon. A cricket chirped faintly, and the croak of a distant frog came from the depths of the forest. Sidonie rowed around the point; the mill and the spreading linden vanished: the castle alone was visible on the left, shrouded in mist. The lake expanded, and was bounded in the distance by a flat meadow, above which blue ghost-like vapours were hovering. Large-leaved water-plants floated upon the water, lifted dripping now and then upon their long stems by the stroke of the oar. Yellow water-lilies waved to and fro in the furrow left in the wake of the boat. Profound peace reigned everywhere in nature; it was an evening to awaken memories of the happiest hours of one's life.

The Professor gazed down upon his hand, still idly toying with the water. "What are you thinking of so earnestly?" asked Sidonie. He was thinking of Katrine, but he did not say so.

Sidonie urged the boat under the drooping boughs of the

overhanging trees, and then, letting it drift whither it would rested upon her oars, leaning her head upon her hand. "What do you think of those people?" she asked, after awhile.

"What people, Fräulein Feinberg?"

"Oh, those people!—my father, my mother, my betrothed, my future mother-in-law, my uncle, my aunt,—no, my aunt is not with us to-day,—but those two Von—what d'ye-call-em's?"

He laughed. "You surely cannot expect an answer?" he said, throwing away his cigar.

"No answer is an answer," she replied, in a low tone, as if half to herself, "as when just now I asked you of what you were thinking."

"I think them all very amiable," he said, evasively, disagreeably impressed by her tone and manner.

"Of course," she rejoined, "very amiable. But, constituted as you are, you could live an eternity with them without being attracted by them. Am I not right?"

"I have so slight an acquaintance with them."

"My father is a man of wealth, which he began to accumulate by stopping the peasants as they passed his door and buying their grain of them before they took it to market. My mother takes four 'Journaux des Modes,' and is always a day in advance of Paris. My mamma-in-law plays the part of a worthy patrician dame excellently well; she does not consider me her equal by birth, and expects me to regard her son Moritz's choice of me for a wife as a great honour. Uncle Otto is a thorough merchant; he foresees every variation in the stock-market, and when stocks fall he would see his best friend ruined without lifting a finger to help him. Moritz——"

"Pray tell me, Fräulein Feinberg, how I have deserved such confidence on your part," Schönrade here hastily interrupted her, excessively annoyed at the turn the conversation had taken.

D*

"Moritz is a good fellow," she continued, without heeding his words, "but I am not sure that good fellows wear very well as companions for life——"

"He is your betrothed——"

"True, that happens to be so. But it might happen to be otherwise: it all depends upon me,—upon what might be called my whim. Very sad, is it not, that so much should depend upon a girl's whim? I should like not to be misunderstood by you. Sometimes I would claim the right not to be judged by their standard. Do you think this presumption?"

"Fräulein Feinberg——"

"Be honest. I can bear blame if it comes from a strong, upright nature. Our acquaintance, it is true, is but a few hours old——"

"That is unquestionably true."

"But I am surely not mistaken in you. You are a man! I recognized in the first moment that I saw you——"

He leaned over, took up the oars, and urged the boat away from the trees out into the open lake. Sidonie laid her hand upon his and prevented his making another stroke. "Oh, don't!" she said; "it destroys the entire illusion. It is as if you wished to drown my words with the noise of your oars. Are you too proud to hear praise, that is indeed no flattery, from the lips of a young girl?"

"Neither flattery nor praise," he said, gravely; "on the contrary, I consider it an insult to call a man manly or a woman feminine."

Sidonie seemed to feel the sting his words were meant to convey. She drew back her hand, and was silent for awhile; then she said, speaking slowly and without manifesting any irritation, "And yet we poor creatures must either expose ourselves to the blame of being unfeminine or die of ennui."

"You exaggerate!" he exclaimed.

She shook her head decidedly. "I do not exaggerate. The ideal woman is best developed in the hard school of necessity, in sordid circumstances, in the grasp of an iron will. The virtue most highly prized in her is entire submission. But now suppose a life fostered in luxury from earliest childhood, a want of all stern training, a longing for freedom, a feeling of self-reliance, and a need of a field of action ; then consider the pitiable inferiority of those who claim a right to rule that life, and what choice is left save a slavish submission to what is despised, or a defiant breaking asunder of the trammels that would bar approach to all for which there is a true affinity ?"

"What that is the whim of the hour must decide," he interpolated.

"Not when it really attracts."

"And when does it really attract ?"

"When it fetters us."

"Nothing is capable of always fettering a human being, save duty. Every pleasure palls."

"The right to be happy is born with us."

"That requires proof, but it may be so. The duty to make others happy is none the less born with us."

"We can only make those happy who choose that we should make them so."

"Or rather, who possess the capacity to be made happy by us."

"Then mistakes are unavoidable ?"

"Most assuredly, Fräulein Feinberg."

"And when discovered to be such, what remains for us ? Resignation ?"

"For gentle natures."

"Or repentance ?"

"For religious temperaments."

"And if one's nature is not gentle, nor one's temperament religious—what then ?"

Schönrade continued to row gently. "I am no doctor of souls, Fräulein Feinberg," he said, evasively; "and—apparently you are not in need of any such."

She sighed. "Let me assist your Professorship. There then remains for us—life. It is ours with all its needs and imperfections, and also with all its chance delights and pleasures."

"And we can play with it until we shatter it," he concluded.

A loud halloo resounded from the shore. The boat had been seen and hailed by the gentlemen. Schönrade rowed hastily towards them, without any opposition from Sidonie. She sat leaning her head upon her hand, gazing into the thickening mist, through which the outlines of the wooded points showed like the landscape of a dream. As she left the boat, she took the Professor's hand and lightly pressed it, as if by way of thanks. To the many inquiries of the two officers, her replies, when she answered at all, were short and monosyllabic.

Frau Barbara Amberger had already driven home: she had entirely disapproved of the row on the lake. This had annoyed Moritz at first, but his easy good humour soon asserted itself. He was rather relieved by the absence of his mother, who, he well knew, regarded with no favour his relations with Sidonie, and, indeed, his entire connection with the Feinbergs. He had long ago given up all attempt to shape his conduct according to her wishes, conscious that, should he do so, his engagement to Sidonie would not last a day; and now that she was not present to watch him, it was far easier to receive his betrothed with amiability and conduct her to her place beneath the linden.

To the surprise of all present, Sidonie expressed a desire to return to town in the carriage. Her mother tenderly trusted that her excursion on the water had not been too much for her, and her father observed, with his own peculiar grace, that "it was deuced folly to go floating about on that swamp in the fog." The young lady, however, assured them that she felt perfectly well and strong, only she did not care to ride again at present. She whispered in her mother's ear, " Ask Professor Schönrade to visit us; he is delightful." And Madame Feinberg was but too well accustomed to obeying such directions from her spoiled darling.

Moritz Amberger uncorked the last bottle of champagne, and insisted upon the Professor's drinking a glass. He seemed to wish to prove to his betrothed that her trip upon the water had not aroused his jealousy, but that he knew how to value a man of Schönrade's stamp. He had drunk considerably, and was jovial and talkative. At last he offered to resign his horse to Otto Feinberg, and to ride Sidonie's mare back to town "lady-fashion," as he called it. The jest was greatly relished by the two officers, and measures were taken for carrying it out immediately. Moritz tied a large plaid about his waist for a riding-skirt, and fastened a handkerchief to his hat for a veil, insisting upon being put into the saddle by Herr von Oschersdorf, who, accordingly, held his stirrup. Sidonie, to whom he waved his hand as he rode off, shrugged her shoulders, but could not help laughing. She seemed tired of playing the languishing fair one, and perhaps regretted having asked for a seat in the carriage.

Schönrade conducted the ladies to the vehicle, and, on the way, Madame Feinberg asked him how long a stay he intended to make in the town, and if she might learn the nature of the business that had brought him hither. He replied that his stay would last but a few days, and then went into some long explanation about a desire to see all the antiquities of the place, and a hope of investigating a new species of infusoria in its waters; by which ingenious fraud he succeeded partly in convincing himself, but produced small effect upon Madame Feinberg, who exclaimed, as he helped her into the carriage, " My dear Herr Professor, if you wish to see the curiosities

8

of the town, you must not miss our house.   It is one of the
oldest patrician mansions.   My husband spent a great deal of
money in buying and rebuilding it a few years ago.   It over-
looks the ancient fosse, and the garden-wall is partly composed of the old wall around the town.   Oh, you must see it!
Heavens! on the lower terrace you see nature, pure nature, on
every side!"   He promised to pay his respects to them, if the
ladies would allow him.   Sidonie followed her mother, and
added, " Pray come, we have nothing in the world to do."
Ignaz was already comfortably ensconced in the back seat, and
gave the coachman a nod to drive off, muttering, by way of
excuse, " The horses will not stand any longer."   " We shall
see you soon?" his wife screamed, putting her head out of the
window as they drove off.

Schönrade mounted his horse, and would have been glad to
have no company but his own thoughts, but it scarcely seemed
courteous to take so sudden a leave, and perhaps an acquaintance with the Feinbergs might further his views.   So he put
spurs to his steed and was soon by the side of the carriage.

Here, in spite of the noise of the wheels, the ladies managed to keep up a running fire of conversation with him, and
shortly afterwards, when the horsemen were overtaken, the
carriage was quite surrounded by riders.   Moritz's lady-like
demeanour was loudly applauded by Madame Feinberg, but
Sidonie ordered him to stay behind in the English garden
until they were out of sight, since she did not choose to be
made ridiculous on entering the town.   He meekly did as he
was bidden.

Upon their arrival at the Feinbergs', a servant darted forward to open the carriage-door.   " Are you engaged to dine
anywhere to-morrow?" Madame Feinberg asked the Professor.
He replied that he had no engagement, and received a pressing invitation to a family dinner.   " And no formal nonsense,"
Sidonie added.

Schönrade rode slowly through the dimly-lighted streets. He did not know his way, and never thought of finding it through the rows of houses with pointed gables, above which the pale moonlight was beginning to gleam. He was buried in thought, and was recalled to himself by his steed, which stopped before a large gate and neighed loudly.

A groom made his appearance, and it was manifest that the horse had wisely chosen to go directly to his own stable since affairs were intrusted to his guidance. It made very little difference; the hotel was close at hand, and the Professor walked home. And these, then, were the people with whom he had to do ; he felt very little attraction for any of them. Frau Barbara Amberger inspired him with a certain respect, but she was the most unapproachable of all. He pitied Moritz as one pities a man whom, nevertheless, he feels no call to assist. He was entirely unlike his brother Philip. As for Katrine,—his Katrine, with her quick intelligence and un-affected gayety,—he could not imagine her in this circle. He determined not to judge her people, however, until he had observed them more closely. The Feinbergs were easier to understand. Sidonie alone was something of a problem. He could not be quite sure whether she was only a frivolous co-quette, with an affectation of singularity, or whether she had some depth of nature and was only spoiled or misunderstood, as she herself declared. Whence her sudden confidences ? What did she mean by singling him out so decidedly ? Was it a custom with her to conduct herself thus with every new acquaintance, or was he specially honoured ? Her self-asser-tion, her caprices, her treatment of Moritz, disgusted him: he did not even think her pretty or attractive ; and yet when he remembered the sail on the lake he could not but admit that he felt a certain temptation to try his influence upon such a wild and unrestrained nature. He could never have the slightest inclination to do more, now that his choice for life was made.

CHAPTER VI.

AFTER a rather restless night, the Professor determined to make no further delay in declaring his hopes to the mother of his love, and accordingly presented himself at an early hour in her drawing-room.

"You returned home yesterday so early and unexpectedly," he began, after the first formal greetings, "that I had no opportunity to bid you 'good-evening.' I hope indisposition was not the cause of your departure."

"You can hardly have missed an old woman," she said, shaking her head, "while you were in such interesting society."

"I did, greatly," he insisted. "Let me confess that I went to Seehausen solely on your account."

She looked at him incredulously. "Then you should not have been persuaded to sail on the lake," she said, "in the mist and darkness with a young lady." She tried to say it jestingly, but her irritation against Sidonie was manifest in spite of herself.

"I could not allow Fräulein Feinberg to go alone upon the water," he said; "and as the other gentlemen were ready for supper——"

"Oh, Fräulein Feinberg would have changed her mind in five minutes," she interrupted him, not without evident annoyance; "I know the fleeting nature of her fancies."

"But if you did not approve of her sailing, why not have told the young lady?"

She sighed. "There are things," she said, "to which we must resign ourselves. Sidonie is very independent, and my son no longer owns my rule. Young people of the present

day do very much as they please, and my opinions—I was
very strictly brought up—would be thought old-fashioned."

"But in this case," he said, bowing, "you may be perfectly
assured that I am not a man to——"

"Oh, pardon me," the matron interrupted him. "I should
rejoice to think you had made a conquest there, did I not
know—— But why speak of the matter at all? Sidonie is
betrothed to my son, and will soon be his wife. She will bring
life into this old house; it has already put on a new dress,
which will greatly surprise my son Philip. Well, it is large
enough; my rooms in it are mine by my husband's will, and
there is space enough in them for Katharina until she——
Let us say no more about it."

"My dear Frau Amberger," he replied, moving his chair
closer to hers, so that she looked up in surprise, "it is of her
that I beg to be allowed to speak. What I have to say lies
nearer my heart than anything else in the world. I pray you
to listen to me."

"How am I to understand you, Herr Professor?" she asked,
in some embarrassment.

He looked her full in the face. "You spoke just now of
Katharina, and of a time when she would no longer need your
protection. Suppose that time were already come——"

"How, sir?"

"You must hear me, madame. I have learned to know
and to love Katharina Amberger during her stay in Berlin; I
have asked her if she can love me, and she has answered
'yes.' In coming here, I had no other aim than to present
myself to you and pray you for your consent. Do not, do not
refuse to give it to me!"

Frau Barbara Amberger sat in her cushioned chair like an
image of stone, her lips slightly parted, her eyes riveted upon
the Professor, who took her hand and carried it to his lips.
"But how can this be?" she asked, after a pause,—express-

ing her astonishment in the words that first suggested themselves.

"Indeed, it would be hard to say," he answered, immediately, infinitely relieved and quite ready to treat the matter gaily. "A philosopher would find it difficult to invent a formula to explain it; but it is a truth, and must be treated as such. I love your daughter, and am convinced that she loves me. These are facts that no consent given or withheld can affect. But it depends upon others whether our love prove fortunate or the reverse, and therefore I entreat your blessing."

Frau Barbara drew away her hand. "But Katharina has never in any of her letters——"

"How could she reveal a secret which she was guarding closely even from herself? I declared myself only the day before my departure. I left her, promising to come hither immediately, madame, to ask her at your hands."

She wrung her hands uneasily, looked down, and seemed to reflect.

"Does any one know of this? Do the Wiesels know?" she asked.

"How should they? They were not at home, and I have not seen them since."

"They do not even know, then, that you came hither?"

"No."

She breathed more freely. "Thank Heaven! Herr Professor, I require your promise that no one—no one else shall learn what you have just told me. Indeed, you owe me this consideration."

Schönrade bowed in assent. "I, too, think that a betrothal should first be made public through the mother of the betrothed."

Frau Amberger moved uneasily in her chair. "You speak of betrothal, Herr Professor," she said, with some hesitation, "but matters have not yet gone so far by a great deal.

Katharina has acted very thoughtlessly,—very. I cannot see how such a *tête-à-tête* could have taken place while she was under the Wiesels' roof. I allowed Katharina to go there because I thought that until her brother Moritz was married to Sidonie she would be safer there than here from all undesirable influences, and now I learn that my daughter has entered into secret relations with an entire stranger, that she has had a *tête-à-tête* conversation with him, and has even shown so little consideration for her mother as to give utterance to words which you, sir, consider yourself justified in understanding as an avowal of affection. Herr Professor, all this confuses and astounds me."

He waited calmly until she had finished; his expression plainly showing how powerless was her disapproval. "Madame," he now said, gently, "I give you my word of honour that nothing has happened that could in any way compromise your daughter's maidenly dignity in the eyes of the strictest parent,—unless, indeed, it be a crime to love me. My declaration was entirely unforeseen by her. I took her by surprise, and in an unguarded moment obtained from her the confession of her affection. Whatever reproach you may think I deserve, madame, Fräulein Katharina and her friends are blameless."

Frau Amberger shook her head. "Our views upon the subject are entirely different, Herr Professor," she replied. " In the circle whose customs and opinions you share, it may be considered correct for a young man and a young girl to engage themselves, if they please, to each other, and then to ask the consent of their parents, who probably have nothing else to give. But in this ancient commercial town, you must know, certain good old customs, that accord but ill with modern ideas, are handed down from generation to generation. There are here patrician families, who have, it is true, lost many of their old municipal privileges, but who still retain

their solid wealth and their pride, and with whom marriages
are contracted after a different fashion from any prevailing
among the common bourgeoisie.　Among the oldest of these
patrician . families the Ambergers and the Vorbringers, of
whom I am one, belong.　I have suffered great pain from
my son Moritz's connection with a plebeian family.　Feinberg is a parvenu, who had no weight on 'Change as long as
my father lived, but his wealth gives him a certain position
now, and Sidonie is his only child ; but my daughter is my
charge, and the disposal of her hand belongs to me and to her
brothers, whom my husband's will endowed with full rights in
the matter.　These are my views with regard to Katharina."

She sat upright and looked haughtily down at the Professor,
whose gloomy gaze was bent upon the ground.　" I could not
have believed that such prejudices prevailed anywhere except
in certain narrow aristocratic circles," he replied, after a pause.
" Let me ask, in my turn, How can this be ?　How can it be
in these advanced times, in which in reality men are divided
only into two classes,—the cultivated and the uncultivated ?
Ask your heart, madame, if you can answer it to yourself to
sacrifice your daughter's happiness to such idols, and then give
me your final decision."

Frau Barbara Amberger compressed her lips and regarded
him sternly.　" You confidently assert, sir, that my daughter's
happiness consists in a union with yourself.　I do not know
upon what you ground this assertion."

" Upon my honest conviction," he replied.　" I know that
I love Katharina unspeakably, and that she loves me.　All
else is of minor importance."

" Not to me," she hastily rejoined.　" How easily we are
mistaken in our own sentiments !　how soon we yield to a fleeting inclination !　An inexperienced girl,—a forward lover,—
an unguarded moment,—and the happiness of an eternity is
arranged : a happiness that is shivered like glass at the first

shock. Your conviction, sir, is no warranty for me. I do not know you, I do not know your family : I heard your name yesterday for the first time ; I do not even know whether I could prudently intrust Katharina's property to your keeping, not to speak of herself. I love my only daughter too dearly to dispose of her so recklessly."

Schönrade smiled sadly. " How shall I explain to you, madame, who and what I am ? I foresaw the necessity of such an explanation, and yet I am unprepared to make it. A man who has been called to fill a chair in a renowned German university, where he is regarded with respect by all ranks of society in our capital,—a man who has expended considerable sums in 'foreign travel to fit him for the duties of his career,— a man who has given to the world the results of his scientific attainments in a work which has passed through three editions in a few years and has been approved by competent critics,—I do not know how to characterize this man who now sues for your daughter's hand, if this does not suffice. Surely you need no further assurance that I am able suitably to support even a portionless wife."

The matron reflected. " All this procures you the respect of your associates," she said, more gently, and somewhat mournfully. " But in an old merchant family——"

" It should do no less," he interrupted her. " There is a patrician rank in science, and princes should not scorn to ally themselves with it."

These proud words impressed her. She cast down her eyes, and drew her golden chain slowly through her fingers. "You must not think it strange," she said, " that I am cautious where I am ignorant. You have an office : so much I understand. Now, in our family we have always attached great importance to entire independence. In old times, an Amberger frequently occupied the position of burgomaster, the family was always represented in the Senate, some of my ancestors served as captains of vessels and of land-troops in the wars of the period ; but such offices were always held simply as posts of honour; they were and they remained merchants. From the time when the civil government was intrusted to hired officials, no Amberger and no Vorbringer could be induced to fill an office. You see, there are offices, and offices, Herr Professor."

" The difference lies least of all, I should say, in whether labour for the common weal receive remuneration or not. If any post may be termed a post of honour, it is, I should think, that of teacher in a great university."

She changed the subject. " Have you any family ?" she asked.

" My mother is still living. Before her retirement she was greatly esteemed as an artist."

Frau Barbara started in horror : " An artist !"

" An opera-singer, madame. The name of Camilla Bellarota is perhaps not entirely unknown to you."

" Camilla Bellarota,—I seem to have heard the name,—in my youth it must have been. Yes, yes, there was a story—— I forget. Your mother, then, was an opera-singer—indeed ! And your father ?"

Schönrade saw all the ground he had gained slipping from beneath his feet. " I never knew my father," he replied, somewhat embarrassed ; " he must have died quite young."

" Indeed ! died ?" she said, coldly. " He was an Italian ?"

The Professor really had not the courage to tell all the truth. " Probably," he said. " He was certainly a gentleman, or my mother would not have married him. But why speak of these things? I am what I am."

" True, true," she remarked, absently and indifferently.

The conversation began to oppress him. He arose, and said, " May I dare to hope, madame ?"

The lady arose at the same time, and stood still, leaning one hand upon the back of her chair and the other upon a table.

. " I will be honest with you, my dear Herr Professor," she said, " that you may not deceive yourself. Judging from the conversation which we have just had, I cannot approve my daughter's choice, and I shall do all that I can to turn her thoughts into other channels. But this ought to give you no offence, for, in the first place, I aet upon principles that are far older than your suit, and, in the second place, I know you too slightly to allow any question of your personal worth to influence me. I believe that Katharina is mistaken, and that she would be far from happy in those circles to which a Professor and a man of science would introduce her. This I must believe until I am convinced of the contrary. In conclusion, my right is more that of refusal than of consent. My husband was very anxious that the inherited and acquired property of the family should be kept together. He therefore arranged in his will that nothing of importance, either of a business nature or otherwise, should take place without the consent of his sons, —two men widely differing in nature and temperament. Although Philip leaves the business, perhaps, too entirely in his brother's hands, I must, in such an important event as Katharina's marriage, appeal to their decision if she should oppose my wishes. Her fortune will then remain in trust with her brothers. Wait until Philip returns from Italy, and make your request of my son Moritz in the mean while. The rest must be left to the future."

The Professor had listened calmly. " Madame," he said, frankly, " I thank you for your candour. If I had only myself to think of, I should say, ' When I learned to love Katharina Amberger, I had no idea that she was an heiress, and it is a matter of perfect indifference to me whether she possesses a penny or not. Were she a poor girl, she is still the only woman in the world whom I would marry, and if she possesses a fortune, not a groschen should ever be used for my household that I did not earn myself.' But I cannot be thus egotistical. It would be a grief to me to cause discord between the girl whom I love and her family, or to leave her dependent upon brothers who blamed her. I shall, therefore, while I do not swerve from the troth I have plighted, do all that I can to preserve family peace and harmony. This, madame, will be my plan of action."

He approached her and kissed her hand. For the first time, a gleam of kindliness softened her expression. "That is spoken like a man of honour," she said, gently, and slightly pressed his hand. He turned to go. "One more thing," she called after him : "I trust you will refrain from disturbing Katharina's peace of mind, and will not seek the continuance of a relation with her which has not received the sanction of her nearest relatives."

Schönrade stood proudly erect. "She shall know," he replied, "that under all circumstances I shall love her as dearly as it is possible for one human being to love another. For the rest, madame, be assured I shall conduct myself towards her like a man of honour."

Her face grew dark again. He bowed once more, and left the house. As he did so, involuntarily the thought occurred to him, "When, and with what emotions, shall I cross this threshold again?"

CHAPTER VII.

It was one o'clock when he reached his hotel, and he would far rather have taken the first train for Berlin than have stayed to fulfil his engagement to dine with the Feinbergs. He was utterly depressed mentally, and he felt physically wearied in consequence. To have to pass hours in the society of those who were entirely indifferent or rather obnoxious to him, was a terrible prospect.

But he could not return to Berlin without first speaking with Moritz. He could not neglect this duty, although it was almost a matter of course that the son, as a good merchant, would share the mother's views. It would be playing a dishonourable part towards Katrine were he to retreat after a first defeat; his own annoyance must have no weight whatever in determining his actions. Nothing would so serve to exalt him in Moritz Amberger's estimation as the attention with which the Feinbergs seemed disposed to treat him, and any neglect of their kindness upon his part would prejudice them against him, and Sidonie's bridegroom would, of course, share such a prejudice,—a result, in the present state of his affairs, greatly to be deprecated. So he made up his mind to submit to be entertained with as good a grace as possible.

As all this was passing through his thoughts, there was a knock at his door. He supposed it was the officious waiter, and called out, rather irritably, "Come in!" when, to his surprise, Moritz Amberger entered the room.

"I lose no time in returning your call, Herr Professor," the young man remarked, quite with the air of an old acquaintance. "I venture to think that your visit of yesterday was not intended exclusively for my mother."

"You are very kind," Schönrade answered, shaking hands with him; "and I thank you for an attention which I hardly had a right to expect. How are you after your yesterday's exploit?"

"Oh, don't speak of it!" the merchant exclaimed, with a laugh. "The jest was tedious enough,—suited to the wits of my military friends. Where did you go? We wanted you to take a glass of beer with us at our bachelor-club, after the fatigues of the afternoon, but you were nowhere to be found."

"My steed carried me whither he would," Schönrade ex-

E   9

plained, "and that was to his own quarters. I am sorry to
have missed the pleasure of your society and the refreshment
of a glass of beer, which I should certainly have appreciated."

Amberger threw himself upon the lounge, and drew off his
glove. "You have not forgotten," he said, as if incidentally,
"that you are engaged to dine at the Feinbergs' this afternoon? Fräulein Sidonie requested me to remind you of it.
You see, she imagines all learned men are very absent-minded,
and that without a reminder you would never remember. Is
she right?"

"Not at all!" the Professor replied, instantly divining the
cause of the present visit. "I have the best memory in the
world for such matters. I am by no means insensible, either,
to the pleasures of the table."

"No bookworm, then," the young man rejoined. "I was
sure of that when I saw how you rode. Yes, yes, in spite of
all that sages may say, meat and drink are as important to-day
as they were a thousand years ago. And no one understands
that better than the Feinbergs, as I think you will admit
after to-day."

"I have no doubt of it," Schönrade replied. "Your future
father-in-law seems to be a man of wealth."

"He is so considered," Amberger answered, with a knowing look; "and yet the half of his resources is not known.
There are very few such heads for business in the world.
Wherever he takes hold he fairly coins money; he knows the
people he deals with, knows all their sources of income, plans
a campaign like a field officer, and manœuvres so skilfully that
his troops always come into play at the right place and time,
and nothing is ever lost except what he has determined shall
be sacrificed. Sometimes I am really very anxious, but in a ·
perfect fire of telegrams he is calm and cool, and sure of conquest. A very remarkable man in his way."

"Is Herr Otto Feinberg his partner?"

" No, not his partner. Ignaz Feinberg will tolerate no one in that position ; even his brother is not allowed to examine his books. But he is his right hand, as I am his left. In all his great projects he sends him to feel the way, as it were, while he himself never stirs from his counting-room, and, as compensation, he gives him a large share of profit, without any risk. Otto Feinberg is a man of excellent capacity, but not very attractive in society,—a man who simply eats when he's hungry and drinks when he's thirsty; it is a perfect sin to waste fine wine upon him,—although he certainly does appreciate a good cigar."

" What did you mean by calling yourself his brother's left hand ?"

" Why, you see, he uses me in another way. The firm of Amberger is one of the oldest and most respected in the country. Its antiquity stands it in good 'stead in the commercial world,—a reputation inherited from father to son for centuries outweighs anything that can be done in a single lifetime. Who knew anything about Ignaz Feinberg thirty years ago? But five hundred years ago the ships of the Ambergers sailed the North Sea. Feinberg, rich though he is, is often glad of the support of an ancient name, and mine stands him in stead. We often do business together, and I should but poorly understand my own interest if I ever refused to go as far with him as he would carry me. In accordance with his advice, I have had less and less to do of late years with the old commerce in grain, which is not nearly so profitable as in former times, and have turned my attention to banking and exchange. I am able to accommodate him with money, and receive large interest for it. My father would open his eyes if he could look into our books to-day." He thrust his hands in his pockets, leaned back among the sofa-cushions, and laughed.

" But the connection that you describe," observed the Professor, " presupposes boundless personal confidence."

"Of course, of course," Amberger assented ; " but I have
a bit in his mouth.   I would not advise any one to follow my
example who was not to be his son-in-law.   He is getting
and gaining for his only daughter, and, as you know, Sidonie
is my betrothed."

In spite of the air of easy confidence with which these
words were spoken, they failed to produce the desired effect
upon Schönrade, who could not but remember what he had
heard from Sidonie herself, that Moritz's position as her lover
was dependent upon her whim.   If it suited her caprice some
fine day to break the slender thread that bound her to her
present choice, he would, to be sure, regain his freedom, but
most disastrous consequences might ensue in his commercial
affairs.

The fortunate lover, however, left him no time to pursue
these reflections.   He took out his watch, held it mechanically
to his ear, although there was not the least reason to doubt its
correctness, and observed, " It is time to go ; shall we walk
together?   At present you possess an immense amount of
interest for Fräulein Sidonie, but her appetite for novelty is
amazing.   You will have to economize your means of entertainment, Herr Professor ; she would so squander the resources
of a millionaire in this respect as soon to make him bankrupt.
I often laugh at my mother's insatiate appetite for romances,
but it is nothing in comparison with Sidonie's greed of
amusement."

Schönrade smiled as he drew on his gloves.   Did Moritz
wish to hint to him that his rapid rise in the young lady's
favour rested upon an insecure basis ?   Were his remarks
prompted by a faint feeling of jealousy, or by the simple humour of the moment?   At all events, he replied honestly enough,
" I should greatly dislike to have to fulfil extraordinary expectations.   An idea that such fulfilment was looked for would
make me unendurably stupid.   Fortunately, my future happi-

ness would not be shattered even by a sudden fall from favour."

"Since you are on the eve of departure, as I hear," the young merchant said, laughing, " it can under no circumstances affect you as it does Messrs. von Otten, Oschersdorf & Co., who have dwindled to mere nebulæ, after careering about for a day or two as stars of the first magnitude."

The Professor regarded him attentively. This young man played his ambiguous part extremely well.

The Feinberg mansion justified the praises bestowed upon it by its inmates. It was really a remarkable edifice, that had been adapted within and on the side away from the street to all the requirements of modern luxury, without destroying the antique appearance of the building. In former times it had been bounded on one side by the town wall, and on the other by a tower in the large garden ; but the wall had fallen to decay, and its ruins had been used to fill up the ancient ditch, while upon its massive foundation a graceful addition of iron and glass led from the ground-floor out into a terraced garden. A single spacious apartment formed the upper story of this addition, and the opposite wall as you entered was occupied by one huge window, extending from ceiling to floor, from which a flight of steps led first to a lower balcony beneath the old tower, and then down into the garden. The table was laid in this apartment. Schönrade expressed his admiration of the room to his hostess, who was evidently looking for a burst of enthusiasm from him. " Yes," she rejoined, " our architect has done extremely well, I think. If you stand here,—just here, Herr Professor, before this wall of glass,—you have nature, pure nature, everywhere. Each pane is eleven feet high, and so well set that you can scarcely see the joinings. The thin gilt frames are made in imitation of slender tent-poles, and the ceiling is, as you see, draped in imitation of a tent. Oh, yes, if you have plenty of money you can really produce beautiful effects and surround yourself with nature."

Sidonie offered her hand to the Professor as to an old acquaintance. She wore a summer dress of some fine thin fabric covered with lace, and a string of large pearls, encircled her throat. Her airy costume threw into strong relief her rather broad face, long nose, decided eyebrows, and her stern mouth, that displayed, when she laughed, teeth dazzlingly white but rather too large. Schönrade had not thought her handsome on the previous day, but in her riding-habit and high hat she had certainly been more interesting than in her present dress. Her eyes, however, struck him as they had done when he saw her first, as possessing a peculiar intensity : she fairly riveted them upon what engaged her attention at the moment. There needed both assurance and ease to parry their glances. " Do you know that I sailed on the water all night?" she said to him, in a low tone,—" in my dreams, of course. I saw the moon rise above the mists, and we sang together the German folk-song, ' I do not know what it foretelleth'—do you sing when you are awake ?—and suddenly a wind blew,—far too strong a wind for the Seehausen mill-pond,—and upset the boat. I was not in the least frightened, however, only frightfully anxious to know whether you would save me. And you did save me, but, very drolly, after you had first composedly put on a pair of kid gloves."

" You see, I knew, Fräulein Sidonie, that you could swim, and, as my task was merely a conventional one, I was anxious that it should be perfectly performed," the Professor answered, in a jesting tone.

Moritz clapped his hands, and cried, " Bravo ! bravo ! That I call true courtesy."

" Nonsense !" she pouted, toying with her fan. " Like a hero in a modern novel."

Ignaz Feinberg was seated in a wheeled chair, an afghan over his knees, looking through the newspapers. He alone, of all present, was not in dinner dress, but appeared in the same gray coat that he had worn the previous day, and which, judging from the inky splashes on the left sleeve, must have been the one usually worn in his counting-room. From time to time he folded a paper together so as to bring into relief some notice or paragraph, which he would hand to Moritz Amberger or Otto Feinberg, as either happened to be near him, without speaking or altering a muscle of his face. From the recipient would ensue a laconic "hm, hm!" "indeed!" "not bad," or words of a like nature. After this fashion Ignaz Feinberg composed for his own inspection a mosaic picture of the business world of the day, and his relish for his dinner depended on the effect of the said picture upon his mind.

The two officers were also invited guests. Sidonie whispered to the Professor, as they entered rather noisily, "For the sake of contrast! And my mother is so fond of a uniform!"

In especial honor of the stranger, old Dr. Sperling had been invited. He was the head-master of the scientific school of the place, and had been town-recorder for many years,—a man, in his host's opinion, eminently well fitted to enlighten a stranger upon all that the town contained of antiquity or interest. His hair was very gray, and his face looked as if it were carved out of wood; he was stiff and angular in his movements, and evidently rather ill at ease in the tight dress-coat that he had donned in honour of the occasion, but there was a grave courtesy in his demeanour, and he was treated with much consideration.

Schönrade's place was between the mother and daughter. Ignaz Feinberg sat beside his wife, Moritz Amberger on the other side of his betrothed. The four other gentlemen occupied the opposite side of the table. "We have arranged a gay

sight for ourselves," said Madame Feinberg, indicating the
gorgeous uniforms on either side of the old Recorder's black
coat.

" I rejoice in not being a lady," the old man remarked, in a
ponderous fashion. " Were I one, the presence of such attractive neighbours would, I fear, spoil my dinner for me." The
jest was very well received; even Ignaz Feinberg laughed
quietly over his soup-plate.

He, the host, never tasted the exquisite dishes that composed the meal, but, to the Professor's surprise, partook of the
simplest fare, served for himself alone, with a single glass of
claret. His wife felt it necessary to explain apologetically.
" My dear husband is very fearful of injuring his health ; he
trusts his friends will excuse him," she said.

" It has nothing to do with my health," he corrected her ;
" I like to eat what I've always been accustomed to. I think
I might be allowed that luxury." Schönrade found it quite
natural, and Sidonie added, " Papa is really a most remarkable
man in this respect; he would have no objection to our con-
juring up here a fairy-palace, if he might have his old counting-
room left just as it is. I could far more easily coax out of him
a check for a hundred thousand thalers than persuade him to
have the threadbare horse-hair covering of his sofa renewed,
or his shabby old desk re-covered. For himself, he clings to
simplicity."

The banker smiled scornfully. " A very fine explanation,"
he said, " but the fact is that I am as superstitious as a play-
actor. On that old sofa, at that old desk, I have come to
occupy my present position,—in which, thank God, I can let
my wife and daughter conjure as they please; but who knows
whether I should find myself as comfortable on velvet and
springs ?"

Frau Feinberg was annoyed by his remarks, but the Professor said, courteously, " Why should you call it superstition ?

It is certain that we depend mentally, in some measure, upon our outward surroundings, and are sometimes actual slaves to trifles. A new carpet in my study might render me incapable for days of bestowing due attention upon my books or writing; and an error in a merchant's accounts is not as readily corrected as a mistake in a scholar's manuscript."

"A mistaken order can throw a whole regiment into confusion," said Herr von Otten; and Herr von Oschersdorf remarked, carefully wiping his moustache after his glass of Canary, "Well, I don't know; I think I can read my novel as easily on one sofa as another, always provided that it is not stupid."

"How can you read novels at all?" asked the Recorder; and the conversation was turned into another channel.

Moritz Amberger and Otto Feinberg both sat silent. The former received hardly a crumb of the lively conversation that his betrothed carried on with the Professor, and, after making several fruitless attempts to join in it, he rather sulkily devoted himself to his dinner. Otto Feinberg treated the Professor with great reserve. He could not believe that he was visiting the town simply for the sake of amusement; it seemed to him significant that he had been seen at the Wiesels', and had here called nowhere except at the Ambergers'. He put together this and that, and the result, although hardly clear, was by no means to his taste. He felt it best to preserve a very formal demeanour in his presence. Schönrade certainly had no desire to alter this.

"What is that remarkable building?" he asked, looking through the wall of glass; "the one to the left, upon the hill. It is too far off for me to decipher those architectural hieroglyphs."

Dr. Sperling cleared his throat; here was water for the Recorder's mill. "That is the ruin of Höneburg, Herr Professor," he explained, "formerly a massive structure, as may still

E*

be seen from its remains, consisting at present of only a small part of the ancient main building, and a portion of the watch-tower, which once arose to a height of one hundred and twenty-three feet above the top of the hill, which there commands the river."

"Why not one hundred and twenty-*four* feet?" Sidonie asked, pertly.

"One hundred and twenty-three feet, Fräulein Sidonie," the old man insisted, with great gravity. "In the archives of the town the account is preserved of how the castle was first injured by the town in 1478, when the Freiherr Botho von Höneburg was taken prisoner by mounted towns-folk. It is all recorded there how that the tower was never again rebuilt to its previous height, although the town suffered severely afterwards from many a lord of Höneburg. You must know that the castle was called Höneburg because it was built for an insult* to the town, and that at one time the lord of Höneburg stretched an iron chain across the river, which could only be removed, giving free passage to vessels, upon payment of a heavy toll. Those were hard times, and the Ambergers were often forced to take arms with their fellow-citizens to protect themselves."

"That would never have done for you, Moritz," Sidonie said, with a sneer.

"To what use could we put our valiant military," he replied, with a glance towards the two officers, "if we bankers donned sword and helmet?"

"The feud between the town and the Höneburg was prolonged through centuries," the learned Recorder continued; "indeed, there never was a formal end put to it. The chain, to be sure, that once spanned the river, now hangs in our town hall, and since the Thirty Years' War there has been no clashing

---

* "Hohn," the German for "insult."

of hostile steel on the meadows beyond the ancient fosse. Not far from here you can see the old gate through which we usually sallied forth to meet our foes; it has always been called the green gate, from its colour, and many an inscription on its battered surface tells of bloody encounters upon the bridge beyond it, and upon the other side of the fosse. The gate has not stirred upon its ancient hinges for many years, and the iron portcullis was removed long since; in later times the strife was continued with other weapons. The Freiherrs lost their wealth, borrowed of the town, could not repay their debt, and were obliged to mortgage acre after acre of the castle territory. Lawsuits innumerable ensued; expensive executions and all kinds of ruinous processes at last left the Von Höneburgs impoverished courtiers and soldiers, with nothing to testify to their past greatness but the possession of those ruins and the sandy hill between the town and the river,—certainly not an enviable piece of property. But the old aristocrats could not rest content, and continued their quarrels with our towns-folk until lately. We have hardly been quit of them thirty years."

"Are any of their descendants living?" asked the Professor, not without interest.

"The last Freiherr von Höneburg whom we can remember was a very gay young officer," replied Dr. Sperling, shrugging his shoulders. "He had an affair with the daughter, or rather adopted daughter, of a most honourable and patrician merchant, Egidius Köstling, whose house and garden you may see there near the green gate, and made a great deal of trouble in his time. But that is a long story." He was not requested to tell it. In the mean time the ices had been served. Herr von Otten reached across the table and offered one end of an explosive bonbon to Sidonie, saying, "Let us recall the ancient feud with the Höneburg by a salvo of artillery." There was a laugh,—bonbon after bonbon exploded, and the hostess arose from table amid a most warlike rattle.

The guests separated into groups. The host returned to his wheeled chair, and was soon buried in his newspapers. Otto Feinberg offered the gentlemen cigars, and carried off the two officers into the garden, whispering, " Be careful, my child !" into Sidonie's ear as he passed her. Madame Feinberg ordered coffee to be served in the balcony of the old tower, retained Moritz by her side, and began a conversation with the old Recorder. Sidonie walked through the dining-hall with the Professor.

" You have seen nothing of the old house," she said, loud enough to be heard by all; "and yet it is twice as worthy of your inspection as this addition. Come, and I will be your cicerone."

She put her hand within his arm and conducted him through open folding-doors into the adjoining room, thence through a dimly-lighted corridor to a suite of apartments the windows of which looked out upon the street and the narrow alley leading to the tower. The furniture was everywhere luxurious, but not distinguished by any special originality. The young lady hastened on, merely saying, with a shrug, " My mother's taste," until they reached a flight of six or eight steps decorated charmingly with drapery and flowers, and leading apparently through a very thick wall. In a niche on either side stood a statue. " Here my Tusculum begins," said Sidonie, taking her hand from his arm and going before him.

They passed through several apartments large and small, with high vaulted ceilings and arched windows with deep embrasures. The Professor approached one of these and looked out. Beneath him was the balcony where the servants were placing the coffee-table, on one side the glass wall of the dining-hall, and in front a distant view beyond the old fosse. He saw that he was in the tower, which had been skilfully connected with the house. " This is my drawing-room," she explained, " this, my library, and here I have a little armory." As she spoke, she drew aside a curtain hanging before a deep recess, where were arrayed upon the wall old shields, swords, and crossbows, with some very handsome pistols richly inlaid with silver and ivory.

" You are a good shot, I suppose?" Schönrade remarked, with a smile.

" Each of my follies has had its day," she replied. " This one went out of fashion some time ago."

The Professor looked around him with the air of a man prompted rather by courtesy than by curiosity. A single glance sufficed to show that these objects in the several rooms had their place there more in the way of decoration than with any eye to their use.

The library contained rows of volumes in the costliest bindings, all shining with fresh gilding. The little studio would have delighted a painter; everything needed was at hand,—even to the life-size lay-figure draped in heavy woollen stuff and maintaining an attitude that could certainly have been taken by none but limbs of wood; but the easel looked as though it were innocent of any picture save the one in a half-finished state at present reposing upon it, and which could hardly have been painted by the untouched brushes thrust into the thumb-hole of the palette that lay close by.

Schönrade did not venture to ask if she were also an artist. Sidonie took from a stand a portfolio, opened it upon a table in front of a lounge, and, motioning the Professor to be seated, asked, " Are you fond of engravings? Here are some rare pictures, if our connoisseurs are to be trusted."

He sat down and turned over a few. " I am no connoisseur," he said, merely glancing at them.

" Nor am I," she rejoined, with an affectation of candour; " but I can tell something about these, like a parrot that has learned its lesson. Here, for instance——" She came closer

10

and almost leaned upon his shoulder, to direct his attention to
the stippling of a Cleopatra.

He disliked being here alone with Sidonie; he would have
disliked still more to be discovered here with her by any of the
guests. He turned over the prints still more hastily, merely
lifting the corners of some of them, as if to show how impossible it would be to examine the entire collection.

Sidonie turned away, drew from a cabinet against the wall
a shallow drawer and placed it upon the table. It contained a
collection of minerals, neatly arranged,—a *bought* collection,
in short. "This is in your line," she said, sitting down beside
him, "and will interest you." She was mistaken, the man
of science detested all dilettanteism; but she had gained her
point: he did not rise.

"Is it true that you leave us to-morrow?" she asked, as he
courteously examined one specimen after another.

"Most probably, Fräulein Feinberg."

"Possibly not, then?"

"My business will be concluded to-day."

"Give us a few more days, Herr Professor. I will promise
you an excursion upon the river that shall be delightful."

"You are kindness itself; but I cannot interrupt my home
labours for so long."

"That is a mere excuse. Confess that you do not find us
especially agreeable."

"How could I entertain sentiments so ungrateful?"

She looked askance at him. "Between ourselves, I am not
very fond of this place myself. I should like to go to Berlin;
although perhaps not, like my future sister-in-law, to Councillor Wiesel's. Frau Wiesel is a fool."

Her mention of Kätharina affected him unpleasantly; he
led away from it. "Where could you be happier or more comfortable than in this luxurious home?"

Sidonie sighed. "Believe me, I grow very tired of it all.

I like well enough to arrange it, but when it is finished there is nothing left but the pleasure of showing it, and I had enough of that long ago."

" You prize the gifts of fortune too lightly, Fräulein Feinberg. You do not appreciate the possession of means sufficient to enable you to shape your surroundings as you please. You do not know what it is to be forced to deny yourself."

A sigh still more profound. " I do not know what it is to be forced to deny myself! Ah, how little you know me, Herr Professor! How poor and unsatisfactory all this frippery often seems to me ! I know that I should have been happier if I were still surrounded by the poverty to which I was born. I should not then have resigned, what I continually miss and long for, but what can never be mine,—a genuine interest in life."

This was the same elegiac mood that had so startled him upon the lake. It did not seem entirely assumed; it might be in some measure the result of genuine feeling. If his heart had been free, he might seriously have pitied her at such a moment, and there might have thus arisen a bond of sympathy between them that even a change of her mood might have failed to sever. As it was, these sudden appearances of hers in a character seemingly foreign to her nature, annoyed and embarrassed him excessively; little prone as he was to self-conceit, they seemed to him baits held out to win him from his intentional reserve.

" It is easy enough," he said, more harshly than he intended, " to desire as an advantage that which is universally regarded as a bar to the enjoyment of existence, if we are perf ctly sure that our lives will always be·without it."

She leaned her elbows upon the table, and her strange eyes looked full and seriously into his own. " Perhaps you are right," she said. " It is easy. But does it follow that this constant longing is any the less painful ? Suppose, for example, that a girl longs to be a man,—is she not wretched in the consciousness of the impossibility of ever attaining her desire, even although the world may regard her as the most fortunate of beings ?"

" I suppose it is so," he said, examining attentively a specimen of quartz.

" I long to be a man !" she exclaimed. " Laugh if you will, I have seriously reflected whether it would not be worth the trouble to simulate at least what I never can become. I might have studied, have proved life in its profoundest depths, have travelled widely ! Aha ! easy enough, are they not, these dreams ? Do you know that I have even arranged the small details of the existence that might have been mine ? I perpetrated, in imagination, the maddest freaks, broke with my parents, outraged society, made myself unendurable as a girl, to be allowed to do as I chose. Still it might all have failed. Ah, you do not know what it is to be the only child of wealthy parents !"

He crumbled off little fragments of the mineral in his hand and dropped them into the drawer. " Excuse me," he said, still more embarrassed by her manner, " but these are dangerous whims !"

" I wish I could find some one to chase them from my brain," she said, as if to herself, casting down her eyes; " perhaps I should not wish to develop the ideal in myself, if I could find it embodied elsewhere. I am capable, I think, of an entire resignation of self." Suddenly she broke off, took the piece of quartz out of his hands, threw it into the drawer, and said, in an altered voice, " Why do you play with that stupid stone ? It annoys me !" He started and looked up at her in surprise, like a child detected in mischief. She seemed to regret what she had done, for she hastily gathered up a handful of minerals from the drawer and put them into his hand, pressing it with both her own. " There, play as much as you choose," she exclaimed, " but listen to me !"

The Professor was about to reply, when Moritz Amberger drew aside the portière and entered the room. He looked vexed, and said, coldly, " Your mother wishes to know whether she shall send your coffee up to you, since it runs a chance of growing cold before you come down to drink it."

" Mamma sent no such message," Sidonie replied, darting an angry look at him as she arose.

" Well, then, I brought it on my own account," he rejoined. " I would suggest that you should not entirely monopolize the Herr Professor."

" And I would suggest," she retaliated, " that you should not intrude upon my special domain unannounced."

All trace of colour left his good-humoured face. " This to me," he stammered,— " and before a stranger!"

Sidonie seemed to fear she had gone too far. " The Herr Professor is no stranger, but a friend," she said, more composedly, with a troubled glance at his grave, disapproving face.

" Then permit me," he said, " to act the part of one, and to entreat you to repair, arm-in-arm, as a betrothed couple should, to the coffee-table. I can find the way by myself."

She reflected a moment, and then offered her hand to Moritz, with a loud laugh. " How he stands!" she exclaimed, apparently once more in excellent humour,—" like some poor penitent praying for mercy. Courage! courage! I graciously pardon." She took his arm, and turning, as she reached the small flight of steps, nodded to the Professor : " It was your wish."

This hasty interruption was the consequence of a conversation that Otto Feinberg had held with Moritz. He remarked the lengthened absence of the pair, and added that the Professor was not to be trusted. The officers contributed their mite to Moritz's annoyance by their badinage, and he forgot the part which he had played so well hitherto, and gave occasion for the war of words in which, as we have seen, he hardly came off conqueror ; and he was painfully aware of this as he conducted his betrothed to the other guests. There was no trace, however, of the scene just enacted in the demeanour of those chiefly interested. Sidonie jested gayly about the cold coffee, Schönrade gratified his hostess by his admiration of her house, and Moritz described how he had found the Professor absorbed in an inspection of Sidonie's minerals. As soon as Schönrade could find an opportunity, he whispered to him, " When can I speak alone with you ? I have an important communication to make." Amberger looked fixedly at him for an instant, pondering what it could possibly be, and then said, somewhat grandiloquently, as if a duel were in prospect, " I am at your service, sir." And the Professor's reply seemed to hint at the same possibility,—" Appoint time and place, if you please,"—only there was not a shade of hostility observable in his expression, which might, indeed, have been assumed.

They walked for awhile in the garden, and then the guests took leave. " This is not the last time we shall meet," Sidonie declared confidently to the Professor, and her eyes flashed and sparkled. " If you do not come here, we shall go to Berlin." And her mother added, " Pray feel yourself entirely at home in this house as long as you are in town, my dear Herr Professor. You may be sure of always finding nature, pure nature, here. Am I not right?" He judged silence to be his best reply.

CHAPTER VIII.

In the street Schönrade joined Moritz Amberger, taking leave of the others, after courteously thanking the old Recorder for his interesting information with regard to the Höneburg. " Where shall we go ?" he asked. " To my hotel ?"

" My house is nearer," the merchant replied, gravely, " and we shall be perfectly quiet there." The Professor assented, and they walked on in silence until they reached the Amberger mansion. Here Moritz produced a key, that admitted them by a side-door.

They were soon seated comfortably in a small room, fitted up as a special retreat for its bachelor owner. " I suspect," Schönrade began, " that in your secret soul you do not acquit me of conducting myself towards your betrothed with a want of due consideration for yourself as her lover. Am I not right ?"

Moritz had by no means recovered from the insult Sidonie had offered him, and half a dozen plans for repairing his wounded honour in the stranger's estimation had been chasing one another through his brain. But they were all very vague and shadowy, and he now replied, with more composure than might have been expected, " Sidonie finds a peculiar gratification in meeting, as it were, upon equal terms, any interesting man whom chance brings in her way. I can make no objection to this, since I myself never belonged to the number of those thus singled out; my relations to her, being of a quite different nature, are not at all interfered with. But the estimation in which she is held by others cannot be a matter of indifference to me, and as, since you leave here so shortly, you can scarcely have any opportunity of seeing how little——"

He hesitated; it was a difficult matter to finish the sentence without either compromising himself or insulting his companion. The Professor came to his assistance. " Pray conclude," he said, with a smile; " you need not be at all afraid of dispelling any illusions of mine. For your entire satisfaction, let me tell you, if you have been suspecting a possible Don Juan in me, that at present I am protected in armour of triple steel against the lightnings of the finest eyes in the world, and am incapable of deserving the trouble that feminine caprice might expend upon me only to make me a target for ridicule after wards. In a word, I come here as a suitor."

Moritz entirely forgot his diplomatic look, opened his eyes wide, and stared in surprise. " As a——?" Then suddenly a load seemed taken from his mind; all his muscles relaxed, and he reclined comfortably in his chair. " May I congratulate you, my dear fellow ? may I congratulate you ?"

The Professor shrugged his shoulders. " That depends upon your ' yes' or ' no,' " he said, looking him directly in the eye.

" Upon my ' yes' or ' no' ?" the young man asked, bewildered. " What do you mean ?"

Schönrade craved his attention, and then unfolded all his hopes and wishes with regard to Katrine, recapitulated his conversation with Frau Amberger, and ended by entreating him not to act in accordance with " prejudices which the world had outgrown."

At first Moritz was influenced by the delight he felt at his own escape from danger; he nodded kindly from time to time; but gradually these nods became rarer, he cast an embarrassed glance now and then at the speaker, and finally the spirit of opposition asserted itself in frequent interruptions of " But——," and " One moment, my dear fellow——," so that the Professor had some trouble in bringing his discourse to an end. When he had finished, Amberger rose, and walked to and fro in the room,

saying, " But this is most unfortunate,—most unfortunate;
not in itself,—good heavens! not in itself; but as matters
stand,"—he ran his fingers through his fair hair,—" as matters
stand,—you don't know—you can't know—oh, most unfortunate!"

Schönrade waited in silence until he stood still before him,
and said, more sensibly and collectedly, " As for my mother's
objections, they are mere nonsense,—not to be disrespectful,
hereditary folly! Patricians! What are patricians? Those
times are past. We are all towns-folk, some with rather larger
incomes than others. One has something, and another nothing,
—and many a one who has nothing is more of a man than
those who have something." The Professor sat quietly regarding him in silence. He had said all that he had to say. At
last Amberger noisily pushed a chair near his guest, seated
himself in it, and seized his hand. " My dear Herr Professor," he said, with a kind of gasp, " I like you very much, so
far,—I do, upon my soul I do,—and if all is as you say, and
I haven't the slightest doubt that it is, it would give me the
greatest pleasure to call you brother-in-law. Why, in my opinion, my dear Herr Professor, we are honoured—the house of
Amberger is greatly honoured—by such a proposal from a distinguished man like yourself. But—but——" He jumped
up, then seated himself again immediately, and continued, in
quite a changed tone, " Let us lay aside all disguises. I am
one man, you are another; let us talk together as man to man.
Why should I inspire you with false hopes? It cannot be,—
believe me, it cannot be. Even if I liked you far better than
I do, it could not be. And I will tell you why,—I will tell
you why frankly, as my regard for you dictates; and I may
rely upon your discretion, my dear fellow, may I not?"

Schönrade gave him the desired assurance as to his discretion, and Moritz continued: " We were talking to-day of my
business relations with Feinberg, and, if I remember rightly, I

called myself his left hand. Now, to be perfectly frank with you, it is no longer a voluntary matter with me whether I will be his left hand or not. If I cease to be his left hand, I am nothing, —no more on 'Change than a severed limb to a body. A humiliating confession enough for the head of the house of Amberger, confound it! I feel that, but I know what I say. My mother has no suspicion of it; with her old-fashioned views she could not understand it. There is no danger so long as we are good friends, but good friends we must remain. Do you suppose that I would tolerate Sidonie's insufferable caprice for——" He paused, perhaps startled by his own temerity, but collected himself instantly, and continued: "Why, you have eyes, and know how to use them; what need is there to tell you what you must know as well as I do? Sidonie's whims are countless, and I must bear the brunt of them, for I am powerless to remonstrate. I *must* endure them,—it is my fate, at least until after our marriage. I am so deeply involved with Ignaz Feinberg that I cannot retreat without ruining myself, —entirely ruining myself. To-day I am a man of weight on 'Change, for he supports me; if he deserts me, I must fall, and drag down my family with me."

The Professor tried to follow his meaning, but it was difficult for him to comprehend complications of this kind. "How did all this come about?" he asked, bewildered.

Amberger moved his chair closer and laid a finger on his arm. "In the simplest way in the world. I inherited from my father an extensive and profitable business in grain and transportation; we owned storehouses, river-vessels, sea-going ships, and had an agency in the nearest seaport. Of late years American competition has been detrimental to our commerce in grain; there was more risk in our ventures. By Feinberg's advice, I closed up that business, drew my capital out of it, and invested it in projects of which he approved. Philip took not the least interest in such matters, but let me do as I

pleased. This banking business, if successful, constantly in-
duces fresh speculation, and numerous issues of paper. Large
profits accrue; but if there is a crisis, one's very means of
living are endangered. I have invested wherever Feinberg
advised,—he is prudence itself,—and am far too deeply engaged for my means; I am the left hand to another man's
head. Feinberg can withdraw without overwhelming loss,—
I cannot. My whole aim at present is to conceal how deeply
I am involved."

Schönrade shook his head thoughtfully. " I pity you," he
said, gravely. " Everything depends, then, upon the continuance of the tie between Fräulein Sidonie and yourself; and
from what I have seen of her——"

Amberger interrupted him. " Did she say anything about
it to you?"

" She knows her power over you, and seems inclined to use
it unless you make every concession that she can demand.
And if you are so indulgent——"

" Don't you see," the young man again interrupted him,
" that I am steering a leaky vessel against wind and tide? I
cannot do as I wish."

" I see. But what has my relation with Katharina——"

" My dear fellow, it has everything in the world to do with it.
Katharina is my chief stay,—unconsciously she is the cause
why my position is not quite so desperate as it would seem.
Ignaz Feinberg has, as you know, a brother Otto, who is
really his right hand. As long as I have a firm hold upon
Otto Feinberg, his brother cannot shake me off, and Sidonie
must pay some heed to what she does. At present I have
this firm hold, for Otto Feinberg loves my sister, and I——
have promised that, so far as I have any influence over her,
she shall be his."

The Professor sprang to his feet, thoroughly indignant.
" What! you could give her—your own sister—to that usurer?

It is absolutely fiendish! Why, with these plots and schemes of yours, you may chance to break her heart,—dear, innocent child, with no thought of wrong, with no idea that her brother can so trade away her life. It is——"

"No matter how right you may be," Moritz interrupted him, uneasily rubbing his forehead, "there is no help for it. Who could foresee that Katharina, young as she is, would make a choice of her own? Why should she not have found Otto Feinberg a desirable partner for life? He has had abundance of time and opportunity to win her. Now I see how unsuccessful he has been, Herr Professor; to my terror, I assure you, for my best hold upon his brother is gone as soon as Otto finds he has no hope. Oh, it is most unfortunate!"

"You certainly would not force Katharina——"

"Force! force! How can I force her? But I must keep my promise, and use, as I said I would, all my influence. If Katharina, in defiance of her father's will, denies my authority over her, I cannot, of course, force her to marry a man of my selection; but most assuredly I shall never give my consent to her marrying any one else,—never! Otto Feinberg, now my friend, would then be my enemy, and I should be lost."

Schönrade folded his arms and tapped his foot impatiently upon the floor. "I expected to meet with opposition," he said, sternly, "but I never dreamed of contending with such views as these. Poor child! Poor child! Is there no way——"

Amberger grasped his hand. "Deliver me from these fetters—I know as well as you do how degrading they are—and I will be eternally grateful to you. I have told you so much that I might as well confess all. I tremble at the idea of a union with Sidonie, whom I do not love, and who does not love me. I know that my weak good nature will soon lose me all show of authority with her, and my own self-respect besides. At times, as at present, my whole soul rises in rebellion against such a fate. And yet—yet—how can I escape it? How can I preserve the honour of the house of Amberger? Only show me how."

The Professor's look was dark and stern. "It seems to me," he replied, after a pause, "that you have lost the courage to make yourself master of the situation, which you doubtless were at the beginning of your connection with Feinberg. You have leaned upon him so long that your own powers have rusted. It may be thus. Throw off his authority by one vigorous effort, and convince yourself that you can proceed without his support."

"Oh, you are no merchant!" exclaimed Moritz. "No merchant would talk thus. You cannot see the importance of this connection, or how much must be thrown overboard if it be dissolved. My mother's and my sister's fortunes are involved. I cannot think of myself only. There is but one possible way, but one, out of my difficulty, and that is too chimerical to be thought of."

"Tell me, nevertheless, what it is," said the Professor.

"If I could embark, without the knowledge of the Feinbergs, independently of them, in some commercial project of vast importance, and obtain firm footing there, I should compel their respect. The undertaking must be sufficiently large to make their friendship or their hostility alike a matter of indifference to me; and it is hardly to be hoped that anything of the kind can be conjured out of nothing for my special benefit. Therefore, my dear fellow, you must follow my example: resign yourself to the inevitable, and be thankful that your fancy is sufficiently youthful not to have taken any very deep root. Katharina must see that it is impossible for me to accede to her wishes, and by-and-by, when her heart has recovered the loss it must sustain, she will be all the more ready to contract a *mariage de convenance* which is in every way——"

" Silence !" Schönrade exclaimed, with such vehemence that Moritz ceased in amazement. " It is as degrading for me to listen to such words as it is for you to utter them. I sincerely pitied you, but I begin to regret having done so. You are upon the point of resigning not only the right of disposing of your property, but also the repose of your conscience."

" Herr Professor !"

" The repose of your conscience, Herr Amberger. Why did your father in his will invest you with such authority ? Because he fully relied upon his son's integrity, and affection for his sister, which should prompt him to think solely of her welfare, without any selfish consideration. But you are selling your sister———"

" I cannot permit this, sir !"

" I say no more. You know what I think ; oppose me to the extent of your will and ability. But do not suppose that I shall look idly on and patiently allow myself to be thrust aside. I will preserve an inviolable secrecy to all save one,— Katharina shall know of your fraternal designs with regard to her, and she will either obey the dictates of her own heart, or owe her unhappiness—to your shame be it spoken—to you. And for yourself, be sure that this corrupt tree of your planting will never bring forth good fruit."

He raised his hand with an air of menace ; his tall form seemed invested with a kind of majesty ; he towered haughtily above the banker, who involuntarily cowered as if he would have sunk into the ground. The jovial expression of his good-humoured face had vanished entirely ; his confession had certainly not procured him absolution. He felt humiliated in the presence of this man who saw into his very soul, and who could be hoodwinked by no such plea as would have found weight with men of his own stamp,—how pitiful such men seemed to him at this moment !

He would have given worlds to be able to stand erect, look the Professor full in the face, and say, " You are right; I was a coward; but I will be one no longer." But he had not the courage; he shut his eyes and stroked his chin. " What can't be cured must be endured," he thought.

When he looked up, he was alone. He arose, dipped his handkerchief in water, and laid it upon his forehead. All his previous hopes and expectations seemed mere folly to him now. How could he ever have imagined it possible that Otto Feinberg could gain his sister Katharina's affection? And how would Sidonie receive himself after the events of the day? What fresh humiliation was in store for him at this woman's hands? What reliance could he place upon Feinberg's friendship? To whom could he turn? What was to be the end of it all?

His excellent physique and the wine he had taken at dinner fortunately solved these questions for him for the present, —he fell asleep.

Schönrade could not so soon find repose from his tormenting reflections. After he had hastily left the room and the house, he began to regret the violence into which he had been betrayed, and which had perhaps closed the door of approach for him to Katharina's family. He remembered with a sigh her close association with these people, upon whom he must have produced anything but a favourable impression. He could not even tell her, without wounding her, what a pitiable figure her brother Moritz had presented during his interview with him. And should she know that he had parted from him in anger, what could she think of such a quick-tempered, impractical lover? He paused for a moment, half inclined to retrace his steps. " But it would do no good; the arguments of each have no force with the other," he said to himself. " Let matters take their course."

He walked on, at first with hasty strides, as if anxious to

put as much distance as possible between the Amberger mansion and himself, then gradually more slowly. He did not
think again of returning, but, as he reflected, Moritz seemed
to him more and more excusable. A suitor for his sister's
hand, suddenly appearing to the detriment of all his plans and
expectations, could hardly be anything but extremely unwelcome to him, and when these plans and expectations were first
formed he could have had no possible idea that Professor
Schönrade would lose his heart during a visit at Councillor
Wiesel's. It certainly was matter for gratitude that he had
not dismissed him with the usual set phrases, but had laid
bare the most secret troubles of his life, that he might explain
his refusal of his suit. And the poor fellow was greatly to be
pitied. Nature had formed him for an easy, good-humoured
enjoyment of existence; he would have been perfectly content never to soar above the commonplace; but in an evil hour
he had been induced to resign the certain profits of his father's
business to embark upon the high seas of speculation, and to
propose to Sidonie Feinberg to share his home, as if she had
been the unassuming daughter of some well-to-do merchant.
And Sidonie! what pains she took to show her lover that she
wore his betrothal-ring solely from caprice!

When he looked around him, he found himself in a quarter
of the town of which he was entirely ignorant. Before him
stretched a long narrow street, lined on each side with tall
houses, and growing still narrower towards the end, where it
was spanned by a gateway. He pondered what he should
do. His business in the town was finished; he could leave at
any moment. But the next train to Berlin left in the night,
and was not an express train. He had nothing to do, and yet
the evening must be passed after some fashion. Anything but
his room at the hotel! He would take a long walk to get rid
of the time; so on he went.

The gateway was connected on the left with a large man-

sion, the last in the street, with quite a stately façade retreat-
ing some feet from the line of the rest of the row, to give room
for a massive flight of stone steps. The simple arch of the
gateway was, in fact, a public passage beneath a wing of this
house that extended across the street to the last of the houses
on the right, beyond which he observed the outline of an ancient tower, not altogether unfamiliar to him. Above the archway were a few small windows with tiny panes of glass,—too
few, however, to relieve the effect of the bare, undecorated ex-
panse of wall, topped by a steep gable, with its little window
near the roof, beneath the rusty weather-cock, that showed in
transparent letters clear against the sky the venerable date
1357. Had he reached the famous *Green Gate* of which
the Recorder had spoken? Its colour was difficult to determine; it might as well have been called brown as green;
many a year must have gone by since the painter's brush had
touched it.

He walked through the echoing archway, and found himself upon a narrow bridge that could hardly have allowed two
carriages to pass each other. It certainly must be the " Green
Gate" through which he had just come, for in front of him
was the hill crowned by the ruin of Höneburg. He looked
back and upwards, directly into the face, carven in stone in
the keystone of the arch, of a knight thrusting out his tongue
maliciously. That must have irritated many a Freiherr of
Höneburg, he thought to himself, and his grave face relaxed
with a smile. There were not lacking inscriptions in Latin
and in German, but he contented himself with deciphering one
only, which stated how a certain Hans Köstling had maintained this bridge with his single spear against six armed
horsemen, until the gate could be closed behind him, and had
then sprung into the fosse and swum across to the town.

Schönrade looked down into the fosse. It was dry, and had
been converted here, as at the Feinbergs', into a garden. Old

trees reared their branches near the railing of the bridge, and the walls were covered with ivy. Far below him, in what had been the deepest part of the ditch, rippled a little brook, winding prettily among the flower-beds, and spanned by rustic bridges. There was a distant prospect beyond the turn of the old wall, which enclosed, in turning, an ancient battlemented tower.

As the Professor stood gazing about him, he became aware, upon the gravel-walk immediately below him, of an old man in a blue broadcloth coat of by-gone fashion and a close-fitting velvet cap. He was walking slowly along, his head bent upon his breast, smoking a long pipe, and pausing from time to time before a rose-bush or to look up at some tree laden with fruit. The most noticeable point about him was that he was followed gravely by two sleek, well-fed cats, who marched at his heels like two dogs, stopping when he stopped and continuing their promenade when he walked on. Evidently he was an old bachelor fond of animals. But why had he selected cats for the companions of his lonely walk? This old man must have a history.

A woman passed upon the bridge. "Who is that?" the Professor asked her, pointing downwards.

"Why, old Herr Köstling," she replied, in a whisper. "Every child in the town knows who he is," she added, as she pursued her way.

He was seized by a desire to visit the Höneburg also. He had time enough, and the afternoon was lovely. He could certainly reach the summit of the hill in half an hour.

CHAPTER IX.

BEYOND the bridge the road forked. To the left it ran along the fosse, apparently skirting the town, and to the right it led directly across the fields, towards the Höneburg. Schönrade pursued the latter road, which was not nearly so much worn as the other. Some hundred paces farther on, he passed a large tile-kiln, and beyond this the ground rose considerably. From the summit of this rise the road turned to the left, leading down to the river, to a ferry, where some tall-masted river-craft lay moored. The Professor looked this way and that, expecting to find some path to the Höneburg, but there was nothing between him and the ruin but a strip of sand, contrasting sharply with the brown heath beyond, overgrown with low juniper-bushes and young birch-trees. There was not even a foot-path across this heath, which extended to the old wall. Schönrade went back and inquired of a man at the tile-kiln his road to the Höneburg. "Oh, no one goes there!" was the laconic reply. He then determined to keep his goal in view and march straight towards it. He was reminded of his pathless future.

The sand covered a stony foundation ; here and there grew tufts of thin grayish-green grass. The most abstemious goat could not have found pasturage here. But farther on there was more tender grass growing, and pale-blue harebells were to be seen among the juniper-bushes on the brown soil. At intervals there was discovered what at first sight seemed a pathway in the right direction, but it always proved to be some old furrow kept open by the rain. Many a year must have passed since the golden grain had here waved in the wind or the ploughshare furrowed these meadows. The birches were six feet high, and among the bushes were the stumps of what had formerly been large trees. It produced a very strange impression, so near a populous town, to come upon this perfect wilderness, and its effect was heightened by the view of the old ruin, that loomed larger upon the vision as one approached it, darkening a portion of the horizon. A solitary lark trilled high in air, a white butterfly fluttered up from a harebell, and a belated bee hummed about the cup of a wild flower; these were the only signs of life around.

The hill upon which the castle had been built, upon a nearer approach, was found to be rather insignificant, but it was the highest point in all the country round, and commanded the turn of the river. The fosse about it was half filled up and easily crossed. On the other side massive foundations supported a wall, crowned here by the lower portion of a tower, its uneven surface overgrown with wild grape-vine. On this side there was no trace of gate or door to be seen.

The Professor walked along the wall to where it turned and made a corner. Here the way was blocked by masses of fallen stones and tiles; two window-slits at some elevation had been boarded up, and were brushed by the boughs of a linden that had struggled up through the heap of ruins. Farther on the wall sloped intermittently to the foundation, and above it nodded and waved the tops of old trees, as if they were growing in a garden within. Here also no entrance was to be seen. A little arched doorway of the olden time had been walled up.

On the southern side, however, an entirely different picture presented itself. Looking quite away from the town, and perfectly protected by the ruin from the north wind, a strip of land on the terraced hill had been carefully cultivated, neatly fenced in, and planted with vegetables of all kinds, fruit-trees, and grape-vines. Lower down lay small fields of potatoes and grain, bounded again by a wide extent of barren heath. The fosse on this side was deeper, but it had been converted into a shady garden, and was crossed at about the centre of the old wall by a bank of earth, probably filling up the place where had stood the ancient drawbridge. Here there was a gap in the old wall which had been repaired by one of modern construction, built of loose stones and broken tiles, and just where the bank of earth led across the fosse an opening had been left in this wall, so flanked by two huge stones, which had probably once formed the arch of a portcullis, that a wooden door could be fitted between them. Two or three stone steps led up to it.

The ruin was inhabited, then,—to the no little surprise of the Professor, who could not remember that the Recorder or any one at table had mentioned it. He passed easily over the ditch, and a low hedge on the other side, and then, as no one was to be seen in garden or meadow, walked up to the door and knocked boldly. He was curious to know who had built a nest here among the bats and owls.

A dog began to bark violently from within as he knocked the second time; a chain also rattled; there was no danger, then, of being attacked.

After awhile a gentle female voice was heard. " Be quiet, Nero ! what is there to bark at ?"

Schönrade knocked again, rather more softly.

" Is any one there ?" the voice asked.

" A traveller begs for admittance," the Professor replied.

" This is not an inn," the voice returned. " The town is near at hand, where there are lodging-houses in plenty."

" I have just come from the town," he rejoined, " where I am in an excellent hotel. I will not give any trouble."

" But what do you want here, then ?"

" I will tell you when I am admitted."

" But I must know before you can be admitted."

The Professor frankly stated that he was a stranger, lured hither by a desire to see the ruins, which he should like to inspect from within.

F*

"There is nothing remarkable to be seen here," was the answer he received.

"I am very tired, and would be glad to have a glass of water." He listened for a few moments, but no reply came. "Are you as cautious here now as in the olden time?" he began again. "Well, then, let me assure you I bring no following of armed towns-folk. I am quite alone, without even a cane by way of weapon."

He heard a low laugh above him, and, looking up, saw a lovely curly head, that disappeared upon finding itself observed.

"What is the matter there, Lena?" a rough voice called out from some distance. "What is the dog barking at, and whom are you speaking to?"

"There is a strange gentleman outside, grandpapa," was the reply, "asking for admittance."

"What does he want?" The question sounded surly.

"Oh, he wants to see the ruins, and drink some water from our well."

"He can see ruins enough outside, and you may hand him out a mug of water."

He was not actually turned away, then. A few minutes afterwards the bolt was withdrawn and the door half opened. A slender girl, the owner of the lovely head, appeared upon the threshold and offered the weary wayfarer a stone mug of sparkling spring water. The wide sleeves of her embroidered white linen underdress were rolled up above the elbow; her petticoat was slightly caught up, showing pretty little naked feet. Behind her, on a slight elevation, stood Nero before his kennel, thrusting his shaggy black head under her raised arm. It was a pretty picture.

Schönrade drank a little water, but did not return the mug immediately. "This water is delicious," he said, beginning another conversation, that he might have time to enjoy the charming apparition.

"Indeed it is," the girl replied, with a smile. "I think you are not very thirsty, though."

"But all the more anxious to see the old castle, now that I have made acquaintance with the châtelaine."

"The true châtelaine is to be seen here only between twelve and one at night. Come by here at that time, if you are not afraid, and perhaps she will wave her veil from the balcony." She laughed, and held out her hand for the mug.

"Stop!" he exclaimed, withdrawing his hand. "This water belongs to me, and until I have drunk it I must ask questions and receive replies."

"Ask, if you please, then."

"Who lives in the Hüneburg?"

"An old gardener, sir, with his daughter-in-law, a widow, and his grandchild, whom you see before you."

"Is there any road from here to the town?"

"Oh, yes; but probably not upon the side by which you came. There was an old feud between the castle and the town, and there was always a waste heath on that side. From here you go down to the river, and there is a road along the bank to the ferry. But pray drink some more; I cannot wait here until the water dries up."

"And I cannot come in?"

"My grandfather will not permit it; he wishes to have as little to do as possible with people outside."

"Does no one know, then, that the castle is inhabited?"

The girl laughed. "We are not quite such recluses, and, indeed, it could not be concealed. Huckster-women come here every morning in summer; many a table in the town is supplied from our garden." She looked up at the sky. "But pray give me the mug, and make haste to go. A storm is coming up, and it may readily overtake you before you reach the town."

He also looked, and saw that she was right. But some

mysterious force seemed to rivet him to the spot. He could not bear to leave without accomplishing his purpose. "If I should wait here until the rain began to fall," he said, in a jesting tone, "you could not have the heart to keep me out in the open air."

She moved the door to and fro upon its creaking hinges, as if about to close it instantly. "Better not try," she said.

"Why don't you shut the door?" the harsh voice was heard again, and a heavy step approached.

"Here comes the grandfather," thought the Professor. "So much the better! I shall soon know if I must go away without seeing the Höneburg."

A bony hand, placed above the girl's, opened the door wide. A man with snow-white beard and hair, but erect and powerfully built, pushed her away and stepped out. It was evident that an angry remonstrance with the intruder was upon his lips; but it died away without utterance. He started as if in terrified surprise at sight of the Professor, knitted his brows, and stood still, the picture of amazement. "Sir," he stammered.

"Your grandchild refused me admittance," said the Professor, "and you look at me as if I were a ghost."

"A ghost," he repeated, darting a keen glance at the stranger. "A ghost,—it might well be so." Then, collecting himself, and passing his hand over his brow, he asked, "May I beg you to tell me your name, sir?"

"Professor Schönrade, from Berlin."

The old man shook his head dubiously. "Schönrade,—Professor Schönrade,—no! 'Twill not do,—'twill not do. But come in, sir, come in. Be quiet, Nero! He is chained. Strange, very strange!"

Most strange indeed the Professor thought this reception, but he said nothing for the present, as he followed the old man up the stone steps into the court-yard. It was a spacious square; on the right there was a little garden, and on the left the remains of the old watch-tower, with a magnificent gateway of carved stone. Partly within this, and partly built against it and the wall of the main building, was a pretty little cottage, with a small stable. The stones from the ruins had afforded a fine foundation, laid above the old castle cellar, where provisions could be stored, and upon them a frame structure had been erected, with a projecting roof, the supports of which were wreathed with wild grape-vines, forming a veranda, beneath which ascended the light staircase. No more unique picture could be imagined than this pretty vine-wreathed cottage in the shade of magnificent old trees, and surrounded by the ancient castle walls, battered and weather-stained by the storms of centuries. There, where the pavement around the basin of the ancient fountain was still preserved, steeds panting for the battle had once neighed, amid the clang of steel and the rattle of harness. Peace had built her nest here in the ruined stronghold of war.

The girl appeared to understand as little as the stranger the sudden change in the old man's mood. Her eyes, from beneath her clustering curls, gazed in surprise at the altered expression of his stern features, that had lost all harshness, in an air of dreamy reverie. He followed Schönrade with his glance, and murmured, shaking his head, "Schönrade!—no—no. I am wrong, I am wrong. It is odd I should be so deceived."

The Professor begged to be allowed to sit down upon the stone seat by the fountain, and the old man assented.

The girl's mother now appeared from the cottage,—a spare woman with a careworn face, but well dressed,—and bade the stranger welcome. She was quite at her ease, and began to talk of what interested her in "the world outside." "We seldom see a newspaper," she said, with a sigh; "we live a very lonely life." In reply to his inquiries, Schönrade learned that her husband had been a sergeant in the army, and had

12

been killed in the last war. After his death she had come with her only child to keep house for her father-in-law. Lena delighted in the life here,—solitude was refreshing to her after her father's death,—and she would not have exchanged it for the gayest life in town. Healthy in mind and body though she was, nevertheless she was by no means insensible to the charm of romance which invested these old ruins; they clothed with life the chivalric stories and fairy-tales of her childhood. The mother, with her sorrowful experiences and her ever-fresh sorrow for her husband's loss, longed for distraction and excitement; she was always glad to welcome a guest in the old ruin.

Had the old man no other son? the Professor asked. Yes, but he might almost as well have had none, for his elder son had left home very early in life, and had finally settled in Italy, where he had married. From time to time they had a letter from him, but of late years they had been written in very bad German,—he seemed almost to have forgotten his mother tongue. He was, however, quite well-to-do in the world. "There is no reason why my father should slave here at his gardening," the woman remarked; "we might very easily live in the town, but he chooses to do it——"

"He *must* do it, my child," the old man declared. "You cannot understand that property that has been intrusted to one's charge must be looked after."

While they were talking, a violent wind had arisen,—it was roaring in the tops of the trees, and whistling in all the holes and crannies of the old walls. Thunder-clouds were banked high in the western sky. It grew very dark, and some large drops fell upon the paving-stones.

"You will be sorry that you did not take my advice," the girl said to the Professor; "the storm will not wait for you."

"Oh, we can't let the gentleman go now," her mother observed; "in ten minutes it will rain so that he would be wet to the skin. He must wait until the worst has passed over." As she spoke, she looked towards the old gardener, who nodded his head in assent. Schönrade was not at all in a hurry.

He was soon seated beside the old man at a round table in a comfortable little room, before the windows of which the vine-leaves were dancing in the storm. The woman placed before him bread and butter, cheese, and beer. The girl had vanished, and reappeared in neat stockings and shoes. The lamp burned brightly, but the rain fell in torrents, and there was a constant roll of thunder.

The Professor, in his turn, now asked his host's name, and learned that it was Vogelstein. " And you have a son in Italy ? In Florence ?"

" Yes, yes ; he wrote us last from there that he had under-taken to keep an inn," the old man replied.

" And I remember now that Signor Uccello told me he came from this part of Germany," the Professor exclaimed ; and then ensued question and answer, by which it was made plain that Signor Uccello was no other than old Vogelstein's eldest son. Of course they were all upon a friendly footing at once. The Professor happened to mention, with a touch of humour, the " Palazzo Bellarota," and on the instant the old man grew attentive, and laid his hand on his arm, as if to arrest the conversation at that point, but, seeming then to bethink himself, shook his head and said nothing. Schönrade introduced the Recorder's account of the Höneburg, in order to learn, if he could, how Vogelstein came to inhabit the ruins. " I suppose," he concluded, " that there is no mystery in the matter ? If there is, I will curb my curiosity."

" Certainly no mystery," the gardener replied. " All is as plain and simple as possible,—too simple to interest any one, even the diligent police. My family has been closely connected in a certain way with that of the Freiherrs von Höneburg for a long time. My ancestors were towns-folk, who centuries

ago possessed great wealth and took their seats at the council-
board. The Feinberg mansion, which you tell me you have
seen to-day, belonged to one of them, and the inscription on
his monument is still legible in the church of the Blessed
Virgin. There is a long story concerning the loss of our
possessions, which I will only lightly touch upon. In a bloody
feud between the town and the Freiherr,—the town had un-
justly thrown two of his followers into a dungeon as robbers,
—my ancestor secretly espoused the cause of Von Höneburg,
to whom he was beholden for many a personal kindness, and
admitted him to the town at night by the green gate. In
spite of his friend's aid, however, Von Höneburg was unsuccessful, and the Vogelsteins were deprived of their rights as
townsmen, and forced to fly. I do not excuse his conduct: I
only tell of it to show how the Vogelsteins came to live at the
Höneburg, first as allies of the Freiherr, and afterwards in his
service. The friendship between them continued when what
had given rise to it was wellnigh forgotten. In later times,
when the lords of the castle were frequently absent at court
or in the army, they always appointed the Vogelsteins their
bailiffs, and this continued as long as there was any land left
to look after. My father was bailiff here, but even in his
young days his master was going down-hill, and farm after
farm had to be sold. Ever since I can remember, poverty was
the order of the day,—very little more than daily bread was
made by cultivating what land remained. I was very young
when I was obliged to serve in the army, and I was in the
same regiment in which the Freiherr von Höneburg was captain of cavalry, and in his squadron. Then the French war
broke out, and we took the field. We rode side by side in
many a battle, and once I saved his life when he would not
have given a pin for his chance. He was terribly wounded,
and resigned from his command, retiring upon his pension to
a small provincial town. He had been married shortly before

the war, and his wife now accompanied him into his retreat
and bore him a boy, to whose education he devoted himself.
As soon as I had served out my time he put me here to take
care of the Höneburg,—that is, all of it that was left to
take care of,—so that a small sum from here was added yearly
to his pension. His son entered the school for cadets, and
was often sent hither in the vacation for the sake of the fresh
country air. After his father's death he came here, a young
officer, and reinstated me in my office for my lifetime; but he
sold a few more acres, so that I am nothing but a gardener.
He led the gay life of a young officer in many a garrison
town, and was finally ordered to this place. What happened
here——"

He interrupted himself, put his hand up to his mouth, and
coughed. Then he looked steadily at his guest for awhile,
moved his lips without speaking, and finally asked, " Do you
not know ?"

" How should I know ?" asked the Professor, in surprise.

" Well, whatever happened," the old man continued, " was,
I plainly perceive, no affair either of yours or mine. I will
only tell you that the lieutenant, my master, came here to the
Höneburg one day, and ordered me to put in order the best
room I could find, for that a young lady was coming here to
stay. I looked at him in amazement, and it seemed to me
that he carried an uneasy conscience in his breast. He saw
what I thought, and said to me, ' There certainly is some
secrecy to be preserved, but it will scarcely result in a siege
of the castle, as in olden times.' I shook my head doubtfully,
and he felt it necessary to reassure me still farther. ' It is
in strict honour,' he said, ' in strict honour ! We are to be
married, but it can't be done immediately. She will be married to some one else to-morrow if we do not prevent it.' It
was my duty to obey, and I obeyed. In the night he brought
her across the moor upon his horse, in front of him, after true

knightly fashion, gave her in charge to us, and returned immediately to the town, as she told him to. He came often to visit her, and one day he brought a priest with him, and they were married, standing upon the site of the old castle chapel, just where the altar-stone lies, beneath the large linden. After that the Freiherr often spent days at a time here, and finally took up his abode here altogether, having received or taken his dismissal from the army."

The old man rubbed his brow, as if to freshen up old memories, or to drive away those that thrust themselves forward unbidden.

" How long ago was it?" asked Schönrade, far more interested in these modern tales of the Höneburg than he had been by the Recorder's revelations.

" Oh, more than thirty years ago," the gardener answered, making a silent calculation, " perhaps thirty-five; certainly more than thirty. I can tell you to a day if I consult my old day-book, where I wrote it all down faithfully, because I was one of the witnesses of the marriage. Certainly more than thirty years."

" And did they live here long ?"

" That depends upon what you call long. Compared with my lifetime it was not long, but they certainly found it so although they were very happy together at first. Oh, what a beautiful lady she was! She had wonderful eyes, so black and flashing, not like the eyes of the women about here, and, indeed, she was only half German. And her hair ! She would sometimes go to the fountain in the early morning with it hanging all unbraided and loose about her. There was a bluish lustre to it, and it was so long and thick that it fell about her like a cloak. I never saw such hair either before or since."

He looked into vacancy with a glow of enthusiasm on his wrinkled face, then nodded his head slowly, and passed his hand across his eyes. "This has nothing to do with it," he began again; "you wanted me to tell you of myself. But, I cannot tell why, I cannot drive it all from my thoughts to-night. Excuse me, sir."

"Oh, go on, pray!" said the Professor, who had grown very grave, and was listening with eager attention. "What happened next?"

"Oh, there is little more to tell," the old man continued. "Although they neither of them could have been used to the solitude of the life here, yet they lived together very happily for a year and more. A little son was born to them, and their content seemed perfect. Sometimes we were rather pinched, for the Freiherr had no pension, and the castle territory was small indeed; the young wife, too, had brought her husband nothing but her beauty and her love. The Freiherr was cross sometimes, and then his wife used to shed tears in secret. Once an official came here from the town about some old debts of my master's, and after that there was many a wretched, unhappy day. 'We shall soon be at the end of everything,' the Freiherr said to me one day, 'and have to leave even this miserable nest,—and what then—— ?' But the Baroness was too proud to complain either to me or to my wife; she devoured her grief in secret, and her beauty began to fade. I am sure that the Freiherr never alluded to her poverty to her; no, no: that was not his way; but she probably accused herself of being the cause of his miserable difficulties. She sang less and less in those days. Ah, how wonderfully she could sing! I once said in jest to my master, 'The Frau Baroness would make a great sensation upon the stage!' But he was very angry with me for my presumption; perhaps she had said something of the kind to him before. At last, when their need was the sorest, a letter arrived that greatly agitated them. A distant cousin of the Freiherr's, whom he had almost forgotten, was dead, and his immense estate, which had been in the family for centuries, in default of nearer heirs, fell to my master. He was also to bear henceforth the title of Graf von Gleichenau. The future of the young couple was luxuriously provided for. The Freiherr hurried off to take possession of his wealth, leaving his wife and child here temporarily."

"And did he never come back?" asked Schönrade, eagerly.

" Yes, he came back once more,—I can't tell how long afterwards,—but not at all as he had left. His beautiful wife may have learned how matters stood from his letters, for she received him so coldly that it cut me to the heart. I heard him in the room speaking loud and violently to her as he never had spoken before, and then I had to go for the doctor, for she was seized with a violent fit of hysterics; and the cause of their disagreement I never discovered,—I never tried to discover it. A notary made his appearance here, with all kinds of papers for signature, but the Baroness refused to sign anything. Then the Freiherr gave me money to have the house put in better order, and to provide for the welfare of mother and child, and again took his departure. Since then I have never seen him."

"And his wife? and the child?"

" They stayed here for some time. Letters came and went; I never knew what their contents were, for she was silent as the grave. Once a packet arrived, with five seals, and a large amount of money written out on the cover of it; but she returned it immediately. A few days after that she took her departure, weeping bitterly as she thanked me again and again for what little kindness I had been able to show her. She drove off with her baby, without saying where she was going. I immediately informed my master of what had occurred, but I received no reply, nor has he ever answered any of my letters since. I send him a yearly statement of my administration here, but apparently he does not wish to be reminded of the Höneburg. I shall die, I suppose, without ever seeing another line from his hand; but I will die at my post, like an old sodier.''

CHAPTER X.

THE Professor rose hastily and left the room. He was greatly agitated, more so than he cared to show in the presence of strangers. Had he just penetrated the mystery of his birth, so carefully guarded from him hitherto by his mother? He was certain of nothing, and yet he could have sworn that so it was.

He stood still beneath the veranda, where the fresh breeze after the storm brought him coolness and refreshment. The drops were falling from the vine-leaves, but the rain had ceased. A few dark clouds were drifting overhead towards the town, but between them the deep-blue skies were clear. He pondered whether he should not instantly leave the ruin and try to forget what he had just heard. But how to leave without making courteous acknowledgment to his hosts for their kindness, when they could not possibly imagine what urged him to depart? And did it urge him to depart? Did it not rather bind him by invisible ties to the spot? A short time ago, all this had been a matter of supreme indifference to him; now he grasped eagerly at anything that could be of advantage to him in his suit. If he was on the eve of what might prove a fortunate discovery, why avoid it? His filial duty prompted no such course. He tapped lightly on the window in invitation to those within, then walked to the fountain and gazed into its depths, where gleamed the friendly sparkle of a star. He hailed it gladly, and thought of her whom he loved best.

The gardener, with his daughter and grandchild, joined him.

"It is time to go," said the Professor, hoping that they would try to detain him. The old man looked up to the skies and remarked that the storm seemed to be over. His daughter happily observed that the meadows and moor were drenched with rain, and that it would hardly be possible to find the shortest path to the ferry. Was it necessary that he should return to the town that night? He replied that there was no need for such haste, and that if he could have lodging here he would far rather remain than wander about the damp moor seeking his way. The woman looked at the old man, who answered her look more kindly than she had expected, with a "Do as you please." Then the young girl joined in the conversation, and suggested the empty room, which, as her grandfather had told her, the beautiful baroness had occupied with her little son. That was just what he would like, the Professor declared, and the two women hurried into the house to make the necessary arrangements.

The old man remained, and seated himself on the stone seat, which was already dry. Schönrade again leaned over the basin of the fountain. "You seemed greatly struck by my appearance when you first saw me," he began, "and I thought I heard words from your lips expressive of surprise. Was I right? and, if so, may I ask what startled you upon seeing me?"

"You were right," replied the gardener, "you were right. But I was wrong, although it is most strange——"

"What is most strange?"

"Your resemblance to—to——"

"To whom?"

"I can hardly say. At first I thought to the Baroness von Höneburg, of whose sorrows I have told you, and then it seemed to me that the Freiherr himself—— But I could not say whether it lay in the face or figure, in eyes, nose, or mouth. And now that I am more familiar with your appearance, it fades, and I see perfectly that I was wrong. You must not take it ill of the man who has been waiting for more than thirty years to see his master and the lord of this castle."

The Professor could hardly control his emotion. After a few moments, he said, " And suppose you had not erred? suppose———"

The old man turned, and laid a trembling hand upon his arm.

" I have no certainty in the matter," the Professor continued, hurriedly, "and nothing can be farther from my thoughts than any desire to impose upon you or myself. But there were some strange coincidences suggested by your story, and my mother, who has always concealed from me every particular of my birth and early infancy, was averse to my coming hither. Do you know the Baroness von Höneburg's maiden name?"

"I do."

" Let me tell you my mother's. She is a Bellarota, the daughter of the singer Carlo Bellarota, who died here in the hospital of the town when she was scarcely ten years old."

" In truth, sir, it was as you say."

" And my name is the German rendering of hers. Schönrade is German for Bellarota."

The old man arose, took off his cap, and bowed low. " Then there can be no doubt," he exclaimed, with heartfelt joy. " Welcome, welcome, Herr Freiherr, to your ancestral home!"

This solemn address served instantly to change the entire tone of the Professor's thoughts, to destroy the melancholy mood in which he was indulging, and he burst into a laugh. The gardener started, and looked half offended. " Forgive me, good friend," said Schönrade. " Indeed, you would laugh as I do if you knew all. Did I not tell you that Philip Amberger believed he had discovered the Palazzo Bellarota in your son's hotel? So it was, and he gravely addressed me there as in the palace of my ancestors. I come to Northern Germany, and

find here evidence to prove my descent from the Freiherrs
von Höneburg, whose oldest and most faithful friend bids me
welcome to my ancestral halls. Is it not better to laugh than
to cry?—tell me."

Vogelstein's face relaxed a little. " Yes, yes," he said, " it
seems strange enough, but many an event in real life seems too
strange for a romance, and why not—— Oh that I should
live to see the day !"

" Do not let us take a well-founded suspicion for complete
proof," the guest said, warningly. " Permit me to remain, as
far as you and yours are concerned, Professor Xaver Schönrade, until——"

" Xaver?" exclaimed the gardener. " It was the boy's baptismal name."

" That, too, strengthens the probability. Nevertheless, let
me remain what I know I am until I receive full confirmation
from my mother and the Count von Gleichenau. I lay claim
to only one proof of confidence on your part: tell me whether
you have any papers in your keeping that may throw farther
light upon this matter. You can safely intrust them in my
hands while I am with you here."

" Yes, there are some papers," the gardener said, after a
moment's reflection, " and they must be just where the Frau
Baroness left them, in the upper drawer of the cabinet, in her
bed-chamber. I kept the key. There are both papers and letters, but she cannot have attached much value to them, or she
would have taken the little packet with her. She left in anger,
and bowed down by grief; she may have forgotten them."

His daughter came to conduct their guest to his room.
Lena was standing on the stairs with a lighted candle, and she
bade him a kindly good-night. Vogelstein brought him the
key of the cabinet, and the two men shook hands in silence.
A moment afterwards the Professor stood within the little
low-ceilinged room where, perhaps, his cradle had once rocked.

He was overpowered, in thus unexpectedly finding his home, by sensations that were both sad and pleasing. For awhile he paused where he stood, near the door, and his eyes grew dim as he looked towards the window where the wretched young wife must have often sat, and at the simple couch where she had passed sleepless nights, and at the wardrobe and cabinet of plainest birch-wood which had contained her belongings. What had taken place here between those two people who certainly had once loved each other dearly? What stormy experience had assailed the heart that had been left here to throb in sickening expectation or passionate grief? He thought he could now understand why his mother had drawn an impenetrable veil over all that far-off time, and had withheld from him the name of the husband who had so saddened her life and deprived her son of his rights. Hitherto he had felt only indifference towards this father of his, now he seemed to hate him as his mother hated him. "It makes no difference," he muttered sadly to himself. "I have no father."

He placed a chair in front of the cabinet, and opened the drawer. He found within, as the old man had said, papers and letters, which he arranged hastily, and then read one by one. From them he gleaned a knowledge of what had happened, but the light and shadow cast upon that past all came from one direction; from Camilla there was nothing save a few words hurriedly written by way of comment on the margin of some of the letters. The Freiherr's tone in writing was uniformly gentle and kind; even when he lamented an obstinate misconception of his good intentions, or enforced some stern demand, his style never ceased to be characterized by a respectful forbearance and a cordial good will, that spoke well for the writer, although they had evidently been but scantily appreciated by the reader. Some sheets were torn in two, and parts of some were entirely wanting. The seals of others were still unbroken; either their contents had been surmised beforehand, or the wife's displeasure upon receiving them had found vent in this sign of an absence of interest. Until long past midnight the Professor sat poring over these papers and unveiling a melancholy past.

It was beyond a doubt that the Freiherr had truly loved Camilla. How he won her for his wife there was nothing here to tell, but in one letter he said that he never could forget that for his sake she had resigned the certain prospect of a life surrounded by every luxury; and this passage was underscored in pencil several times, by the same hand, evidently, that had appended to it a mark of interrogation. The son knew his mother too well not to suspect that her proud and passionate temperament might but too probably have been the cause of disagreements in her married life that had cooled the ardour of a husband not especially constant in character. The fine bond of union must have been somewhat frayed when the event occurred which necessitated the Freiherr's absence. True, there followed from Castle Gleichenau the tenderest letters, that in their constant reference to the idyllic life in the old ruin were not without a deep tincture of romance, and that painted in glowing colours the happy future that should be passed in the midst of wealth and plenty. But soon the communications grew less frequent and more common-place, being often confined to excuses, scarcely received as sincere, for delay in writing. Camilla had apparently answered these with bitter reproaches, requiring that her husband should return, or should send for her and her child, for the Freiherr renewed his excuses, at first eagerly, then more coldly, postponing the day of his return, and entreating her not to think of coming to him until the castle should be ready to receive her.

At last, in answer probably to renewed inquiries as to the cause of his delay, came a letter of grave import. It appeared from an investigation of the title-deeds to the large entailed estate of which the Freiherr had just taken possession, that it could devolve only upon heirs noble on the side of both the father and the mother, who must themselves be able to prove a certain number of noble ancestors. The Freiherr apparently informed Camilla of this fact simply as a preamble to what followed; he thought he had heard her say that her father belonged to an ancient Italian family of rank. She well knew how little importance he himself attached to noble birth, how small a value he had placed upon his own, but, now that this large estate of Gleichenau had fallen to him, it was of moment to know whether his son could inherit it, or whether it must devolve at his death upon another branch of the family. Camilla, perhaps smarting from a sense of previous real or fancied neglect, appeared to have suspected in this letter a regret upon her husband's part at having contracted an unequal marriage, for his next letter contained a remonstrance with her for her intemperate outbreak of passion, and for her accusations, which were certainly as yet without foundation. This " as yet" was again strongly underscored in pencil, and attention was called to it by exclamation-points on the margin of the paper. She must have replied, however, that her family was indubitably noble, for the Freiherr, although he expressed himself as by no means convinced, promised her that he would go immediately to Italy, and make all possible inquiries there, that she might be reinstated in her rights, praying her, until that should be done, to remain in the Höneburg, since he desired to present his wife to the noble families in the neighbourhood of Gleichenau in a manner that should insure her a suitable reception from them.

This last communication must have greatly irritated Camilla, and, indeed, one might easily conclude from it that the new Count of Gleichenau was nowise inclined to submit to any social rebuff for his wife's sake. She must have discerned in such an ignoring of herself a greater want of affection than even his previous coldness had prepared her for, and she clearly saw the loss that threatened her child. In a short memorandum in her handwriting she accused her husband of treachery in wishing to make use of the law of inheritance, to which he referred, in order to rid himself, in his changed circumstances, of wife and child. There was, besides, the copy of a letter to a famous advocate, inquiring whether such conditions of inheritance would hold good in a marriage contracted before coming into possession of an entailed estate. The answer was not to be found, but it could scarcely have been satisfactory, since there were several notes from various Italian cities, proving that Camilla, in her distress, had instituted inquiries there upon her own account.

And certainly any impartial judge would have agreed that the Freiherr spared no pains to discover traces of the Bellarotas. There was a good-sized roll of papers,—information procured from magistrates and priests,—from which it was clear that a noble family of the name did assuredly exist, —but no link could be discovered by which Carlo Bellarota could be associated with it.

Meanwhile, time widened the breach between the husband and the wife. It was undeniable that the Freiherr was strongly influenced by his new surroundings, and was growing more and more familiar with the thought of breaking a bond which his wife's constant mistrust, complaints, and reproaches threatened to convert into a galling chain. His proposal for a separation was not surprising. On the margin of this letter Camilla had written, "Never! never! never!" There were some lawyer's letters, offering a generous maintenance for mother and child; several of these were much torn. A letter with them from the Freiherr was still unopened.

His return to the Hüneburg must have interrupted the correspondence. The old gardener had told of the meeting.

Then came an agreement, carefully drawn up, the conditions of which were most favourable to the wife, signed by the Freiherr, but not by Camilla. Beneath his signature this sentence in his handwriting bore a later date: " I hold myself bound to all these conditions, even without Camilla's expressed acquiescence." Xaver knew that his mother had never received any means of support from this source, and he must therefore conclude either that his father had broken his word or that his mother had been too proud to receive anything at his hands,—which last supposition was the more probable. With this contract he found another paper, that occupied his most profound attention.

It was an official document, made out with all the legal formula, in which the Freiherr von Höneburg and Graf von Gleichenau, after a short explanatory introduction, irrevocably declared that, in the event of his legal separation from his present lawful wife Camilla Bellarota, whatever opinion might be entertained concerning blame to be attached to either party, he not only acknowledged his son, Xaver von Höneburg, born of this marriage, as his sole heir to all that he, as Freiherr von Höneburg, should possess at his death, but that he wished hereby to make over to him at the present time the Höneburg, with all the buildings, gardens, fields, and waste lands thereto belonging, upon the sole condition that the boy's mother should be allowed the use and control of it during his minority. "Small in value as the gift is," the paper concluded, " it is all that now belongs to the Von Höneburg race, and by this act I wish to convince my son, for whom I hope to provide abundantly from the income of the Gleichenau estates, that my love endows him with all over which I have power of disposal." The Professor read this paper three or four times, examining the seal and the notary's signature. Unquestionably, here was a document the validity of which could be proved in any court of law. According to it, he was lord of this ruin of Höneburg, in which he had been offered a shelter for the night,—he had been so for thirty years, and learned the fact now for the first time. The document had been given into his mother's keeping, and she had valued it so little that she had left it behind her when she left his birthplace. Was it because the place had seemed to her so worthless? Hardly. But she hated the man who had given it to her son, and she had left the Höneburg, evidently resolved that her son should bear her name and should grow up in ignorance of that of her thankless and faithless husband.

It was strange. As the heap of letters laid aside as read accumulated on his left hand, his sentiments underwent an astonishing change. He cordially loved his mother, he was grateful to her for her care of him, the many sacrifices she had made in his behalf, and the thousand proofs of her tender affection; he could not but admit that one of the chief causes of her grief and despair had been the thought of her child who was to lose a father; her love for her husband had been most fervent and passionate,—her sufferings had been great in proportion; and after her life had been shattered, as it were, the manner iu which she had relied solely upon her own efforts, and refused all other aid, was proof of extraordinary force of character; and yet he could not but feel more and more that the man who had wrought all this wrong was something to him, that he could not be as angry with him as he seemed to deserve, and that he could not refuse him a large share of sympathy. Those two people, he reflected, could have made each other happy only for as long as their several peculiarities of temperament were held in abeyance; if all this had not happened to separate them, they would not have pursued life's pathway much further arm-in-arm,—they would have become estranged, and perhaps neither would ever have reached any desirable goal. Camilla Bellarota was a born artist.

The further course of events, so far as it was to be gathered from these papers, strengthened him in this idea. The Freiherr declared that during the short period of their marriage he had become convinced that an enduring union between them was impossible. He could not compel his wife to consent to a divorce, but he should henceforth live away from her, and he hoped that time would bring her the power to see and judge more clearly as to her course. Her reply to this must have been the announcement of her intention to go upon the stage, for a letter from the Freiherr ensued, evidently written in extreme irritation, in which he distinctly and emphatically forbade any such step on her part. Several others, all occupied with the same subject, were found, until at last he briefly and sternly declared that persistence in her determination would constitute a sufficient plea for a divorce from the Count of Gleichenau, and that he should not fail to avail himself of it. This was the last letter in his handwriting, and it was blistered here and there with tears. According to the old gardener, Camilla had delayed her departure from the Hüneburg for some time after receiving the letter containing money, of which he had told. Perhaps she had pondered long whether she should disregard the menace, which was certainly the result of stern determination on her husband's part. But at last she had thrown all consideration to the winds, and had gone forth into the world with her child, to pursue the vocation for which she was born. The Count of Gleichenau had doubtless shortly received intelligence of the singer's brilliant success, and had easily obtained a divorce.

The candle had burned low in the socket; the Professor extinguished it, and, throwing the window wide open, leaned out into the cool night-air. The heavens were clear, sprinkled with glittering stars, a gentle breeze rustled among the tops of the trees, and from a crevice in the ruins a moping owl sent forth its melancholy cry. Was his Katrine asleep and dreaming? How little the dear child knew of what was now agitating his very soul!

Not until after an hour spent in deep reverie did he betake himself to bed, where he slept until late the next morning.

The gardener's daughter had twice served the coffee, and twice cleared it away, when he at last appeared for what was almost a mid-day meal. His healthy nature had recovered its wonted tone after his hours of sleep; his nerves were no longer shaken by the agitating revelations of the previous evening; he was even ready to jest again. "Bygones are bygones," he said to himself as he dressed; "those tears were dried long ago; those sighs—there is not even an echo of them left. Each of those two has long passed the meridian of life, and is upon the downward path; the chance that revealed all that vanished time to me thus late made it present to me last night. What influence it may have upon my life is most uncertain. In the clear light of to-day I will let it take its place for me also in the past."

Accordingly, he did not fail to compliment the sergeant's widow upon the excellence of the coffee and the breakfast, or to observe that Lena was this morning attired very prettily and quite like a town-bred maiden. He discovered also that the girl was remarkably well educated, more thoroughly and carefully than many a daughter of the aristocracy who had masters by the dozen at her command.

"Where will your pretty daughter find a lover in this solitude and seclusion?" he jestingly asked the mother.

She sighed. "It is indeed very lonely and quiet here, but sometimes we mix with our kind. Almost every Sunday we go to town to church, and I see many a fine gentleman turn to stare after my Lena's pretty face. One and another comes here from time to time; but the girl holds her head very high, because the Vogelsteins, she says, have patrician blood in their veins. And yet I do not say that an upright, honest man, with his heart in the right place, would be unwelcome to us all."

Lena brought a basket of ripe cherries, fresh from the garden. Her grandfather, in the joy of his heart, had let fall something of the previous night's conversation, and she asked, in a tone of gay raillery, " Are you our Freiherr, then, or not? How can we pay you due respect unless we know?"

" Oh, if the Professor does not inspire respect, Fräulein Lena," Schönrade said, with a laugh, " the Freiherr will come off but poorly. You are too familiar with the length and breadth of his noble possessions."

" We cannot tell what they may be worth," the old gardener gravely interposed. " Not long ago there were some gentlemen here surveying the meadow and the sandy tract. There was some talk of a new railroad, and they wanted space for a depot and machine-shops. They thought I had the disposal of the land, and offered me a sum for it that I should hardly dare to mention. And yet I rather think they hoped to drive a close bargain with so poor a man. They probably had recourse to the Graf von Gleichenau."

From these words the Professor concluded that Vogelstein knew nothing of the deed of gift. He might have put the paper in his pocket and carried it off, but he could not for a moment contemplate such an abuse of confidence. He took the old man up-stairs and delivered up to him again all the papers, showing him the important deed and commending it to his special care. " I cannot ask you," he said, " to let me take this paper, for I am still only a stranger to you, and must make good my claim, although I am sure that I could easily satisfy your mind on this point. But I am not yet certain whether I shall find it best, in my own interest, to vindicate my rights here; and therefore you will certainly not object to my taking a copy of this deed, and referring, if necessary, to the original in your possession."

G*

The gardener gladly consented. "I am sure you are our Freiherr's son," he said, "and I only pray Heaven to grant its blessing upon all you undertake."

He brought paper and pen. In an hour Schönrade had finished, and bade good-bye to his kind hosts. He reached his hotel in time to pay his reckoning and leave by the express train for Berlin.

On the long journey he had sufficient leisure to think over all that had occurred, and to form his plans for the future.

CHAPTER XI.

THERE were many surmises in the villa in the Thiergartenstrasse as to the cause of the Professor's absence for two consecutive days. The Councillor's wife received his card, left for her with the servants, but had heard nothing further from him. Katrine judged it best to mention having seen him, as he had of course been observed to enter the pavilion, but she naturally made no further reference to his visit, and no one felt any curiosity on the subject. Who could suspect that those few minutes had been a crisis in two lives?

"You must stop at his rooms as you come home from 'Change," the Councillor's wife said to her husband. "He may be ill, and it would be very unkind to take no notice of his absence." She found the evenings very tiresome, and had constant headache again.

Mr. Fairfax offered to call on the Professor.

"But why?" Lilli inquired. "He might think——"

"What might he think?" her mother asked, with more asperity than the timid remark seemed to warrant. "The Professor is our dear friend, and it is no more than proper that

Mr. Fairfax, who has learned to value him, should ask after his welfare."

Lilli made no reply. She had not altogether regretted Schönrade's absence, since she had not been the cause of it. These few days of uninterrupted intercourse with the young Englishman, during which she had seen very little of Katrine, who had been busy with some embroidery and seemed to like to be alone, had convinced her that the society of the man of science was not necessary to her happiness. The young people were growing very intimate, and, although no formal declaration had as yet been made, there were many signs of an approaching betrothal. The Councillor's wife observed this with satisfaction; her husband's wishes were on the eve of accomplishment.

Mr. Fairfax inquired at the Professor's rooms, and found that he was absent from the city; his landlady could not tell whither he had gone or how long he would be away. Frau Wiesel thought such a sudden departure very odd,—leaving no address, either. "Did he say nothing to you about it?" she asked, turning to Katharina; "it is extremely strange." The poor child felt the blood rush to her cheeks, and bent her head low over her embroidery, as she replied that she had seen him but for a few moments, and that probably some sudden occurrence——

"Of course, of course!" Frau Wiesel assented; "we shall soon learn that there is no cause for our anxiety. One grows so accustomed to seeing people, and then, in turn, to their absence. He could not have gone to Wiesbaden with us, at all events." Her thoughts were again occupied with the contemplated pleasure-trip.

Katrine had put the rose that Xaver had given her in a glass of water, in her own room, and tended it carefully. Before it withered, he must be back again, she thought. Lilli wondered at the care thus bestowed. "Why are you so devoted to that one rose?" she asked; "there are hundreds far finer in the garden, and you can have as many of them as you like every day, you know."

Katrine laughed archly. "This rose is very different from the rest," she replied; "can't you see that?"

"Not at all. I think it faded and poor-looking."

"It has a very rare and peculiar fragrance."

"That is pure imagination."

"Perhaps so."

The next morning Katrine found a rose in a vase of water in Lilli's room. "You too?" she asked.

"Oh, dear!" she replied, with some embarrassment, "Mr. Fairfax plucked it yesterday and gave it to me. It is very silly to save one rose, when there is a garden-full; but then he did it so kindly, and said——"

"What did he say?"

"Oh, I can't tell you. I ought to have thrown the rose away, I know."

"Yet there it is in water, and there it will be, I wager, until, it is entirely faded and its fragrance is all gone. Then it will probably be pressed and preserved."

"What nonsense!"

Katrine shook her finger at her. "Oh, Lilli, how faithless you are to your Professor——"

"Katrine!"

"Out of sight, out of mind!"

"You must confess that all that was very stupid——"

"With pleasure, my dear."

Lilli was struck by a sudden idea. "Tell me—that rose of yours——"

"Make yourself easy. Mr. Fairfax did not give it to me."

Lilli pouted prettily. "I'm quite sure of that."

"Oh, indeed!"

"But did some one else——?"

Katharina laid a finger on her lips. "Don't ask yourself riddles, my dear, that all your wisdom will never solve."

"What! you have secrets from me! And I tell you everything! Down upon your knees and confess!"

Katrine sighed. "Yes, if you could only give me absolution." And that was all she would say.

That very day the post brought two letters for "Fräulein Katharina Amberger." She took them hastily from the servant, glanced at their addresses, and put them, unopened, into her pocket. "From my mother," she said to Lilli, who was with her.

"And the other?"

"From my brother in Italy," she replied, instantly, without looking up.

"It did not look like a German hand; it seemed to me more French."

"Oh, Moritz often uses the Italian characters."

"Moritz?"

"I meant to say Philip."

"But that letter had a German post-mark. Let me see it."

"How curious you are! I will go up-stairs and read it."

"Why not read it here? I'll not disturb you."

Katharina gave her a kiss, and hurried out of the library.

She locked herself up in her own room, threw herself into an arm-chair by the window, and looked at the two unopened letters in her lap, delaying the decisive moment that their contents would surely bring her. She was not familiar with the Professor's handwriting, but she never doubted that the second letter was from him. Yet she opened her mother's first, for she knew it would be the more important of the two, and she would read her lover's words when they might be needed as comfort. Frau Barbara Amberger wrote:—

"MY DEAR CHILD,—I have received a visit to-day from a
certain Professor Schönrade, who has said some very strange
things to me,—unfortunately, having reference to you. I cannot at all imagine that you have given him the encouragement
which he speaks of having received : you could not have so
far forgotten what you owe to your family and to your own
self-respect. At all events, I must interpose my authority to
prevent any continuance of your intercourse with him, and it
is inconsistent with my sense of maternal duty to allow you to
remain any longer beneath a roof from which I have no right
to exclude such bold intruders. To avoid all remark, I do not
recall you to your home, but shall come to Berlin to take you
with me upon a journey, which we can afterwards shorten at
our pleasure. I have informed Frau Wiesel of my plans in a
manner that can awaken no suspicion ; and it is your part, my
dear child, so to conduct yourself that neither we nor you may
experience further annoyance from this disagreeable occurrence. All discussion I will postpone until we meet. In the
mean time, hoping to find you the same good and obedient
child that you have ever been, I am your loving mother,

BARBARA AMBERGER."

Katharina knew it all now,—her worst forebodings were
fulfilled. The letter dropped from her trembling hand into
her lap ; the enclosure to the Councillor's wife fell upon the
floor. Her eyes grew dim as she looked out of the window at
the acacias waving in the breeze, across the glass containing
her poor rose, the leaves of which had fallen off in the previous night and were strewn upon the window-sill. She did
not wonder what was to be done,—what the future had in
store for her if she obeyed or resisted her mother's will ; her
thoughts were simple sadness for her happiness destroyed.
Now she saw how, in spite of all her prudent foresight, her
heart had been in reality filled with hope that her lover's

powers of persuasion would have won to him both her mother and her brother. The dream was over. She burst into tears, and not until they had relieved and soothed her did she open the second letter and read :

"My Dearest,—No oak ever fell at the first stroke of the axe; no need, therefore, to lose courage. Certainly it was rather rash to invade an old patrician house with a modest demand for the hand of its only daughter ; but there must be a beginning to everything. The fact is that I have not prospered in my suit,—there is no disguising it. But I do not at all despair of victory in the end, if you will only be true and steadfast. Let no reproach disturb you, my darling ; you have done right in following the dictates of your heart. Some of Frau Barbara's objections I am sure I could remove by bringing to my aid a few facts with regard to myself which I have just discovered by chance. Your brother Moritz has selfish views with regard to you,—so selfish that I cannot but look upon his opposition with contempt. But even although this letter were a thick book, I could hardly tell you all in it, —I must speak with you face to face, my own love,—must let you know all that has happened, and advise with you as to what is next to be done. I have no doubt that your mother will do all in her power to separate us. This can do no harm if we are sure of each other, but we must have one confidential talk to arrange future communication with each other, in spite of all the Argus eyes in the world. Where shall we meet for such an interview ? Hardly at the villa,—I cannot think it advisable to make a confidante of Frau Wiesel. She would not lend her assistance to what your mother disapproved, and even could we persuade her to befriend us, we should incur too weighty an obligation by doing so. We had better act independently. I propose that we should meet at my mother's, to whom I will tell all, and who will delight to know the girl in whom her only son's hopes for a happy future are centred. She loves me, and she will dearly love you. To-day I shall pay my usual visit at the villa. I shall at least see you,—ah, what a joy that will be! But even if we have an opportunity of saying a few confidential words to each other, they will be so few that I write you now that you may be ready to let me know whether and when you can come to my mother, or if you can propose any better plan. Courage, dearest Katrine, courage, and just as much daring as will assure me of your acquiescence in my plan. Always and forever your

Xaver."

This letter, unsatisfactory as it might be thought, nevertheless comforted her extremely. After what her mother had said, the announcement of her lover's want of success was no shock to her, and all the rest that he wrote was so reassuring. She kissed the paper again and again ; no misgiving that her own resolve could be affected by the opposition of her family troubled her soul. He loved her and she loved him,—here was a truth for which it was a duty to endure the worst that could befall. It was only when this first ecstasy of delight in the consciousness of her lover's strength and fidelity began to yield to graver reflection, that she could not resist feeling anxious and troubled. Not only must she patiently endure and wait, but she must devise some plan for seeing Xaver in private, and this after her mother's written injunctions forbidding all intercourse with him. Reared as she had been in the strictest obedience to the parental rule, she could not meditate, without absolute terror, any plan for a secret rendezvous which might, after all, be detected. She knew that she was incapable of deceit, and to what might she not be exposed? She must so arrange matters that malice itself should find no cause for blame in her.

Then she accused herself of too great a dread of consequences. Of course she would deal frankly and openly with her mother; in spite of her displeasure she would confess her love, and that no power on earth should force her to be false to it. Love demanded self-sacrifice, and it was hardly a sacrifice to conquer her timidity sufficiently to devise means for an interview with the man in whom she reposed absolute confidence. And the interview would take place in the house of his mother, a woman universally esteemed, whom she should be proud to know and love. But how should she explain her desire for a lonely walk so long as would be necessary for the meeting? What if she made a promise that she was unable to perform? Suppose the Councillor's wife should not permit her to go out alone? There were a thousand difficulties in her path. The more she pondered them, the more fanciful all her plans for disguising her intentions seemed to her.

At last she decided that it would be impossible to accomplish anything without Lilli's assistance. Surely she might tell her friend all, and make her her accomplice, as it were. To be sure, Lilli was not the wisest friend in the world, but she had been greatly interested in the Professor, and she was certainly falling in love with Mr. Fairfax. She would understand her and feel for her, and, above all, be silent. Yes, her friend should know her secret and assist her.

She arose to look for Lilli in the garden. But as she unlocked her door she seemed to herself over-hasty. She would wait until the evening: by that time Xaver might have changed his mind and thought of another plan more easy of fulfilment. She seated herself at her desk, selected her smallest sheet of note-paper, and, in case any word of mouth should be impossible with all the family present, she wrote, " I have had a letter from my mother, and she is coming to take me away upon a journey in a few days. But I shall be true to all eternity. I know that we must speak together, and that we have no moment here unobserved. To-morrow forenoon, then, at the appointed place,—if I can succeed in arranging a means of getting there. If I do not come it will not be my fault. I am very sorry, and very happy. God grant all may turn out well! Forever your Katharina." She folded the note so small that she could easily conceal it in her hand, put it in her pocket, and then, taking the letter from her mother to Frau Wiesel in her hand, she went down to the drawing-room, where she knew she should find the lady of the house.

Frau Barbara's note gave the Councillor's wife no cause for suspicion of any kind. "I am sorry," she said, "that we are to lose you so soon, and Lilli will be inconsolable. But I cannot wonder that your good mother wishes you to accompany her upon this journey, which she has been so long desirous of taking. I rather think she is pining to see Philip, and means to surprise him at Naples or Rome. Well, I congratulate you upon so delightful a pleasure-trip. Oh, if my husband would only consent to let me have our travelling-carriage packed too! This terrible atmosphere will be my death."

Her maid brought in a new gown which had just arrived from the most fashionable dress-maker in Berlin, and for a moment or two the lady luxuriated in fancy in displaying it at Wiesbaden. Then, bethinking herself again of Katrine, she said, "Is your wardrobe quite in order for the journey, my dear child? People dress so much nowadays, and one doesn't like to be behind the fashion. Your mother writes that she shall spend barely a day here; there will be no time to do anything then."

It suddenly occurred to Katrine that here perhaps was an opening for her. She had thought of that, she replied, and she should like to add somewhat to her stock of laces and ribbons; upon which Frau Wiesel declared that the carriage was quite at her service.

Oh, what a long day it was! The sun seemed resolved

never to leave the zenith; no occupation sufficed to kill the time. Again and again Katrine held her watch to her ear, convinced that it had stopped. At last the streets began to grow gay with equipages and passers-by. The Councillor came home, and with him Mr. Fairfax. Dinner was over at length, and coffee was taken in the pavilion. One more hour must pass.

"How restless you are to-day!" Lilli remarked. She was playing chess with the young Englishman, but her eyes were everywhere. "Sit down here by me, Katrine dear, and see me checkmate my adversary. How many more moves do you give him?"

Katrine leaned over her and looked at the game. "Mr. Fairfax takes the greatest pains," she said, "to be beaten. You cannot avoid being victorious."

"How mean of you!" Lilli exclaimed. "Mr. Fairfax really plays a much worse game than I do." And, as she spoke, she captured his last remaining castle. The Englishman smiled contentedly: he knew he was winning the only game he really cared for.

Suddenly Lilli moved her chair, and so jostled the little table that the chess-men tumbled about upon it. "The Professor!" It was no news to Katharina, whose sharp eyes had already detected him making his way towards the house through the crowd of passers-by. But the Councillor's wife put up her eye-glass. "At last!" she said, in a tone of satisfaction; "he has not forgotten us, then."

Schönrade exchanged one hurried glance of intelligence with Katharina, and then kissed Frau Wiesel's hand with as easy a grace as if he had only taken leave of her on the previous evening. "Do you call it well-behaved," she asked, "to leave us as you did, without even letting us know towards what quarter of the globe we might send after you our wishes for a successful journey?"

" I hardly hoped I should be missed here," he replied. " I am greatly flattered by your reproof, madame."

She held out her hand to him again. " Let it be of service to you, then."

Katharina took her seat upon a low chair opposite him, a little behind the others, where she could now and then return his glance unobserved by the rest. To her surprise, he was easily induced to speak of his absence from Berlin; but she soon saw his reason for this want of reserve. A friend had told him of a deposit of coal lately discovered in a part of the country where he thought any such deposit impossible. He had been greatly interested, and induced to interrupt his work for several days. As he had supposed, however, his journey was fruitless; the coal proved to be only a remarkably hard species of peat. " But do you know, Fräulein Amberger," he said, turning to Katharina, " that my road led me past your native town, and that out of regard for you—solely, I assure you, out of regard for you—I stopped two days there?" Every one wanted to hear more, and he told all that he could,—how he had accidentally met the riding-party, of the leap across the ditch, the supper at the mill, his row on the lake with Fräulein Sidonie Feinberg,—at which point in his story Katharina showed signs of restlessness,—and of his visit to the Höneburg. Evidently he wished to inform Katharina of all these indifferent matters, that their future interview might not be occupied with such details. She understood him, and was grateful. The others were greatly entertained, especially with the account of the Höneburg and its latest possessor, which he related just as it had been told him by the old gardener, and which produced the effect of a romance. Of course he made no mention of either his mother or himself in the matter. Twilight set in before any one was aware of it.

A walk in the garden was proposed, and the Councillor unwittingly did the Professor a great favour by offering his arm to his wife. Mr. Fairfax, of course, never left Lilli's side, and, as a matter of course, the Professor escorted Katharina. To be sure, the conversation among the party was to a degree general; still, there was an opportunity now and then for a low question and reply, and, as Xaver and Katrine walked behind the others, they could saunter more slowly, and the Professor could press the little hand that lay upon his arm without fear of being observed. It was indeed a delightful evening.

"And you will come?" he whispered, when the conversation between the others was louder than usual.

"I ought not," she answered, in as low a tone.

"But you will come? My mother expects you."

"Does she know?"

"She knows all."

Frau Wiesel asked a question of the Professor, and they were interrupted. Xaver took Katrine's hand, and she slipped into his her note. "It will tell you all," she whispered.

"Thanks, a thousand thanks!"

"And your mother lives——?"

He gave her the number of the house.

It was high time that this important communication should be made, for the Councillor's wife now complained of the narrowness of the paths, that forbade more than two people to walk abreast, and, to remedy this, proposed a change,—setting the example by leaving her husband's arm, and waiting for the Professor, who disguised as best he could his dissatisfaction with this new arrangement. Wiesel, of course, offered his arm to Katharina, and this degree of change appeared entirely to satisfy Mr. Fairfax and Lilli, who were by this time arm-in-arm,—Lilli not at all sorry to demonstrate thus to the Professor the hopelessness of his passion.

Thus they remained until they all repaired to the supper-table. The Councillor's wife had uttered all her choicest commonplaces, selected from her beloved romances, about life and the world, and, feeling that she had been excessively interesting, applied herself to her supper with an excellent appetite. Wiesel could not but remark this. " I shall have to engage you for my family physician, Herr Professor," he said, with a sly glance at his wife.

" Doctor though I am," said Schönrade, not understanding immediately, " I am, as you know, no physician."

" Your medicines are purely sympathetic," his stout host continued, facetiously. " See how they suit my wife. For some days she has lived solely upon lemonade."

" That is of no consequence," his wife remarked, with a languid smile that was meant to convey a great deal to the Professor. It was provoking to have Wiesel joking so at her expense; but she was not sorry that Schönrade should thus learn what his society was to her.

" If I am really fortunate enough to be of service to madame without any merit of my own," the Professor said, gallantly, " I am doubly sorry that my daily visits here are almost at an end."

" You are going to deny us the pleasure of seeing you thus regularly ?" asked the lady, rather surprised at this unexpected turn of affairs.

" I am the greatest sufferer," he continued, in the same tone ; " but there are duties——"

" Duties ?"

Lilli blushed, and glanced timidly at Mr. Fairfax, her next neighbour.

" Duties, madame," the Professor continued, " which certainly do not add to the charm of existence, but which, if neglected, revenge themselves as certainly. For several weeks past I have not been as diligent as I should be, and the publisher who has announced my book for this autumn is growing very urgent. If I am to keep my promise to him, I must omit some of my walks during the next month or two." He wished to pave the way for the cessation of his visits after Katrine's departure. Lilli supposed he was devising a fitting pretext for withdrawing, but entertained her own views as to the cause of this withdrawal on his part. She gave a little nod to Katharina, who would understand it all too, she thought.

"Why, we shall be lonely indeed," said the Councillor's wife. "Do you know that Fräulein Amberger wants to leave us too?"

"*Must* leave you," Katharina corrected her. "My mother writes me that she wishes to travel for awhile, and that I am to accompany her. Perhaps she may be here by to-morrow evening." This was for Schönrade's information.

"You will enjoy yourself greatly, and never miss us," said Frau Wiesel.

"And whither do you go?" the Professor asked.

"I think mamma hardly knows that yet herself. She seldom makes any plan of travel, but follows the inclination of the hour. She enjoys travel more in anticipation than in reality, I think. She is used to the regularity and order of a home-life, and she soon wearies of railway-carriages and hotels and longs for her own peaceful rooms. I foresee that our present journey will not be a long one: we shall soon turn our faces homeward." This plausible declaration would, she thought, forestall any future expression of surprise if the journey with her mother should, as she suspected it would, come to a speedy termination.

"By the way, I am forgetting to tell you what your story of the Höneburg reminded me of," exclaimed the Councillor, when there was a pause in the conversation. "You spoke of a Count von Gleichenau. Do you know that there is a gentleman of that name in Berlin at the present time?"

Schönrade listened attentively. This might be important news for him.

"Perhaps not the one you spoke of," Wiesel continued.

" My physician mentioned paying frequent visits to a Count Gleichenau staying here with his son, who is ill, and whom his father is moving heaven and earth to keep alive."

" If I am not mistaken," the Professor remarked, evasively, "there are several noble families of that name in Germany. It would be of small consequence, either, even if the man so strangely connected with the old romance I have told you should really be in Berlin, since we do not know where to find the young Baron Höneburg. And, besides, who knows whether the old hermit of the ruin was not, after all, amusing himself at my expense?" He was sorry to have told the story and mentioned the Count's name. He certainly had not reckoned upon his sudden appearance on the stage.

The party broke up late in the evening. The lovers were obliged to content themselves with a slight pressure of hands; but Xaver had no need of even this to assure him of his Katrine's fidelity, and he had in his pocket her letter, containing, as she had told him, a consent to his wishes. He took a long walk in the Thiergarten before returning to his lodgings.

CHAPTER XII.

As Lilli was undressing, she heard a knock at her door. " Is it you?" she asked, knowing that it must be Katrine.

" Let me in," was heard in a whisper; " I want to speak to you."

The bolt was withdrawn. " Oh, this is delightful!" said Lilli, embracing her friend. " Shall we put out the light?"

" If you like. It is bright moonlight."

" Oh, magnificent moonlight!" She extinguished the candle

and opened the window-shutters. " Come here and take this big arm-chair, and I will sit on this little one at your feet. There,—now what have you to tell me?"

" Can you keep a secret, Lilli?"

" I can be silent as the grave." She laid her hand on her heart, and nestled close to her friend.

" This is a very important secret, my child."

" So much the better, dear, so much the better."

" And our friendship would be destroyed forever if you should ever betray to any living creature——"

" You need say no more : you know I never tell anything."

" Not to your mother, nor Mr. Fairfax."

" Mr. Fairfax, indeed! It's likely I should speak of such things to him!"

" You soon may. Promise me——"

" I promise—yes, yes—I promise!" She was too impatient even to wait to know what it was she must promise so solemnly.

Katrine leaned towards her, and whispered in her ear, " I am betrothed, dear."

Lilli started. " You are—betrothed? I don't believe it."

" Privately."

" To whom? to whom?"

" To Professor Schönrade."

An earthquake could hardly have produced a more startling effect than did the utterance of this name. Lilli sprang up, overthrew the little chair upon which she had been sitting, and stood in her white night-dress, tall and slender in the moonlight, like a ghost. She seemed actually terrified. " To—— ?" she ejaculated, in what was little more than a whisper. For the moment she could not pronounce the name.

" Certainly it is nothing so very dreadful," her friend said, soothingly, startled in her turn. " *You* do not love the Professor."

H   15

" No, no! I do not love him! I hate him now!" Lilli exclaimed.

" Because he loves me?"

" No, no! because I imagined—because I told you——" She covered her face with her hands, and hid it on Katrine's shoulder.

" Oh, never trouble yourself about that," Katharina reassured her. " You conducted yourself with such perfect propriety that the Professor never suspected your preference for him. You ought to be very glad, dear, that I did as you begged me, and diverted his attentions from you, for your heart is now——"

" Oh, don't say anything about that!" Lilli pouted; " you have deceived me,—and it is very vexatious to have taken such pains for nothing."

" You would have liked to repulse the poor Professor, and to see him waste away in despair."

" Oh, men don't waste away in despair. Who knows but what, if he really had——"

" Oh, are you jealous? But the mischief is done now."

" Yes, it can't be helped, and I must endure with heroism. Oh, you traitors! But now tell me—confess—explain—how could it all come about and I know nothing of it?" She pushed the low chair nearer to her friend than before, and seated herself again.

" Are you entirely reconciled?"

" I must be. Tell me all,—begin!"

Not until the placid moon had sunk behind the trees did Katrine slip off on tiptoe to her own room, where she soon slept calmly, for a plan of operations had been arranged, which the next day was to see carried into effect. Lilli had shown herself even more skilful in devices for assisting the lovers than Katrine had expected, although, as she gave her friend a last good-night kiss, she solemnly declared that she would never look upon the Professor again.

The Councillor's wife had finished her breakfast the next morning when the young girls entered the breakfast-room. Katrine soon left it to write a few lines to her brother, and Lilli made use of her absence to carry out the plan formed the night before. She wished, she said, before her friend left her, to present her with some token of her affection, and, as Katrine had mentioned that she was going to spend the morning in shopping, she proposed to accompany her, and discover what gift would be most agreeable to her. Her mother thought it an excellent idea. "And then I need not leave the house to-day," she said; "I had meant to accompany Katrine in the carriage, but really I feel so languid and exhausted that it is a great relief to have you go in my place. Buy her something very pretty,—she is a dear child." The simple plot was entirely successful.

A little after eleven the two girls were driven from home,— Lilli in most exuberant spirits, Katrine very grave and silent, —to a large shop which possessed the double advantage of being very near the house occupied by Camilla Bellarota and of opening upon a parallel street at the back of the salesroom. "You can leave me and pass directly into the back street," Lilli instructed her friend, "as soon as we have asked to see the laces. I will linger here as long as possible, and then drive to the other shops, mentioning to the footman that your business here is not yet concluded, and that I am to return for you; so you will have plenty of time to pay your visit to Madame Bellarota. Don't hurry too much, dearest Katrine, —you shall have a whole long hour. My regards to your Professor, and tell him that he is a most objectionable person, to induce young girls to disobey their mothers."

The plot was an eminent success. Katharina was admitted by Madame Bellarota's old servant, and conducted to the little drawing-room, where the Professor received her and presented her to his mother. Camilla held out both hands to her, and kissed her on either cheek. "What a beautiful woman!" thought Katharina.

Immediately upon his return to Berlin, Schönrade had confided his love to his mother. He would have done so even had he not felt the need of her assistance, for he could not endure the thought of reserve in such a matter with a mother who had always been to him so tender and devoted. Camilla was surprised,—is not every mother surprised when her son comes to her with a confession of his love for another?—and perhaps if the course of his love had run smoothly her old antipathy to everything connected with Katrine's birthplace would have aroused her antagonism. But that his suit had been denied by the merchant kinsfolk of his love, a suit that her maternal pride prompted her to feel conferred honour where it was proffered, produced an effect upon her mind most favourable to her son's wishes. She instantly enlisted herself upon the side of the young people against Frau Barbara and Moritz Amberger, was indignant at the narrowmindedness and cold hearts of "those trades-people," and evinced the liveliest interest in the girl upon whose steadfast fidelity in the face of all opposition Xaver placed such implicit reliance. He had a warm partisan in his mother.

She knew nothing as yet of his experiences at the Hüneburg. He would taste the delight of presenting these two, dearer to him than all else in the world, to each other before any awakened memories of old sad days should have cast a gloom over his mother's mind and aroused her passionate regrets. Let her think that he was occupied solely, as he was chiefly, with his wooing in that old town, and she could for the present look back with equanimity upon his visit there, in view of which her thoughts had been filled with such sad forebodings. His course in the future should be guided by circumstances.

Camilla was all gentleness and amiability. The charm of her

manner, her caressing kindness, soon placed Katrine entirely at her ease, and called forth her son's grateful glances. There was only one cause for discontent on his part,—he was not left alone with his Katrine for a single instant; to be sure he could take her hand, draw off her glove, and imprint kiss after kiss upon her little rosy palm, but here were two people pledged to each other for life whose lips had never once met to seal the bond between them.

The time was limited, too limited to allow of any range of topics of conversation. Xaver reported every particular of his interviews with Frau Barbara and Moritz, and felt it his duty to inform Katrine of her brother's views with regard to Otto Feinberg. " I do not believe," he said, " that Moritz likes the man ; he certainly has no real friendship for him, but he is weak, and seems to be entirely influenced by these business associates of his, to whom he is under certain obligations.   His relations with Sidonie seem to me most unfortunate, although in the interests of his business he is disposed to make every concession to her.   I think he will be greatly to be pitied if he ever marries her, for the entire happiness of his life will be sacrificed by such a union ; and yet it would be the best thing that could happen for us, for Ignaz Feinberg would be obliged to stand by his son-in-law, whatever his brother Otto might say.   If, on the contrary, anything should occur to sever the connection between Moritz and Sidonie, Otto Feinberg would be your brother's last hope, and he would do everything in his power to make you yield to his wishes.   You shake your head, dearest Katrine.   I know that all his efforts would be vain, but, depend upon it, Moritz would present the matter to you under aspects that might cause you many a hard struggle.   Least to be dreaded in the case will be the loss of your property.   In addition, he will probably tell you that the hostility of the Feinbergs will bring ruin upon the ancient house of Amberger, and this consideration will induce your mother, who at present has no liking for these parvenus, to join her voice to your brother's in entreating you to sacrifice for their sakes your own inclinations. I dare not conceal this from you, and you must judge yourself whether your heart is brave enough to endure the struggle, and whether its sufferings will not be too intense even in victory."

Katharina looked gravely at Camilla, who was eagerly awaiting her answer.

"I will never be Otto Feinberg's wife," she said, after a pause, in a low tone, as entirely devoid of passionate inflection as it was of faltering or indecision ; "and I will love you while life lasts. God grant I may be yours one day !"

"Your being so," he replied, "depends upon yourself alone."

She looked at him with eyes full of fervent affection, and slowly shook her head. "Not upon myself alone. My heart is free to choose, and will always insist upon its rights, but I will never stand before the altar without my mother's blessing. I came resolved to tell you this. If you love me, never try to make me false to this duty."

"I will do all that I can," he replied, perhaps not altogether satisfied, "to win her consent. But if she persists in her opposition, if neither prayers nor argument can move her——"

Katharina laid her hand upon his arm. "Do not let us think of that to-day. Let us believe, as you wrote me, that everything will come right in the end. I will bind myself by no promise that could offend my conscience ; and I will not force a decision which is unnecessary at present, and which might grieve you. Trust me, I desire nothing more fervently than to be yours ; and in resigning such happiness I should be the greatest sufferer. Indeed, you may trust me."

"Right, right, dear child !" Camilla exclaimed, embracing her. "Xaver is my only son, and dear to me, Heaven knows, as son can be to mother. I hold him incapable of an unworthy act, and yet—— Whoever has once built up the fabric of life upon what has seemed steadfast rock, and felt it crumble like sand beneath the foot, can never counsel rash or daring measures, but will rather urge the claims of prudence and duty. No, no! Do nothing rash, Xaver, nothing that can cause yourself or this dear child a future pang of remorse. Promise me this!"

"Katrine does not, cannot understand you, mother," he said, half in reproof; "do not disquiet her unnecessarily."

"You are right," she said, controlling herself. "You can neither of you understand or know what wretchedness I prepared for myself by ruthlessly following where passion led. I will not sadden your hearts with my woes, my children. I will not say a word to shake your firm faith in each other; but the chosen of my son shall know that his mother feels as she does. If my mother had been living, perhaps——" She did not finish the sentence, but turned to Katrine and kissed her forehead. "Enough, enough!" she said, checking herself; "every trial repeats itself in this world; and yet the reverse is true also, that the same experience never occurs twice." Then, extending her hand across the table to her son, she said, "You are honest and true, Xaver. He is the best son in the world, dear Katharina, the very best. And a good son will be a good husband. I can testify to his noble nature——"

"Mother! mother!" he interrupted her eulogium.

"Your mother, my son," she went on, "has a right to speak thus, and your love may listen. It is only because they do not know you that the Ambergers do not receive you with open arms. The time will come when they will be proud to count you among them, and Katrine will be envied——"

"Dearest mother, indeed this is more than enough," he interrupted again, with a laugh. "In a few moments more you will have them all at my feet begging my pardon for not appreciating me. No, no, that is the least of our troubles. There are great material interests in the way of our happiness, and my chief care must be to remove these obstacles, if possible. If I succeed here, they will all find me quite charming,—although Frau Barbara Amberger will hardly emulate my dear mother's enthusiasm."

The beautiful woman nodded gently in assent. The dark fire in her eyes glowed still, but more calmly. Katrine looked at her in admiration, and whispered, " Give me a little of the love you bestow upon him."

" But what can you do," Camilla asked her son, " except show them what you are ? If you wait until your books and lectures make a Crœsus of you, Katharina's heart may well be sick with hope deferred."

" I will try to influence them in another way," he replied. " I have lately discovered several clues that may, if followed out, lead to very unexpected results. In science we often thus accidentally come upon something which signifies little in itself, but, in connection with other facts, reveals some important truth."

" Do not speak in riddles," said his mother.

" I must for the present," he answered, " for I am not yet clear in my own mind. But I rely upon my dear mother's support."

" What ? Upon my support ?" she asked, surprised. " Am I to go upon the stage again to make a fortune for you ? My voice might still find favour, it is true, but what am I to do with this old face of mine ?"

" Oh, no," he said. " When I think of all I have cost you, I see what wonders you have already accomplished. We will consult together some other time upon this matter. The principal point to be discussed at present is how to arrange a correspondence between Katrine and myself when we are apart from each other. I think even my stern and strict mamma will admit that we ought to be able to establish a confidential correspondence between us."

" Yes, lovers must write to each other," she replied, " or they pine in despair."

" I can tell how it may be safely arranged," Katrine observed, glad of this important concession.

" Quick, quick ! what is it ?" Xaver said, kissing the little hand he held in his.

" Lilli Wiesel is my devoted friend. I have told her all, and am sure I can rely upon her silence and assistance. We owe it to her that I am here now without being missed from her home. My mother will think it very natural that I should write to her from time to time, and I can easily slip an enclosure to you into my letters. She will contrive that you receive it."

" Admirable !" he exclaimed. " But why from time to time only ? It seems to me it will be very cold-hearted to refrain from a constant interchange of letters. And can I too rely upon her for my messenger ? In that case I shall take delight in still devoting a portion of my time to visiting at the villa. Lilli is a charming girl."

" Have you just found that out ?" she asked. Of course he could not divine her thoughts as she put the question.

The hour allowed Katrine fled all too swiftly. She started up as she heard the clock strike in the adjoining room.

" Good Heavens, it is time I were away !" she cried. " I must not get Lilli into trouble ! Good-bye !" She embraced Camilla, and leaned her head for a moment upon her breast.

" My dear good child," Camilla repeated, caressingly, several times, as she stroked her cheek, " I have been very inhospitable, I'm afraid. I have given you nothing to eat, for fear of interrupting you. The next time when you come to me you shall be better treated."

H*

" With lemonade and cake," laughed Xaver.

" Quite enough to sustain you in Katrine's society," she retorted. " And now, children, I am going to look out of the window for one minute,—only one." She turned away, and walked towards the other end of the room. Xaver threw his arm around Katrine's waist, drew her lithe figure towards him, and pressed a first lingering kiss upon the lips that did not shun his own. " Mine forever !" he said, and her happy but tearful eyes replied, " Amen."

" Now, go," said Frau Camilla, turning towards them, and, taking Katrine's hand, she conducted her to the door. " Stay where you are," she said to the Professor, who would have followed them. " You ought to be satisfied."

He patiently obeyed.

The same evening an important event occurred at the villa. Mr. Fairfax presented himself with Lilli upon his arm, before her father and mother, and implored their blessing. " Are you surprised at my betrothal?" Lilli whispered in Katrine's ear as they separated for the night.

CHAPTER XIII.

It cost Frau Barbara Amberger a very considerable effort to resolve upon this journey. And yet to resolve was not, after all, the difficult part, for her ideas of maternal duty left her no choice in the matter, but, with her domestic habits, it was hard to leave her home. At first she thought of snatching Katrine away from Berlin, if possible, before the Professor could contrive to see her again ; but so hasty a departure from home was hardly possible ; the letter announcing her intention was dispatched, and then several more days were spent in preparations for the journey.

She discussed the subject with Moritz, whom she found in a very strange and cross humour about it. He sneered quite offensively at all her objections to the marriage, and spoke of the Professor as if no more desirable son-in-law could be imagined, and yet he went on to say that the thing was impossible, not to be thought of, and that he had prevented any renewal of the suit, without stating why he disapproved of the suitor. Naturally enough. He knew he should have to encounter from his mother objections to his own plans. The time was not ripe for their disclosure. But this was not all that made him irritable and sulky. His *tête-à-tête* with Schönrade had produced an effect that he could not away with. The truth had been told him for once, and that not by a man upon whom he could look down, but by one whom he was obliged to respect as his superior,—and, what was worse, who was in the right. The Professor was right. Disguise it as he might, he was playing a base part towards his only sister, for whom he had a genuine fraternal affection, and he was wronging himself, even while acting only from self-interest.

He had tried his best to shut his eyes as long as he could to all that was humiliating to himself in his connection with the Feinbergs; he could do so no longer, since it had been immediately manifest to an entire stranger. Ignaz Feinberg treated him like a child, used him, and tossed him aside; Otto Feinberg was a coarse fellow, who stooped to transactions in business that even his brother would scarcely undertake; and Sidonie did not think it in the least worth her while to consider his claims upon her when it suited her to ignore them; she endured him only so long as he made no assertion of his rights. He raged inwardly as he plainly admitted all this to himself. He had serious thoughts of calling "these insolent upstarts" to a reckoning, of demanding that Ignaz

Feinberg should balance certain accounts between them, and of taking Sidonie to task for her treatment of him; but any step in this direction was sure to turn out a disastrous one for him, and he persisted in the inaction for which he despised himself, until his life grew almost unendurable.

And to crown all, there came a letter from Philip, that was by no means welcome in the present state of affairs. Philip, who was wont to be the most economical of men, suddenly declared himself in want of considerable sums of money. He talked of purchases and orders to the amount of thousands, of removing and sending to Germany the entire wainscoting of a room in Florence, and more nonsense of the same kind. Philip doubtless supposed himself fully justified in his demands, but Moritz had disposed of all the available means of the firm, and could not raise the sum he asked for without drawing upon Feinberg. Of course his draft would be honoured, but it was wretched to place himself under such an obligation. He had never felt so utterly weak and dependent.

A few days after the Professor's departure, Madame Feinberg surprised him by the intelligence that she was going with her daughter to Berlin to pass some time there. In summer? —it seemed strange. A visit to some watering-place might be desirable, but to go voluntarily in warm weather to a large city,—he begged to know their reasons for the plan. " I like what is odd," Sidonie replied, with a shrug. " Any fool can find amusement in Berlin in autumn or winter,—I want to see how a large city looks when no one is at home. I like to play the country-girl come to town to see the sights, to visit museums and galleries, catalogue in hand, to stare at the strange beasts in the aquarium and zoological gardens, and to give the droschky-drivers something to do. Why should I not? Often as I have been to Berlin, I have seen very little of it."

Moritz thought any further discussion entirely superfluous.

His private opinion could not be publicly expressed ; but he would have given a deal to be able quietly to remark that Professor Schönrade was privately betrothed to his sister Katrine. To see the face with which this intelligence would be received would have indemnified him for all he had suffered. What a trump card it would have been! He thought of Katrine, and swallowed his vexation.

Madame Amberger could hardly believe her eyes when, upon driving to the railroad-depôt from her home, she found the Feinbergs, mother and daughter, already descended from their coupé and about to enter a railway-carriage. She had not neglected to pay them a farewell visit, but had received no intimation of this project of theirs.

"A sudden resolve, my dear," Madame Feinberg explained. "You know Sidonie hates long preparations."

"Quite a surprise for Moritz," said Frau Barbara, rather tartly.

"Oh, he knows we are going, and will not, I trust, allow us to leave without coming to bid us good-bye. There he is!—rather late, to be sure. He has paid Sidonie but scant attention for some time, it seems to me: it is well that he should miss her for awhile. Will you get in with us, my dear? we have taken the whole carriage, so as not to be annoyed by intruders; pray—— "

"I thank you, no," Frau Barbara replied, coldly. "My maid has arranged my place in the next carriage." And she bowed and passed on.

"We shall see each other in Berlin," Frau Feinberg called after her, and Sidonie settled herself in her place as Moritz came up.

He passed them with a bow, and went to see that his mother's arrangements were completed, returning as the signal for departure was given, to exchange a few indifferent words with his future mother-in-law, as she looked out of the carriage-

16

window. Sidonie was leaning back in a corner, selecting a
cigarette from a package of them which she had taken from
her travelling-bag. She nodded carelessly as Moritz bade her
a rather formal adieu.

. " Do not forget to give my regards to Professor Schönrade,"
he could not help calling in at the window after the train was
in motion.

Thus it happened that Madame Amberger and Madame
Feinberg, with her daughter, paid their first visit at the Councillor's villa upon the same forenoon. Frau Wiesel received
them with all due courtesy, only lamenting that they could
not make their home while in Berlin at her house. To tell
the truth, the household had been rather agitated by a surprising event—Lilli's betrothal. Mr. Fairfax was forthwith
presented and congratulated, and Lilli was kissed again.
Naturally enough, the young couple were the chief objects
of interest, and Katrine could retire to the background, to
her great content.

She had never liked Sidonie. Not because of any influence exerted upon her by Frau Barbara, for that good lady
felt it inconsistent with her maternal duty to give utterance to
any criticism of her son's betrothed; but it had required only
a very short acquaintance with her future sister-in-law to
convince Katharina that the greatest caution was necessary
in her intercourse with her. She had no taste for Sidonie's
masculine airs and affectations; she was disgusted by her
coquetry, and she thought her deceitful, if not absolutely
false-hearted. It was an entirely superfluous precaution on
Frau Barbara's part to remove her daughter from the influence
of such an example; there was not the slightest sympathy
between the two girls. In the beginning of their acquaintance Sidonie had affected a passionate attachment for Katrine,
which had cooled almost instantaneously, and she was only
deterred from openly sneering at her by a degree of haughty

dignity in Katrine's bearing. Since then there had been just as much courtesy exchanged between the two as the fact that they were future sisters-in-law required, and no more.

Meeting now as they did, beneath a strange roof, the interchange of a few remarks was unavoidable.

" People are so tiresome when they are just betrothed," said Sidonie, taking a seat by Katharina's side. " You must be glad you are to have no more of them."

" I like to be alone," Katrine replied, " and therefore such happy young people never tire me. It is delightful to see Lilli so happy and her father and mother so satisfied."

Sidonie replied, " ' Ah, might they ever verdant prove!' I should think life in England would be very tiresome."

" That depends upon what one expects."

" What a philosopher you are! Have you learned all this wisdom in Berlin?"

" One need hardly come so far from home to learn so much;" and then, changing the subject, Katrine asked, by way of something to say, " Shall you make a long stay here?"

" Long enough to see if I too cannot learn something here," Sidonie replied. " It has seemed to me lately that I know very little of a great many things that are worth knowing. A few private lessons could do me no harm."

" What do you mean?"

" What do I mean? Why, just what I say. A very clever Professor dined with us lately,—why, you must know him: he visits here,—Professor Schönrade."

Katharina felt a sudden sinking of the heart; she remembered the evening sail upon the mill-pond, of which Xaver had told her. She flushed, and then grew pale. She could not have told why she so detested to hear Sidonie speak of him, but she would have liked to get up and run away, to put an end to the conversation.

Sidonie observed her change of colour. " Oh," she said,

"you seem to take an interest in him; and no wonder: he is the most interesting man I have ever met, and I do not deny that it is partly on his account that I wish to spend some weeks here. He condescends to initiate certain young ladies into the mysteries of science, and he shall find me an apt pupil, if he will consent to be my teacher."

"So far as I know, he is occupied at present in writing a book; at least, I think he made that an excuse the other day for not coming here so often as heretofore. You must conside, Sidonie, that any interruption of his work at present can hardly be welcome to him."

Sidonie tapped her lightly on the shoulder with the ivory head of her parasol. "How careful you are for the poor Professor! But I understand all this. Nothing is more welcome to these learned scholars than to be gently obliged to shut up their books and beguile their time in ladies' society. Oh, the Professor is a man of the world, however he may consider it his duty to knit his brows upon his students in the lecture-room; no one knows him who has not seen him at a dinner-party. I will lure him from his retirement; he must dine with us, drive with us, show us the sights of Berlin; and he shall have time and opportunity to expatiate upon the properties of the surface of the globe upon which we saunter, or upon the nature of the fixed stars that shine above us on these lovely summer nights. It will be delightful!"

Sidonie would probably have said all this even if she had known of the pain she was causing; but Katrine could not at present accuse her of malicious intent. What could have occurred to justify her in speaking thus of Schönrade, in forming such expectations for the future? For a moment she was startled into wondering if Xaver had been dazzled and misled at first—— What folly! It was impossible. She knew Sidonie, and had often been a witness of her arts to attract every stranger. Xaver was quite innocent; and yet

——this much was certain: Sidonie had come to Berlin
on his account, and would do all that she could to entangle
him in her net, whether she thought it worth while to keep
him there or not. The Professor would be frequently thrown
into her society, while Katrine herself must be far from him,
travelling about with her mother, who hoped thus to estrange
him from her. Had she anything to fear from Sidonie? She
could not tell. There were those who praised her beauty,
admired her eccentric style of dress, thought her manners attractive and her wit brilliant. And Xaver——? How had
he ever loved herself, if he could find any attraction in her
opposite? No, she had nothing to fear from Sidonie, although
she could not feel quite easy in thinking of her.

Madame Feinberg arose to take her leave. Sidonie was
quite ready to accompany her: Katrine was not entertaining;
her thoughts were evidently elsewhere. Frau Wiesel begged
them to repeat their visit often, and, before they had reached
the garden-gate, made various critical remarks with regard to
them, which were not at all interrupted by the gracious nod
she gave them as they drove off. "Frau Feinberg would be
a dear creature," she said, "if she only had a little more culture. She is a good soul, but very weak where her daughter is
concerned. I suppose Sidonie rules the whole household at
home,—everything she says is regarded as oracular. What a
pity it is to spoil a child so! She is not in the least like a
young girl, but really conducts herself like a woman of the
world. I should be very sorry to see Lilli dressed so, either,—
all to produce a startling effect. It is well they are so rich, or
her husband would have a hard time of it."

Frau Barbara Amberger could have subscribed to every word
of this, but she replied only by a half-smothered sigh and a
troubled face. The Councillor's wife understood these mute
signs, and began to trumpet forth Katharina's praises. "The
dear, good, modest, unaffected, sweet-tempered child had stolen

her heart, and as for Lilli, she doted on her. She could not bear the idea of losing her so soon."

Frau Barbara might perhaps have enjoyed this eulogium more thoroughly if she had not been aware of the fact, of which Frau Wiesel was fortunately profoundly ignorant, that the "dear, good, modest child" was at present entangled in a love-affair, and deserved a severe reproof, which her mother was prepared to administer as soon as she could see her alone. She wished to take her back with her to the hotel and leave Berlin that very afternoon, but this the Councillor's wife would not hear of. So sudden a departure would really offend her. Lilli's betrothal was to be celebrated the next day, or the day following that, by as large an assemblage of friends as could be gathered together at so unpropitious a season, and the entire evening would be spoiled for the dear child if Katrine, her best friend, her confidante in the whole affair, were absent. Lilli added her entreaties, and Mr. Fairfax proffered the same request for Fräulein Katharina's presence on the happy occasion. Frau Amberger was prevailed upon to consent in spite of herself, and to permit Katrine to continue in her present abode until their departure. Of course her mother must consider the villa as her real home in Berlin, and only the nights were to be passed at the hotel. "I hope to persuade my husband," Frau Wiesel concluded, "to take me to Wiesbaden after the betrothal celebration, for the sake of my health, which has been very poor lately. Why not go with us, my dear Frau Amberger, and take a course of the waters to prepare yourself for your journey—to Italy, I suppose? We have hired an entire house there, and I shall be delighted to let you have some rooms in it." Frau Barbara thanked her kindly, but could not so prolong her absence from home.

Katrine was by no means pleased with the prospect of this trip to Wiesbaden. What was to become of her fine plan for carrying on a correspondence with Xaver through Lilli?

Perhaps he would not even be reminded of her by a letter, while Sidonie would see and speak with him every day. She was sad and down-hearted, and would gladly have avoided all gayety.

The day after his interview with Katrine, Professor Schönrade paid his mother another visit, and found her most cheerfully disposed. She had been very favourably impressed by Katrine's grace and loveliness, and her first words after her kiss of welcome were, " I cannot believe, Xaver, that Madame Amberger will withhold her consent long, after she sees how truly Katrine's heart is your own."

" In fact, she is only acting like a prudent mother," he replied. " She does not know me as you know me, and may well doubt whether Katrine has sufficiently weighed all that in her estimation are very important considerations. If that were all, we could look forward with confidence to the future ; time would smooth away all difficulties. Unfortunately, however, there are deep-rooted prejudices to be overcome, which we, indeed, from our point of view, may regard lightly, but which, nevertheless, are insurmountable obstacles in my path. The Ambergers are an old patrician family, and Frau Barbara is proud of her name."

" I think Bellarota is hardly inferior to it in antiquity," Camilla observed, rearing her head haughtily.

" It may be," he replied, with a shrug; " but you know we have no means of proving that to the world."

" It is the truth !" she exclaimed. " My father was incapable of falsehood, and he frequently referred to the antiquity and nobility of his name. You show but scant respect for your grandfather if you do not believe his word."

" My belief in the matter is of very little consequence," he replied, calmly. " And you must certainly admit also that it is hardly an agreeable thing for me to be obliged to refer to my mother's ancestors for my name———"

Her face grew dark. " You have every right to bear your father's name," she said, " and a name that would abundantly satisfy Frau Barbara Amberger. But I cannot bear it,—I cannot."

He did not answer immediately, but left her time to become familiarized with the thought that there must no longer be any secret between them. Then, taking her hand in his, and stroking it as if to beg her to be calm, he said, " Mother dear, I have always respected your desire that I should ask you nothing concerning your marriage and my birth. Chance has lately revealed to me all that I ought to know. I only need that you should simply admit certain facts——"

" Chance—chance?" she interrupted him, hurriedly. Her brow was moist from nervous agitation.

He told her of his walk to the Höneburg, and of all that he had learned there,—confining himself to a bare statement of the facts as he had gathered them. " Was it all so, mother?" he asked.

"It was all as you have said," she replied, in a firm tone. " And the judgment you passed upon it, Xaver?"

" Do not ask me for it, mother."

" But I do ask you. Was I right, or did I rob you when I deprived you of a name which brought me only pain and remorse? No, my son, I obeyed the dictates of a mother's love. You were all that was left to me, and I could not be to you what I ought and wished to be if you daily and hourly reminded me of the traitor who——"

" Mother," he gravely interrupted her, " remember you are speaking of my father!"

" Oh, I loved him!" she exclaimed, and her eyes flashed fire. "I loved him as only a woman can love, and he betrayed me. I have a right to sit in judgment upon him, and to condemn him."

" I know how you have suffered," he said, soothingly, " and

I will do no violence to your feelings, mother. I will not try to excuse my father to you, for he offended you bitterly, wounded you to the very heart; but do not forget——"

"From those letters, which should have been destroyed," she interrupted him, passionately, "you learned much of my misery; but they could not tell you all. You know that we were happy, and that he threw away that happiness when it excluded him from the hope of securing to his name the possession of a newly-inherited estate; but you do not know all that I had gone through to secure this happiness, which I fondly dreamed was for eternity,—how I had destroyed, annihilated the hopes of others to pave the way—— No, no! enough of that! I will not make you your mother's accuser, my son, and I have atoned for the wrong I inflicted. Oh, God! I have atoned for it!"

Xaver placed himself beside her, and put his arm around her. "Is it so hard to forgive, then?" he asked, gently. "Must what has once been dear be so hated? Must *I* hate what has never even been dear to me,—what until a few days ago did not even interest me? Do not require what is unnatural of me, mother dear; remember that I cannot share your emotions if I should encounter the man who is my father, whose errors it is not my part to condemn, and upon whom you revenged yourself by depriving him of the child whom, if his letters did not lie, he loved tenderly. Witness the deed that gave me all the property over which he then possessed any right of disposal."

The proud woman's eyes were bent upon him with an expression of bitter pain. "You are not thinking, Xaver," she said, in a voice that she controlled with difficulty, "of seeking out that man,—your father?"

He felt his hand tremble and his heart throb as in the presence of some imminent peril. He knew that it would afford intense delight to the mother whom he fondly loved if he could only throw himself into her arms and declare, " No, no ! I will never know him, never utter his name again." But he could not allow himself to be so enthralled to her hate as to be untrue to himself in pity for her suffering, and play the part her passion would have assigned him. He must not admit feeling to any voice in this matter,—he must see only its practical side. " The reasons are obvious why I must certainly think of presenting myself to Count Gleichenau," he said, with composure, " since I need his confirmation of my right to the arms of the Von Höneburgs, and to all that remains of their estates. What use I may make of them I cannot say, but you can certainly see clearly, mother, that in my present position they are of great value to me. Frau Barbara Amberger will not reject the Freiherr von Höneburg as a suitor for her daughter's hand."

Camilla reclined wearily upon the couch. " You will sacrifice your mother's honour," she said, gloomily. It did not sound like a reproach, but like a wail,—she saw that further opposition on her part would be fruitless.

The Professor arose, and paced to and fro in the room, pausing from time to time, and then continuing his walk. He suffered much in thus giving his mother pain ; he had taken counsel a thousand times with himself, before coming to her, to try to avoid it, but it had always seemed to him that this frank, open course was the only one to pursue. Now she knew what he intended, and could assume what attitude seemed best to her with this knowledge. He had not hoped that she would approve his intention, but, even although she did all that in her lay to deter him from fulfilling it, he could do more calmly and easily what he felt to be right than if from a desire to spare her feelings he had acted in an underhand manner and kept her in the dark as to his line of conduct. He was relieved to know this, and, approaching her again, he leaned over her, and said, tenderly, " We know each other, mother dear! You have confidence enough in me to be sure that I could never have the heart to take any action or to concede anything that could offend your keen sense of honour. I can promise more. I will do nothing that can prevent you from pursuing your own path as proudly as ever. I will speak and act for myself alone, and my own pride, which is of a different nature, will never allow me to resign my position as a man who owes all that he is to you."

She sighed, and turned upon him a face that, for the first time, looked to him as old as her years would make it. He had always rejoiced that she never seemed to grow old, and this change terrified him. She held out her hand, and said, wearily, "It is not easy to see all our hopes fade, when each hope was born of agony. My pride is broken. Before my son I am a weak woman, who hardly dares beseech indulgence. Follow the dictates of your heart,—I—forgive you."

He kissed again and again the hand that lay so languid and cold in his own. Camilla arose,—she evidently wished to be alone to go through the struggle with herself, that could no longer be postponed. He understood her mutely-expressed desire, and took his leave.

CHAPTER XIV.

In his own home he found upon his writing-table two delicate little notes. The first was an invitation from Councillor and Madame Wiesel to their daughter's betrothal festivity. Would Katrine be there? It would be easier to speak with her unobserved in a large assemblage than in the home-circle. This invitation pleased him.

The address of the other, a pink billet-doux, was in an unknown handwriting,—apparently a woman's. Still occupied with thoughts of Katrine, he opened it without curiosity. Instead of a sheet of paper it contained merely a visiting-card. Madame Feinberg had the honour to inform him in pencil, beneath her engraved name, that she, with her daughter, was at present in Berlin, and looked forward to his society in seeing all that was worth visiting there. On the other side of the card another hand had inscribed, " We are longing to see Professor Schönrade. Pray come soon, and have a great deal of time for us. S."

He looked at the card with a smile,—a smile not of self-satisfaction, but of satirical humour. He felt sure that Sidonie was here on his account, but his vanity was not at all gratified : he was annoyed, feeling that he was likely to be hampered by the attentions that would be expected of him. He was not at all what is called a " society man," but was apt rather to neglect social duties, to leave visits unpaid, and letters and notes unanswered. He longed now to plead his multifarious occupations to excuse him from playing cicerone to the ladies. But he had accepted hospitality from them, he was sure to meet them at Fräulein Lilli's betrothal festivity, and it was better to do all that the conventional rules of courtesy demanded. He would surely be able to confine his duties within strictly formal bounds.

He did not go the same day. The next was the one preceding that of the festivity at the villa, and he presented himself at the hotel just after the dinner-hour,—the time of day which was most at his own disposal. The ladies had just retired to their sitting-room from the table-d'hôte, and had ordered coffee. The Professor made his appearance, preceded by the waiter carrying a tray.

" Oh, here you are at last, my dear Herr Professor !" Madame Feinberg called to him from the sofa where she was lounging. "Waiter, another cup for Professor Schönrade. You will take coffee with us? We expected you at dinner, and had the seat next us reserved for you. But I am afraid you are so spoiled in this huge city that our society presents small attractions."

Sidonie sat at the window, looking out into the street. On a chair beside her, and upon the floor, were a multitude of boxes filled with laces, feathers, and flowers, which had apparently just been purchased. She turned her head after the waiter had left the room, and with a supercilious air said, half in jest, half scornfully, "For Heaven's sake don't believe a word mamma says! We no more thought of you than did the chair beside us, which remained unoccupied because no one ventured to approach us, except a Russian Jew, whom we frightened away by saying the seat was reserved."

"Your cruel explanation, Fräulein Feinberg," he replied, "was entirely unnecessary to convince me that I was not missed. I see evidences here of the interesting nature of your occupation before dinner."

She pushed the boxes off the chair, and thrust them all into a heap on the floor with her foot. "Oh, do not look at this nonsense!" she said, with a laugh. "Is it not hard that we girls are expected to deck ourselves out like dolls? and for what? To please the big children who parade in gay uniforms or fashionable black dress-coats. Sit here, Herr Professor; you will be more comfortable than in that creaking arm-chair. Well, shall we see you to-morrow among the big children?"

"If my dress-coat may be admitted into the category you allude to, after the good service it has done me," he replied, as he kissed the hand held out to him in welcome. "It has already had the honour of appearing before the ladies."

"You must be very fond of it, to take it with you even upon a business trip," Sidonie said, laughing; and her mother made several luminous remarks as to the ungraceful cut of the gentlemen's coats of the present day, animadverting upon the taste of their inventor.

Sidonie interrupted her by calling the Professor to account for not paying his respects to them earlier.

"I am so very much occupied, Fräulein Feinberg——" he began.

"Oh, I can't listen to that!" she said, breaking in upon his explanation. "As long as we are here, you must not think of your work. Throw away your pen, and let your ink dry up. Listen to Goethe : ' The lowest of the human brood will teach you you are a man amongst your kind.'"

The Professor frowned. "Mephistopheles says that, Fräulein Feinberg,—the cousin of the serpent. But, after all, the lowest society is not as dangerous as the best; and the safest for a man of science is his books."

This the ladies would in no wise grant. They declared that they would be generous enough to give him all his forenoons for himself, but that he must dine with them every day, and devote to them the afternoons and evenings. He fought desperately to retain his freedom; but their persistence so far conquered him that he was obliged to promise to dine with them that very afternoon, then to go to a theatre where a new farce was performing, and to finish the evening by a supper at a favourite restaurant " unter den Linden."

Half an hour later all three were seated in a barouche, driving through the Brandenburger Thor. They went to Charlottenburg, and sauntered about the garden there for some time, and then drove directly across the park. "Return through Thiergarten Strasse!" Sidonie called out to the driver.

Of course they were obliged to pass by the Wiesels' villa. Sidonie hoped they should be seen by Frau Wiesel or one of the young ladies, and her mother loudly expressed her desire to this effect. The Professor devoutly wished that the vehicle might lose a wheel, but he said nothing. He could not endure the thought of being seen by Katrine in his present company, and hardly liked to look towards the villa as they approached it.

And yet it was no other than Katrine upon whom the ladies lavished their most gracious nods and smiles. Schönrade took off his hat with as piteous an expression as his features could command. Was she expecting him in spite of the next day's festivity? What would she think of his spending his time in driving out with these strangers? It was excessively annoying.

"Katharina is a dear girl," Madame Feinberg remarked, as they passed the pavilion ; "I think her the most agreeable of the family."

"Yes," said Sidonie, carelessly, "very pleasant,—a trifle commonplace."

"A little affected, 'tis true," her mother added; "don't you think so, Herr Professor?"

This was almost too much. He raged inwardly. "I am a great lover of simplicity, madame, and therefore Fräulein Amberger seems to me a very charming young person."

"She is! she is!" both ladies said, in a breath.

"People are not all alike," Sidonie added.

The farce and the supper fortunately came to an end,— the Professor insisting that both should be at his own expense, in hopes that the ladies might be unwilling to renew their obligations to him.

Madame Feinberg declared that now he could not refuse to dine with them at their hotel the next day. On the contrary, he proposed to conduct them to a really remarkable restaurant, where he hoped they would be his guests.

"And if we consent this time also," Sidonie said, triumphantly, "you cannot possibly refuse to come with us afterwards. We will accept, mamma."

" But, my child——"

" Good heavens ! we will take our revenge afterwards. So take care, Herr Professor !"

Thus it was settled. As he accompanied the ladies to their hotel, Schönrade wondered where he should find the "remarkable restaurant" to which he was to conduct them.

It was discovered, however, the next day, "unter den Linden," and every preparation was made for a Lucullan banquet.

As they were entering the place, they accidentally encountered an old school-fellow of the Professor's, with whom he had never been intimate, but whom he was in the habit of seeing from time to time. Ernst von Fuchs had been in the army, but his debts had obliged him to leave it, and for some time he had been living principally upon his title of captain and his social accomplishments. Although he had run through his property, and had no visible source of revenue, he lived like a lord, dressed like an exquisite, was intimate at the best houses in Berlin, kept a riding-horse, and gave out that he was studying for the post of engineer in a large manufacturing interest. He certainly was a man of intelligence, and had been a constant hearer in the Professor's lecture-room during the previous winter. Schönrade could not avoid presenting him to the ladies.

As he was conducting them to the private table provided for them, a fiendish idea occurred to him. Why not invite this entertaining " man about town" to join them, and so provide a door of escape for himself ? Ernst von Fuchs was the very man to captivate them by his manners and conversation. On the instant he asked the ladies whether they would permit him to add his friend to their little company,—a proposition that met with a ready assent.

He then returned to his old school-fellow, and proffered his invitation in a low tone. " Who are they ?" asked Herr von Fuchs. " Oh, you may be perfectly easy," said Schönrade ;

"the elder is the wife, and the younger the daughter, of a millionaire."

"The deuce they are! and in Berlin only to amuse themselves? My dear fellow, I accept your invitation with the greatest pleasure." A fourth cover was laid, and the lobster-soup was discussed amid a buzz of lively conversation.

It was a perfect success. Herr von Fuchs rattled away; his small-talk was admirable, and now and then quite witty, and he soon found such favour with Sidonie, always attracted by novelty, that the Professor took but a second place in her attention. Before dinner was over, the Captain knew that she was an enthusiastic horsewoman. He proposed riding to Ruhwald the next day. " We can ride beside your carriage, madame," he said to the mother, who could make no objection to this plan.

" Provided the Herr Professor will drive with me," she said.

" Oh, he must ride with us," Sidonie declared; " we will run a race."

" I have no chance with the Captain," he replied, evasively.

" You know how little time I have," Schönrade whispered in his friend's ear, after they had risen from table. " I pray you to take the ladies in charge; they are delightful, as you see."

" Of course, of course, my dear fellow," the Captain replied, with a chuckle. " I will call upon them at their hotel to-morrow. Heavens! what a sage you are,—never away from your books! Well, so much the better for me; you might be in the way. Farewell; I will attend them, and it is your own fault if I supplant you."

The Professor shook hands with him, and helped the ladies into their carriage.

But the evening at Councillor Wiesel's showed him that he was by no means yet extricated from his difficulties.

It was a wretched evening. First he had to undergo a meeting with Frau Amberger, whose distant bow revealed no change in her sentiments as yet, and then with Katrine, to whom he so longed to say one confidential word, but who could not possibly escape her mother's Argus eyes. She looked so pale and sad that it grieved him to the very soul. And when Madame Feinberg and her daughter arrived, and had been duly received, Sidonie entirely ignored every one else, and seemed determined to converse with him, and him only.

She had selected another *rôle* for this evening, and tried its effect upon him. An assemblage like the present always made her melancholy. It was so sad a spectacle,—all these people, gayly dressed, met together for the sake of enjoyment, and really not knowing where to find it. They stood until they were tired, staring about to find out that there was nothing to be seen but what they had seen hundreds of times already; they changed their places to say the same phrases over and over again; they could not really converse, for fear of being interrupted; they ate and drank in the most uncomfortable attitudes, or went hungry; they were sleepy from fatigue, and had to wear happy faces; all would say, Thank God! when the time came to tell their hostess what a delightful evening they had passed, and to depart; yet, with all this dreary experience, they would accept the next invitation. And six or eight of these people, well selected, might have such a delightful evening together, without all this expense and show.

Schönrade only half listened to what she was saying. "We must do as others do," he said.

"Not at all!" she exclaimed, so loudly that it recalled him to himself. She put her hand upon his arm, and pointed to two vacant chairs. "Let us at least," she said, "take the liberty of isolating ourselves in the midst of this crowd." He could do no less than take one of the chairs, while she seated herself in the other. "If ever I have a house of my own," she continued, "I shall break the fetters of this conventional society and order my life with a view to higher aims." And she painted this life so vividly that he could not but compliment her upon the picture.

" If only true friends can be found to uphold your efforts," he remarked.

" Yes, yes !" she exclaimed, " but those who can be true friends can find true friends. Have you ever felt the want of such ?"

He evaded the question, and asked what she thought of Herr von Fuchs. She did not wish to form too hasty a judgment, but he seemed quite endurable. And then she made various inquiries concerning him, to which Schönrade gave prudent replies. Sidonie did not let the conversation flag; she seemed determined to retain him by her side, while from time to time he could see Katrine's grave face in the distance.

Frau Amberger in the mean while was obliged to listen to eulogiums upon the Professor. Frau Feinberg kept near her, and spent the time in glorifying him, and telling of his attentions to her daughter. Really, " dear Moritz" had some cause for jealousy this time. Apparently she wished to prepare the way for events that were not impossible. Frau Wiesel, as soon as his name was mentioned, joined her voice in his praise to what Madame Feinberg said, and prophesied a brilliant future for him. Privy-councillor Bachstelze, a member of the government and a friend of her husband's, who approached to utter his congratulations, spilling his wine on the lady's silken train as he did so, declared that Schönrade was one of the celebrities of the city, and an ornament to the University. Frau Barbara listened in silence, but by no means in indifference, to what was said.

She entertained her own private opinion when Katrine came to her a little later in the evening, complained of headache, and begged to be allowed to retire to her own room. Sidonie and the Professor had arisen, and were walking in the garden.

"I am afraid your absence will be observed," Frau Barbara remonstrated.

"I have told Lilli," the poor child replied, "and she will make my excuses, if necessary."

Her mother as she looked at her could not doubt that she really felt ill, and let her go, in hope that half an hour's rest would enable her to return to the drawing-room.

"If Sidonie would only keep the Professor forever," Frau Barbara mentally ejaculated, "I should have both my son and my daughter again."

Xaver soon missed Katrine, and his restless anxiety was so great that he scarcely returned intelligible replies to what Sidonie was saying. "You are very preoccupied, my dear Professor," she said. "Where are your thoughts at present? Evidently not with me."

"Oh, I am not well,—I am quite unwell," he said, by way of excuse. "I ought not to have come here."

She proposed that they should sit down in an arbour; but just then two or three officers of her acquaintance came up to speak to her, and Schönrade took the opportunity to excuse himself and retire from her side, leaving her to the care of her military friends.

He found Lilli among her guests upon her lover's arm. "One second, my dear Fräulein Wiesel," he begged, in a low tone.

She said a few whispered words to Mr. Fairfax, who nodded and resigned her to the Professor.

"I pity you from my heart," she said.

"You know all, Fräulein Lilli," he rejoined, going at once to the point. "Where is Katrine?"

"In her room, I believe."

"Not ill? She looked so pale."

"Nothing of any consequence is the matter,—at least, as far as I know ; but in her place I should be pale too to see you spend the entire evening with a lady——"

"But, my dear Fräulein Lilli, you must have seen," he interrupted her, "that this lady herself—— Oh, I am vexed beyond endurance! And to-morrow Katrine will be gone, with Heaven knows what thoughts of my conduct. If I could only speak to her for two minutes!"

Lilli reflected. "Really, only two minutes? I am very sorry for you. I am half inclined to risk something in your behalf."

"Oh, my dear child——"

"Hush! hush! You don't deserve it of me, but nevertheless—— Come here." She led him through a concealed side-door to a winding iron staircase. "Go up," she said, "and knock at the second door on the left. I will keep guard here for you. Remember, only two minutes!" He hastened up.

Lilli heard him knock—twice in vain, and then the door was opened. She seemed to have waited a long time, when she again heard steps in the corridor. "Well?" she asked.

"Katrine is quite recovered," he replied, with a beaming face. "We have just decided that I am to take her to supper in spite of everything and everybody."

"Bravo! bravo!"

He took her hand and pressed it gratefully. "Oh, how I thank you! Pray go up and bring Katrine down. I will disappear through this door, to meet you by chance in the pavilion and take charge of Katrine in the face of all the world."

"But what will Frau Amberger say?"

"We will think of that to-morrow. To-day is our own."

"Go, go, then!" She closed the door behind him, and ran up-stairs to help her friend efface all traces of her tears. "Am I not a fool?" poor Katrine asked.

Frau Barbara could hardly believe her eyes when she saw her daughter calmly going to supper upon the Professor's arm. "I brought her down," Lilli explained, "and begged our dear Professor to take charge of her. He will soon make her well again."

1*

The old lady turned away with a frown. " We ought to have left Berlin yesterday," she said to herself.

Sidonie sat at the supper-table in anything but a pleasant humour. What was the Professor thinking of, to take " such an insignificant girl" to supper?

CHAPTER XV.

COUNCILLOR WIESEL had spoken of a certain Count Gleichenau who was staying in Berlin on account of the health of his son. Upon inquiring, the Professor learned that this was, in fact, the possessor of the large entailed estate bearing his name, and that therefore a journey thither might be avoided.

Count Gleichenau had hired a luxurious house in the Viktoriastrasse, which combined all the elegance and comfort of a winter residence with the requirements of a summer home. The gardens around it were carefully kept, and there was an immense retinue of servants, but the life led there was most retired. The Count received no visits, and never left the house except to take the drives with his son ordered by the physician, whose vehicle might be seen several times a day standing before the mansion, and, when the weather permitted, the father wheeled the invalid about the garden in a low chair constructed for the purpose.

The Professor had passed this house several times, less with the expectation than in the hope of meeting the Count, for he could not endure the idea of presenting himself as a son to a man whose face he had never seen since his infancy. His exterior at least must be no longer strange to him. One day, at noon, he passed just as the Count was driving off,—a tall, spare figure, dressed in gray, with a head which would have been very handsome but for a certain prominence of the nose and chin. His gray felt hat was pressed down over his eyes, his hair was cut short after the military fashion, and his yellowish-white moustache was drawn out into two long points. The pale lad beside him leaned back among the cushions of the carriage, and, despite the warmth of the day, the old man enveloped him carefully in a thin woollen wrap. As Schön-rade passed, he lifted his hat, an attention that evidently took the Count by surprise. He returned the greeting with the hurried air of one recalled to a duty he had neglected, and then apparently searched his memory for a recognition of the stranger, for as the carriage drove off he turned on the seat and looked back.

The next day the Professor went to the house and sent in his card. He was instantly shown into the library, where the Count arose to receive him, the card still in his hand. For an instant he appeared to remember having seen him before, but then slowly shook his head in utter ignorance of his guest's person.

Schönrade for a moment could find no words in which to open the conversation. His father stood before him, and the next few minutes would decide whether he had done well or ill in presenting to him his son. The Count looked worn and anxious; there were deep furrows in his forehead and cheeks, and the green hangings of the room increased his natural pallor. This man had passed through bitter trials, and their traces were graven deeply upon his countenance.

"You are looking at my card again, Count Gleichenau," the guest began, at last. "Does the name upon it—suggest——"

The Count put down the card and motioned the Professor to take a seat. "The name—I cannot remember—Professor Xaver Schönrade—I must have heard the name frequently, but—my memory is very poor—very poor. Xaver, to be sure —Xaver—but that has nothing to do with it. It is rather an

unusual name—and I had a son——— But that has nothing
to do with it." He put up a thin right hand, and reflectively
rubbed his forehead,—then dropped it by his side with a slight
inclination, as if to entreat an explanation of the visit.

The Professor thought any longer preparation entirely unnecessary. It needed but a single word to turn in the right
direction the Count's surmise, already busy with memories of
his son. "The name Schönrade is only a translation of the
Italian Bellarota," he said, in a tone which he vainly strove to
preserve free from emotion.

"Bellarota!" exclaimed the Count, sitting erect in his arm-
chair. "Bellarota," he repeated, more gently, sinking slowly
back again, while his eyes never strayed from his guest's countenance. "Why—do—you tell me that, sir?"

Schönrade bit his lip with a strong effort to conquer his
agitation. "To preface a disclosure," he said, with as much
composure as he could command, "that is thus tardy only
because I have but lately become aware of certain facts. Let
me premise, Count Gleichenau, that the practical importance
of this disclosure concerns yourself alone. I am entirely independent, and have created for myself in the world in which I
live a position of which I conceive I have some right to be
proud. I confess that this circumstance had weight with me
when I resolved to seek you out. It must render impossible
any suspicion that this step could be prompted by unworthy
motives. I desire nothing save the acknowledgment of my
rights; any use that I may make of this acknowledgment
will certainly meet with your approval. Will you allow me
to speak?"

"Go on, go on!" the Count exclaimed, his haggard cheek
flushed with crimson. "Your mother———"

"Is Camilla Bellarotta."

"Camilla——— !"

"The divorced wife of the Freiherr von Höneburg."

" My wife !"'

The Count leaned back in his chair, his face grew ghastly pale, and he pressed his hand upon his eyes. " Camilla—Camilla——" he murmured.

Xaver was touched. He arose and approached him. " Count Gleichenau," he said, gently, in a low tone, " what I say requires proof. If I can produce this, and if you are that Freiherr von Höneburg, I have the right to call myself your son. But do not be startled by the idea that you must play the father to a man whom you have not seen since his infancy, and who can be no more to you than any other stranger who may happen to present himself before you. I fully admit that nature, in such a case, does not assert her claim,—filial love is largely gratitude, and gratitude I owe you none. All that I, at my age, can hope for is that I have found a man whose friendship I shall be glad to win, and who may in time value me as a friend. In time, Count Gleichenau ! It must take time. Permit me to lay these papers upon your table, and to take my leave. I shall hold myself aloof until you see fit to send for me."

" Not yet ! oh, not so quickly !" the Count entreated, as he took his hand within his trembling grasp and drew him towards him. " Did I not seem yesterday, when I saw you first —when you bowed—you bowed to me, did you not ?—did I not seem to be for one instant in a dream of the past, that I could not explain ? I know now what called it up. Your mother's features,—as a little child you were like her." He stood up, and drew aside the curtain from before a picture that hung above his writing-table. " Look," he continued, " here is all that is left me of Camilla,—her picture. She could not take it from me, because at that sad time it was still in the artist's possession. How lovely she was,—how lovely !"

. Xaver could hardly master his emotion at finding his mother's memory thus preserved.

18

"She is still a beautiful woman," he said, "although——"

"Where is she?" the Count interrupted him, letting the curtain drop, and turning towards him. "Where is she? While she was upon the stage, the newspapers told me of her whereabouts; but for years now they have said nothing of her art or of her."

"She withdrew long ago from the stage," Xaver replied, "and has since been living in great retirement, here in Berlin, upon the income of her earnings."

"Here!" cried the Count. "And I never knew it! But how could I? I am a hermit. Take me to her! I must see her; I must learn from her own lips that she has forgiven."

The Professor avoided meeting his eye. "Count Gleichenau," he said, "my mother knows that I am come to you, but she does not approve my doing so, and she does not desire to have any part in the consequences of such a step. I cannot judge her——"

"She is still angry, then!" the Count interrupted, and the frown appeared again upon his brow. "She will never forgive. But I will not relinquish all hope, now that I have an intercessor in her son." He took Xaver's hand and gently forced him to sit down again, standing the while himself. "Stay, stay awhile," he said; "give me at least a superficial glance at your present life. I too trust we shall be friends."

"Will you not first, for my own satisfaction, look through those papers?"

The Count took them from the table and glanced over them hurriedly. "What do they signify? A baptismal certificate; a certificate of the confirmation of Xaver Bellarota; teachers' testimonials as to your diligence and acquirements; a diploma. I have no doubt that you are Professor Xaver Schönrade, who sent me in this card, '*alias* Xaver Bellarota,' as your diploma has it, and that you are Camilla's son and mine, as this baptismal certificate attests. What possible reason could a man in your position have for deceiving me? I know that Camilla refused to allow her son to bear my name, and, since I learn that you have only lately discovered what this name is, I know that she fulfilled her threat, to keep her child in ignorance of it. God forgive her for taking such a revenge!"

The Professor related all that he thought worth hearing of his life and pursuits, detailing every particular of his visit to the Höneburg.

The Count listened attentively, giving from time to time a nod of assent. "Yes, yes; it was all as you say," he said, when the story was concluded. "You have learned from those letters and papers all the particulars of that sad time, and from your manner in relating them I see that you do not entirely justify the offended wife. Oh, I could complete that corre-. spondence by producing Camilla's letters to me, but I will not try to excuse the wrong I did by adducing evidence of that passionate intemperance of thought and word that cooled the ardour of my affection for her. I grant that the sudden acces- sion of fortune which transformed me from a needy retired officer, burdened with debt, to a very wealthy man, from the possessor of an ancient name, and of nothing else, to a member of the landed aristocracy, dazzled and bewildered me, confusing for awhile my estimate of the real value of everything. Per- haps in time I should have recovered myself, had there been a gentle, patient hand to lead me back to the right path. As it was, nothing was more to be avoided, headstrong as I was, than a hasty misconception of my motives and a passionate op- position to plans that were but half formed at the time; and Camilla—— But I will not allude to her errors,—you see how difficult it is to look merely objectively at one's own past. Possibly I regard my conduct now from a point of view that would then have been impossible to me, and which I have gained only through the hard trials and bitter experiences of years. Let me simply acknowledge that I was wrong. But to you, my son, I must recall the fact that at least I left no means untried to soften the wrong I did. It surely was not my fault that Camilla sternly refused at my hands every means of support for herself and our child. I endowed her with a yearly sum which would have maintained her independently and suitably as the mother of the Freiherr von Höneburg. I sent her this quarterly, but my letters and enclosures were always returned unopened. The mediation of friends and of lawyers was alike fruitless. Once, when I heard from a source to be relied upon that she was in absolute need, I myself went to entreat her at least to accept of a loan; but she refused to see me, and preferred to take her father's name and wander about the world as a singer. Every intelligence of her son's welfare was denied me. I could do nothing save deposit with a banker the yearly sums I had appropriated to her and your support, and hope that in future years the property thus accumulated might be of some use to you or to your heirs. I was powerless opposed to her pride,—she humiliated me at every turn. And yet I must confess to the admiration with which her force inspired me. I could not redeem my fault,— I bore it always with me, a burden that increased with years, like the money that was deposited upon her account. And now I hear from her son that she is still implacable."

Xaver heard him without interruption,—he saw how great a relief it was to the man to pour out his grief in this way. Every word carried with it conviction of the kindly disposition of the speaker. "Why cannot my mother learn to know you as I see you now?" he said. "But her heart remains untouched by what moves mine. I have only one hope in the matter: she loves me tenderly ; her pain in knowing me, in spite of all obstacles interposed by herself, united with my father, will be overcome,—she surely will not be able to close her heart forever to the friend of a son so fondly loved. This is my hope."

The Count pressed his hand, and sat silent for awhile. The Professor arose and took his hat. " Permit me to retire," he said ; "you need rest, and I too—— Farewell. May I come again ?"

" May you ?" exclaimed the old man, arising and approaching him. " I trust you will not allow a day to pass without coming to this house. If you knew how sad—— But no more of this." Another idea seemed suddenly to occur to him ; he looked about as if in search of something. " Wait one moment," he then said ; " I must present my dear companion to you." He opened the door into an adjoining room, and called, " Kunibert !"

The pale lad whom the Professor had seen in the carriage appeared upon the threshold. It was plain to see from his languid air that he had outgrown his strength. " What is it, father dear ?" he asked, in a weak, husky voice, with a shy glance towards the stranger.

" My poor invalid boy !" the Count said, leading him up to Xaver. " You need fear no teasing questions from this gentleman, Kunibert ; he is a professor, but no physician. Who do you think he is ? Look at him well. I trust we shall see him daily."

The lad looked down, embarrassed. " I cannot tell, sir."

" Of course, of course ; how should you ? But if I should tell you that your brother Xaver has been found——"

The lad looked up quickly, and a flush of pleasure coloured his pale cheek. " My brother Xaver ? And this gentleman——"

" Is he," the Professor concluded the sentence, offering him his hand. " Do you think you can be friends with him ?"

" Easily," the boy replied, after a short pause, regarding the Professor with boyish frankness. " It will be a jolly thing to have a real brother of my own. But you are so much older than I—and——"

He was again covered with confusion. His father laid his hand caressingly upon his shoulder. " It is a great surprise for you, my boy ; we shall need time to discuss all this together quietly, and when you meet again I trust it will be like old acquaintances."

The Professor took his leave, the Count accompanying him with every mark of cordiality. His emotion seemed at last to master him ; he seized his son's hands, wrung them in his own, and turned away, greatly agitated. " To-morrow !" the Professor exclaimed, as he left the house.

The next forenoon the Count returned his son's visit. He found Herr Ernst von Fuchs with him, using all his eloquence to induce him to throw aside his work in the evening and accept an invitation from the ladies Feinberg to a *petit souper* that they had arranged. " Don't attempt any excuse, my dear fellow," he said ; " it will not be received. Fräulein Sidonie would be too much disappointed by a refusal, and would, besides, entertain but a poor opinion of me as a messenger. Heavens ! what a man you are ! Here are the ladies perfectly raving about you, you have only to close your hand upon the prize that is ready to drop into it, and you retire and take airs upon yourself like a young girl with a wooer of sixty."

" I have already given you to understand," Schönrade replied, " that I have no mind to appropriate this prize. The field is yours, Ernst."

" Oh, I understand," the other exclaimed : " you believe you can insure your conquest by seeming to prize it lightly."

" If my tactics are wrong, so much the better for you," said the Professor.

" This seems to be a very odd dispute," the Count remarked. " Each wishes to accredit the other with assured success."

Xaver laughed. " And all about a young lady who is already betrothed."

"Bah! betrothed!" exclaimed Herr von Fuchs. "I do not believe in that betrothal."

"You, of course, have a right to your opinion," rejoined the Professor; "I can only assure you that I know her lover, —a young man of unexceptionable family and large fortune."

"And is that what deters you from frequenting the girl's society, desirous as she is of charming you to her side?"

· Schönrade paused for a moment. "That does deter me," he then replied, decidedly.

"Oh, pattern of chivalrous honour!" exclaimed the gentleman. "Is it possible that you do not see that the ladies have come hither solely on your account? I found that out the first hour we were together."

The Professor made a deprecatory gesture. "A very fleeting interest, I assure you! One could hardly find any foundation there for setting aside the claims of her acknowledged lover."

"Which no one seems to value less than the lover himself."

"However that may be, my dear Fuchs, however that may be——"

The gentleman spoke in his ear. "May I hint to Fräulein Sidonie the reasons for your conscientious reserve?" he asked, with a sly glance. "Of course with all due discretion——"

"I empower you to be as indiscreet as you please," said Schönrade, aloud and evasively.

The ladies' ambassador was not yet content. "And you will come this evening, my dear fellow?" he insisted.

"Do not forget that you have promised me this evening," the Count remarked, coming to his assistance.

"You hear?" said the Professor, with a shrug.

But Herr von Fuchs was not so easily appeased. "We shall keep it up very late. Surely you can sacrifice an hour's sleep to a charming young girl——"

The Professor shook his head.

"Then you must excuse yourself to-morrow morning on the plea of sudden illness," the ambassador concluded. " I dare not carry back a decided ' no.' "   He thereupon took his departure.

" I hope you were not constrained in any way by my presence ?" the Count remarked.

" Rest assured on that point," Xaver replied. " I have weighty reasons for not leaving the lady in question in any doubt as to my sentiments."   And in a few words he explained matters to his father.

" I have seen this Herr Otto Feinberg," said the Count, reflectively.   " There was some project for a new line of railway afoot, and he came to me in its behalf, to ask for my name in the undertaking : there was something, too, about their wanting the land now occupied by the ruin of Höneburg. I did not like the man, and I made inquiries of one of my friends in the ministry about his brother's business status and the chances of his project.   He is thought a very wealthy man at present, but there is no confidence in the stability of his plans, and obstacles were therefore intentionally placed in his way.   There was another reason why I could do nothing for him, to which, of course, I did not allude.   The Höneburg does not belong to me."

The Professor sat silent, although his father seemed to expect some expression of surprise on his part.

" It belongs, and has done so for thirty years, to my son Xaver," the Count continued.

" To be frank, I found your deed of gift among the papers left at the Höneburg by my mother," said Schönrade, in some embarrassment.   " The gift was not accepted, and must, of course, be considered as recalled."

" By no means," the Count rejoined.   " I expressly made any such recall impossible.   Who knows whether that heap of sand and strip of waste land may not be worth something, now that——"

Schönrade laid his hand upon his arm. "Do not let us speak of that now," he entreated.

"You are right," the Count said, kindly. "Rather let me hear something of my learned son's occupations and interests. You must not take it amiss that I have never read your book, —every line interests me now, and I have already written to my bookseller——"

"Unnecessary extravagance," Xaver interrupted him, taking from his table a book wrapped in thick paper. "If you do not scorn a gift that costs me nothing——"

The Count thanked him cordially, and they were soon deep in scientific matters. They might have been old acquaintances, from the tone of the conversation.

CHAPTER XVI.

DURING the following days the father and son spent many hours together. The Count did all that he could to testify to Xaver his delight in his new-found son, and the Professor forgot more and more the reserve of manner which he had resolved to maintain. He must have been cold indeed if the old man's kindness and evident desire to do all that he could to win a place in his affection had not touched him to the heart.

There was no occasion to decide upon which side lay the blame of the mournful separation that had hitherto estranged father and son. They owed it to a fortunate chance that they were at last together, and every day strengthened the bond between them, by an intercourse that was a source of mutual

pleasure and profit. Kunibert too, happy in seeing his father
no longer a prey to constant depression of mind, and cheered
by his brother's society, grew less listless, and more disposed
to second by his own exertions the efforts of his physician,
while he began to manifest an interest in the world around
him, and an intelligence that surprised and pleased both
father and brother.

The Count soon had no reserve with his new-found son.
Xaver learned that his second marriage had been productive
of but little happiness. Kunibert's mother had been one of
a prominent family in the circle of which the young Count
of Gleichenau found himself a member. Within its charmed
bounds the social and political aspects of the present were
entirely ignored ; mediæval modes of thought were encouraged,
and everything tending to progress was discountenanced and
disapproved. It would have needed the moral force of a re-
former, and the assured calm of a philosopher, to endure such
an atmosphere or to attempt to dispel it. Young Gleichenau's
only thought was to enjoy a life of luxury, from which his
poverty had hitherto excluded him. No wonder that he had
dreaded to introduce Camilla to this new circle, especially
since she herself heaped proof on proof of her unsuitability
for such a sphere.

As soon as he saw how hopeless it was for him to swim
against the current, he determined to swim with it as far as
was possible. He presented himself as a suitor in one of the
most conservative of these ancient families. The lady upon
whom his choice fell had been educated to consider pride,
arrogance, and a haughty demeanor aristocratic virtues, and,
in addition, she was far from strong physically, and was very
irritable. Still, the marriage might have been a happier one
if the wife had been able to refrain from making claims upon
an affection of which her suitor had frankly admitted to her
he was no longer capable. She soon discovered that his heart

was sore from the loss of his divorced wife, and she tormented him with her jealous fancies. He came into repeated collision with his associates, whose narrow-minded views with regard to life and the world he was not made to share; and the loss of three or four children in infancy still further saddened and embittered his existence. What, after all, was the life worth for which he had sacrificed so much? When, however, after eight years of marriage, Kunibert was born, and father and mother in him found a common interest, their life became far more harmonious; and the boy had never suspected disunion between them, so that after his mother's death, which occurred when he was fourteen, he felt it no insult to her memory to learn from his father that he had been previously married, and to be shown a picture of the first wife, as a carefully-cherished relic. Kunibert's delicate health was the cause ‧ of constant absence from Gleichenau, and the Count had come to Berlin in hope of effecting a permanent cure.

With all his duties, the Professor found time to visit his mother and to pay his respects to the Councillor's wife. Of course he contrived to exchange a few confidential words with Lilli, who, two days after Katrine's departure, conveyed to him a letter from her and took charge of his reply. Katrine wrote resolutely but sadly. She had been duly reproached and catechised by her mother, but had borne herself bravely, refusing to make any concession of her sentiments. Therefore they were to travel longer than had been at first intended. Schönrade could tell her that he had found his father, and was ready to follow her to the ends of the earth, as soon as he felt himself master of the situation. This he was not as yet, and he begged her not to require him for the present to appear before Frau Barbara as the Freiherr von Höneburg. Everything with regard to this matter must remain a profound secret for awhile. "But we can have the satisfaction of knowing, my darling, that this anchor of hope"

—thus he concluded his letter—" can be made use of, in case of danger, at any moment."

His line of conduct towards his mother was difficult. At the first few interviews that he had with her after' their last important conversation, she seemed estranged from him, she received and dismissed him with unwonted formality, she ostensibly led the conversation to dwell upon commonplace matters, and refused to second any effort of his to make it more confidential.

He on his part, however, refused to be deterred from entering into all the particulars of his daily life, telling how he had found the Count, and how kindly he had received him; but he was not at his ease while he talked. It was a gain, he thought, that Camilla did not absolutely forbid these communications, but listened without contradicting his favorable judgment. And our Professor learned to be diplomatic. He knew that we forgive most readily when we find the wrong that we have suffered avenging itself. He knew she must find a certain satisfaction in the knowledge that the wrong-doer had not found peace in his wrong-doing, but had reaped a plentiful crop of thistles, and he painted the Count's sufferings, not as if appealing to her pity, but as if to appease her sense of justice. Sooner than he had hoped he accomplished his design, which was not merely to inform her of all that he had learned, but gradually to temper her resentment and predispose her to gentler judgments. Of course he did not forget to touch upon the fact that the Count still cherished her portrait; and when he found it produced a favorable impression, he dwelt upon it with more emphasis.

One evening when he went to bring her home from the theatre she surprised him by the intelligence that she had received a grand visit. At first he supposed that the Count had been unable longer to restrain his impatience, and he was the more startled to learn that Madame Feinberg and her daughter had done themselves the pleasure of waiting upon "the famous singer, Camilla Bellarota," the mother of "the well-known Professor Schönrade." "I really did not know I was a Berlin celebrity," Camilla said, gaily. "If Fräulein Sidonie has any brains, she must have inherited them from her father, for her mother, in spite of the fashion-plate that she makes of herself, is extremely tiresome. She admired greatly my flowers in the window, and declared they were all nature,—as if it were natural for any plant to grow in a flower-stand and be shone upon through a window by a Berlin sun." Her son laughed. "She begged for permission," she continued, "to come often to take me to drive. Well, you know my fancy for driving. But both the ladies complained bitterly of you. I was to tell you that you are a most discourteous man, and that you do not deserve that they should inquire after you, and a great deal besides. I promised to use my maternal authority to lead you back to the paths of duty; but I know better than any one else how little my maternal authority is worth of late." And she sighed.

The next morning he received a delicate little note; the address was in Sidonie's hand. She wrote, "Your friend has availed himself of your express permission to be indiscreet, and my resolve was taken instantly. Set your conscience at rest. *I am free.* S."

He was startled,—he hardly knew at first by what. Lately his head had been so full of other things that he really had some trouble in recalling the solution of this riddle. His friend——? Who was his friend? Oh, probably Ernst von Fuchs, although in his heart he had never accorded him that title. What was his conscience to be set at rest about? The last words, "I am free," were intelligible, and they were what startled him. He could not but understand why she told him this, and it was a most startling thought that Sidonie might have understood his reminder to her of the bonds that his conscientiousness respected as a desire that she should break them.

The affair was still more complicated when, towards noon, to his great surprise, Madame Feinberg presented herself.

Her ordinary placidity had given place to a feverish agitation. She looked pale and miserable. " What will you think of me, my dear Herr Professor," she began, refusing his offer of a seat on the sofa, and sitting down in a chair near the window, " for coming to you here? But I wanted to speak with you confidentially,—it could not be at the hotel, for Sidonie must never learn the step I resolved to take,—never. I should lose her confidence forever. It is about something that she—— How shall I tell you ?"

" Compose yourself, madame," Schönrade entreated ; " I trust nothing unfortunate—— Rely at least upon my desire to serve you."

She held out her hand and gave him a look that would have melted a stone. " You are our friend," she wailed, " yes, you are our friend. I knew to whom I had to come. You know all our family affairs, and can judge. Oh, if I had only refused to let Sidonie take this journey, now that I see what she meant by it ! But I am a weak mother, a very weak mother." And she smiled tenderly above the handkerchief with which she lightly touched first one eye and then the other, as if to dry an imaginary tear. " You know that Sidonie is betrothed, —betrothed to Moritz Amberger. You know Herr Moritz Amberger ; he is a very good, amiable man in his way,—of an excellent family,—the best match in the town, it is true ; but for Sidonie——" She shrugged her shoulders. " I was afraid she was too hasty when she said 'yes' to him, but her father was so determined ; you see, that is the difficulty. Feinberg is a man of business ; he looks at things from a different point of view from ours. He has no love for nature ; he is devising plans all the time, and when he has thought them out they must be carried out; but the female heart——"

He interrupted this torrent of, words. "Pray consider, madame, that I——"

"The female heart demands its rights," she continued, more glibly than before; "and Sidonie has a true and tender heart. Good heavens! that child will have—entirely between ourselves, Herr Professor—a million at least; she is a match for a prince; but she takes no pleasure in wealth,—pomp and show leave her as cold as ice,—as cold as ice, I do assure you!"

Here she paused, and appeared to expect some remark from her auditor.

"Fräulein Sidonie has sufficient intellect——" he began, in embarrassed assent.

"Intellect!" she interrupted him. "Oh, what an intellect she has! Poor Sidonie! her intellect is her misfortune,—her great misfortune. If she had no intellect her heart would be lighter. Woman needs a stay, a support, some one to revere; she must be all nature, all idealism. She cannot love her inferior, and Moritz—well, you know him. He is Sidonie's inferior,—she cannot love him."

"It is very unfortunate," he remarked, cautiously, "that Fräulein Sidonie at this late date——"

"Oh, most unfortunate!" she assented. "It was not until she saw the contrast between—— Oh, do not misunderstand me, my dear Herr Professor, if I say that you—you, entirely unconsciously, unintentionally—first opened her eyes to what she was doing."

"I, madame?"

"You, you! I do not mean to flatter you, but you are a man of intellect,—a man——"

"Madame——"

"A man of superior talent; and it chanced that an opportunity occurred of comparing you with Moritz. From that

hour Moritz lost all hold upon Sidonie. I do not say it was
your fault,—you cannot help being what you are. I only
wish to explain how it was that Sidonie came to leave home;
and now—— Can't you guess ?"

He had no need to guess : he knew what had occurred; his
silence was sufficient answer.

"Oh, yes; you guess," the lady continued, encouraged.
"Sidonie has broken with Herr Amberger. She is no longer
bound to that insignificant man, whom she never loved."

She looked at him as if she expected from him some exclamation of delight. This utterly confused him.

"I take an interest in all you are good enough to tell me,"
he rejoined, in a dejected tone; "but if, as it appears, you
fear disagreeable consequences will ensue upon your daughter's
unexpected dismissal of Herr Amberger, I really cannot see
how I—— It would be a great pity that Fräulein Sidonie
should be over-hasty."

"Over-hasty——?" Madame Feinberg repeated, in a long-
drawn tone that betokened the greatest surprise. She had
evidently expected an entirely different rejoinder. But she
collected herself immediately.

"Yes, over-hasty! If indeed she has been over-hasty,
my husband will be furious. He was resolved upon this connection,—it was so convenient for his business; he will call
her refusal caprice, and will accuse me of helping to destroy
his plans. It was this that brought me to you as a *friend.*"
She emphasized the last sentence. "I beg you to talk with
Sidonie; she has such implicit confidence in you. Tell her
what you think; tell her everything,—frankly, frankly, just
what your heart—— I don't mean that,—just what your
clear judgment dictates in the way of advice. And if the
poor child remains firm, — heavens! her mother could not
blame her for it. Then I pray you advise me how to write to
my husband and Moritz Amberger, and to represent the affair

to them so as to cause as little of a breach between them as
possible. We might, I think, make every possible concession
to Herr Amberger. Good heavens! the whole matter, viewed
in a certain aspect, is perfectly reasonable. My husband
wishes his only child to be well cared for. He would give
her his blessing upon her marriage with a man whom she
loved,—whom she *loved!* That is the chief consideration.
I can see no reason why our son-in-law must be a merchant.
Sidonie has intellect; she has education; she is at home in
cultivated society." She coughed behind her handkerchief.
" But why speak of all this? Do not, I pray you, think
hardly of an anxious mother who, in her agitation, may say
more than—— You are our friend! I entreat you to talk
with Sidonie."

She had arisen and seized his hand, which she pressed to
her heart, and then, waving her lace pocket-handkerchief,
slowly walked towards the door, and took her leave without
awaiting his reply. In her carriage her face lost the amiable
look it had worn as she bade her "friend" farewell, and grew
vexed and angry. She had not gained the end she had in
view, but she hoped she had not betrayed too much, if a retreat should prove necessary. Some kind of an explanation
must ensue.

The Professor was left in a most unenviable state of mind.
He could not believe that this was all a farce, in which Sidonie
was playing the principal part. Was her mother's distress
real, or affected? and, after all, what did she desire him to do?
He could not remember one intelligible sentence in all she had
said. She had, of course, wished to sound him,—whether
with or without Sidonie's knowledge he could not say. His
situation was unendurable.

" A stop must be put to all this!" he exclaimed to himself.
" I must be clearly understood, and that immediately. I owe
it to Katrine and to myself, and perhaps to Fräulein Sidonie.
19*

As yet she has not compromised herself. It is my duty to
tell her the truth."

His resolution once taken, he hastened to fulfil it. On
the steps of the hotel he encountered Herr von Fuchs, just
leaving it.

" Are you going up ?" the gentleman asked.

Schönrade replied that he was.

" Very melancholy mood to-day,—highly tragic ; have just
had a profound discussion upon the subject of death."

" I trust Fräulein Sidonie has no serious thoughts of
dying?"

" There's no knowing.   Meanwhile, she has decided that I
must take a box for her for this evening in the Friedrichs-
Wilhelmstadt theatre.   They are going to play ' La Belle
Hélène.'   Fräulein Sidonie finds burlesque the only endurable
thing at present."

" Has Madame Feinberg returned ?"

" Yes ; how did you know she had gone out ?"

" Another time, my dear Fuchs.   Go get your box."

He shook hands with him, entered the hotel, and sent up
his card.   He found Sidonie alone.

" You have come at last, then, faithless man !" she called out
to him as he entered the room, sitting erect as she spoke, and
throwing a book upon the table at her side.

" Of course, since I am to offer congratulations."

" Congratulations?" she asked, bending a searching look
upon him, as if to read the thoughts concealed beneath those
dark curls, the meaning of the smile that played about his
mouth.

" I am sure you meant I should congratulate you upon the
news you wrote."

" Hush !" she interrupted him, " my mother must not
know."   She pointed, as she spoke, to the door into the next
room, which was ajar.

" You are free," he continued, in a lower tone. " I confess, to be frank, that the intelligence did not greatly surprise
me; I did not think that tie would last long."

" You knew that my only safety was in breaking it ?"

" And yet——"

" Yet ?"

" One must not deceive one's self, Fräulein Sidonie. There
are natures that are forever longing for what is unattainable,
—their only enjoyment is in desiring what they have not.
For them the chain that is lightest will be the most easily
endured."

She cast down her eyes and bit her lip. " And such a
nature you think—I possess."

" I do not know you well enough to say,—I have no right
to judge. I can only say that my own organization is so entirely different that I must ask for your congratulations upon
my being bound in the strongest of fetters."

Sidonie looked up shyly, and played with the books upon
the table. " You speak in riddles," she said.

" But there is no need that you should take the trouble to
solve them," he continued, with as much easy assurance as he
could assume. " In exchange for your ' I am free,' Fräulein
Sidonie, I have quite as confidential but a very different communication to make : ' I am betrothed !' "

" Betrothed !" she exclaimed, and her features were con-
vulsed for a moment. " You—are—betrothed ?" she repeated,
slowly, from between her teeth.

" Privately,—to a charming girl whose name I cannot give
you quite yet. I need not tell you how perfectly happy——"

Sidonie, with an angry gesture, forbade him to proceed.
Her brow was contracted in a frown, and she strove in vain
to rise. The Professor's kind heart was touched to see her thus
agitated,—her self-control all gone,—and he could not continue
to play his part of unconscious ease. He went up to her and

laid his hand upon her arm. "Fräulein Sidonie," he said, gently, "surely no word or act of mine——"

At that moment Madame Feinberg appeared at the door of the adjoining room, her face aflame and her eyes flashing. "Sidonie!" she called, in a tone of command.

Sidonie threw off his hand and arose. Casting upon him a look of utter hatred, without speaking a single word, she left the room, and he heard the door bolted behind her.

Schönrade stood for one moment as if stunned; he had done no wrong, and yet he felt guilty to have inspired even the capricious affection of which alone Sidonie was capable.

He gravely left the hotel, to go to his father, whom he usually visited at this hour.

CHAPTER XVII.

KATRINE'S secret was not so well kept as Lilli had promised it should be. Of course Mr. Fairfax was informed of it in the deepest confidence; what girl could keep such a secret from her lover? The Englishman could not quite approve, as matters stood, and advised prudence, but nevertheless allowed himself to be made use of on occasion to deposit the precious letters in the post. He cordially liked the Professor, and was willing to do what he could to serve him; there was no treachery to be apprehended from him. But Lilli's head was too full of her own affairs to pay all the attention to her friend that she had promised. She did not write as regularly as at first, and if she was at her desk when the servant announced Mr. Fairfax she would leave it hastily, without closing her portfolio, where, perhaps, a half-finished letter of her own, or an enclosure to Katrine, directed in the Professor's round, scholarly hand, would be lying so as to meet the eye of any one who happened to be in the room. Not until hours afterwards would she bethink herself of what she had done.

Several times this had happened, and chance had befriended her,—no discoveries had been made; but upon one occasion her mother came to her room for the third volume of a novel that she was reading, just after Lilli had left her desk in this careless fashion. Naturally, her eyes fell upon the open portfolio, and, although she was no more curious than most mothers, it occurred to her that this would be a good opportunity to discover what the two girls could find to write such long letters about. She found Katrine's latest letter, arrived only two days before, a sealed envelope addressed to the Professor, and a sheet of paper, upon which Lilli had begun: " Dearest Katrine,—I expect the Professor this evening, and will give him yours, which has just arrived. He is sure to come whenever I have something for him. As he will certainly bring a letter for you, that I will send to-night, if possible ; I write now, because Mr. Fairfax will be here in a little while, and——" This was enough for the Councillor's wife.

This was the reason, then, why Schönrade had been so frequent a guest at the villa, and why he could so seldom spare an hour of late ; Katrine Amberger had been the magnet that now attracted only his letters. This had all been going on under her very eyes. They were even privately betrothed, and they had dared to make an accomplice of her own daughter. It must be confessed that she had reason to blush when she reflected that Frau Amberger might possibly suppose that she had "connived at such disgraceful goings on." Thus, at least, she explained her irritation to herself; but it was none the less true that mortified vanity had a great deal to do with it. It was too provoking that she should have been so deceived as to suppose she had any influence in bringing the Professor so frequently to the house, when all the while he had paid at-

K*

tention to her only that she might be kept in a good humour and further his plans. He had dared to make a tool of her. It was unpardonable!

She never distinctly admitted in thought that she had not dreamed of permitting herself in any way to compromise her husband by receiving an undue amount of attention, that she had only hoped to find some stimulant for her relaxed nerves, or that the Professor had never by word or look attempted to establish, as she would have liked, a more confidential intimacy with her. She did not touch upon this delicate subject at all in her conference with herself; it must be blotted from her memory as if it had never existed. But even as she withdrew the sting that she had planted in her flesh, she felt that the wound was painful. She might persuade herself that the pain proceeded from some other cause, and take comfort, if she could, in this new form of self-deception.

She was not at all doubtful as to what was to be done. She could speak to Lilli upon the subject at any time; but the Professor must be dismissed as soon as possible. She put Katrine's letter to him in her pocket, determined to take care that it reached its destination.

Lilli never thought of the letter in her portfolio until the Professor made his appearance in the afternoon at the garden gate. She remembered also hearing her mother ask for the novel, and that she had afterwards seen it in her hand. Begging her lover to receive the guest, she ran with a beating heart to her room. There lay her letter on the table, and the envelope containing Katrine's last to the Professor was gone. All search among her papers was fruitless. With tears in her eyes she returned to the garden.

Mr. Fairfax came to meet her to tell her that her mother had requested the guest to give her a few moments' private conversation in the pavilion. She could see them there through the open door, and Frau Wiesel was just handing him a letter, which was undoubtedly the missing one. " Oh, what have I done ?" the poor child said, turning away.

The lecture that was to have been read the Professor became considerably modified and abbreviated in his presence. The sharpest remarks were forgotten as he kissed Frau Wiesel's hand as usual and inquired after her health. True, she replied that she had felt quite unwell for several hours, and that he was to blame if she should have a return of her nervous attacks; but the words were not sufficiently severe to prevent him from bewailing his involuntary fault with exaggerated contrition, and offering his services as physician. She had no longer any confidence in his method, she rejoined, and then proceeded to dwell upon the proofs of confidence he had always received in her house, a confidence which, she regretted to say, had been shamefully abused. " You will need no further explanation," she said, " than this letter, which Lilli was to have given you, and which accident has placed in my hands."

She had told him all. But if she expected her words to produce an annihilating effect upon the Professor, there was certainly nothing of the kind to be observed in his countenance. On the contrary, it beamed with what looked almost like merriment as he took the letter from her hand, and, bowing, expressed his thanks. " I am delighted," he continued, " that chance has revealed to you what I certainly disapprove of keeping secret. You, madame, whom I have to thank for so many proofs of friendship, would have been the confidante of my choice; but I owed it to you to be silent. Katrine was your guest, and you can hardly wonder that I wished to save you from the alternative of either becoming our secret protectress or—forbidding me your house."

" But such an unfortunate occurrence !" she exclaimed, irritated still further by his composure. " Good heavens ! when I consider to what danger I exposed my own child !"

" What danger ?" he asked, in surprise that was not without

hauteur. " Certainly you would not have considered it unprincipled if I had come to you with the intelligence that I had won your daughter's heart, and a request that you would grant me her hand; else your opinion of me must have undergone a great change lately."

" Herr Professor," she replied, hastily, " I never thought of anything of the kind."

" Of course not," he rejoined, with a smile. " Fräulein Lilli's hand was already appropriated, and you could not possibly regard me in the light of a suitor. But suppose that Katrine had been your daughter——"

" Impossible, Herr Professor!" she interrupted him. " The question is not how I, kindly disposed as I am to you, might have regarded the affair, but how Frau Amberger has regarded it. This correspondence is carried on without her knowledge, through my daughter's connivance. My course is clear."

He opened his pocket-book, put in it Katrine's enclosure, and took from it a letter of the same size. " May I pray you, madame," he said, offering it to her, " to dispose of this contraband article as if chance had also thrown it in your way ?"

" Do you suppose, Herr Professor——"

" Certainly not that you will send this letter to Katrine, as Fräulein Lilli has done hitherto. Of course not. But I beg you to betray our love-affair. If you will send this letter to Frau Amberger, telling her at the same time of your indignation at discovering that such secret transactions have been carried on in your house, she can have not the smallest doubt of your innocence. Perhaps there may be a little room left on the margin of your letter to say what you may be kind enough to state in conclusion, that Xaver Schönrade is, after all, a well-meaning fellow, and that assuredly he cannot be blamed for losing his heart to such a girl as Katharina Amberger."

This was not the way to appease the Councillor's wife. "You seem to find the matter very amusing," she replied, tartly. "I regret not being able to share your enjoyment of the jest."

He put the letter in his pocket-book again, and arose. "In the course of a few weeks," he said, gravely, "I hope to send you the announcement of a betrothal which there will be no reason for keeping secret. Until then——"

"I suppose we can scarcely hope for the pleasure of a visit from you," she continued his sentence, "since there can no longer be any interchange of letters here with Fräulein Katharina Amberger."

He replied to her by a look that she could not meet. Then he seemed to regret it, and, offering her his hand, he said, in his former gay tone, "Let us part friends, madame."

She turned away sulkily. He shrugged his shoulders, bowed low, and took his leave. "Can she feel personally aggrieved?" he asked himself.

Nevertheless, he was glad that all secrecy was done away with. Of course he could not expect the irritated lady to be silent.

No, indeed! She was too indignant not to take advantage of the favourable opportunity that occurred the next morning. Madame Feinberg and Sidonie paid her a visit, the aim of which was soon apparent. "Have you heard the latest news, my dear Frau Wiesel?" the mother asked. "Professor Schönrade—ha! ha! ha!——"

"Is betrothed," the Councillor's wife hastily concluded, that she might be beforehand with her friend.

"And privately," Sidonie added. "A most juvenile affair!"

"You are so intimate with him, my dear," Madame Feinberg went on, "that of course you know to whom,—or perhaps even to you he has——"

"One can't prevent people of that sort from pretending to

intimacy," the Councillor's wife observed. " But, really, we ought to pity dear Frau Amberger——"

" Frau Amberger?"

" Yes, indeed. She must be greatly vexed to find her Katrine engage herself in such a low affair in a strange house, like some common governess, or—— But what is the matter, Fräulein Sidonie? You are very pale."

" Oh, nothing, nothing," Sidonie declared, leaning back in her arm-chair; " the day is so sultry, and I awoke this morning with a headache."

" Indeed she did," her mother added, little disposed to continue the subject of conversation after exchanging glances with her daughter. Katharina Amberger betrothed to the Professor! Here was a revelation indeed, that must be discussed in private conference.

Sidonie's indisposition shortened their visit. That same day a long letter to Herr Ignaz Feinberg was dispatched from their hotel.

Katrine wrote from Munich. It was probable, she said, that her mother, instead of going to Switzerland as she had intended, would cross the Brenner to Italy. Philip seemed to have taken up his abode in Florence,—no one could understand why from his letters. This was what had caused their journey to be extended. In a postscript she said, " Indeed I should not love you less, dearest Xaver, if you would let this letter be my last until we have no more need for secrecy. I suffer more than I can tell you in behaving with a want of candour to my mother, to whom, indeed, I have declared that I shall love you for ever and ever, but who has no idea that I tell you the same thing almost every day. Do we need to write to each other? Consider, and decide."

This was all as it should be. He knew that Lilli would tell her of what had occurred; but he must himself answer her request and set her mind at ease. One way was left in which he could do this. Before Frau Barbara and her daughter should arrive in Florence he must have a partisan there. The time had come to apprise Philip Amberger of his hopes, and there was no danger that a letter enclosed to him for Katrine would not reach its destination.

And it was time, too, to have no reserve with his father. He longed to tell him everything; and he took advantage of the first time they were alone together to do so.

The Count was much moved by this mark of his son's confidence. " At last you know that you have a father," he said, shaking him cordially by both hands. " Of course you have my blessing, which I trust Heaven will ratify. But there seem to be obstacles in the way which daunt even a sage Professor. Let us consult together, my boy, as to what is to be done."

" I have full faith that the Freiherr von Höneburg, with whom I should else have very little to do, will meet with a favourable reception from Frau Barbara Amberger," Xaver observed, " and the poverty of the Freiherr is of very little consequence. But Moritz will get into terrible trouble on my account." He then told his father all the circumstances of the case, and concluded, " Now, my entire possessions as Freiherr consist of the Höneburg, since you do not recall your gift, and, unfortunately, it is no longer strong enough to stand a siege from poor Moritz's creditors, if the Feinbergs determine to ruin him."

The Count rubbed his forehead. "Did I tell you," he said, after some reflection, " that there are contingencies in case of which the Höneburg may come to be very valuable ? Land is needed near the town for a railway-terminus, for store-houses and workshops, and what remains will be enhanced in value by the vicinity of these buildings. First of all, a wide and convenient road to and from the town must be arranged ; and this shall be Moritz Amberger's care. Let him privately buy

up all the houses on the right side of the narrow street leading
to the green gate; if he conducts the purchase with caution,
their price will not be high. The old wall can be destroyed
to fill up the ditch and make a road which will replace the
bridge, no longer needed as a defence against the Freiherrs
von Höneburg. This all seems perfectly feasible. Amberger
can widen the street, and build in addition a row of shops,
which will bring an excellent rent; for, as you may recollect,
the gables of the buildings there front on the street, and the
houses are very deep. As for the necessary capital, my banker
is yours, and my credit too, if you require it. This is not
enough. Nothing that I can see hinders us from undertaking
the new railway ourselves. Of course without the Feinbergs. There are moneyed men enough willing to take part
in such a project as soon as the way is made plain for them.
It is time that men of honour and family interested themselves in these projects for the common good. The railway is
an acknowledged necessity. Let us build it."

Xaver listened to his father with eager attention, and at
the same time with the greatest surprise. "I am astonished,"
he said, "to discover a financial genius in Count von Gleichenau. How in the world did this plan, which really looks
as if it could be carried out, occur to you?"

The Count smiled. "I will be honest," he replied, "and
confess that it is not the product of my own brain, and that
for this very reason I am disposed to think extremely well of it.
The projected railway, which it appears is important not only
in a mercantile but also in a political point of view, has a
staunch advocate in an influential member of the government,
who is an intimate friend of mine. His home is in that part
of the country through which the road is to pass; he has
various relatives and connections there, and is not only interested in the undertaking, but also understands and is possessed
of ways and means for promoting it. He is a capital financier,

—an indispensable qualification for success,—and thoroughly honest. When he was applied to lately by a committee from certain merchants contemplating this undertaking, he gave the matter his earnest attention, and refused to have anything to do with it, because he saw clearly that the projectors were working solely for their own advantage. He came to me afterwards and tried to induce me to take the matter in hand with several other moneyed men, giving me the outlines of his plan, which certainly is excellent. At that time, depressed as I was, I took no interest in it, and declined all his offers. Now I am another man. Say the word, and I will ask my friend to dinner to-morrow, present you to him, and he will enter into all the details with you."

Xaver gratefully acquiesced. His only misgiving was whether it would be possible to find the capital necessary for so large an undertaking. But the Count convinced him that it would be entirely possible. "There is your acquaintance Councillor Wiesel," he said, "a cautious man, who refused to be drawn into Feinberg's net, but who is very well inclined towards any speculation patronized by the government. In the same way we could command a large amount of English capital. There is a London firm, 'Fairfax & King,' if I remember rightly——"

"Fairfax?" the Professor interrupted him,—"that is the name of the Councillor's future son-in-law. He is a friend of mine."

"So much the better; our negotiations with them will be all the easier. We have enemies in the distance, but friends near at hand. I am ready to give you my name, which has some weight in the stock-market. To-morrow, then, the triumvirate shall be inaugurated."

And so it was. The Count's friend, a Privy Councillor, proved to be as wise and as willing as the Count had described him. The first thing to be done, he said, was to obtain pos-

20*

session of all the old town-buildings that must be cleared away to insure the government a free broad road for traffic, and, besides, of the green gate, the bridge just beyond it, a part of the ditch, and the meadow between it and the Höneburg. The tile-kiln beyond the gate must also be purchased, to give entire control over a large extent of land. Of course all this property could be procured upon moderate terms only by keeping secret for the present the view with which it was purchased. In the mean while, he would so arrange matters that when everything was thus prepared, the charter should be forthcoming without delay. He advised that Xaver should not yet appear as Freiherr of Höneburg, who should empower Professor Schönrade to act for him, which would enable him to proceed at once to the purchase of the tile-kiln and the land beyond the gate in the interest of the proprietor of the ruin. A report could be put in circulation as to the Freiherr's design to erect a factory upon his estate, which would satisfy any curiosity that might be excited. In the town Moritz Amberger must attend to matters, and play into his friend's hands.

There were long and repeated conferences before Schönrade was fully instructed. Then he provided himself with all the necessary documents, and took his departure from Berlin.

CHAPTER XVIII.

Since Frau Barbara's departure the windows in the upper stories of the Amberger mansion had been closed. Moritz had occupied exclusively his own apartments, and was much more frequently to be found in his counting-room than had been his custom of late. Any one seeing him at work among his ledgers or walking about on 'Change would have supposed him ten years older than he really was, he had become so much graver and quieter. He himself knew well enough the cause of this change. Since his talk with the Professor his mind had dwelt constantly upon the words then spoken. Once having been face to face with the truth, he could no longer veil it from his eyes. In Sidonie's absence he experienced a sense of relief, more freedom to collect his thoughts and frame his resolves. He knew that he had nothing to fear from the Professor, and if Sidonie should, by any chance, be taught a lesson in self-control by some humiliating repulse, it would be all the better for himself. But there were moments in which he doubted whether she would ever return to him; and these were his happiest. He acknowledged frankly that he had no genuine pleasure or satisfaction in the life she delighted to lead, that the butterfly existence of a man of her world was abhorrent to him, that his tastes were for simple domestic pleasures, and he could have sighed like a sick girl at the emptiness and loneliness of his heart.

He applied himself diligently to his neglected business, conducted a part of his correspondence himself, reviewed his ledgers, and became convinced that his entanglements with the Feinbergs were even more hopeless than he had given the Professor to understand. At the same time he discovered that his book-keeper and chief clerk had been acting far more in the interest of the Feinbergs than in that of his master,— perhaps influenced by secret inducements. He could not dismiss him immediately, but he watched him narrowly, and threw less responsibility upon him. Feinberg perceived the change, and gave him to understand that he was of very little use to him, and that it would not cost him much to dissolve all business connection with the house of Amberger.

Sidonie's letter breaking their engagement decided matters. It increased his anxiety, but the die was cast, and he knew certainly what he had to deal with. To be sure, Sidonie's letter was full of diplomatic sentences, designed to leave the door open for a change of mind; she spoke of doubts which had arisen within her as to whether they were fitted to find happiness together, said that she needed more time for reflection, and that she must be allowed freedom to follow the impulse of her soul. This meant that he was to consider himself still bound, but that she was entirely free from blame if she chose to withdraw from her engagement. The blood rushed to his cheek as he read, and he replied immediately and briefly that he considered their engagement ended.

He of course expected that Ignaz Feinberg would at once announce to him the dissolution of their business connection; but he could see no change in the man's behaviour towards him. Moritz could not tell whether the prudent man of business judged it best to ignore the change of affairs, or whether he was without information from his wife and daughter. His own situation meanwhile was a most anxious one; and his thoughts would have been far more gloomy if just at present they had not been occupied in a way that drove business from his head at times.

The day that he dispatched his final letter to Sidonie, two strangers from the country desired to see him. He supposed that they wished to deposit their savings in his bank, and referred them to his book-keeper, but they sent in word to his office that they wished to speak to the gentleman himself. By no means in the best of humours, he consented to receive them.

His visitors, an elderly woman and a young girl, were entire strangers to him. Their dress was plain, but in good taste, and the servant was evidently in doubt whether to designate them as "ladies" or "persons" The elder introduced herself as the widow Vogelstein. She, with her daughter Lena, had business in the town, and desired to deliver into his own hands a letter which she had for him from Italy. She laid a certain emphasis upon the word Italy, as if he could see from it how important the letter was.

Moritz recognized his brother's handwriting on the envelope. "Are you in communication with my brother?" he asked, surprised both at their errand and at the great beauty of the girl. Could Philip have any private love-affair in this direction? If so, he certainly had shown an immense deal of taste.

"We do not know Herr Amberger," the woman replied, "but he is staying in Florence with relatives of ours, who have enclosed to us this letter from him to you, with the request that we would deliver it into your own hands. My husband's elder brother left home very young and married in Italy, in Florence, where he now keeps an inn and seems to be very well-to-do in the world. It chanced that Herr Philip Amberger took lodgings there, and, finding that his host came from the same part of Germany, they were soon very friendly together,—and—I think the letter will tell you all there is left to tell."

"My grandfather would have brought it himself," Lena added, "but he does not like to come to the town; and, besides, he objected because——"

"Because he did not know how the family might receive the news," Frau Vogelstein completed the sentence. "My

brother-in-law has given us some hints that cannot be misunderstood.   He has a daughter——"

" Ah ! And this daughter—— ?" Moritz exclaimed, a suspicion suddenly dawning upon his mind of the cause that kept
Philip so long in Florence.

" This daughter, judging from her photograph," Lena said,
" must be exquisitely beautiful, and her father is a man of
means.   There would be nothing so very strange——"

" Hush, hush, Lena !" her mother interrupted her.   " There
are two opinions upon that subject.   There were once wealthy
merchants in this town who bore the name of Vogelstein and
were held in high honour, sitting at the council-board, as your
grandfather has told you, with the Ambergers.   But times
are changed,—very much changed ; we earn our living now
by gardening, and no one cares whether we live or die."

" That cannot make us anything but what we really are,
mother," said the girl, standing proudly erect.

This pleased the young merchant, whose admiration of independence of spirit was just now very great.   " Excuse me
if I read my letter," he said, courteously.

" Pray do so," the widow replied, " that we may know what
to write to Florence."

Moritz, really curious, opened the letter, which, although
scarcely a page in length, was not easily dispatched.   The
contents required to be well weighed before they were pro-
nounced upon.   At the first few lines the reader's face expanded into a smile, and he muttered between his teeth, " I
thought so ;" then he grew very grave ; and when he had concluded he said, with an air of embarrassment, " My brother
tells me that he is formally betrothed,—betrothed to Signora
Lucia Uccello, in Florence."

" Uccello and Vogel are the same name," the girl remarked,
observing him narrowly.   " Vogel or Vogelstein, it could make
very little difference in Italy."

Moritz bowed. "Signora Lucia is your cousin, Fräulein Vogelstein; I comprehend it perfectly, and I should express my pleasure in making the acquaintance of so near a relative of my brother's choice, if I only knew——"

Lena looked at him with so much expectancy in her large eyes that involuntarily his own fell before her. "If I knew," he went on, in a lower tone, "what impression this news will make upon our mother, who is absent from home, travelling. You may imagine," and he turned to Frau Vogelstein, "that this engagement will take her by surprise, and that she will hardly bestow her approval upon it until she has more exact information concerning it."

"Of course," the widow assented; "it would perhaps have been better if he had asked his mother's permission before speaking to Lucia,—any dissension in his family might then have been avoided."

"That would hardly have been the part of a man," Lena declared, decidedly. "Lucia could not have smiled upon a lover who asked his mother for permission to woo."

Frau Vogelstein, who preserved all through the interview the most perfect placidity of demeanour, cast a reproachful glance at her daughter. "You must excuse her," she said. "Lena is a country-girl, and has not learned to suppress her opinions. But I know more of the world, and I am not at all surprised that your first thought is of your mother, since your father is not living. We ourselves hardly know our Italian relatives; but if my brother-in-law at all resembles his father and brother, he must be an excellent man, worthy of all confidence."

"And Frau Amberger," the girl added, "must know her son well enough to feel sure that he could not choose unworthily."

"You are right, Fräulein Vogelstein," said Moritz; "it should be so. As far as I am concerned, I have no desire to dictate to my brother. He writes me that the affair is entirely settled, and I know how firm he is after he has decided upon a course of action. I hope he may find all the happiness in life that he anticipates. You must not take it ill of me that as a merchant I hoped he might choose a rich wife."

"It seems to me Herr Philip Amberger is rich enough," Lena remarked, in a tone of wonder, "to be indifferent to money considerations."

Moritz shrugged his shoulders, and the corners of his mouth twitched slightly. "Supposing that to be the case," he said, after a pause, "a merchant—and Philip is a merchant, although perhaps only in name—is seldom so sure of his property that he may not lose it in a day." He seemed considering whether he might or ought to say more. Then he held out his hand to Frau Vogelstein, and made a friendly inclination towards the young girl, whose cheeks glowed with earnestness. "It might not signify much, perhaps," he continued, "if something of the kind did happen, for Philip is a philosopher, and could, I believe, live as contentedly as Diogenes in a tub. But we must consider whether the fair Lucia would be equally willing to resign the adornments of life."

He then asked where the gardener Vogelstein lived, and was not a little astonished to hear that it was in the Höneburg ruins. "Can women live in that old robbers' nest?" he asked, gaily. "Diogenes' tub is a comfortable villa in comparison. I imagined that old heap of stones too dreary even fir owls, and here it contains a treasure——"

Frau Vogelstein sighed, and Lena looked at him so gravely that he could not continue in this tone of easy gallantry. "I really pity you," he said, with an answering sigh.

"We are not at all to be pitied," the girl rejoined. "A house like this in the town seems to me a heap of stones. One may live and breathe in it, but where is the comfort and retirement that we enjoy in our hiding-place, where we allow no one to intrude?"

"No one?" asked Moritz, as the idea occurred to him that he should greatly like to pay a visit to the ruinous old castle.

"No one!" the girl replied, contracting her eyebrows, while her mouth laughed archly. "We have a very savage watch-dog, and no one who does not know how to propitiate him dares approach the place."

"Lena!" Frau Vogelstein admonished her.

"Has no one succeeded in doing so?" Moritz eagerly asked, more and more interested in his conversation with the fair châtelaine.

"A little while ago, a Professor," she replied, after a moment's reflection; "but he was a very learned man."

"Not Professor Schönrade?" he asked, with a laugh.

She nodded.

"Did even the savage dog respect him?" he went on. "Oh, I know him, and I shall beg him to teach me his magic formula."

"It cannot be taught."

"You must not let the Professor cast a glamour over you."

"Herr Amberger!" Lena arose as she spoke.

"Be careful; he has already lost his heart."

The girl threw back her head haughtily. "That is his own affair."

"Unfortunately, mine too," sighed Moritz. "He loves my sister." He was startled at this sudden confession of his, but he said it involuntarily, feeling that he must, he knew not why.

"Your sister?" Lena asked, evidently surprised and pleased.

"Oh, it is a secret," he replied, lightly touching his lips with his finger. "How could I be so indiscreet? However, it is safe with you." He was glad to see that she did not change colour.

"Then you know too who he really is?" she asked.

" Who he is ? Why, Professor Xaver Schönrade. Who should he be ?"

" I keep *my* secrets better," she rejoined. " Come, mother dear, our errand is concluded; we will not disturb Herr Amberger further."

Frau Vogelstein took a formal leave, while her daughter hurried away. " We shall soon meet again," Moritz said, as he accompanied them to the door.

He seemed to be dreaming. Had Philip's letter not lain open upon his desk, he might have thought he had been sleeping. Now that he was alone he read it again, and made no effort to control his sentiments. His first impression had been that Philip had acted very foolishly, and this feeling now returned upon him in full force. He thought his brother a thoroughly impractical man; he knew how averse he was to ladies' society, and he had believed firmly that he never would be married; and now, in his travels, in an inn, he had evidently been allured by the arts of some vulgar coquette, and induced to contract a most unsuitable alliance,—it must be so. Perhaps he had resolved not to return home, intending to live upon his income in Florence, believing himself a rich man, and making his arrangements accordingly. So it would seem from his recent demands for large sums of money ! And all this to happen just when his own engagement to Sidonie was dissolved, his hopes of a wealthy marriage thus suffering woeful shipwreck; while his business might shortly receive a shock the consequences of which could not be estimated ! Scarcely an hour had elapsed since he had dispatched his note to Sidonie, and he was already considering whether he had any right to think of himself and wish for freedom.

And what a strange dispensation it was by which the man whose daughter Philip had learned to know and to love hundreds of miles from here should have a father in this very place, about whom he seemed to have troubled himself little until this most unfortunate time for reviving his interest! He remembered to have heard that an old gardener lived in the Höneburg ruin, leading the life of a hermit there; nay, he even seemed to recollect visiting the place as a boy with some school-fellows and being frightened away by the watch-dog. It was many years since, and these memories might have faded entirely but for this recent event. Old Vogelstein might be the best of men; but what would his mother say? Philip should have acted more considerately towards her, and begged Signor Uccello to continue to neglect his family. But it was just like Philip to act as he had done, with an entire disregard of all annoyances of this kind.

Thus clouds were rising all around his horizon; the only question was how soon the storm would burst upon him from all sides.

In the anxious days that ensued, it was strange that the beautiful country-girl constantly occupied his thoughts. Beside her, the free, healthy child of nature, Sidonie seemed like some painted overdressed doll. He could scarcely see how he had ever thought a union with such a heartless coquette possible. He certainly owed it to his brother Philip to return the visit that had been paid him, and, accordingly, one afternoon he ordered his horse and took his way towards the Höneburg. Since Sidonie's departure, the animal had never left the stable; it was only with an idea of pleasing her that he had played the enthusiastic horseman; and now he would rather have driven out to the ruin but that he feared there was no carriage-road thither, and he did not like to let his people know where he was going. For the same reason he did not take the shortest way, through the green gate, but by a distant bridge and a circuitous route to the tile-kiln. His steed was very lively, and needed a firm hand upon the bit,—all the more

necessary as there was scarcely a bridle-path on the latter part
of his way.

He arrived at the ditch quite safely, but judged it best to
dismount here and lead his horse, who pricked his ears sus-
piciously, across it and along the hedge bounding the garden
of the ruin.   The dog, who must have heard him, began to
bark, and sprang up against the wall.   Instantly a voice
that he knew called out from among the trees, "Who is
there?"

He turned towards the direction whence it came.   Lena
started upon seeing a man and horse so near her, but laughed
gaily when she recognized him.   A white handkerchief was
wrapped around her head, and she had in her hand a hoe, with
which she had just been weeding the beds.

"How you startled me!" she said, while he had some ado
to control his horse, terrified by her white kerchief and the
barking of the dog.

He excused himself as well as he could, but she still affected
displeasure.   "What has such a fine gentleman from town to
do with an old owls'-nest like this?   Did I not tell you that
no one was admitted here?"

"Yes; and it was just that which provoked me to try whether
you would not let me be a fortunate exception.   It is well
that I have surprised you here, giving you no time to barricade
yourself in the castle."

"We have no desire to do anything so rude," she replied,
approaching the horse and patting him on the neck.   "And
it is kind of you," she went on, "to come to see my grandfather; he will be glad to see you and to receive you hospi-
tably.   He is proud of his ancient lineage, and cannot be
embarrassed by the presence of wealth and station.   Surely
those people who can value one another need not be strangers
because one possesses more worldly wealth than the other.
Thus he thinks with regard to my cousin Lucia and Herr Philip

Amberger; and I think difference of nationality of far more importance than any that money can produce. It must be hard to make use always of a tongue that is not one's own. I can get along very well in English and French, which I learned at school; but as soon as I wish to speak from my heart, my tongue is only German. Your brother must speak Italian perfectly?"

"He has learned it, then, in Italy," said Moritz, with a laugh. "He was but poorly provided with that language when he left home."

"I suppose Lucia is so pretty," Lena observed, "that it is enough to look at her. You must see her picture; it can do you no harm."

"Why not?" he asked. "On my brother's account?"

"No, no," she answered, with a bright blush; "but you are betrothed. Oh, we hear even up here of such important matters."

"But what if your information be incorrect?"

"What?"

"It is so. I am not betrothed."

"You had better not let that reach the ears of Fräulein Sidonie Feinberg——"

"She would confirm what I say. It is not long, indeed, since the tie between us was broken; but we have known for much longer that we were not at all suited to each other, and therefore you startled me, almost, when you alluded to our engagement."

She looked down, as if reflecting whether to pursue the subject farther, and then, suddenly raising her clear eyes to his, she said, frankly, "Do you know I am glad to hear this?"

"You are glad?" Moritz repeated, in some surprise, but none the less pleased.

"Yes; on your account," she said, with a nod of girlish

wisdom. "Of course, now that my cousin is to marry your brother, I take a certain interest in all his family; that is not to be wondered at, is it?"

"On the contrary," he declared, "it is your duty, Fräulein Vogelstein, to take the deepest interest in every one bearing the name of Amberger."

"Well, then," she continued, gravely, "I may tell you that I never liked the little I have seen of Fräulein Sidonie Feinberg. No one likes her,—she is haughty, and as heartless and false as her father, whose wealth was not all honestly gained. I can see it in her face."

"Heartless and false—— Yes, yes!" Moritz muttered to himself. "You are right." He held out his hand to the young girl: "Thank you."

"For what?"

"For being glad that I am free once more."

"Oh, indeed! Then I ought not to have said it. I must keep a better guard upon my tongue."

"Do not do that," he entreated; "we are to be very good friends, and must begin by being frank with each other."

"Perhaps," she said, blushing again. "But I am keeping you here. I will go and tell my grandfather. I wonder he has not come to see what Nero is barking at. We must take your horse into the court-yard and tie him at the fountain. They will wonder where I got this steed." And, without heeding Moritz's remonstrances, she took the animal's bridle, and led him across the bridge through the gate of the court-yard.

A moment afterwards the old gardener appeared, with a courteous welcome. "Our chronicles tell," he said, "of an occasion where one of the gentlemen of the Amberger family was brought within these walls a prisoner; since when, I believe, this castle has never had the honour of a visit from them."

"I can easily imagine being a prisoner here," rejoined

Moritz, with a laughing glance at Lena; "but I am curious to see how you have made life endurable in these old ruins, not only for a recluse, but for a gay young girl."

"The garden is the pleasantest part of our domain," said old Vogelstein; "but I shall be glad to do the honours of my dwelling to you."

His manner was so full of quiet dignity that Moritz entirely forgot the idea he had formed in his mind of the old "gardener." He was more like a gentleman of the old school, living in retirement after a busy and active life, occupying himself with his garden as an enjoyment, not as a duty. The widow now appeared, and invited the guest into the house. But, before they went, Lena, with her own shapely arms and hands, drew a bucket of water from the fountain, and from it filled a smaller one, to satisfy the thirst of Moritz's horse.

"Why not call the servant?" her mother remonstrated.

"I like to do it," the girl replied.

Moritz found the little cottage charming. In his present mood he thought it would be easy enough to live there both summer and winter. To the widow it seemed lonely, and she often longed for a town life. Lena brought Lucia's photograph, which she took from a small portfolio full of her own pencil sketches. Moritz looked through these, while the conversation turned upon the Florence relatives and Philip. Vogelstein, with great good sense, remarked that he was, of course, glad that his grandchild should be so well married, but that he could not blame the family here if they should object at first. Moritz, who was fast forgetting how he had thought of the affair, spoke out bravely in defence of the rights of the heart, taking a most democratic stand, and, by way of reward, received not only an approving glance from Lena's bright eyes, but also permission to carry away with him a sketch of the interior of the ruins.

"I value such things highly," he said, "taken directly from

nature as they are, even when faulty in execution; but this seems to me capital."

Lena was not at all embarrassed by his praise, but replied that it was easy to see he was no connoisseur.

Vogelstein asked his granddaughter to pluck them some ripe strawberries from a bed in the garden. "Although they taste much better fresh from the stalk," she said, rising to do his bidding. Moritz agreed with her that fruit eaten from a plate was very poor, and she offered to show him the way to the berries,—an offer which was gladly accepted. The mother called after her child to remind her to tie her white kerchief over her head.

"Oh, mamma, the winter is long enough to bleach me white again, and the sun is very low," the girl remonstrated.

"But the kerchief is so becoming," said Moritz.

"In that case——" she replied; and, tying it on, she turned and curtsied to him, with the merriest laugh in the world.

The gentleman from town was very awkward about plucking strawberries. He had to be shown all the best places, and his eyes were anywhere but upon his work.

"Oh, child of cities," Lena cried, "let me show you!" and she plucked a handful and poured them into his hollowed palms. Then they walked through the garden admiring the flowers and the loveliness of the declining day. At last it was time to take leave.

"You shall have a nosegay to carry with you," said the girl. "Your knife, if you please, grandpapa."

"Only a single bud," Moritz said.

"Well, then, let it be the loveliest."

"The one plucked by you must be the loveliest."

"No, no;" and she blushed deeply. "You must say only what you mean. As a punishment, I shall give you no rose at all."

Vogelstein led the horse through the gate, and across the

bridge to a path which ran tolerably smoothly along the ditch. The animal was very restive as Moritz mounted; but he held him still, while he promised to come soon again and bring to Philip a letter, which Vogelstein could enclose in one to his son. As he was about to touch his hat in farewell, Lena handed up to him a rose-bud that she had cut privately. He pressed the little hand that gave it to him, and stuck it in his button-hole. "And now, good-by!" he called out, as he turned his horse and gave him a light cut with his riding-whip.

It was quite superfluous. The restive animal started off, rushed to the edge of the ditch, then shied, and reared so that the rider, off his guard, lost his stirrups and was thrown. He heard a low scream, and saw his steed galloping across the moor. He rose instantly, but immediately felt an intense pain in his left ankle. "It is nothing," he reassured his hosts, who hurried up to him. "But how am I to get my horse again?"

His foot soon became so painful that he was obliged to lean for support against the trunk of a tree. "The ankle is not broken, I trust?" said the old gardener.

"Only slightly sprained," Moritz replied. "But what shall I do? I cannot go home." Again he tried to walk, leaning heavily upon Vogelstein's arm. Lena, pale with terror, supported him upon the other side. "It must be bandaged," her mother said; "you must stay here until we can procure a vehicle of some kind."

He assented, with a slight pressure of the pretty arm upon which he leaned. "I thought," he declared, "that I should be a prisoner here."

CHAPTER XIX.

No bone was broken ; but by night the foot was much swollen and very painful. A couch was prepared for Herr Amberger in Vogelstein's room, and the old man arose many times in the night to renew the cold-water bandages that en- abled Moritz to gain some sleep. In the morning, although it was no worse, the foot was altogether too painful to use at all, —at least so its owner averred when the widow offered to go to the town and order a carriage for him. " Keep me here a few days, I pray," he begged. " The cold water from your fountain is so healing, and the pure air so invigorating. I think I never knew what really pure, fresh air is before, and when I think of sitting for days in my own room, where the sun does not even come, with my foot up on a chair, the pros- pect is too dreary. If only my mother were at home, it would not be so bad."

Vogelstein made no objection to his remaining, only he was afraid they might be anxious about the master at his home, especially if the horse had found its way to the stable. The widow offered to call at Herr Amberger's counting-room, as she was obliged to go to the town to make some purchases ; and Moritz, seated comfortably in a huge arm-chair, with his foot on a rest, wrote a note to his book-keeper, directing him to send a small portmanteau by a servant, and giving him necessary instructions for the next few days. " There !" he exclaimed, as he handed her the letter ; " they will know where I am now. Let them go on for a few more days as they have been doing ; a change of affairs will shortly be made. And could you not, my dear Frau Vogelstein, order the servant to bring a basket of wine from my cellar ?" The old gardener, however, forbade this, stating that the stock of wine in the castle cellar had not been exhausted since the days of the former Freiherr.

At the tile-kiln Frau Vogelstein learned that the horse had been caught and taken to town. The *chef* did not seem to have been much missed in the counting-room. The book-keeper sent word that all should go on as usual.

In the mean while, Moritz sat beneath the vine-covered veranda, and was taken care of and entertained by Lena. The hours passed quickly enough. The old man worked in the garden, but paid him a visit now and then, and joined in the lively talk. At noon the patient was given a book, and told to read, since his nurse was to be busy elsewhere. " I shall examine you upon it this afternoon," she said, archly, shaking her finger at him. But when the time came, he knew nothing of the book. His thoughts must have strayed, she told him.

" Not very far," he excused himself; " only into the kitchen, where you were."

" Ah, then I suppose you were busy with hopes as to your dinner. How disappointed you must have been !" was her mocking reply.

In the evening, which was lovely, there was a great deal of talk about personal matters. The old man told many stories of his early youth, and of his life before the young Freiherr brought his bride to the ruin, upon which subject, of course, he did not touch. His son's widow had many relatives, well-to-do people in the country round, and had much to tell of them and of the virtues of her deceased husband. Moritz spoke of his business undertakings, and regretted having deserted his father's sound business principles,—letting his hearers perceive that he was by no means so solidly established as was supposed. Lena asked the real meaning of the words " commercial speculation," of which he had several times made use, and his explanation was far from satisfactory. " Why, chance seems to be the speculator's best friend," she said.

" And sometimes his worst," he added.

He passed an excellent night. At breakfast he assured Lena that, strange though it might appear, he had dreamed delightful things of her all night long. " The reality will seem all the more commonplace," she declared, as she presented him with a bouquet of roses fresh from the garden.

" I dreamed this very thing just before morning," he replied, " and that you allowed me to testify my gratitude by kissing your hand. Let me make that a reality too, I pray."

But this proposal found no favour in her eyes.

The foot was reduced to its original size, but its owner maintained that the ankle was still painful. Vogelstein advised him to walk a few minutes at a time, now and again, so as gradually to regain the full use of it. This would be impossible, Moritz said, alone, but if Fräulein Lena would lend him her arm—— This she did not refuse to do, although she thought a cane would have answered the purpose as well. In order to complete his sense of due support, he clasped her hand and held it tight. Thus the promenades beneath the veranda grew longer and longer, until they were extended to the fountain, and to a pretty little seat beneath the trees, just within the garden wall. Here he must rest, Moritz said, and here they sat down.

" Do you know what I have been thinking, Lena?" he said, omitting the Fräulein, as if unintentionally.

" How should I, Herr Amberger?" she asked, in her turn emphasizing the last two words.

" You love these ruins, do you not?"

" Indeed I do. I look to end my days here."

" Ah !"

" And why not?"

" You are so young yet."

"I have all the longer to stay here, then."

"But suppose you should be enticed to town."

"How?"

"By some one whom you could love better even than these dear old ruins."

"But what were you going to tell me you had been thinking of? Something very wise, I hope."

"I have been thinking that I would buy them; they cannot cost so very much."

"Oh, that would be a very bad 'commercial speculation.'"

"Who could think of it as such?"

"I suppose you want to sell the stones for building."

"Do you think me so prosaic, Fräulein Lena? I wish to own these ruins, that they may never be disturbed, and in summer I can come here always."

"And drive us away? How kind of you!"

"That I never said. What would it be here without you? I value the place because it pleases you."

"Yes, but if you——"

"We will restore the tower, with its crown of battlements, from which there must be a charming prospect."

"I once climbed up upon a ladder that I placed against the inside wall, and peeped through one of the narrow windows. The view was lovely."

"But you must never do that again, Lena; you might have fallen. We will have a pretty winding-stair, with a hand-rail up to the top, where shall be a huge flagstaff, and on all festal occasions we will hoist a flag that can be seen from the town. What do you think of having a large L and an A upon it?"

"Oh, I do not think of it at all. Fortunately, the Höneburg is not for sale. But we have rested enough." She arose.

He took her hand and tried to draw her down upon the

22

seat again, but she resisted. " I have so much to say to you," he declared.

" Come to the fountain, then,—there is a seat there too, and we can see better what is going on in the house."

" And can be seen, too."

" Yes ; that is an advantage."

And he did as he was bidden.

Towards evening, Herr Vogelstein came in from the garden with the information that a light vehicle was coming across the moor towards the Höneburg. Moritz could not guess whom it could bring, for of course it must be coming with some visitor of his. He was supported to the bridge, and exclaimed, as soon as he looked at the approaching carriage, " That is one of Feinberg's equipages ! What can he want of me ? Probably something unusual has happened on 'Change."

Some hundred paces away from the garden hedge the carriage stopped, and a gentleman, whom Moritz instantly recognized as Ignaz Feinberg, descended from it, to come the rest of the way on foot. " Take me to the arbour outside the wall," Moritz begged the old gardener, " and tell my visitor where I am to be found." Frau Vogelstein and Lena withdrew, pacifying Nero, who was barking furiously.

" What in the world have you been about?" Feinberg called out, as he approached the arbour where Moritz was sitting, certainly looking just at that moment quite ill. And, as he spoke, he tried to assume an expression of hearty good will, in which he succeeded but poorly. " Riding out here, entirely alone! Sidonie will never believe it. Why not confine yourself to the high-road, if you must emulate a cavalry officer ? I thought you rode solely to please my daughter, who has many a wild freak, silly girl that she is,—but here you are. I hope your hurt is nothing serious—eh ?"

He was wonderfully loquacious. Moritz wondered what could be the reason for his change of demeanour, as, instead

of his usual two-fingered shake, he grasped his hand cordially.
With certain people one always asks, " What is the reason of
this?" before accepting any token of friendliness from them.
The repeated reference to Sidonie, too, was not unintentional.
Moritz thanked him with some reserve.

" I should like to carry you away from this old owls'-nest,
my dear friend," Feinberg continued, glancing at the ruins.
" To think of my losing my way in this wilderness in pursuit
of my adventurous son-in-law,—ha! ha! ha! Well——?
Will your foot let you get to the carriage if we support you?
My coachman will drive us back to town without upsetting
us,—quite a feat, it is true. Oh, you will be glad enough to
get back, even although the jolting may not be very pleasant.
Come, then!"

He offered his arm to Moritz, but the young man refused
it, and beckoned to Vogelstein, who was standing near, uncertain whether or not to withdraw. "I am capitally taken
care of here," he said; " and, thanks to my kind host and his
family, my foot is much better. Allow me,—Feinberg, this
is the castellan of the Höneburg, Herr Vogelstein."

The wealthy merchant bowed, with a scornful smile, as
if to say, " This was scarcely necessary," and asked, " You will
help me, my good man, I hope, to support the invalid to my
carriage?"

" You seem in great haste," Moritz remarked, keeping his
seat. " It is by no means the case with me. I am extremely
comfortable here, and I shall remain until I can return to
town on foot, unless Herr Vogelstein turns me out." He held
out his hand to the old man.

" You shall stay as long as you please," Vogelstein replied.
" I am but a plain man; but until you tire of my society——"

" There is no need of all these compliments," Feinberg interrupted him. " You can show your gratitude to this good
man another time, and in another way than by subjecting your-

self to further inconvenience. The first thing to do is to hurry to town, where you can consult a physician. So make no more delay, dear friend."

" I desire no gratitude," Vogelstein replied, not without a degree of offended pride. " Herr Amberger is quite aware of that."

Feinberg buried his chin in his cravat. " Then I cannot see why——"

" I am sorry," said Moritz, "that you should have taken any unnecessary trouble on my account. I have no wish to change my delightful quarters at present, unless my presence in the town is urgently necessary."

" Hm! hm!" Feinberg growled. " A merchant's place, I should say, is in his counting-room."

" Have you any important information to give me?" Moritz asked, in a rather uncertain tone.

Feinberg glanced towards old Vogelstein. " I did wish to speak with you; and, since you will not drive to town, I will stay here a few minutes. If we could be——"

" I will withdraw," the old man observed, as he went off to his work.

The merchant sat down beside Moritz, whose eyes were bent gloomily upon the ground. Feinberg's plebeian manners had never seemed so repulsive to him. There must be an end to this, he thought, and sat in dread of the coming conversation.

" Has anything happened in the office?" he asked, with some hesitation.

" Not that I know of."

" I thought, as you wished to speak——"

" We have other things to speak of."

" Then you know——?"

" What is there for me to know?"

A pause ensued. Apparently, neither wished to put into words what was in his mind.

"I supposed," Amberger began, at last, "that Frau Feinberg might have told you of the change which—which——"

"Well? Say what you have to say."

"Which Fräulein Feinberg has seen fit to make."

"Frau Feinberg—Fräulein Feinberg! This formality is odd. I believe Sidonie is your betrothed."

Moritz felt suffocated. "She *was*," he answered, driven to speak clearly; "but Fräulein Feinberg has given me to understand——"

"Oh, nonsense, my dear friend!" Feinberg interrupted him, briskly. "Women are full of whims,—we all know that,—and commit follies for which they are afterwards very sorry. I believe in my heart that they went to Berlin after that Professor they were so wild about. Now they have had enough of him. No need to have any anxiety about that."

"If you had read Fräulein Sidonie's letter to me——"

"Oh, yes, yes; I've no doubt there was an immense deal of nonsense in it. Women are women, and they seldom write anything worth reading. You ought not to have answered it."

"But I have answered it."

"Of course, in your first moments of anger. I suppose your reply was hardly worth reading, either."

"Herr Feinberg——!"

"But now you can listen to reason? Or perhaps not quite yet. Unfortunately, I heard of the matter to-day for the first time, from my wife, with marginal notes which I will not betray. If I had known about it sooner it should never have gone so far. Sidonie had entire freedom of choice. I put no force upon her in your case, much as I desired the match. If she had wished to marry Herr von Otten, I should have said 'yes.' But after she had decided, it was a very different affair. I have treated you in a business point of view as my son-in-law, and I am not going to have my plans interfered with."

Moritz began to understand, and the decided emphasis laid

upon the last sentence told him that there was no expectation
of any opposition on his part. This was an emergency for
which he was unprepared. What should he—what could he
reply?

Feinberg left him no time to decide. "The business world,"
he continued, "is used to hearing the names of our firms connected, and such customs can never be laid aside without dis-
advantage. I say nothing of the fact that this connection at
present is of use, I may say indispensable, only to yourself.
I am of a grateful disposition, and do not forget that it has
served me in former years. In conclusion, I do not wish, my
dear friend, to have striven for your benefit in vain. You will
reap the harvest with me. These are very plain and simple
considerations. I think we understand each other."

" I understand you," Moritz replied, hopelessly, swallowing
his indignation.

Perhaps the tone in which he spoke was not sufficiently
submissive, for Feinberg thought it necessary to cast upon him
a keen glance of inquiry. " Well, then," he began again, " you
understand me. It is fortunate that only the writers themselves, my wife, and I know of the letters that have passed
between Sidonie and yourself. My wife will be silent, I will
be silent, and as for the betrothed couple themselves——"

Moritz drew away from the hand which he was about to
place upon his shoulder.

" As for the betrothed couple themselves, my dear friend,
I am not at all afraid that they will not know how to forget
this little mutual misunderstanding."

" But Sidonie——"

" Sidonie thinks no longer as she did a few days ago. In
view of her character, I think that on the whole you did well
to return an instant and decided answer to her letter, instead
of appealing to her father. She did not expect it, and it impressed her. She needs to be impressed: she tires of constant

indulgence and submission. Now she sees what you really are, and the effect is evident. My wife tells me that if she had not written that unfortunate letter to you, it never would be written now. What does that mean, eh?"

To Moritz it seemed as if some serpent were winding its coils about him body and soul. "It may be," he said, almost with a gasp, "that Sidonie repents her-precipitation."

"What! Precipitation?" Feinberg exclaimed. "Repent! You talk like a school-master or a priest. Why take a whim so seriously? You must make allowance for young girls, and show your own superior wisdom. Come to town, take a sheet of paper and write to Sidonie as if those warlike epistles had never been exchanged, and I will insure——"

The young man forgot his lame foot, and sprang up involuntarily. "What! you would have me——?" he exclaimed, indignantly.

Feinberg regarded him with extreme surprise, half closing his eyes, as if to observe him more distinctly. "Yes; you cannot wish Sidonie to ask pardon,—you know the girl."

"And you require me, a man, so to humiliate myself——"

"Pshaw!" Feinberg interrupted him, drawing him down upon the seat again. "Let us talk like practical people. Is it of consequence that the old relation should be restored,— yes, or no?"

Amberger looked away, and made no reply.

"Yes, I say," his tormentor made answer. "Yes, in your own interest. This being so, my dear friend, the question is, how this is to be brought about; and you can hardly fail to see that the first step towards reconciliation must be made by yourself, especially since I have treated you with such frank cordiality. Or do you not agree with me?"

Moritz still looked away. He knew perfectly well what his reply should be, but he also knew the consequences of Feinberg's departure in anger. For one moment he succumbed to a weak despair. Should he give an evasive answer? What good would it do? Just then he thought he saw something moving on the other side of the garden wall; and, sure enough, it was Lena's curly head that appeared for an instant and then vanished. He heard her speaking to Nero, and the gentle sound of her voice warmed his heart. It was as if the wall were transparent and he could see her caressing the dog's shaggy head. He had often envied the animal the light touch of those pretty fingers. He could not feel her so near him and still pause irresolute. He turned to Herr Feinberg with a face greatly changed in expression. "I will tell you frankly what I think," he said, firmly. "There never ought to have been any engagement between Sidonie and myself. Now that it is dissolved, dissolved by her, it must stay so,—it is much better for both. Sidonie does not love me, and I—I no longer feel towards her in a way that would justify me in offering her my hand again. This is my reply as an honest man."

Feinberg had raised his head so that he quite looked down upon his bold opponent. "You had better have said so at first," he said, with icy coldness. "Why let me waste my words? You *wish* the engagement broken. Yes, that is quite another affair."

"I do not *wish* it broken," Moritz replied; "it *is* broken."

"Then you do not wish it renewed. That amounts to the same thing." He arose slowly, and began to draw on the glove which he had hitherto held in his hand. Perhaps he wished to give his rash antagonist time for reflection.

"Remember that the welfare of your only daughter——" Moritz entreated. The words died in his throat.

Feinberg went on composedly putting on his gloves. "I am not accustomed to act without due reflection. Do not overlook the fact that I have offered you an opportunity for the adjustment of the affair, and that you have refused to embrace it, and that the matter at stake is my daughter's hand,—a very delicate matter. I am driven to suppose that you wish to insult me, if you——"

" Herr Feinberg !" Amberger interrupted him in terror.

" That you wish to insult me," the banker repeated, in the same cutting tone, " if you reject the attempt at a reconciliation that only requires you to stretch out your hand. Of course you can expect no further tokens of friendship from a man whom you insult ; and when two men of business like ourselves can no longer work together, of course you understand that they must be opposed to each other. Well, I think I shall be able to bear it."

" What ! you would——"

" I shall show the business world that there is no reason whatever for my coveting the honour of calling you my son-in-law. Of course I owe this to myself when this broken engagement becomes the town-talk."

" You would ruin me ?"

" If it comes to that, I must take care of myself. That hardly suits you, it seems ? Hm ! Do you wish time for reflection ?"

Moritz was silent.

" I will give you time for reflection," Feinberg continued, with a smile that was by no means pleasant to see. " You shall have forty-eight hours. There need be no word of excuse or entreaty,—only send me a letter to Sidonie, and I shall consider your part in the affair concluded. If not," and his voice grew loud in menace, " I shall publish abroad the next morning that Sidonie has dismissed you. Adieu !"

He touched his hat, turned, and went down the path to the moor where the carriage was standing. Moritz heard him whistling a gay opera-air.

CHAPTER XX.

THE young merchant felt annihilated. He sank back on his seat and buried his face in his hands. " Time for reflection." What was there to reflect upon ? The only question was whether he should suffer ruin as a man or as a merchant. And he no longer had only Sidonie to think of; his heart seemed almost breaking when he thought of the hopes that he might have to sacrifice.

Thus he sat for awhile, lost in a sad reverie, when a merry voice addressed him. " Are you asleep, Herr Amberger ?" He started and looked up, to see Lena standing before him. His face must have worn a pale and dejected look, for she instantly asked, anxiously, " But what is the matter ? You are pale as a ghost."

He held out his hand, and nodded sadly. " I cannot——" he muttered to himself, " I cannot."

" You cannot what ?" the girl asked, compassionately.

He drew her down upon the bench beside him, and she made no resistance. " If I only knew——" he said, looking into her clear, frank eyes, that slowly fell before his own. " Lena, dear Lena——!"

She recoiled. " But, good heavens—— !"

" Do you know who the gentleman was who has just left me ?"

" My grandfather told me."

" And do you know what he wished me to do ?"

" Not——?" She raised her head.

" Yes! yes!" he assented. He saw that she guessed rightly.

She grew very grave and thoughtful, her white teeth resting upon her under-lip.

"Something must have happened," he began again, " to make Sidonie change her mind. For I am convinced that she and her mother are the contrivers of this plan. It may perhaps suit the old man very well, since he has made up his mind to this marriage, and knows his daughter well enough to know where the fault lies. His social position is not yet sufficiently well assured; he would avoid a scandal and stand well with the respectable part of the community. Therefore he has consented to play the go-between, not a *rôle* very much to his taste. He will be all the more resolved upon my ruin if he has taken this trouble in vain. And he can ruin me. I have allowed myself to become too deeply involved with him. What shall I do, Lena? what would you do in my place?"

She had let him finish without stirring. Now, her hand trembled slightly, and she turned her face more away from him. "If you can hesitate," she said, in a low tone, "there is only one advice to be given you: Go back to Sidonie."

"You advise that?" he exclaimed. "You, Lena——!"

A tear fell from her eyes into her lap. "I am sorry for you, but——"

"You advise me thus! Because you think me a heartless man, you do not believe in——"

"Because you hesitate," she replied, interrupting him. "I understand how much courage is required to withstand such a temptation, and you are not brave enough."

"Lena!"

"Examine yourself. You are not brave enough to risk position, wealth, and a brilliant future, only that you may earn your own self-approval."

"Do not forget, Lena, that my mother's, my sister's, and my brother's property is at stake——"

"I do not forget it."

"Yet you blame——"

" I do not blame you. How could I?"

" But you say I am not brave."

" I do not say that you could not be brave."

" It is impossible, Lena."

She made no reply.

" Quite impossible that I should yield. A week ago, per-haps—I cared very little then what became of me. I did not know. If I only knew now, Lena!" She arose.

He took the hand hanging by her side in his own. " It might be," he said, " that I could lose all, and yet be supremely happy in the possession of a heart worth all else that can make life dear. I might be brave enough to be true to myself in poverty, if this poverty were shared by a love that would make me rich indeed. If I ask you, Lena——"

" Do not ask!" she exclaimed, hastily, and her voice and her hand both trembled. " You must think of your mother and your sister, and of yourself. You are still undecided; what may seem impossible to-day, because it finds you unprepared, may seem so no longer to-morrow, after cool reflection. Do not make your decision more difficult. I am but an ignorant girl, and have never pondered such matters; but I think in your case I would not ask any one to share the responsibility of my decision, least of all any one whom I cared for."

" You know, then, Lena, that I care for you," he said, carry-ing her hand to his lips; " and I must not ask whether you care for me?"

" No, you must not," she replied, hastily; " and you must promise not to speak of such things while you are our guest here, or I must go to town and not return. Will you promise?"

" But only think——"

" Will you promise?"

" Well, then—yes! if I may have the smallest hope——"

" Unconditionally."

"Very well! I will trust to your clemency. I will rely upon your angelic kindness, your——"

"You must rely upon nothing, but must consider prudently and quietly what you owe to every one. Fortunately, you owe me nothing, not even a compliment."

"Oh, you are cruel!"

"It is my duty to be so. And now lean upon my arm and let me lead you in. Do not disturb my mother or my old grandfather. Why should they know anything about this? Your foot will be quite well by day after to-morrow, I think, so that you can go to town, and if you are very good until then I will go with you as far as the green gate." He ventured to press her hand.

"If you are very good, you understand."

———

All through that evening Lena avoided any *tête-à-tête* with Moritz, and the next morning she was very busy. She had never seemed so lovely to him as now, when he could only follow her with his eyes. She was evidently determined to leave him quite to himself; but there was nothing stern or forbidding in her demeanour; on the contrary, a happy smile continually played about her mouth, as if her thoughts were occupied with pleasant subjects. Before retiring to rest on the previous night, Moritz had done his best to reconcile himself to his position; but his mind was too full of Lena to admit of other considerations. Sidonie seemed like some far-off delusion, which could never take possession of him again. All there was to consider was, what the consequences of a break with Feinberg might be, and whether they could in any way be averted or mitigated. For this he must examine his books afresh, and that could be done as soon as he returned to his counting-room. The elasticity of youth and a kind of blind reliance upon the chances of trade stood him in good stead in contemplating his future, which did not look so black as it had done formerly. If the worst came to the worst, it was but being a small merchant instead of a great banker, and there was consolation in the thought that there would then be no objection to Katrine's engagement to the Professor.

Affairs wore a more serious aspect when, towards evening, he received a visit from a young man in his employ, upon whose honesty he could depend. He was the son of a man who had been one of his father's most confidential clerks. He came because, as he said, he could not answer it to his conscience not to put his chief and benefactor upon his guard. He had long known that the book-keeper was false to the interests of the business, and that he was even engaged in speculations with funds that could hardly be rightly come by. He himself had received orders to make certain entries which he could not understand, and in answer to his questions had received replies which had strengthened him in his suspicions that the books were falsely kept. Nor did it look well, either, to have the book-keeper receive almost daily letters from Herr Feinberg that were not filed with the rest of the correspondence of the house, or that he should have long private conferences with Herr Otto Feinberg. So long as his chief was in the counting-room, he had not felt it his business to interfere, but in his absence these suspicious circumstances forbade him to be silent any longer.

Moritz urged him to tell him everything that had come to his knowledge, assuring him of his gratitude even although it should be found that he was in error. The young fellow then related that on the previous evening Feinberg had been closeted in the counting-room with the book-keeper until far into the night, and that to-day various changes had appeared in the books, in the way of descriptions of stocks, etc., that plainly showed they had been made in Feinberg's interest. They consisted mainly of an exchange of perfectly safe paper

for what Amberger had always considered, even in opposition
sometimes to Feinberg, as unsafe, and would really be of little
consequence if the two firms continued to act in concert, but
would be ruinous to Amberger if any division should occur
between them. Moritz had no doubt that Feinberg had made
use of his absence and of the reputed intimacy of the two
houses to cripple his former associate; and he even doubted
whether the treacherous book-keeper could be called to account,
since he could plead ignorance of any possible breach between
the two houses.

Thus much was ascertained,—that he could not, without culpable neglect, resign himself any longer to the *dolce far niente*
which he had enjoyed for the last few days; and which had
not been without its advantages, since it had helped him to
become more resolved and self-reliant. In his first indignation against the man who had so grossly deceived him, he sat
down at Vogelstein's desk and indited a letter to Feinberg, in
which he entirely relieved his mind. He required an immediate restoration of the stocks for which Feinberg had substi-
tuted what he knew to be worthless, and declared all further
business connection with him dissolved,—concluding, " I now
understand why you gave me time for reflection. I did not
need it: you did. Whatever I may have to endure from
your hostility, I will never again consent to wear the unworthy
fetters which I regret having borne so long. Begin the campaign : I am ready for everything. But expect no mercy
from an antagonist whom you would endeavour to trample
under foot after having, by his aid, attained a position which
you intend to use for his ruin."

Without reading over the letter, he gave it to the young
man to take to town, directing him to leave it that very evening at Feinberg's door. He himself would be at the counting-room the next morning. His cheeks glowed as, after his
clerk's departure, he approached Lena, who was seated by the

fountain, engaged in shelling a basket of peas. His foot was much better, and he limped only very slightly.

" You have had some important news?" she said, looking up.

" Most important," he replied, his agitation vibrating in his voice. "Feinberg is acting a Judas' part towards me. He has not even awaited the conclusion of the truce, but has broken into my stronghold in my absence. I must go to town early to-morrow morning."

" What do you call early ?"

" I must be in my counting-room by nine o'clock."

" And it will take full an hour to walk to town."

Moritz sat down by her, and took a handful of unshelled peas from her basket. He opened one after another of the pods,—rather awkwardly, to be sure. Lena looked at him with a smile.

" You take too much pains with them," she said. " See how easily they open if you only press the right spot."

He leaned towards her, and watched her busy fingers.

" Nothing is difficult if one only understands how to do it," he said.

" Try, then."

" May I help you ?"

" As much as you please."

He soon grew expert, and the basket was emptied.

" Now you will relish your supper," Lena remarked.

" The last——"

She sighed almost inaudibly.

" The last must always come."

" You have not forgotten your promise to go with me as far as the town ?" he asked, after a slight pause.

" Did I promise ?"

" Oh, you would not break your word, Lena ?"

" But if your foot is well,—and it seems to be so,—you will not need me."

"If you say that, it will grow alarmingly worse; and I really do limp a little still."

"Well, then, if I really promised——"

"Oh, thank you!" And he arose, as she did.

She took up the bowl of shelled peas, and said, "Will you not carry the basket for me?"

"With pleasure." And he followed her to the house.

Vogelstein came from it towards them. "You have a grand servant," he said, shaking his gray head.

"And he has no wages, either," she said, archly, as she took the basket from him and entered the house.

"Who knows?" he called after her. "I will serve like Jacob."

The evening was exquisitely lovely. The little family sat together till a late hour. Moritz forced himself to forget his cares. Lena hummed an old folk-song in a low tone, and he hummed it with her. She sang aloud, and he joined in a powerful second. They sang, "Count the stars in heaven's vault shining," and "Far in a pleasant valley a mill-wheel gaily turns," all through. It was quite pathetic to hear them declaring that they would "die far rather," and "all would then be still," and really feeling as if the words had some application to themselves, although they never dreamed of dying, and would far rather be happy together. It rang in his ears after he had retired to rest, that "Oh, I would die far rather, and all would then be still," until it really was still, so far as he was concerned, and he dropped asleep.

The next morning, when he left his room, Lena appeared in her Sunday costume. "I shall do you no discredit if we are seen together," she said; "my mother and my grandfather have given their consent to my going nearly as far as the town."

The widow's coffee and biscuit were delicious, and Moritz

had an excellent appetite, since he had a whole hour's *tête-à-tête* with Lena in prospect. He thanked his hosts for their kindness, and would have kissed Frau Vogelstein's hand, but she would not permit it. Nero's shaggy head was patted, and they crossed the bridge and walked along the ditch, past the place where the horse had shied, and out upon the moor.

The sun was quite high in the cloudless sky, but the air was cool and refreshing; the dew-drops were still clinging to the bushes, and fell like rain upon Moritz's feet as he brushed past them, leaving to Lena the centre of the narrow path. How lovely she was, with her slender, girlish figure and her wealth of fair hair! He offered her his arm, but she did not accept it; nor would she admit that there was any further need of his being supported by hers.

This was rather a disappointment, and they walked along silently for awhile, until she seemed to regret that she had so repulsed him, and while with one hand she gathered up her skirts to keep them from the dew, she let the other hang down by her side. His own touched it as they walked, and he began to talk gaily enough, his fingers the while enclosing, as if half unconsciously, the little hand that was not withdrawn. He went on talking, but his words grew more and more confused; he felt that it was so, yet she did not ask any explanation. After awhile he ceased speaking, and they walked along silently hand-in-hand, amid the songs of the moorland larks and the humming of the bees, not daring to look each other in the face.

The tile-kiln was not very far distant. On the edge of the moor there were lying huge blocks of stone, singly and in groups, covered with moss, and forming very inviting seats. " Shall we not rest here?" asked Moritz.

" No, you ought to be early in town," Lena replied; "we must not loiter." He made no demur.

There was still a strip of sand to be traversed before they reached the road, along which people were passing, and where Moritz saw it would be impossible to unburden his heart, which he must do before they parted. " Lena," he began, after several more steps, " you know that I wrote to Feinburg yesterday."

" You said so," she answered,—" upon business."

" Not only that."

Her hand trembled in his, but the other drew her broad hat down over her face.

" I gave him my decision with regard to what he said to me the day before."

" Indeed ?"

" Yes, Lena; I wrote to him that everything was at an end between Sidonie and myself, and that I needed no time for reflection to be convinced that it was so."

" But did you weigh well what you said, Herr Amberger ? I think you were agitated by the discovery of his treachery."

" No, Lena ; that only hastened my reply. My mind was entirely made up beforehand,—had been made up some time before, I assure you."

" You will be sorry for it when you get to your counting-room and find how many annoyances and trials await you."

He pressed her hand. " I shall not be sorry."

" I think you should have waited," she said, timidly.

" What for, Lena ?" he asked, gaining courage from her shyness. "All delay was dangerous. I am rejoiced to return to the town a free man ; that is——"

He stooped a little, to look beneath her hat, which shaded her forehead and eyes. Perhaps she did not see this ; at all events, she did not raise her head.

" That is, Lena," he said, with some hesitation, " when I say a free man, you know well, in a certain sense that is far from literally true,—do you not ?"

"I know nothing," she said, in a low tone, and her head bent still lower, although he imagined that a smile played about her mouth.

He hastily raised the hand that he held, and pressed it to his lips. She would have snatched it from him. "You must not," she said.

He refused to release it. "I shall hold you fast," he said softly in her ear, "until, Lena, you hear all I have to tell you. The first time I ever saw you, you awoke within me sensations that I had never before experienced, and in these last happy days I have clearly learned how poor I was, and how blest I am now in knowing that I love,—love from my very heart. I cannot see how I can love without being loved in return. And if you will love me, Lena, nothing will be hard to bear. I can meet every tempest fearlessly. So tell me, dear, that I may hope that you care a little for me, and that one day you will be mine, dear, dearest Lena——"

"Oho!" a manly voice near them called out. "Here you are! This is delightful."

They started and looked up guiltily. Absorbed in each other, they had not noticed that some one was approaching; and now, there he stood just before them. "Herr Professor!" they both exclaimed, in a kind of terror.

It was Schönrade. In their flushed faces he plainly read that his presence was ill-timed, and, holding out a hand to each, he said, in excuse, "I see I intrude, but indeed I could not turn away without speaking."

Lena was the first to collect herself. "If we had known you were coming to the Höneburg, Herr Professor——" she began.

"What, then? You would not have allowed our friend here to walk alone to town with his sprained ankle! I have been to your house, and heard there what has happened. I am so sorry."

" Oh, there is nothing to be sorry about," said Amberger, not quite able to control his irritation at the interruption. " My foot is quite well."

" So much the better," said Schönrade. " Your few days of country air seem to have been of great benefit to you. You are looking incomparably better than when I bade you good-bye."

Moritz was pleased to hear this. " You never bade me good-bye, if you remember," he replied, with a smile, " but——"

" You are right," the Professor interrupted him. " We parted in storm and rain, not in the best of humours. Since then the weather has cleared with me,—and here too, I rather think, eh ?" He looked meaningly at Moritz and Lena, who cast down their eyes. " Those surprises for which we are least prepared are often the pleasantest. Well, I can keep a secret."

" Under certain circumstances, an excellent trait," Moritz remarked, " especially when those most interested——" He hesitated, and glanced at Lena's blushing face. " Why did not you wait three minutes longer ?" he blurted out.

" I will leave you this instant," the Professor said, " and never even look back."

" Then I will go with you," said Lena. " If I guess aright you were on your way to the Höneburg, and I must return."

" You promised to go as far as the green gate," Moritz eagerly interposed.

" But I did not know that I might have a companion on my way home," she returned, with a glance entreating silence.

" I must admit, fair châtelaine, that I was not going to the ruin on your account," said the Professor, " great as is my pleasure in seeing you again. My visit is to Herr Amberger, with whom I have very important business. I arrived last evening, and, not wishing to impose another guest upon the Höneburg, I waited until this morning. I did not anticipate meeting you upon the way."

M*

"I should like to turn round and go back whence I came with Fräulein Lena and yourself," said Moritz, dolefully, "but——"

"But Herr Amberger has pressing business in the town," the girl continued his sentence,—"business which demands his immediate presence there."

"The young man seems to be well taken care of," the Professor remarked, drily.

"Unfortunately, Fräulein Lena is right," Moritz said, with a laugh. "I must go to my counting-room, where, it is to be feared, most unpleasant revelations await me."

"It is all the more important, then, that I should speak with you," the Professor insisted. "I propose that you permit me to accompany you the remainder of the way, in spite of your present aversion to my society, and that Fräulein Lena——"

"Can find her way back to the Höneburg alone," she interposed, turning away. "Adieu, Herr Professor! Adieu, Herr——"

"Stay!" cried Moritz, barring her way. "Not so fast,—I must have your hand in token of farewell,—your hand, Lena!"

"Take it. And now——"

"May I interpret as I please?" he asked, in a low voice.

He felt her hand press his, and as she raised her eyes for an instant, he seemed to look into her very soul. "I am brave now, Lena," he said.

"And now," and she curtsied to the Professor, "adieu."

"We shall see you soon again," the latter replied, as he offered his arm to Moritz.

The girl hurried away. Amberger turned slowly towards the town. "Is all right?" Schönrade asked.

"I hope so," Moritz replied. "Are you still of the same mind with regard to Katrine?"

"Of course."

" Well, then, I may make you my confidant."

"And I offer my heart-felt congratulations. But now we must cry truce to all thoughts of love for awhile, and sternly address ourselves to business. Give me your undivided attention. There is a railway——"

Amberger was soon an eager listener.

CHAPTER XXI.

" I CANNOT imagine why mamma suddenly seems so irritated with our dear Professor," Lilli remarked to her lover. " It is really no such great crime for him to love Katrine. Even if it were her own daughter——" A faint blush appeared on her cheek, at the thought that this had once not seemed so very improbable.

Mr. Fairfax nodded carelessly. " Have you heard the strange report there is about him ?"

" No ; what is it ?"

" They say he is the son of a very wealthy Count von Gleichenau."

" Ah !"

" It certainly is true that he frequents the Count's house as if he belonged there."

" But his name is Schönrade, which is the same as Bellarota, and Katrine has told me that his mother is Camilla Bellarota, the former prima donna, whom Sidonie and her mother have lately been to see."

" Yes, Camilla Bellarota is his mother."

" But how——"

" My dear child, Count von Gleichenau may have—— It really is no affair of ours. I only tell you what I hear."

" Do you know the Count ?"

" I saw him yesterday at a business meeting, where proposals were made to our firm. A really hopeful railway project was under consideration."

" Is my father concerned in it ?"

" Not yet. I think he is busied with other things. The Feinbergs are laying siege to him. I don't know,—those men do not greatly please me. He ought to be cautious."

" Can you not warn him ?"

" It is scarcely my place to do so. My estimate of them is not sufficiently well founded. Although the behaviour of the head of the firm to Moritz Amberger——"

" What about it ?"

" Why, there are very damaging reports in circulation. Amberger has dismissed his principal book-keeper, and writes to several business friends here that the man was bribed to defraud him. He claims certain papers as his property that Feinberg was disposing of here. At all events, Feinberg is leaving no stone unturned to undermine Moritz's credit and to ruin him, and has appealed to your father for aid in certain matters."

" And all because the match is broken off, I suppose."

" Yes; but Madame Feinberg runs about telling every one that Fräulein Sidonie herself dismissed Amberger, and it is easy enough to see why."

" You mean about Herr von Fuchs ?"

" It is very evident that Sidonie accepts his attentions. He goes everywhere with her and her mother."

" Yes, he always comes here with them. He must have a great deal of time to spare."

" He has all his time to spare. A fine son-in-law for Feinberg he will be; he will soon set his money circulating."

" But how can Sidonie be so infatuated ?"

"Perhaps she was not in earnest at first. She is a thorough coquette. Every one is talking about them now, and Herr von Fuchs is the very man to tunr this to his own advantage, and compel her to an engagement. Is not that Herr Otto Feinberg? He, too, is breathing threatenings and slaughter against Amberger, because he did not favour his suit with Fräulein Katharina."

He was right. It was Herr Otto Feinberg coming towards them, with his hands in his coat-pockets and his hat on the back of his head, as usual. He immediately asked after the Councillor, and, when he heard that he was not yet at home, hoped he might see the lady of the house.

Frau Wiesel had been suffering from a renewal of her nervous attacks. When she was not occupied with her dress, which, fortunately, disposed of a large part of her time, she reclined upon a sofa, turning over the leaves of a novel, or reading scraps from newspapers and magazines. Intimate friends, like Otto Feinberg, she received without more ado than languidly raising her head from among the cushions.

"Have you had letters?" she asked.

He answered, with a toss of his head and a smack of his lips,—a characteristic habit,—"Plenty of letters, but the news is scanty and not greatly to be relied upon."

"Amberger is still afloat?"

"Still afloat. It is inconceivable how he has kept up for the last three days. My brother was convinced that he would sink at the first blow, and he knows his affairs even better than the young man himself. But he has suddenly developed resources of which we had no idea. Until now he seems to have redeemed all his paper with perfect ease. The question is, how long it will last. To operate efficiently, we must know from what source he derives his means, and how soon it will be exhausted. I have had several clues, as I thought, but they have thus far led to nothing. If the Councillor would only display a little more energy. But he has suddenly become prudence itself."

" Has my husband really any influence?"

" He could gain it if he chose. He delays proceedings that would certainly cause Amberger extreme embarrassment and help to run the fox to earth. But what annoys my brother still more is, that the Councillor has lately refused the unlimited credit he has always accorded him. He has suddenly grown very careful in the examination of securities, almost offensively exact. He has even refused some of our best paper, in consequence, I believe, of a stupid report circulated by Amberger or his unknown friend. As he stands high on 'Change here, we are very much crippled by his want of confidence. If you, madame, would try to interest him more in our behalf——"

" I? You know that in all business matters my husband admits of no advice or interference. I have said what I could; but what can a poor invalid do?"

Feinberg stroked his pointed chin. " Something decisive must be done if we would avoid defeat. In his last letter my brother says he suspects that Amberger has some scheme in hand from which he looks for entire rehabilitation. His manœuvres thus far seem senseless enough; but there's no knowing what may come of them. It is possible that he only wants to inspire confidence in his resources; but he may have some project in view that has been hatched in a more brilliant brain than his own."

" Is Professor Schönrade there still?" the Councillor's wife asked, after a pause.

" He is there still," Feinberg replied, in a tone of annoyance. " We cannot make out that man. His betrothal to Katharina Amberger is at the bottom of the whole difficulty. If he had been free——! My niece Sidonie took a fancy to him, and my brother could easily have shaken off Moritz Amberger."

Frau Wiesel listened eagerly. " For the sake of the Professor ?"

" I think so."

" And Sidonie ?"

Feinberg smacked his lips again. " Really, I scarcely know what I am saying. Mere fancies of mine,—half-spun schemes, no more. But the fact is that this Professor is a dangerous man. The money, it is true, that Moritz has so suddenly at his command, cannot come from his pocket. I know he has no property; and a simple Professor cannot possess much credit."

The Councillor's wife had grown thoughtful. Otto Feinberg had dropped a word which, in spite of his eager denial of any knowledge, was quite worth remembering for private consideration. If Sidonie were concerned, it explained much in the conduct of the Feinberg ladies that had seemed incomprehensible. Self-deceived as she was, she was ready to blame others for a want of honesty in their intercourse with her, although she had no claim upon their confidence. She would so like to think that all her annoyance arose from feeling herself deceived by those whom she had trusted.

When the Councillor came home and learned from Mr. Fairfax and Lilli, in the garden, that Feinberg was with his wife, he made a wry face. " You were right," he said to his son-in-law, " in advising caution : the Feinbergs seem to have gone very far,—how far is not known at present." And he went into the house without waiting for a reply.

His reception of his guest was more formal than usual. " Have you heard the latest news ?" he asked, as Feinberg began to talk of business.

" What is it ?"

" Moritz Amberger, after dismissing his chief book-keeper, has denounced him to the public authorities."

Feinberg started.   " Is he mad ?"

" Why mad ?"

" I should think he would hardly like to have all the world
cognizant of his most private affairs; and you know that whatever is brought into court——"

" Gets into the newspapers," Wiesel concluded the sentence,
stroking his smooth chin.

" Certainly."

" Hm !   He must feel very secure, then."

" Do not believe that, my dear Councillor ; on the contrary,
it is the recklessness of despair; there could be nothing worse
for him."

" It may be so.   But in the letter I saw,—not addressed to
me, it is true——"

" What did it say ?"

" Oh, some odd things.   The man seems very confident.
There is a talk of a large undertaking,—and there are ugly
stories."

" Ugly stories ?"   The thin face grew longer still.

" We will not forestall judgment.   What I wanted to say
to you is, that—hm!—it seems to be taken rather ill of your
brother that he took the man into his service at an unusually
high salary immediately after Moritz Amberger had dismissed
him."

Feinberg started.   " And the inference is—— ?"

The Councillor shrugged his shoulders.   " I do not know ;
but your brother and Moritz were formerly the most intimate
business friends, and it is not usual in such cases——"

" My brother's reason for breaking with him is well known,
I think," Feinberg interrupted him.   " His insulting withdrawal from his betrothal——"

" Hm !   There are several opinions on that head.   Many
say that Fräulein Sidonie dismissed him, and by letter, too,
from here."

" Because his conduct made a continuance of the engagement impossible."

The Councillor seemed to have but little desire to pursue the conversation further; he opened a small cabinet and took out a box of cigars. " Will you smoke ?" he asked.

Feinberg declined. "I should like to know," he said, returning to the subject, " what conclusion you individually draw, my dear Councillor, from the fact that my brother has engaged a competent book-keeper, of whose possible delinquencies he could not have the slightest knowledge ?"

Wiesel had lighted a wax taper, and was taking a great deal of time to light his cigar by it. " Are you sure you will not smoke ?" he asked, evasively.

" By-and-by, perhaps. If you will be kind enough to answer my question——"

" I think I gave no opinion," the Councillor said, still evading an answer.

Feinberg persisted. " You certainly mentioned certain facts in connection with each other that you seemed to think——"

The Councillor puffed out volumes of smoke, and rejoined, " Will it satisfy you if I assure you that I really have no opinion in the matter ? Amberger has claimed as his own— whether justly or not I cannot say—certain papers that are at present in your brother's hands, and the book-keeper is accused of having contrived their transfer. Doubtless your brother, my respected friend, will explain clearly how he came into possession of the papers in question—doubtless ! But you can easily understand that for the present I am only a spectator,— you can readily comprehend this."

Feinberg looked irritated and annoyed. " If that is the case, I might have spared myself the trouble of coming here to-day," he said, taking his hat. " My brother thought he had a right to more confidence; he will be surprised to find you confine yourself to the part of a spectator ; he relied upon your

active support on 'Change. Fortunately, he does not lack
friends, and I have no desire to interest you in his favour if
you are at all disposed to hold back. I must remind you,
however, that among business men it is my turn to-day and
yours to-morrow. Ignaz may choose to play the part of spectator some day."

" Pray assure him of my unaltered esteem," the Councillor
said, courteously ; " I should be sorry to be misunderstood
by him in any way."

Just then Frau Feinberg and her daughter were announced.
Herr von Fuchs accompanied the ladies. The Councillor's
wife arose, with a sigh, to receive them ; she looked weary and
vexed. Otto Feinberg took his leave.

" I am come to-day to see your good husband," Madame
Feinberg said, after the first greetings. " May I have a few
moments' conversation with you, my dear Councillor ?"

Wiesel bowed.

" I will not disturb you," said his wife. " Come with me
to the pavilion, Sidonie."

" No secrets," Frau Feinberg called after them, " no secrets, I assure you ; only not in the presence of the young
people——"

" Permit me also to withdraw," said the Councillor's wife.
" I am not curious." Herr von Fuchs gallantly offered her
his arm, and Sidonie followed with Mr. Fairfax and Lilli.

Madame Feinberg seated herself on a sofa, and the Councillor took a chair opposite her. " What can I do for you,
madame ?" he inquired.

" Oh, nothing of any great importance," she said, easily.
" I wanted to ask a favour for one of my friends."

" Pray let me hear how I can be of service."

" It will not cost you anything beyond a few words of
recommendation. I wish some suitable position for a man
of excellent family and great natural talent,—also, if I am not

much mistaken, of extensive information and distinguished social ability."

Wiesel played with the seals dangling at his watch-chain. " A suitable position,—ha ! hm !—— May I ask, madame, what you understand by that ?"

The lady furled and unfurled her fan. " Good heavens !" she said, smiling, " I should think there could be no doubt about that. A suitable position is, of course, some office of distinction, with an income corresponding to one's needs."

" The needs of human beings are so various, madame."

" Of course ! Well, then, my dear Councillor, we will assume that these needs are not the most modest of their kind. I speak of a man belonging by birth to the privileged classes, and who cannot conform his life to limited means. Imagine, then, his possible connection with a family sufficiently wealthy indeed to attach no great importance to the amount of his income, but who would nevertheless like to see him in a position commanding means enough to secure him a certain amount of respect in business circles. Now you perfectly understand ?"

He assented, gently nodding his head. " Will you intimate more distinctly, madame, in what line I can serve you? I am 'a merchant and a banker. My influence, if I have any, is limited."

" Not in the direction where it will serve me," she hastily remarked. " You are not only concerned in, but at the head of, various companies, and there are new undertakings contemplated. I hear something of a new bank, with an immense amount of capital. You will, of course, have the disposal of many profitable places among the directors or managers ; and, even if you can do nothing yourself, you have such influential friends. A salary of five or six thousand thalers would do, with a share in the yearly profits. As I said before, the pecuniary compensation is of less importance than a position

in the commercial world. I am sure you will do everything
you can to help me."

The Councillor's face still wore the same friendly but un-
meaning smile as at first. " The young gentleman who has
the honour to be under your protection is, I suppose, well
skilled in commercial affairs?" he asked, apparently quite
innocently.

Madame Feinberg looked up from her fan in surprise.
" How could he be? I told you—— Good heavens! since
when has it been necessary to be so qualified for such offices?
The man's superior intelligence will teach him in a very short
time all that it is necessary he should know. Surely I am
right?"

" Most probably," Wiesel replied, settling himself in his
chair. " You know the world, madame; I am only a little—
a very little—surprised that you do me the great honour of
applying to me, when your husband possesses at least as
much influence——"

" Oh, there is a reason for that," she said,—" a very good
reason. My husband would take the greatest pleasure in
being of service to you in a like case, but in this particular
instance he does not wish to be the one to whom Herr
von—the young man owes his position. I cannot explain
myself more clearly to-day, my dear Councillor, and, after a
little, you will not need any explanation. I pray you be content with my mysterious hints, leave my husband out of the
question, and regard this as a matter in which I solely am interested. There will be no danger of any want of gratitude
for your kindness on my husband's part."

She held out her hand to him as she spoke, and he did not
neglect to carry it to his lips. " 'No guerdon at your hands
I ask,'" he quoted, without thinking how little the quotation
suited his desire to be especially courteous. " Of course, as
soon as occasion offers, I shall, in spite of the multitude of

such applications that are made to me, do all that I can to fulfil your wishes. You cannot doubt this. May I now ask the name of the promising young man?"

Madame Feinberg smiled sweetly behind her fan. "Of course," she said, "you must know who he is. Do you not guess? Herr von Fuchs possesses every qualification to make him worthy of my recommendation."

Wiesel had suspected who the man was, but he judged it best to feign astonishment. "Herr von Fuchs?" he asked, sitting erect. "The same Herr von Fuchs who——"

"Whom we have introduced to you before, and who accompanies us hither to-day. A most charming young fellow."

"No doubt, no doubt——"

"A cultivated man, who can talk well upon any subject."

"Certainly! But——"

"But?"

Wiesel looked meaningly at the eager lady, and appeared to reflect whether or not to speak out. At last he said, drily, "Do you know the amount of his debts, madame?"

She seemed amazed. "His debts? No."

"Nor do I, madame. And I have little desire to know."

"Herr Councillor——"

"Which, however, does not in the least prevent me from thinking him a most courteous cavalier, and, upon your recommendation, a very talented man."

Again she opened and shut her fan. "And after all, my dear Councillor, what are a few thousands, when the man could not possibly have a very extensive credit——"

Wiesel put his head on one side. "Yes, madame; but if the gentleman with a limited credit has gone so far, what would he do with unlimited credit? If I understand Herr von Fuchs aright, he is one of those who always need more than they possess. Such people are not to be trusted with a great deal, madame."

Madame Feinberg moved uneasily in her chair. " But Sidonie is our only child——" slipped out before she was aware of it.

"Oh, Fräulein Sidonie?" Wiesel exclaimed, apparently all amazement. " Forgive me, madame; I never dreamed——"

" Good heavens! what have I said ?" she interrupted him, actually growing pale. " Forget what I said, Herr Councillor; forget it entirely."

" Be assured of my entire discretion," he replied.

" There is a faint possibility," she said; " nothing more. I do not even know whether Sidonie—but a mother, you know —my eyes are everywhere, of course——"

" Of course, madame," he said, soothingly.

" No one must suspect——"

" No one. I have heard nothing; I know nothing——"

" And if there should be any opening, you will——"

" Hm! hm! Certainly. I should like to show your husband how glad I am to be of service to him, where such service is consistent with my principles." And he bowed low.

Frau Feinberg thanked him with a cordial pressure of his hand. He offered her his arm, and they walked through the garden to the pavilion, where Herr von Fuchs was the life of the little party. Sidonie was very silent. Perhaps she was hiding her own light under a bushel that her companion's might shine all the more brightly.

After a little while the guests took their leave, upon the elder lady's plea that the horses would be tired of standing.

" What did Madame Feinberg want of you?" the Councillor's wife asked her husband, as they walked back from the garden gate to the pavilion.

Wiesel replied by the question, " What do you think of Herr von Fuchs?"

" Oh, he's agreeable enough," she answered, in an indifferent tone. " Why ?"

He half closed his eyes, with a sly expression. "Do you suspect nothing?"

Her attention was roused. "Is there anything to suspect?"

"Yes; but I must not tell."

She began to understand. "What!" she exclaimed,—"this Herr von Fuchs—— ?"

"Will soon be one of the directors of a new stock company, with a salary of five or six thousand thalers, and a large proportion of stock. I am glad you like him. But I must not tell,—you understand, my dear?"

His wife made no reply, but smiled to herself. This was news to occupy her mind.

CHAPTER XXII.

IN the mean while, Moritz Amberger and Professor Schön-rade were labouring together steadily in the old house with the cupola, not only to foil Feinberg's repeated attacks, but also to prepare a crushing blow in return.

The Professor had come just at the right time. True, there was no need of his influence in determining Moritz's decision, —the final breach had been boldly made between the young merchant and Sidonie; the Professor could but confirm his suspicions as to the reason of Sidonie's journey to Berlin, and her attempt, or rather her mother's, to retract her withdrawal from her engagement as soon as she knew herself disappointed with regard to the Professor. Sidonie's written card to the latter was an entire refutation of all slanderous reports concerning Moritz's share in breaking the engagement, and gave him a certain sense of security, since Feinberg was entirely unaware of this evidence, which could be adduced in case of necessity.

The Professor, however, was able to encourage and assist him in his counting-room; the plan that he unfolded to him there was most gratefully received, and the material help that he proffered him tended not a little to restore the self-reliance of the young merchant, who had almost given himself up for lost.

In this last particular it was clearly Schönrade's duty to act with the greatest caution. The Count of Gleichenau had most liberally placed large sums of money at his disposal, but it rested entirely with himself whether or not they should be appropriated to Moritz's use. If bankruptcy could not be averted, they must be held in reserve for some new commercial undertaking. Here were novel and difficult tasks for the man of letters; but he did not evade them. He could not determine how to act without examining and judging for himself.

His practical good sense and his clear analytic brain stood him in good stead. "We must understand matters thoroughly," he said to Moritz, who would have been content with a more superficial examination of his affairs. "We must be sure of every figure if we would secure a firm basis for our operations. However bad your case may be, we ought to know precisely how bad it is; nothing is so unwise as to attempt to gloss over the real state of affairs. If I am to advise you, I must be sure how far my assistance can be of service to you."

Moritz admitted that he was right. He consented to a thorough revision of his books and ledgers, and the two men sat together hard at work, day and night, labouring to throw some light upon statements that had evidently been intentionally made vague and confused. The Professor put himself to school to learn all that there was to be learned of the merchant's trade, and Moritz, his teacher, soon found the advantage of having a pupil whom nothing less than a full and free explanation would satisfy. After forty-eight hours of assiduous application—they scarcely took time either to eat or to sleep—they were able to compare results and strike a kind of balance.

Amberger's case was certainly bad, but it was not quite hopeless. The Professor might feel himself justified in appropriating to his assistance the ready money which the Count had placed at his disposal. Of course it would not suffice for any unexpected misfortune; but there was an equal chance of unforeseen good fortune.

The next few days were full of anxiety. Feinberg opened his campaign on 'Change, after spreading abroad the news that Moritz had no chance of ever becoming his son-in-law. This was quite enough to induce many who knew how dependent Amberger was upon him, and who attached great importance to the friendship of the millionaire, to turn their backs upon the young merchant. Significance was now attached to circumstances before considered quite natural,—as, for instance, the absence from home, first of Philip Amberger, and then of Frau Barbara and her daughter,—doubtless after insuring their own property from all possible harm from commercial fluctuations; some of the wisest were quite sure that the fall from the horse was contrived to arrange for Moritz a hiding-place in the old ruins from which Feinberg had dragged him; he had suddenly dismissed his chief book-keeper in the most insulting manner, to weaken the value of the man's testimony against him; and various other nonsensical statements were made. Of course Feinberg did nothing to gainsay any rumours of the kind.

As soon as he gave the signal on 'Change for the attack, all his associates gathered about him and proffered their services. Every creditor of Amberger clamoured for payment; no one would trust him with money without security more than sufficient. Of course this state of affairs was made public. The house of Amberger had had a reputation for such solidity that many had deposited their savings with the firm ; the counting-house was besieged by people reclaiming their deposits. It required courage indeed to brave the storm.

Feinberg had been sure that Moritz could do so only for a few days. He was mistaken. To his daily-increasing surprise, he redeemed all his paper, returned whatever deposits were reclaimed, and was ready with his payments on 'Change even before they were due. The millionaire and his friends shook their heads; public confidence began to be restored; many who had hastily withdrawn their money brought it back again. Feinberg was in a rage, and sent his brother to Berlin to prepare fresh plots. While he was away, Amberger had the insolence to publish abroad the fact of the unauthorized exchange of stocks,—nay, even to denounce to the authorities, the book-keeper who had effected it, and thus to induce an investigation which might easily compromise Ignaz Feinberg himself. No wonder that he redoubled his efforts to overthrow an opponent whom he could no longer despise.

"We must do nothing by halves," said the Professor. "As soon as the tempest lulls, we must launch our vessel, the cargo of which shall indemnify us for the loss the storm has caused." Moritz, who was in a state of feverish excitement, all the more intense because he was forced to show a smiling countenance to the world, was ready for everything, but wondered whether it would be best for him to begin to purchase houses as if for himself.

"Our chief aim," Schönrade declared, "is to proceed so quickly in the matter as to preclude all possibility of Feinberg's interference. It will do no harm if people do talk. Moritz Amberger certainly cannot be in such desperate straits if he is buying houses." They resolved at last to begin their work simultaneously, and to conclude it as quickly as possible.

The Professor called upon the Burgomaster, an excellent

and honest magistrate, in his own house, informing him that he had expressly avoided going to his office, as he wished to consult him about a matter that must for a time remain a secret. He then disclosed to him that the Freiherr von Höne-burg desired to purchase the meadows and the tile-kiln between the ruin and the green gate, for the purpose of carrying out an industrial project that would be of vast service to the town. He offered to fill up the fosse before the green gate, or to con-struct a wide bridge over it, which should be maintained at his own cost, and to establish a broad, convenient road from the highway to the river, which should be free to all. The magis-trate acknowledged the advantages that would ensue to the community, and accepted the offer. The town-architect was called into council. The Professor did not greatly demur at the rather extravagant price demanded by the owners of the tile-kiln for their land, and matters were soon so far in train that there would shortly be no further need of secrecy.

Meanwhile, Moritz had been negotiating with the owners of the houses and land in the narrow street leading to the green gate. Some of them were quite willing to dispose of their property for a moderate price; but, by the Professor's advice, their offers were not closed with at first, the purchaser stating that he wished to buy a certain number of houses on this street; which they were, should be determined by the terms upon which they were offered. In this way it was easy to learn beforehand whether any opposition was to be met with, —a necessary precaution, since one obstinate landholder would have ruined the whole scheme. The results of this caution were most satisfactory : each householder began to underbid his neighbour in hopes of being preferred, and before a week was over, Moritz owned as many bills of sale as there were houses in the street.

Of course Feinberg heard of these doings. At first he laughed, as at the folly of a man with no head for business.

He supposed facetiously that Amberger wished to divert attention from the public squares, where he was playing so poor a
part, to a side-street. But when he learned that property had
really been purchased, he laughed no more, but set his spies to
work, and soon discovered that some scheme was afloat, which
for the present was to be kept extremely private. " I will lay
a cuckoo-egg in his nest," he thought, and gave orders to buy
one of the houses in the middle of the street. There was not
one for sale : Amberger had purchased them all. Then came
the surprising piece of news that the Professor had purchased
the meadows and the tile-kiln outside of the town for the
Freiherr von Höneburg. It had all been kept so secret that
when he heard of it the transaction was concluded. There
was no doubt, then, that Amberger and Schönrade were acting
in concert. This Professor had suddenly come to be a very
dangerous man.

"And now we can take a little holiday with clear con-
sciences," the Professor said, one afternoon, when the papers
completing their purchases had all been " signed, sealed, and
delivered." " Let us enjoy a little relaxation."

Moritz was overjoyed. At last he should see his Lena
again.

As they walked along the narrow street, they examined their
property. " In a short time," Amberger remarked, " there
will not be one stone upon another here. After a few years the
men who walk along a broad pavement lined with shop-win-
dows in this place will hardly believe that our forefathers and
we ourselves could have been content with so narrow a passage. I am still nervous lest we have reckoned without our
host, and should have difficulty with the government about
our charter.

" That is my father's affair," said the Professor ; " we may
rest assured, I think, on that point."

They walked through the archway towards the bridge, and

Schönrade, looking up, called attention to the wide slit where the portcullis had formerly hung. "Those were odd times," he said, pausing for a moment, "when they kept that thing there ready to crash down upon the skull of any Freiherr von Höneburg who should dare to ride beneath it."

Moritz laughed. "And now some peaceful mason, with his pickaxe, will destroy it and throw it stone by stone into the fosse. We must have a good photograph taken of it first."

"It is perfectly certain, is it not," inquired the Professor, suddenly turning to him, "that this old gate belongs to the fosse and to the bridge, and can of course be pulled down by the town? Nothing has been said about that."

"To the fosse and to the bridge?" Amberger repeated, surprised. "I think not."

"What?"

"The gate belongs, I think, to the Köstling house there; the bridge only is the town's, and the public has the right of way through the gate."

Schönrade thrust his cane into the ground. "The gate is private property, and this is the first I hear of it?"

"But I thought——"

"A fatal error. Of what use will the meadow and the street be to us if we do not own the gate?"

"But the gate is worthless to its owner. He will surely be delighted to have us pull it down and open a view from his windows of a broad road and the railway buildings. I took it for granted there could be no difficulty there."

"My dear friend——!" The Professor shook his head and looked anxious. "We never ought to take anything for granted in such matters. Worthless or not, we need a consent here that is as likely to be withheld as to be accorded. If I had dreamed that this gate belonged to a private house——"

"We are quite in time for all that," said Amberger, impatiently pursuing his way. "I know old Köstling. It was not worth while to go to him until everything else is settled."

Schönrade did not stir. "Matters of such importance should not be postponed an hour longer than is absolutely necessary," he said. "Let us go to Herr Köstling immediately."

"Not now!" Moritz exclaimed, dismayed at the prospect of any longer delay. "The old man admits no one at this hour, —I know that. He is very eccentric, but good-natured and amiable enough if you do not attempt to transgress his rules. How could he possibly object to the tearing down of that ugly old gateway? It is the merest formality to ask his consent. Do not spoil our delightful evening. I will attend to it to-morrow."

The Professor hesitated. "Are you sure that we should not be admitted at this hour?" he asked. "I hoped to go to Berlin to-morrow to report upon the affair, and to have nothing left to settle. My father wrote me that the railway project could no longer be kept a secret, and I answered him in good faith that the application for a charter might be officially made to the government. Suppose it should be made before we are sure of matters here?"

Amberger repeated his assurance that there was nothing to fear, took his arm, and tried to lead him on. "This is folly," Schönrade declared. "We have the whole evening before us; why delay this matter of business?" He turned round and drew Moritz with him to the corner formed by the Köstling house and the wall of the gateway. The steps were broad and much worn. "It has not always been so quiet and deserted here as now," the Professor remarked, tapping them with his cane.

After they had rung several times, the door opened only just far enough to allow the head of an old woman to peer out. "What do the gentlemen want?" a harsh voice inquired.

"Herr Professor Schönrade, from Berlin, wishes to see Herr Köstling," Moritz explained. "Pray announce us, Frau Lutter. My friend leaves town to-morrow."

The old woman glanced at the stranger. "The master is in the garden," she replied. "Herr Amberger knows that I dare not disturb him there."

"But my business is urgent," the Professor rejoined. "Perhaps you will make an exception——"

"No business is so urgent that it cannot wait a single day," she replied, composedly. "The gentleman may be in a hurry, but we are not."

"Will you not ask?"

"There is nothing to ask. I know my duty, and it is plain enough. To-morrow noon, gentlemen, to-morrow." And the door was shut in their faces.

"There! was I right?" Moritz asked, triumphantly.

"At any rate, I shall not have to reproach myself with procrastination," said the Professor, slowly descending the steps with downcast looks.

As they were crossing the bridge they saw Herr Köstling taking his walk in his garden. The cats were following him as before, waving their tails and now and then humping their backs. "I greatly fear," the Professor remarked, in a low tone, "that that eccentricity will not be easily managed. I mistrust a lover of cats: he is always apt to partake of their nature."

"He is not a bad old fellow," Moritz said, confidently, "only you must know how to deal with him, and not intrude upon him when he wishes to be alone. Hermits have strange tastes. Cats are always the special favourites of old maids, are they not? And why should not old bachelors prefer them too?"

"Has he never been married?"

"No. There is some story of an unhappy love-affair; but no one really knows anything about it. I have never known him except as we see him to-day. I believe he is hardly sixty, yet he looks as old as Methuselah." He began to whistle a merry tune; with every step he grew gayer and more restless. The thought of seeing Lena again would have driven any anxious care from his mind, and, after the hard labour of the last week, his cares were no longer very anxious. Sanguine as he was, the relief from his entanglements and the prospect of a few happy hours were enough to flood all his future with rosy light. The green gateway might have been far narrower and gloomier than it was, without depressing his spirits.

He induced his friend, who was still grave and thoughtful, not to pursue the direct path to the Vogelstein garden, but to make a détour and come upon it from behind, so as to surprise the inmates of the ruins. They reached the bridge unobserved, and Moritz sang out boldly a trumpet summons, that served to rouse Nero instantly. His violent barking was silenced, however, as soon as he recognized his friends.

" Who is there ?" Lena's voice inquired.

" Open, trusty châtelaine !" Moritz called out. " The young Freiherr von Hüneburg approaches, and asks admittance through me, his faithful squire."

The castle gate flew open. " Welcome, Herr Freiherr !" Lena exclaimed, with a beaming smile. " Is it really so ?"

" It is really so," Schönrade assented ; " but pray do not drop the Herr Professor."

" Have you no word for me ?" Moritz asked, holding out his hand. " Heaven knows I wanted to come far more than he did !"

" I am not sure of that," she said, blushing, and casting down her eyes.

Grandfather Vogelstein received with a respectful air a letter from the Count von Gleichenau, and broke the seal on the spot. " At last ! at last !" he said, and a tear rolled down his furrowed cheek. " And you, honoured sir, are really his son ?"

" And your very devoted friend, my good Vogelstein," the Professor replied, shaking him warmly by the hand.

Moritz and Lena had strayed off together. The widow Vogelstein hastened to make preparations for a supper worthy of the guests, and Schönrade, with the old gardener, went up to his mother's room, where he took possession of the papers and letters to which he had now established his right. He informed the old man of all that had occurred, and of the changes that were to take place in the neighbourhood of the ruins. They were to be left as they were, he assured him,— a memorial of a warlike age happily gone forever. He offered him a responsible post in the new railway-depôt; but Vogelstein refused this, preferring, he said, old as he was, to remain a simple gardener in charge of the old place. He could not weary of asking questions about his old master, the present Count von Gleichenau, and Camilla. Nor could he be made to understand why they had never met since the son had found his father.

Before the hour preceding supper had elapsed, Moritz and Lena had come to a thorough understanding, and the summons to partake of the evening meal found them sitting on the bench beneath the trees, hand locked in hand, and beaming with happiness,—a happiness so evident that as soon as they appeared at the table the Professor asked, in a loud tone, " May I not congratulate ?"

" Indeed you may," Moritz answered, greatly relieved. " Grandfather Vogelstein, and you too, Frau Vogelstein, Lena loves me, and I ask her at your hands."

The old man was really surprised, and Frau Vogelstein considered it her duty to seem so. The Professor came to the rescue of the party, imprinting the kiss of a future brother-in-law upon Lena's hand; then, filling up the glasses of all with Rhine wine, he proposed the health of the newly-betrothed couple. " God bless you, my children !" the old man said,

N*

with much emotion, and tears of maternal pride sparkled in his daughter-in-law's eyes, although she did not forget to remind all present that their supper was getting cold.

A second bottle of wine was brought up from the castle cellar, and the happy party did not separate until late in the night.

The moon was high in the heavens as the friends took leave of one another on the bridge. " I should like to go with you across the moor," said Lena, " if my grandfather will let me."

" Do," said Moritz, eagerly; " and I will escort you back again."

" Stop !" exclaimed the Professor. " Another time you can try how long it will take you to reach town after that zigzag fashion. To-night I play Wallenstein to your Max and Thekla. You must part !"

Moritz sighed. " Till we meet, then !"

As the two men passed through the green gate, Schönrade said, " I must leave to-morrow afternoon, and all this matter must be arranged first."

" What ?" Moritz asked, as if awaking from a dream. " Oh, yes," he added, recollecting himself. " Yes, indeed. To-morrow forenoon. 'Twill not take long."

" If only——" the Professor muttered to himself. He could not feel at ease beneath the shadow of the narrow archway.

When Amberger returned the next day from a lengthened visit to Herr Köstling, there was not a trace in his countenance of his former confidence.

" Well ?" the Professor asked, eagerly.

" Deuce take it !" Moritz exclaimed. " Old Köstling will make us trouble."

" Trouble ?"

" He refuses to have one stone of the old gate touched !"

Schönrade uttered an exclamation of dismay, and struck the table with his hand. " I thought so !"

CHAPTER XXIII.

ɪɴ the Palazzo Bellarota, as well as in the Höneburg, there ⟨ʷᵃˢ⟩ a happy betrothed pair; and it is quite necessary to the levelopment of this veracious history that the two lovers should be brothers, their two loves near relatives, and that there should be certain relations between the Palazzo Bella- rota and the Höneburg, all centring in the person of a com- mon friend. Most extraordinary combinations and revelations, those will declare who think their own lives as full of inci- dent as is natural. But if this were so, the story-teller's prov- ince would be greatly contracted.

Philip's love for the beautiful Lucia so transformed the man that he pleaded his cause with an eager confidence quite foreign to his nature; and he must have pleaded well, for Lucia un- derstood him in spite of his imperfect Italian, and consented to leave her native country for his sake. Her mother hesi- tated, at first, to resign her only child, lest the " Signor Am- bergero" should not be all he represented himself; but her husband easily satisfied her doubts: he knew well enough the consideration in which his countryman was held at home, and that his daughter would be well cared for.

At first Philip had no thoughts of ever carrying his bride to Germany. It seemed to him far better to stay in sunny Florence; Lucia could not be at home, he thought, beneath those gray northern skies and among his formal countrymen. He liked always to see her in the little room with the dark carved wainscoting, where he had visited her first, and would often induce her to stand upon the threshold, as he had then beheld her. He made acquaintance with a very clever painter, occupied in copying at the Uffizi, and engaged him upon a picture of Lucia, which, as it progressed, was strikingly like some masterpiece of the Venetian school of art in the six-teenth century.

To be sure, Moritz's letters, although they by no means revealed the whole truth, caused him some anxiety, and sug-gested a question whether he were justified in withdrawing his share from the business, and so adding to his brother's per-plexity. Philip was no business man, but he had sufficient understanding of business matters to see that some peril was impending, which it was a partner's duty to help to avert. As he was about to incur new responsibilities, he could not but take a more practical view of life. Moritz ought not to be left to do all the work ; he felt that he must put his own shoulder to the wheel, at least until he could see his way clear to retire from the firm without injury to the business, and live upon his means. Florence or Rome was the goal of his desires, but he gradually came to be reconciled and to reconcile Lucia to a sojourn in his native country before this goal could be reached. He would make it as short as he could, he told her for her consolation.

At all events, as much of the Palazzo Bellarota as could be transported without inordinate cost should be carried across the Alps. The wainscoting of Lucia's room could certainly be transferred thither. There was a room in the old house by the hill of about the same size and height, he remembered. If this exquisite carving could be set up there, the windows hung with old tapestry, and the room filled with Lucia's fur-niture, she would feel really at home. The young people were both delighted with this plan ; they examined the carving closely to find how to divide it into small pieces with least injury to the beauty of the work. Signor Uccello's consent was easily gained. Although he had formerly branded the whole room as " stupid rubbish," he began now to affect the air of a connoisseur to enhance the value of his gift, reckoning it as part of Lucia's dowry. "There will be nothing finer of the kind in Germany," said he.

Philip's surprise was not all pleasure when, one day, there was brought him from the great hotel "Italia" a note in which Frau Barbara Amberger announced her arrival in Florence.

He knew that she was travelling, but he had had no idea that she would seek him out. The Professor's letter to Katrine he had smuggled to her at Munich, whence he had supposed his mother had intended visiting the Salzkammergut. Since then he had not heard from her, and he readily guessed the reason for this. Certain hints in his own letters had not pleased her. He thought he knew why she had come, and hastened to her, not without some trepidation.

Her reception of him was, as he had anticipated, rather cool. "I have come for you, Philip," she said. "You seem to have forgotten that you have a home."

"The ties that keep me here are stronger than you think, mother dear," he said, resolved to come to a speedy understanding

"I trust," she rejoined, sternly, "that you do not contemplate lightly assuming serious responsibilities——"

He immediately interrupted her. "Gravely assuming the most serious, mother, and I beg to be allowed to present my future bride to you."

Thus at their first meeting dissension arose between mother and son, which Katrine vainly attempted to soothe by begging them at least to take pleasure in seeing each other again, after so long a separation. Frau Barbara's pride was too deeply wounded by her son's betrothal to an "innkeeper's daughter." "My children conduct themselves after a most extraordinary fashion!" she exclaimed; "my daughter has a secret understanding with a schoolmaster, and my son falls in love in an inn. What would your father have said? But I will not suffer it; I have some right to speak,

26

and I will see whether my children love and honour their mother."

" There is no doubt on that score," Philip said, " even although we obey independently the dictates of our hearts. I am pledged, and my word is sacred ; but even were it not so already, I confess it would make no difference with me, for Lucia is worthy to be the choice of an honourable man, and other than an honourable man I do not desire to be."

Frau Barbara had never heard her gentle Philip speak thus before. He, formerly the most docile of her children, suddenly seemed to ignore her sway entirely. She grew angry —she forbade—she scolded—she entreated : in vain.

" Only see my Lucia," was his reply.

" I will not see her !" she exclaimed. " I will leave here to-morrow. Do not have our trunks unpacked, Katharina,—we are going away immediately." This threat was also fruitless.

" I have no power to keep you here," her son said, " but consider, it will be regarded as a positive insult if you refuse even to see my future bride. You will never be able to avoid seeing my wife, for I shall assuredly take her to our home."

" Then you will compel your mother to leave it," she replied,—not, however, with all her former decision.

He went up to her and put his arm around her. " Be kind, mother dear," he entreated ; " you will not refuse to see and judge whether your Philip has chosen well? You may be so happy in your children's love ! Do not spoil their chief pleasure in life !"

His tenderness so far soothed her that she listened to what particulars he had to tell of his love, of the worldly estate of his future father-in-law, and of Moritz's letters,—little reassuring as they were. Frau Barbara was certainly glad that the engagement with Sidonie was broken, but she was not at all pleased at the tone in which Moritz spoke of the Professor, calling him his only friend in need. She could not imagine the need, or how the Professor could come to be of assistance as a friend.

But it was most welcome news to Katrine. She had exchanged no letters with her lover for several weeks ; and she now learned that he had been busy indirectly in her interest. The first minute that she could speak privately to Philip, she begged him to tell the Professor where she was, and to assure him of her unalterable regard.

" Why not write to him yourself, child ?" Philip asked.

Her face beamed : it was too much for her principles. " Oh, will you take charge of the letter ? And perhaps he may write a few lines to you———"

" Of course, of course. Only write ; I'll take care of the rest."

" But our mother ?"

" It is our mother's fault if we have to plot and contrive. I trust she will forgive us by-and-by."

He pondered whether a surprise might not operate in his favour. Lucia, to whom he of course painted his mother in a most favourable light, declared herself quite ready to pay her a first visit. Philip had no fear that in his mother's presence she would meet with want of courtesy. Frau Barbara was polite under all circumstances. It suddenly struck him that he might prepare her for the surprise after a fashion that would deepen its effect. " Let us postpone the visit until to-morrow forenoon," he said. " There is no need to be in a hurry. When my mother has seen something of Florence and its sights, she will be more in sympathy with its inhabitants."

He betook himself again to the Hôtel Italia, and invited his mother and sister, if they were sufficiently rested, to take a walk with him. Frau Barbara's mood seemed more encouraging, and she said nothing further of leaving immediately. She took her son's arm, and he conducted them along some

of the finest and most interesting streets in Florence.   His
mother was soon tired.   " Why not drive ?" she asked.

" Because we lose half the beauty of the place when we go
along so swiftly," said he.   " Let us rest in the nearest café, or
—stay,—we are close by the atelier of an artist friend of mine.
He has a charming picture upon his easel just at present;
would you not like to see it ?   It is by some sixteenth-cen-
tury artist, and has lately been discovered in the attic of an
old palazzo, where it has lain for more than a century, and has
been admirably restored.   It has created quite a sensation,
and, in the style of the painting, will remind you of the portrait at home of our ancestor, Jacobus Amberger, sheriff in
our good town in the time of the Danish war.   That must
have been the work of some Venetian artist upon his travels.
We are very near the atelier, and you can admire the picture,
which is a great favourite of mine, until you are thoroughly
rested."

Frau Barbara was interested in his description, and followed
his lead willingly.

The ladies were shown into the atelier, and Philip gave his
friend, the artist, a hint to be silent.   Lucia's picture, which
stood against the wall all ready for packing, was hastily placed
upon the easel, and the light arranged.

Frau Barbara sat down opposite it in a large arm-chair,
Katrine stood beside her, and Philip and the artist took their
places near the easel.   The group made an excellent genre
picture.   The young girl was lost in admiration ; the elder
lady murmured, " Lovely,—very lovely,—most beautiful in
deed !"   And Philip smiled contented.

" Which do you so much admire ?" he asked his mother:
" the execution or the subject of the picture ?"

" Oh, both ! both !" she said, eagerly.   " The colouring is
exquisite, the tone so pure.   When we remember that it has
been painted for hundreds of years——"

" It is far more like a beautiful copy of an old painting or a successful imitation of the Venetian school," Katrine continued her mother's remark. " I think if you could compare it with other old pictures——"

" You doubt its genuineness?" Philip asked.

" I have no right to do so; and yet there is something— something—I cannot explain myself perfectly, but I have a sensation in looking at it as if I might meet this very girl in the street to-day, and the old portraits that I have seen before do not impress me thus at all."

The artist did not understand German. Philip translated for him what his sister had said, and he smiled significantly.

Frau Barbara did not agree with her daughter.

" The picture is only admirably restored. We ought to send our old portrait to this artist: it would be greatly improved." She regarded the picture still more attentively. " This young girl is exquisitely beautiful. We rarely see such beauty in our time. Not that we do not see beautiful girls and women nowadays, but they seldom possess that distinguished air, that refined grace, which characterizes this portrait."

Philip with difficulty retained his gravity.

" She must have been of an ancient line," his mother continued. " You can see that in her whole carriage. The dress, to be sure, is not very costly,—of some blue woollen stuff, if I see rightly ; but the chain about the neck, and the lace ruff, give style to its simplicity. I should never tire of looking at that lovely face, that graceful figure."

Philip asked, " Shall I buy the picture, then, mother?"

" Oh, the price will be too high."

" I think not; it is the property of my friend the artist here, and he will let me have it quite reasonably. We had better secure it."

Frau Amberger was much pleased.

"We shall be envied the possession of this treasure at home," she said.

"I should rather have the original," said Philip.

"The original? You said——"

"I mean the signora herself."

"Oh, the signora herself," his mother repeated, with a smile. "Yes; I should be glad of such a daughter-in-law."

Philip shrugged his shoulders and sighed, glancing meaningly at Katrine, who did not seem entirely convinced. He thanked the artist for his trouble, and then left the studio, conducting the ladies to their hotel by a roundabout way past the Palazzo Bellarota. He could not help saying, as they passed it, "This is the building where the painting was found. It is now a hotel."

His mother merely glanced up at it; but Katrine exclaimed, noticing the marble figures at the entrance, "There are the men with the ornamental circlets of which——"

Philip turned to her and put his finger on his lips. "You will have an opportunity soon, I hope, of observing them more closely."

He was quite satisfied with the success of his ruse, and looked forward eagerly to the visit to be paid the next day. Lucia, by his desire, was dressed in the blue gown in which she had been painted.

"Wait one moment," he said to her when they had mounted to the door of his mother's room in the Hôtel Italia: "I will announce you: it will only take a moment." He knocked at the door and entered, standing near it, hat in hand. "A lady of Florence wishes to see you, dearest mother," he said to her. "May she come in?"

She looked at him in surprise. "A lady of Florence—— Me? I know none here."

"Oh, yes, you do! You will soon see that."

Her face grew dark. "Philip, I cannot believe——"

" What ?"

" That you would force me to receive——"

" Only see her."

He threw the door wide open, and Lucia appeared upon the threshold. Frau Barbara started in absolute terror, gazing at her visitor as at some apparition. " But that is——" she stammered.

" Signora Lucia Uccello,—my Lucia ; the loveliest and the best girl in Florence."

He took her hand and led her forward. " Did the artist flatter her ?"

His mother could hardly yet understand. " I never should have thought——!" she murmured. " There is certainly a most striking resemblance to the old picture !"

" For which she sat," Philip said, with a laugh.

Lucia, who did not understand this reception, looked embarrassed.

" Is this your mother ?" she asked.

" My mother ; my sister. I will tell you by-and-by why they look so amazed."

Katrine put a stop to a scene that was beginning to grow painful, by hastening to embrace Lucia.

" We saw your picture yesterday," she explained. " Philip played a little trick upon us——"

" And my mother was enchanted with so much beauty and grace," he completed her sentence. " I hope, mother dear, the original will please you even better than the painted presentment."

" But I thought the portrait in the studio was an old painting," she said, still confused.

Philip took her hand. " You cannot but be glad," he said, gaily, although with inward trepidation, " that my love is not three hundred years old."

" Your love ?"

" Receive her as such, mother dear. You cannot find in the world a daughter-in-law who will love your son more truly, or who will be more devotedly loved by him."

Frau Barbara appeared to perceive that all further opposition would be useless, and held it wisest, under such circumstances, to yield with a good grace. She did not withdraw her hand when Philip placed Lucia's within it, but drew the beautiful girl towards her and kissed her brow.

" I cannot tell whether you understand my German, my child," she said, as an excuse for her hesitation.

Lucia assured her that she understood her father's native tongue, and that, in a short time, she hoped to express herself in it with ease.

" I pray you to be patient with me for awhile, dear madame," she added. " I shall surely learn quickly, for Philip's sake."

This pleased Frau Barbara. She stroked Lucia's cheek, and led her to the sofa.

" I frankly admit," she said, " that I have been vexed with my son for seeking a wife in a hotel. It is a fortunate accident that——"

" Are not marriages made in heaven?" he interrupted her. " Do not let us speak of accident, but of Providence. Eh, Katrine? Providence takes care of us."

" Take care," his mother said; " do not speak too lightly." But the tone of her reproof was gentle; now that she had resolved to make the best of it all, she was glad to open her heart to her new daughter, with whom she was more and more pleased. At the end of the visit, an appointment was made for the next day, to see together the wonders of Florence. " The most curious and interesting of Florentine relics is the Palazzo Bellarota," Philip assured his mother gratefully, kissing her hand, " which I discovered myself."

Frau Amberger understood him, and presented herself duly

there the next day. She found in Signor Uccello a man who, as she was forced to own, in spite of his being "an inn-keeper," was by no means to be despised, and the preliminaries of the marriage were soon settled. It was to take place sooner than had been at first proposed, in order that the mother and sister of the bridegroom might honour it with their presence.

Of course the removal of the wainscoting of Lucia's room was immediately undertaken. Frau Barbara, who privately counted the cost of transportation, scarcely approved; but Philip was fired with the idea of reproducing her southern home for his bride in the land to which he was about to carry her, and heeded no remonstrance. A skilful cabinet-maker was employed to loosen all the carving from the wall and pack it safely. The work went bravely on, until a certain panel, in the middle of the wall opposite the windows, resisted the efforts of the workman to loosen it. Additional force was used, and it was so far stirred from its place as to allow of a peep behind it. "I see what is the matter," said the workman: "there is a little wooden cupboard built into the wall, firmly connected with the panel." Philip admitted that he was right.

"That cupboard must have had some practical use," he said. "It must have been opened from the room. Let us find the door." They examined the panel minutely; in vain. "There is some secret lock," the cabinet-maker declared, "purposely concealed by the florid carving. They were very skilful in such work in those days. I am sure some spot, some projection, is movable; we have only to find where it is to come upon the means of opening the cupboard." This, however, was no easy task.

The two men pressed, pushed, and turned every projection in the carving, to no purpose. Lucia brought a light and examined slowly every figure, to discover some clue to the

mystery. " It seems to me," said the workman, with whom
it was a point of honour not to be baffled, "that one of the
cheeks of this Eve, who is gazing up at the coveted apple, is
smoother than the other parts of the figure, and her necklace
of berries is suspicious too; a joint might be hidden there, and
the whole head turn like a rosette. May I use a little force?"
Philip, whose curiosity was greatly excited, assented; but for a
long time all their endeavors were without result. They were
just on the point of giving up this spot as hopeless, when an
accidental pressure pushed the whole head below the surface of the rest of the carving, and it was there easily slipped
aside, revealing a key-hole. Every key to be had was tried
in vain. A locksmith who was called in found it impossible
to unlock it with a pick-lock. It could not be forced without
injury to the carving. " Let us preserve the panel intact,"
said Philip; " the cupboard is not of much consequence; it is
probably quite empty, and certainly cannot contain a treasure.
Those who knew how to open it doubtless took good care to
remove its contents."

The cabinet-maker said there was no reason why the cupboard could not be taken out of the wall: it was less securely
fastened there than to the panel. This was attempted, and
with success,—the whole cupboard was removed from the wall.

When, after its removal, they shook it to and fro, it was
plain enough that there was something inside that changed its
place with the motion. The desire to see what this was took
possession of the whole party, including Signor Uccello and
his wife, and Frau Barbara and Katrine. " Let us open the
cabinet at the back," said Philip, " even if we have to use the
saw."

"That is what I must do," replied the cabinet-maker; " the
work is so admirable."

The by-standers encouraged him to make no delay; the saw
was put to use, and in a few moments the board at the back

of the cupboard fell to the ground. Every one pressed forward to see what the thing contained.

Within lay a roll of paper and a leathern purse. The latter was scarcely half full. Its contents poured out upon the table elicited a simultaneous " Ah !" from all present. They consisted of various articles of jewelry, precious stones, rings, buttons, seals, chains, etc., of gold. Upon several of the rings and seals was cut the same device that was to be found everywhere in the palazzo,—a richly-ornamented wheel. " Here we have the inheritance of the Bellarotas !" Philip exclaimed, eagerly. " Oh, if the Professor were only here ! He would believe me now. I never had the smallest doubt about it in my own mind."

He unrolled the papers and looked over them while the rest were busy with the contents of the purse. " Here is an important discovery for some people," he said, after awhile, holding up a sheet of manuscript. " All these manuscripts have reference to the Bellarota family. Here is a genealogical tree, bringing the name down to a certain Annibale Bellarota, ducal chamberlain, who died about a hundred years ago ; and then we have the baptismal certificates of his son Pietro and his grandson Carlo. If I remember rightly, Professor Schönrade told me those were the names of his mother's father and grandfather ; yes, it was Pietro who was imprisoned for political offences, and died in confinement. Schönrade's mother has a missal, bequeathed by him to his son Carlo, in which his name is written by his own hand. Good heavens ! and in this paper he mentions that his imprisonment is certain, that his death is probable, that he can bequeath to his son Carlo nothing beyond these few family relics, since all that he possessed has been spent for political aims. Perhaps his son may one day amass fortune sufficient to re-purchase the old family estate. ' But,' he concludes, ' my time is short. I shall take with me the missal that belonged to the man who, in happier days, adorned this palazzo with many works of art, and who contrived this secret repository. No one knows that under the movable boss on the cover of this book, that apparently serves only to confine in its place the ivory head of Christ, lies the little key to this small receptacle. They cannot refuse to promise me that after my death this book, from which I shall derive consolation in my last hours, shall be sent to my son Carlo,—my only legacy to my well-beloved son,—and they will keep the promise, for the legacy is valueless. God grant you a happier life, my Carlo, than mine has been!'

"Carlo must have been elsewhere at this time, and perhaps his father had no opportunity of revealing to him the mystery of the cover of the missal; the key may still be concealed there. It would then be proved beyond a doubt that the Carlo Bellarota who was a singer in Germany and died there in want was the Bellarota to whose baptism this certificate testifies,—Pietro's son, Annibale's grandson——"

"Xaver's grandfather," Katharina interrupted him. "Oh if Camilla learns this——!"

"What,—what,—what?" Frau Barbara asked, eagerly. "Xaver! yes, it must be Professor Schönrade who said he was a Bellarota,—yes. And he is really descended from the ancient family who owned this crest? Can it be so?"

"It seems certain," said Philip. "He himself takes very little interest in such matters, but his mother attaches great importance to them; and who knows what may come of this unexpected discovery?"

"Who knows, indeed?" Katrine observed. "If Professor Schönrade does not care for it, this baptismal certificate may be very useful to the Freiherr von Höneburg."

Her mother looked at her in amazement. "The Freiherr von Höneburg? What has he——"

"Oh, I ought not to have said it!" the girl exclaimed, ter-

rified at what she had done; " but the words came before I
thought, and it cannot be a secret much longer. Xaver
was too proud to tell you this after you had repulsed him.
Camilla Bellarota is the divorced wife of the Freiherr von
Höneburg, and Xaver is his son, the son of the present Count
Gleichenau."

" And you have never said one word of all this to me,
—your mother?" Frau Barbara exclaimed, in great agitation.

" I was forbidden to speak, dearest mother. Perhaps Xaver
could not enter into explanations as yet, and then he hoped
to win you over to his side without them."

" Yes! yes!" the offended lady declared. " I am sure of
nothing; he might have persuaded me to give my only child
to a Professor,—it is possible. But if he really has the
right to call himself Freiherr von Höneburg, if his mother
is the grandchild of this noble Pietro Bellarota,—why—I am
quite bewildered."

" You mean, dearest mother," said Philip, " that you will
no longer refuse to listen to the dictates of your kind heart,
that you will approve Katrine's choice, and that I may write
to my friend——"

" Stop! stop!" she interrupted him; " not too fast. I shall
wait and see whether the Freiherr von Höneburg asks me for
my daughter. If he does,—why—then, indeed, I will forget
that we have ever met before."

Katrine threw her arms around her and kissed her. She
did not repulse her, but looked grave, and said, " For all that,
you are an obstinate, naughty girl."

" At all events, the Professor must have these papers," said
Philip. " I will write to him, to Berlin, this very night. Who
will send him a message?" He looked, as he spoke, at Katrine; but she made no reply, except by a look of arch entreaty
at her mother.

" Well, I have no objection," Frau Barbara agreed, with a
o

smile. "It is fitting that I should congratulate him upon the discovery. But say nothing else."

"I will take care of all that," said Philip, as he kissed her. "Had we not better invite him to the wedding?"

"Oh, that would be delightful!" Katrine exclaimed, with sparkling eyes.

"Signor Uccello and his wife are the persons to decide that matter," Frau Barbara declared, quite formally, and there the conversation ended.

CHAPTER XXIV.

IF the Professor had only suspected the contents of the letter that the post was bringing to him across the Brenner, he would certainly have been less depressed, or, at least, have dismissed his cares for awhile. Now he could not forgive Moritz for his want of caution with regard to the green gate, and he was still more provoked with himself for his negligence in being uninformed upon the subject. The gate barred the street: it must come down, or the whole project of opening a free entrance to the city on this side was a failure. A long row of houses had been purchased, a vast amount of capital expended to no purpose, and the money had been intrusted to him by his father, who had a right to exact prudence and caution in its use. More than that, the Count had already made application to the government for the charter, and he would be heavily compromised if he could not keep his promises.

To a man like Schönrade, the idea of failure through any fault of his own was intolerable. "We must not despair," he said to Moritz. "I will try what can be done with Herr Köstling. I ought to have gone to him before."

Moritz looked incredulous as to his success, but made no reply. He was greatly depressed, and disposed to forebode the worst. Köstling's refusal had been so decided that he dared not hope he would change his mind. His answer would have been the same, he was convinced, if they had gone to him at first; but then, to be sure, much time, trouble, and money would have been saved.

So Professor Schönrade presented his card to the old house-keeper, whom we know, in the house by the fosse, and waited for a long time before he was told that the master was ready to receive him. He was shown through several darkened rooms, furnished after the fashion of a bygone day, decorated with mirrors made in many small pieces, and huge glass chan-deliers, till he found the old man in a small apartment over-looking the garden, the windows of which were almost entirely obscured by dark curtains. It seemed to be the only inhab-ited room, for in a back corner stood a bed, beside it a set of book-shelves, and a sofa covered with black hair-cloth ; and where a single ray of sunlight was allowed to penetrate stood a writing-table. Chairs with carved feet and high backs stood stiff against the walls, which were hung with family portraits so blackened with age, for the most part, that white ruffs and yellowish faces were all that could be distinguished of them. On the window-seat beside which stood the writing-table, the two cats sat opposite each other, immovable as Egyptian sphinxes; they might have been stuffed.

Herr Köstling surveyed the visitor with a look of mingled surprise and suspicion. "I do not know whether you really desired to speak with me, Herr Professor," he said. in a low, grating voice ; "but sit down. From Berlin, I believe,—from Berlin. Am I righ ?"

"I occupy a chair in the university there," the Professor replied, unable to master a certain uncomfortable sensation, but speaking with force l calmness. "My speciality is natural science, geology in particular. I am not here, however, in the interest of science, but partly of friendship. In brief, I am betrothed to Katharina Amberger, and am of course anxious to assist Moritz Amberger in certain undertakings, which are approved by my Berlin friends, and upon the success of which much depends. May I explain what they are?"

This question was justified, for at the mention of Amberger's name Herr Köstling had turned away, and his brow had contracted in such a heavy frown that it might well be doubted whether he wished to hear more. "As you please, as you please," he said, crossly; "but if you come on the same errand that brought Herr Moritz Amberger here yesterday, about the gate adjoining my house, you may spare your pains. Never, never, never!"

This did not sound encouraging. "Let me explain the matter to you, at all events," the guest entreated: "perhaps you may see it from a new point of view——"

"There is only one point of view for me," the old man interrupted him. "The gate belongs to me, and I will not give it up to be removed,—I *will* not."

"I am ready to offer a very high price for the old relic," the Professor said, half as if to himself. "Name a sum."

Köstling laughed aloud,—so loud that the two cats, as if surprised at the unwonted sound, turned their heads and pricked up their ears. "A very high price!" he exclaimed. "What does that mean? A price that far exceeds its real value? Of course. What real value does the thing possess? To look at, it is but a heap of old stones and mortar. How many times would you multiply its value to make a very high price? How many times?"

"It is not the gate which is of value," the Professor replied, "but the spot on which it stands. Its value is relative."

Köstling drew his head down between the points of his high

collar, as into a snail-shell. " What do I care for that? I am
a man who has really no wants, with money enough to gratify
even an extravagant love of pleasure. I have neither father,
mother, brother, sister, wife, nor child; I am alone in the world.
This huge house is empty. I live in this one room, my stom-
ach is content with the most frugal fare, my books are so good
that I can always read them anew, my garden supplies me with
more fruit than I want, and my friends there," and he pointed
to the two cats, " are as easily satisfied as myself. What good
would some thousands more thalers do us? We have too
much already." His voice grew lower. " Alone in the world,
—alone !"

Schönrade felt that nothing was to be gained in this direction. " Well, then," he said, " for the sake of the common
good, give up a possession that is of no possible use to you,
but which is in the way of an enterprise that will be of the
greatest benefit to the town. Herr Moritz Amberger was not
empowered to make known to you our plans, but I will not
hesitate to communicate them to you. Listen to me quietly
for a few minutes." He then explained with great clearness
the plan for the proposed railway, and showed the necessity
there was for a wide road to the new depot. " Every obstacle
is removed," he concluded, " except the old gate. Give your
consent to its destruction, and you will confer a benefit which
must give you also satisfaction."

Köstling had closed his eyes; now he opened them, as if to
see whether the Professor had finished. " Do you think so?"
he asked, in a drawling tone. " Even if all you say is correct,
what do I gain by the change? A noisy street before my
house, above my quiet garden a bridge groaning and creaking
all day with passing freight-wagons, and a railway-depot not
very far off, where locomotives are whistling and shrieking all
day and all night. I love quiet, solitude, and seclusion; everything that I may still call pleasure depends upon the gratifica-

tion of this desire of mine for repose. And you would have me—— Oh, let us say no more about it!"

There was a strange melancholy in his words. Although they certainly were not intended to move compassion, they nevertheless did so. "I perfectly understand," the Professor said, gently, "how little sympathy you can have with our undertaking. But when you reflect upon its real importance, does it not seem to you culpable egotism to prevent so great a work, simply that you may secure for yourself a quiet room and a peaceful garden? If you will take this into consideration——"

"Egotism!" the old man interrupted him. "Yes, I am an egotist; but I have a better right to be one than you and all the others who fill the world with clamour that they may enrich themselves,—yes, to enrich themselves. It is their only aim, however they may gloss it over with fine phrases. I am an egotist, for I have nothing but myself, and want nothing but for myself, in the world. I have been left entirely alone; what have I to love save myself? Whom have I to cherish save myself? Who, save myself, is there to expend a thought upon me? Look up at these walls. Those are my ancestors,—and I am the last. My race perishes with me. I have no future; the past alone is mine. Leave me, then, what belongs to the past; a part of life that can still gladden these old eyes. I do not wish to die while my body still lives."

The Professor shuddered involuntarily. What had been this man's life, to have induced such a state of mind? He did not know how to reply.

"The old gate!" Köstling continued, after a moment, lifting his head a little, while a dim fire gleamed in his gray eyes. "The old gate! To whom, save me, is it of the smallest account? Who, besides myself, can read the story that it tells? The history of my race is written upon it, Herr Professor.

Shall I destroy the story of my line before I, in my person, have made an end to it? Centuries ago the town bestowed the gate upon a Köstling, as a token of high honour, because he had defended it against an attack from the Freiherrs von Höneburg with his blood and the blood of his sons, four of whom were left dead upon the field,—bestowed it upon him for all time, as the ancient document has it, the seals of which are still well preserved. The Köstlings were the guardians of the town, and have repeatedly defended the gate and bridge against the attacks of the knightly Höneburgers; and the gate is thus a memorial of loyal citizenship. Is it valueless as such? To you, I suppose, it is. What do you care about the archives of this town and my family? But I know that they are filled with quarrels between the Höneburgers and the Köstlings, with battles about this gate. And the enmity survived even to my own time, as I know by bitter experience. I owe to it a desolate old age." He arose, pulled aside the window-curtain, and pointed out.- "There are the ruins of the Höneburg. The castle and the gate have confronted each other in menace for almost five hundred years. Well, then? The gate shall not be destroyed while one stone of the Höneburg is left upon another. They belong together."

For awhile the old man maintained his attitude at the window, gazing out at the ruined tower in the distance. If the Professor could have seen his eyes, he would surely have been daunted by the hatred that gleamed in them. But he was pondering the last words that had been spoken, so full of menace, and yet, perhaps, capable of being turned to his advantage. "And if I should take you at your word?" he cried, yielding to a sudden impulse. "If the ruins of the Höneburg are utterly destroyed, may the gate fall too?"

Köstling hastily withdrew the hand that held back the window-curtain, and turned an astonished face upon the inquirer. Some strong expression hovered upon his lips, but it was not

uttered. He smiled compassionately. "Ah! you would promise what you cannot perform," he gravely said.

"You can put it to the test," the Professor replied. "I
propose a formal exchange. If the ruin falls the gate falls."
The old man shook his head. "How would you——?"

"The ruin belongs to me."

"What? Has the Freiherr sold it, then?"

"Sir! But you do not know,—I am the Freiherr of Höneburg, the youngest of the name."

Köstling sank back in his chair and stared at him in wide-
eyed amazement. "You are——? No, no, no!"

"I am Xaver von Höneburg: there is no doubt of it; the
proof is at your command."

The old man's expression grew terrible in its intensity.
"You are," he faltered—"you are——? And this other
name, this——" He snatched up the card. "Schönrade——"

"Bellarota," the Professor translated for him. "My
mother——"

"Your mother—Camilla Bellarota?" Köstling almost
shrieked. "Oh, it is too much! too much!" His head
fell back against the high chair, his eyes looked faint, and
his arms hung by his side.

The two cats leaped from the window-seat, across the table,
upon the floor, and purred about their master's legs, humping
their backs and licking his feet and hands. The Professor
was so startled by the effect of his communication that it was
only after the lapse of a minute that he hastened to help the
half-unconscious old man. At his touch the form quivered,
the head moved. "Is it true?" he faintly asked. "Are you
really Camilla's son, Camilla, who—who——? Yes, yes, those
are her features. And you do not know—oh, you do not
know?" His eyes filled with tears: he could not speak; but
he began to cough convulsively.

"What do I not know?" the Professor asked, after a few

minutes, during which Herr Köstling had partly recovered himself. " May I not learn it now.?"

" No ! no !" the old man gasped. " Oh, Camilla, Camilla ! Is she alive ?"

" She is living."

" And—your father ?"

" The Count von Gleichenau is also living."

" They are divorced, are they not ? Divorced !"

" Unfortunately, they are. They have not seen each other for more than thirty years."

" Ah ! it is the justice of Heaven !" exclaimed Köstling, clenching his raised hand. " It could not permit them to be happy, my mortal enemy and my—— Begone ! begone, young man ! I repent my words. Leave an old man alone with his memories."

The Professor grasped his hand. " No," he said, with warmth, " I will not leave you now. Heaven is my witness that I never meant to wound you ; I had no idea of any connection—— Speak, I entreat you ! The son of your mortal enemy has a right to learn the cause of this enmity."

" You have heard," Köstling exclaimed ; " it is centuries old, and bequeathed from generation to generation. How should he and I escape the curse ? Do you not feel it in my presence ? You ask of me—what I must refuse; and you will cross that threshold my enemy. So be it !"

Xaver gravely shook his head. " Not your enemy. It were a crime to believe that such dissensions cannot die. You say you are the last of your race; but my father, if he has injured you, is not the last of his : I am living, and am innocent of all that has occurred. For my sake speak, and tell me what atonement I can make during your life."

" No atonement is possible," said Köstling; " there may be some consolation in the thought that we are all alike unhappy. Crime separates, misfortune reconciles."

o*

"Let me guess, then," said Xaver. "You loved my mother."

The old man sighed heavily. "And she——" He broke off, arose, and walked through the room. Then he seated himself upon a chair near the bed, beside the second window, the curtains of which were closely drawn. "Yes," he said, in a low tone, "you shall learn all that words can tell. You will at least understand then why I—— But I cannot foretell your opinion. Perhaps you may judge of such matters like a genuine Freiherr von Höneburg, and not at all after my fashion."

He reflected for awhile, and then began : " My father was a great lover of opera and of the drama, and he not only went regularly to the theatre, but he sought the society of artists and actors who ranked well in their profession, and opened his house to them (it was not so lonely then as now), besides often affording them material aid. Remember, this was at a time when the actor's profession was not so esteemed as at present, and when those belonging to it were, with a few brilliant exceptions, excluded from aristocratic society. Of course my father, in a town full of old patrician prejudice, had many annoyances to encounter ;—but he persisted in following his inclinations and listening to his own kind heart. More than forty years ago a singer appeared on the stage here, calling himself Carlo Bellarota. He was something of a celebrity, and my father valued him, not only because of his fine tenor voice, but also because he was a man of artistic culture and excellent breeding. Unfortunately, he soon entirely lost his voice. The public, always heartless in such cases, hissed him, and the director dismissed him. Pain at being thus ill treated, and anxiety for the future, made him ill. As he was entirely without means, he could not pay for his lodgings, and would have been turned into the street but for my father, who paid his bills and procured him admission to the hospital, where he saw that he was well taken care of. But his spirit was broken, and his body did not long survive. He died, and my father, his only friend in his need, had him buried, not in the pauper burying-ground, but in the churchyard."

Here Köstling paused, overcome, it would seem, by painful memories. "This Carlo Bellarota," he at last began again, "had a daughter: her name was Camilla, and she was then ten years old. The child had been her father's companion in his wanderings, and had received but very imperfect instruction, spending most of her time at the theatre among the actors and actresses, and even dancing in public now and then. The director of our theatre would have kept her to be educated for the stage; this, however, my good father would not allow; he took Camilla home and informed his household that she was to be regarded as his child, very much in opposition to the advice of his friends, who thought he would do enough, and more than enough, if he sent her to a boarding-school. But my father had no daughter,—he hoped that Camilla would fill a daughter's place in his life,—at least she would be grateful.

"I was then fifteen or sixteen years old, just at the impressible age, and here was a sister who was, after all, not really my sister; the gayest of companions, who, in spite of her youth, knew so much of which I was ignorant, and who was beautiful,—so beautiful. Yes! Camilla was exquisitely lovely even as a child. Her large dark eyes, her waving masses of black hair, her airy, graceful figure,—before long she was my only thought, and as she grew in intelligence and beauty, and in time became the darling of every one around her, the very apple of my father's eye, I felt sure that Heaven had sent her to me, and that I should be the happiest mortal in the world if she could only love me.

"I dared to believe that I was beloved,—I believe to this day that I was beloved. All the time I could command was spent in Camilla's society. I played with her so long as she enjoyed childish amusements.　I read with her, studied with her.　I could not sing with her, for a voice had been denied me, but I was always by when she took her singing-lessons, and accompanied her on the piano when she practised.　She was mine by every tie of the spirit; I advised and guided her; she confided to me all her little woes, and I shared her every joy.　'You are the elder, Lorenz,' she used to say, 'tell me what to do.'　When she went into society her gayety did not separate us.　She was passionately fond of dancing, but I never moved gracefully, and preferred to stand aloof and watch her at a ball.　How often she has left the dance to walk and talk with me, until I myself would beg her to return!　As she waltzed, if I stood near, she would smile and nod at me, and I was happy in her happiness.　The next morning we would sit together gravely over our books.　I had mastered the tongue in which she had always talked with her father, and I used it in conversing with her.　How grateful she was!　'You are the only one,' she used to say, 'with whom I can speak from my heart.'　She liked to consider herself a daughter of Italy, and her mirror told her she was right.　Wherever she went she was the cynosure of every eye, but she seemed to care nothing for general admiration,—I was always her only cherished friend.　Had I not a right to believe myself loved?

"On her seventeenth birthday, this house was filled with the fragrance of flowers.　How her face beamed with happiness when, upon enterin the drawing-room, she found the household assembled there to offer her their gifts and congratulations!

"'How kind you are to the poor orphan!' she said, when we were alone together.　'How shall I ever repay you?'

"'By loving me, Camilla,' I replied, more boldly than I had ever spoken to her before, and impelled to a confession of what filled my heart.　She seemed not to understand me, for she put her hand in mine, saying, 'I do love you dearly;' and as she spoke, the tears came into her eyes, and she gazed into mine, until she must have read my heart there; for she suddenly withdrew her hand and cast down her eyes. Then I threw myself at her feet, and told her that I loved her more than life itself, and that she must be mine forever. The storm of passionate expression coming from one usually so calm amazed her. 'I never thought of this,' I heard her say, as if to herself. But when I implored her to give me the answer I longed for, she did not withstand me, but threw herself into my arms, and whispered, 'Yes, it must be so; I can have no truer friend in this world!'

"'God knows you cannot, dearest!' I cried, in a rapture of delight, as I clasped her to my heart."

As he recalled this, the happiest hour of his life, Köstling became greatly agitated. He had arisen, and held his hands aloft, as if actually calling Heaven to witness, while his whole figure seemed loftier and more dignified than before. But now he sank down in his chair again, and rested his head on his hand. Thus he remained, silent, for awhile. The Professor did not venture to arouse him from his reverie. "She did not love him," he said to himself. "She was self-deceived."

"I had expected," Köstling began again, much more quietly, "that our betrothal would have been a cause of heartfelt joy to my father. I was mistaken. He seemed, on the contrary, disagreeably surprised, saying, as Camilla had done, 'I never thought of this.' He loved his adopted child, and would have provided handsomely for her, but it had never occurred to him that the daughter of the public singer who had died in the hospital could become the wife of his only son. Free from prejudice though he was, there was a point where his old patrician pride made itself heard, and it suddenly opposed a bar to the fulfilment of my hopes.

"My father said everything to me that fathers are accustomed to say to their sons in such cases; but I refused to listen. Nothing availed to shake my resolution. The property that I had inherited from my mother made me independent of my father in a worldly point of view, and I now offered to leave him, that he might be relieved from any responsibility with regard to me. This conquered him. 'No! no!' he exclaimed, 'I yield,—be happy! Whatever my son does I will uphold before the world.' Camilla had known of and justified his opposition, but he now greeted her as my future wife, and arranged for a large *fête* here, at which our betrothal was to be publicly announced.

"There was present at this *fête* an officer who had been stationed in the town for awhile,—the Freiherr von Höneburg. He, as well as his brother officers, had paid his respects to my father upon his arrival, and had, of course, received an invitation. The two men had laughed over the ancient enmity between their two houses, as at some shadowy tradition. 'We robber knights had the worst of it,' the Freiherr jestingly observed. 'There lies our castle in ruins,—a study for a landscape-painter, while the green gate stands stout and stiff, like a soldier on parade; and the Messrs. Köstling are enthroned in their counting-room, while the last Höneburg, like George Brown in 'La Dame Blanche,' is reduced to his lieutenant's pay.' This careless good humour pleased my father.

"'Your inheritance is a noble name,' he replied; 'and your sword, which can make it glorious in defence of your native land, for which I too would give my wealth.'

"'If we could only have a war! The whole world is weary of this stupid peace,' Von Höneburg exclaimed.

"It was at this betrothal festivity that Camilla and the Freiherr first met; and afterwards they saw each other often in my father's house, where Von Höneburg was continually invited, and at all the gatherings made in honour of our betrothal by our friends. There were very friendly relations established between the young officer and myself; he constantly made decided efforts to obtain my friendship, and I never took it at all amiss that he paid particular court to Camilla,—danced with her continually, and evidently liked to sit next her at table. Why should she not receive his attentions graciously? The daughters of the first families of the town were proud to be distinguished by him, and he knew well how to recognize talent and beauty. Was not Camilla my own? What had I to fear? Oh, forget—forget that she is your mother!

"There was nothing to prevent our marriage. My father, however, wished it postponed for a year, and I could not refuse to yield this to him, who had yielded so much to me. He told me afterwards that he wished to give us each time to test our affection,—a dangerous precaution; the reasons then given me were Camilla's extreme youth and the preparations to be made for our future establishment. What happened in the course of this year, the longest I had then lived, I can only surmise, and I tell you the result of these surmises as briefly as I can. The Freiherr was true to the traditions of his house; he trampled our rights beneath his feet; he stole Camilla's heart from me; he beguiled her with his honeyed words, poisoned her ear with flattery——"

"He loved Camilla," the Professor interrupted. "I know that he loved her."

"He had no right to love her," the old man passionately exclaimed, "for she was mine. And he never loved her as I did, for he left her, after she had sacrificed everything to him, even her conscience. Oh, her conscience warned her and tormented her for a long time. I could not understand her sudden changes of mood, from warmth to coldness, her half-stifled sighs, her hastily-dried tears, her laughter, misleading even herself. I attributed it all to girlish whim, to nervous irritability, to vexation at the postponement of our marriage.

Unfortunately, I was obliged to leave home for a month upon business. When I returned, I found Camilla greatly changed, but she evaded all my anxious inquiries. She did not go at all into society, and I noticed that the Freiherr no longer visited at the house. Why was it? 'I desired that his visits should cease,' she said, and her eyes filled with tears. 'Has he been guilty of any rudeness to you?' I asked, astonished. She shook her head waywardly, and answered, 'Beware of him: he is a Höneburg!'"

"I tried to interpret her words innocently; probably some unguarded remark of his had offended her. I begged my father to shorten our time of probation, and the day for the marriage was at last appointed. Camilla seemed glad of this, and for a week she was almost her old self again. Then I learned one day that, while I had been busy in the counting-room, the Freiherr had spent an hour with her. 'Are you reconciled?' I asked her, gaily. She looked strangely at me, and replied, after a minute, 'Yes!'—nothing but 'yes!' But it sounded as if there was much more to say,—I could not understand what. During the next few days she was very restless, secluding herself for hours at a time in her own room, and even when she was with me seeming absent in thought. I remember one conversation that I had with her, that gave me food for reflection at the time, although I did not understand her. She asked me whether, in my opinion, the duty of gratitude ranked higher than the duty to live. I could not answer her, and she added, 'Men commonly expect gratitude for the kindness they show us, and yet they are more our debtors than we theirs.' I thought this view rather selfish, and Camilla, her thoughts evidently wandering, said, sadly, 'When parents lose a dearly-loved child, are they not consoled by the thought of the joy it has been to them? It should console us for the loss of those we love that we have had the delight of loving them.'

"'Strange fancies,' I thought,—'born of her agitation on the eve of a step that is the most important that can be taken.' I was soon to learn—— But why probe that torment to its depths? There is little more to tell. On my marriage morn we awaited the bride. Why did she delay so long? I knocked at the door again and again; in vain. I ventured to open it,—she was gone."

Köstling hid his face in his hands, and his frame trembled with agony. In a few minutes, however, he looked up with a profound sigh, and said, "It is past. Upon her table I found a letter. 'I cannot be yours,' she wrote, 'as you wish I should. I have had a fierce struggle, and, even now that I have decided, my heart bleeds. I love, and I cannot be your wife with another love in my heart. It would pain you to deceive you, it pains you to tell you the truth. What is to be must be. Call me thankless; blame, despise, forget me! I cannot struggle any longer——" I was prostrated as by a stroke of lightning. Weeks afterwards I began slowly to recover from a violent attack of brain fever. I never have been well since,—I never shall be while I live.

"As soon as I could stand upright, I challenged the traitor. We fought with pistols in the room above the green gate. I forced him to make no allowance for my weakness. Three times my trembling hand missed its aim; twice he intentionally shot wide; the third time he disabled me without wounding me dangerously. Why, oh, why did not his bullet find my heart?

"Thus blood flowed again upon the spot which had seen bloody strife between the Freiherrs von Höneburg and my forefathers. The old enmity was sealed afresh, and now, when I look up from my garden at the gate and the old bridge, the thoughts that fill my life crowd upon me. Do not ask, young man, that I should look for them in vain, before my eyes close forever."

28*

He arose, and, walking to the window, stood -gazing at the
ruin, absently stroking the cats, who had taken up their previous position on the window-sill.   The Professor felt that
any further discussion would be useless, and that it was time to
take his leave.   "I thank you for these revelations," he said,
"which have explained much that has been a riddle to me
hitherto.   For the first time I now understand my mother,
and how she came to hate the husband she surely loved once.
I understand your suffering: you lost a bride and a sister at
one and the same blow; but if years cannot dull the pain, is
there not some consolation in what Camilla said, ' I have had
the delight of loving' ? "

He shook his head. " Cold comfort! No, no; I do not
choose to be so consoled."

The Professor approached him.   " Can you give your hand,"
he said, with gentle cordiality, "to the son of those who have
so wronged you, or must that wrong be visited upon him ?"

Köstling hesitated ; then, giving him his hand, hastily turned
away, saying, harshly, " Farewell ! but we must never meet
again."

Schönrade made no reply ; but a voice within told him this
could not be.   As he left the house, he looked up involuntarily
at the little leaded panes of the window above the gateway.
There the first act of the tragedy had been concluded.   He
knew it all now.

CHAPTER XXV.

IN very melancholy mood Professor Schönrade returned to his friend Moritz Amberger with the result of his endeavours, —only the result; Moritz was not sufficiently near a friend to be informed of all that Köstling had told him. "The old man has his reasons," he said, "and from his point of view they are valid. At all events, they must suffice us."

Moritz took a certain kind of satisfaction in learning that the Professor had effected nothing more than he had been able to do. "What shall we do?" he asked, more cheerfully than the situation seemed to warrant. "It is too provoking that we cannot get round that old heap of stones."

"Would it not be possible to leave it on one side, and carry the street past it?" asked Schönrade.

"Impossible! we should trench upon Feinberg's property."

"Well, then,"—and the Professor shrugged his shoulders, —"I have nothing more to say."

"Could we not obtain from the government a right of appropriation?"

"By no means!" the Professor exclaimed, indignantly. "Take away the old man's property? By no means! I would have nothing to do with such a measure."

"But if we are governed by considerations of delicacy——'

"Better give up the whole project," the Professor declared, "which, indeed, I never should have taken up, had I known our opponent and the trump-card he holds in his hand. I shall return to Berlin, and write from there as to what is to be done next."

Thus matters stood. Even when Moritz returned from 'Change and reported that the railway-project was now public gossip, and that Feinberg was mustering his forces for a fresh attack, Schönrade was firm in his determination not to use the law as a weapon against the old man. He could scarcely hope for a peaceful adjustment; but by nothing save a peaceful adjustment would he consent to attain their end.

He set out for Berlin with a heavier heart than he had brought thence. Wherever he turned, trouble seemed to await him.

But when he reached his lodgings, he found there a package of letters that instantly absorbed all his attention. It came from Florence, and contained Philip's and Katrine's communications, with the papers found in the Palazzo Bellarota. Philip described with great minuteness exactly how they had been found; but it is to be feared that Xaver scarcely displayed sufficient interest in that part of his package. Katrine joyously informed him that she had betrayed his secret at the right moment,—that her mother was most favourably inclined towards the Freiherr von Höneburg,—and that a few lines from him to Frau Barbara would surely meet with a gracious reception. Then came the invitation to the wedding, and a pressing request not to let the long journey prevent his accepting it, and a commission to select a wedding-present for Lucia, that must be " very northern in character," and congratulations for Camilla, which he did not understand, for he had not yet read Philip's letter through. He looked through the documents; they entirely confirmed his mother's statements. For one moment he rejoiced for her sake; but the next he asked himself, with a shrug, " What then ? We are what we are. If Frau Amberger values such things, so much the better for Katrine and me. It is of no real importance."

Greatly cheered by this episode, he added Katrine's letter to the others from her hand, which he always carried with him in his letter-case, and then, refolding the old documents, took them with him to his father. An explanation with him seemed more desirable even than a visit to his mother.

The Count was delighted to see his eldest son again, and Kunibert was unaffectedly rejoiced to welcome his brother. Xaver thought him looking much stronger than when he had left him, and the Count explained that a change in his condition for the better had undoubtedly taken place. " I ascribe it in great part to your influence," he continued; "you have cheered and refreshed my poor boy, who was doubtless affected by my own melancholy mood. He is beginning to have some confidence in himself, and that will prove his best medicine."

" I wish," Xaver replied, " that I were always as successful. Unfortunately——"

He began a detailed account of all that had happened. The Count listened attentively, but without eager interest until mention was made of the green gate. Then, at the name of its possessor, he was evidently disturbed, saying, " Yes—yes ! it belongs to the Köstling house. The Köstling house—there is a sad story—and I and your mother—— But go on: I am prepared for everything."

Xaver thought it right to repeat to him his conversation with the unhappy old man. " Thus the matter stands," he concluded; " and I admit that I felt the deepest compassion for Herr Köstling, although I am convinced that my mother did not love him, and that neither would have found happiness in their union."

" True, true," the Count eagerly confirmed his words. " I will neither defend nor deny the wrong I committed. When I first knew Camilla, she was betrothed, and I, who knew that she was so, did not shun her as soon as I felt myself passionately attracted by her, but I trampled upon her lover's right in striving to gain her affection. There is nothing that can excuse me but the strength of my passion, which he can hardly

be expected to take into consideration. It is, however, perfectly true that Camilla loved him only as a friend and brother,
and that even when she promised to marry him she had a
foreboding that she could not make him happy as his wife.
If I had not appeared, Camilla would have come to understand her own heart, and would not have sacrificed herself
to her feeling of gratitude, or she would have had even
more unhappiness in that marriage than I afterwards caused
her. We loved from the first moment that we met, with au
intensity against which it was in vain to struggle. As we then
felt, suicide would have been preferable to separation."

" But why such secrecy?" Xaver ventured to ask. " Would
it not have been better to confess frankly——"

" I advised it," the Count interrupted him ; " but Camilla
would not listen to me, and it is only justice to her to admit
that our shares in such a confession would have been very
unequal. I owed nothing to the Küstlings, except what was
due from a guest who had been kindly received beneath their
roof, and I was quite ready to be held accountable for my
actions. Camilla, on the other hand, was not only breaking
with a lover, but she was requiting with a blow the kindness
of those to whom she owed a vast debt of gratitude, and from
whom, should she confess, she could not expect absolution.
The thought was intolerable to her of remaining a day, an
hour, beneath their roof after such a revelation. ' If they
would cast me off in anger,' she once said to me, ' I would tell
them all. But they would be gentle and kind to me ; they
would assail me with entreaties to consider, to take time for
reflection ; they would torture my heart, and at last, when it
was all in vain, their patrician pride would prompt them to
play a part before the world that would be sad indeed. No,
I will seem as guilty as I am ; they shall be justified in de-
spising me.' I still hesitated, for I felt that my position as an
officer required a different course ; but what did any consider-

ation avail against the strength of my passion? An elopement was arranged, and that very day I sent in my resignation from the army."

Xaver sighed. "And all the evils that have been the result of the act may be explained, but not averted. Köstling will not be persuaded. The failure of the house of Amberger is certain, and your losses will be by no means small."

The Count did all he could to console him upon this score, reminding him that the railway undertaking was only postponed; the green gate must come down some day, and there was no need of putting a stop to the preparations that were making. There must be a conference with Fairfax and Wiesel, who were now won over to the enterprise, and if Amberger still had time——"

"And his mother and sister are perfectly ignorant of the misfortune that threatens them!" exclaimed Xaver. He then told his father of the contents of Philip's and Katrine's letters, and thus came to speak of the discovery of the papers, which he now laid upon the table.

For his own part, he attached very little importance to the facts they established; his mother would doubtless exult, he said, in jest, that she had been in the right; he did not grudge her that innocent pleasure. But the Count took an entirely different view of the matter, judging from his grave face and the eager attention he paid his son. He did not immediately make any reply, but unfolded the papers, and began to examine them. "There is no doubt of their authenticity," the Professor remarked, by the way, "and there really is very little to interest you in them." His father pursued his examination, however, only asking an explanation, from time to time, of certain words, the significance of which he found it difficult to understand. When he had finished, he arose and walked to the window, where he stood with his back to his son, apparently lost in thought. Whence this sudden change of mood?

Could these papers——? Xaver looked them through again for the sake of occupation.

After awhile the Count returned to him; he was very pale, and walked unsteadily, regarding his son with great earnestness as he approached him. "Did you bring me these papers for a special reason?" he asked.

Xaver looked up in amazement. "For a special reason?"

"With any especial aim——? Tell me."

"Not that I know of. I bring you the papers because I have just received them, and because the manner of their discovery was curious."

"And you care nothing about them?"

"Nothing whatever! You know that I have made no use as yet of my Freiherr's crest, and this influx of Italian blue blood does not interest me much."

The Count slowly shook his head. "Inconceivable!" he muttered to himself. "Will you leave these papers with me?" he asked, after awhile.

"Certainly; but——" and he hesitated.

"But what?"

"I hardly like to keep them from my mother, who will take much more pleasure in them than I do."

"Do you think so? And why?"

"Good heavens! Why, you know that she really took great pains to have these facts established."

"To be sure,—to be sure!"

Xaver could not comprehend him. "I cannot understand your emotion, and still less why you should appeal so to me. These papers——"

The Count hastily took his hand. "Forgive me, Xaver," he entreated. "You cannot see that—— Enough, we will not speak of it now. At some future time, my son. Will you intrust these papers to me?"

"If my mother——"

"If your mother consents, you would say. But I do not mean to keep them, except until she sees them, and I pray you to allow me to take them to her."

" You, father?"

" I myself."

" You would——"

" Take advantage of an opportunity that may never occur again of approaching her. These papers will be of real significance to Camilla only as coming from me."

Xaver sprang up. " You will go to her,—to seek a reconciliation?"

" It has long been my desire and intention," the Count replied, gently, " but I could hardly hope for any result from my efforts if I went of myself, alone. Now I have an errand, and, even although I gain nothing of what I desire, I shall not be entirely disappointed. You see I do not wish to rob Camilla."

The Professor rolled up the papers and handed them to him. " I wish you all success!" he exclaimed. " If my entreaties can avail anything, they shall not be wanting. I will go to her immediately, and try to soften her mood. My letters have been full of all that I could think of that might lead her to gentler thoughts of you."

Thus he took his leave, quite cheerful again, and his father repeated to himself, as his son left the room, " Inconceivable! inconceivable! Is it possible," he thought, "that he does not see the immense importance to himself of the discovery of these papers? Has his practical sense deserted him on this occasion? or does he affect ignorance? No, no! he is all frankness and honesty. There is not a drop of falsehood in his blood. He deserves that fate should deal brilliantly with him,—and, thank God, I can atone for the wrong I committed." He opened the door into the adjoining room, where Kunibert sat writing, and, approaching him, laid his hand caressingly upon his head. " My poor boy!" he said, compassionately.

The lad turned and kissed his father's hand. "Why am I your poor boy?" he asked. "I feel really well to-day. Has Xaver gone? I hoped he would want to see what I have been doing while he was away."

"Just at present he is very much occupied with his own affairs," the Count replied. "He will soon come again."

After a pause, he asked, "Are you very fond of him?"

"Very fond," the lad replied.

"Would your affection stand a test?"

His son looked at him with surprise in his large eyes. "Any test, I think," he answered.

His father put his hands on either side of his head, and kissed his brow. "Oh, how little we know!" he said, with a sigh, as he went to his room.

CHAPTER XXVI.

THE Professor was glad to have finished his business report to his father, and, as he walked along the street towards his mother's house, he recapitulated, in thought, Katrine's letter, and then reflected upon what course he should pursue to prepare his mother for the visit she was about to receive. So preoccupied was he that he scarcely heeded the passers-by, but walked along with eyes bent upon the ground, when suddenly an equipage drew up to the sidewalk, so close beside him that he started, while at the same moment he heard his name called.

In a very elegant vehicle, drawn by a pair of horses, sat Sidonie Feinberg, by the side of Herr von Fuchs. She held the reins, and, leaning forward, nodded to Schönrade.

"Is it really you?" she exclaimed, with a laugh. "Oh, I know; you have been away, and have given my poor Moritz, who was in a bad case, a helping hand. Very kind of you, I'm sure. Is it true that he has some romantic liaison with a gardener's daughter? I congratulate him. An admirable thing for him! When will you tell us all about it, my dear Herr Professor?"

"Fräulein Feinberg, the street is hardly the——"

"Hardly the place? True, my steeds are much too impatient. But you will come to us soon, will you not? Good heavens! this is really the only way to catch you. By the way, Herr von Fuchs, take off your hat to your old friend. I have the honour, my dear Herr Professor, to present to you my future bridegroom. Why do you laugh?"

"Because your announcement is made so drolly. Permit me to——"

"For heaven's sake, do not congratulate us in the street. That would be too droll. But come as soon as you can, O most conscientious of men! You see I am no longer in the slightest danger from you. I shall, I trust, see you soon." She nodded again, gave her horses the rein, and drove off.

"'Birds of a feather,'" the Professor thought to himself, as he continued upon his way. "This Fuchs! his debts never troubled him much. It was written in the stars that he was to marry an heiress, and there she is. They will be very content together as long as the paternal million lasts."

His mother was in her most genial mood, busy at her piano, reading some new music that greatly interested her. She invited her son to lunch with her, and he accepted her invitation, to her surprise, as she immediately betrayed. "What! will you really stay?" she asked, with mock dismay. "I was not prepared for this. But so much the better. I asked you in good faith. If I am not mistaken, we shall have a couple of very little birds. We will share them. There will be a profusion of sweets, at all events." She gave the necessary orders to her duenna, and settled herself comfortably in the corner of the sofa. "And now, my child, tell me all," she said.

This was rather a difficult task; her thoughts continually took a turn suggested by some word of his, and she interrupted repeatedly. He liked to talk thus with her, however; and there was much to say, for he told her of Katrine, and Katrine was in Florence; Florence, Italy, Italian music, the Italian opera, Carlo Bellarota, wicked men,—each subject followed the preceding one so naturally; and thus they got back to the Ambergers' native town, and Xaver ventured to speak of Moritz and his affairs, at first only generally, then more particularly, but always without touching the point uppermost in his mind. He did not wish to spoil his mother's luncheon,—and he succeeded admirably; she ate her bird with evident relish, and gave her son the largest half of the sweet omelette, of which, to her great content, he did not leave a morsel. But when the meal was concluded, it was time to speak of graver matters.

He then grew absent-minded, not in appearance only, but in reality, and scarcely heard her as she criticised the candied fruits and declared that they were nowhere so delicious as at Venice, until at last she asked him what he was thinking of. "Anxieties of various kinds, mother dear," he replied, with a sigh. "I forget them for awhile, when we are so happy together, but they will return and demand attention. I am sure you know how this is."

"Indeed I do," she answered, looking at her son with an air of tender apprehension; "but I thought you had everything that your heart could desire."

"My heart!" he said, lifting his eyebrows. "Hardly that, while I see my father and mother alienated——"

"Not a word more," she entreated, casting down her eyes; "you promised me——"

"What I am unable to perform," he interrupted her.

"There are other anxieties too, dearest mother, of a more worldly nature, and they depend upon circumstances about which we may be silent, but which are none the less real. Do you remember the green gate?"

"The green gate? By the—Köstling house? What of it?"

"It is in our way, and if it does not come down a large amount of money will be sacrificed; Moritz Amberger will be bankrupt, Frau Barbara Amberger a poor woman, Katrine's inheritance lost, and Philip will have but a melancholy wedding."

Camilla listened eagerly. "But what connection——?"

He tried to place clearly before her the importance of the old structure, or rather of the spot upon which it stood, and then spoke of its possessor, whom he had visited and had found entirely inexorable. Camilla did not interrupt him, but sat perfectly still, with tightly-compressed lips. When he paused, she looked up, as if terrified, for an instant to his face. "And do you know all that?" she asked.

"I know all that," he replied; "Köstling has forgotten nothing, and withheld nothing from me. He is greatly to be pitied."

"He is greatly to be pitied," said Camilla, resting her head on her hand. "It was his misfortune to love me, who could not love him in return. But perhaps I might have learned to love him in time."

"No, mother, I think not!" exclaimed Xaver; "I think not. I felt convinced, from Köstling's own words, that you never could have truly loved him. A union with him would have been contrary to your nature; it would have been misery as soon as you really understood yourself. But it is greatly to be deplored that the sisterly affection which you gave him, and which might have blessed both your lives, could not last. Now, after such sorrowful experiences, when you have survived the tempests of life, and can think and feel more calmly, you may suspect yourself of having made a mistake. But it was no mistake! The heart—the heart that loves—rejects the idea. None the less does Köstling deserve our compassion, for, whether wrongly or rightly, you were the cause of grievous woe to him,—a burden of woe, which, faithful to his sorrow, he bears about with him to this day."

Camilla shook her head sadly. " I cannot acquit myself," she said,—" I cannot. Then I thought otherwise; I would sooner have died than have stood before the altar with him. But I owed it to him to tell him the truth. His pain might not have been less, but I should have been spared the re-proaches of my conscience." Again she leaned her head upon her hand, and said, as if to herself, " I loved him as a brother ; suddenly he was my lover, and my own heart was unchanged. I hardly knew that he did not possess my entire affection until I had to struggle with a genuine passion, while my feel-ing for him was unchanged. It was only when I knew that he had a right to expect of me more than I could give that I began to suffer unspeakably. I could not tell him. It seemed too much to hope for that he should forgive me. I would not ask him for pardon; if I were guilty, let him know me so. Afterwards I felt the agony of that sting."

" Its pain would have been less if you could have found the happiness that you expected in your love," her son ob-served, taking her hand in his, and leaning towards her. " It would pain you less now if you would be reconciled to him for love of whom you transgressed an irksome duty,—if you——"

" You speak of your father," she again interrupted him, in a sterner tone. " How is a reconciliation to be thought of? Can he himself seriously desire it ? And upon what grounds could it take place ? He *cannot* be just to us,—*cannot!* Can we grant that he was right ? I do not wish to hinder you from kissing the hand that thrust you forth,—it is your father's; but I am bound to him by no ties of nature, and those which we ourselves devised have been wantonly severed."

" They are *not* severed, mother!" Xaver exclaimed. "They exist indestructibly in *me.* Blot me from existence, mother, and then say that that year at the Höneburg was a dream,—a space of time to be regarded as some illusion of fancy. Am I not my father's and my mother's son? And shall those two, who in me are indissolubly united, live eternally apart because, as frail mortals, they erred? Ask your inmost heart, mother, could you hate my father as you hated him had you not loved him as you loved,—had not your love lived on, and ever and again revolted at his fickleness? And if in his heart he never has been faithless to you, and if of late his thoughts have been filled with you and you alone—— Mother! Is it impossible for you to forgive?"

As his words poured forth, full of eager entreaty, he sank down upon his knees before her, and looked imploringly into her face, which she tried to avert, as if unwilling to yield to an agency that was asserting its power over her.

" Not thus, my son," she said, " not thus! Rise, I pray you! Do not torture me. Rise!"

" Mother!" he exclaimed, throwing his arms around her, " if you love me!"

Her hand stroked his black curls, but her face was still turned from him; and there was a dreamy fire in her dark eyes.

" Rise!" she repeated; but her voice faltered.

He only clasped her closer in his arms. " If you love me. mother, forget,—forgive!"

" I cannot," she replied; but so low and faint was her voice that her words scarcely reached his ear. She put her arm around him, and endeavoured to raise his head. He would not lift it, but buried his face in her lap. At this moment the bell rang loudly. Camilla started. Xaver looked up, without rising from his knees. " Be kind, mother!" he implored, seeking her eyes.

The door opened, and the old servant announced, " A stranger wishes to——" Then she paused, amazed at the posture of mother and son.

" I am at home to no one," Camilla said to her,—" to no one at present."

Xaver arose, and took his hat. " To no one?" he asked, eagerly. " Mother, if——! Let me see who——" He opened the door wide, and held out his hand to some one standing upon the threshold.

" So soon?" he asked, in an agitated voice. Then, taking the stranger by the arm, he led him into the room.

"Mother, it is my father!" he said, in a clear, distinct tone, like the sound of a bell. " If you love me, mother——!" His eyes completed the sentence. He hastily left the room, and closed the door behind him,—ran down-stairs, past the wondering servant, and left the house.

Camilla had sunk back upon the sofa; the Count stood for awhile motionless in the middle of the room, regarding her with eager anxiety. Here were two persons who had loved each other, who had worked each other much woe, and who now met again, after more than thirty years. Ah, what a meeting was this! Where was the youthful form that had lived so vividly in the memory of each,—a mark for affection, sorrow, anger, and hate? Here were but the ruins of past glory and beauty,—majestic ruins, 'tis true. Had they but grown old together! An abyss of time, that might have swallowed up the space of an entire human life, was to be bridged over in a few minutes. It was better thus; the change was too great to allow of their taking up their lives where passion and anger had divided them. All illusions vanished, and the real clamoured for its rights. That dignified matron was not the girl, glowing with love and youth, whom the Count had adored; the spare, proud man, with gray hair and furrowed brow, was not the faithless lover whom Camilla hated. Something like amazement, that quickly faded into melancholy, appeared in the countenance of each, to see the other grown so strangely altered.

And yet there were the same features, only sharpened in outline, faint in color. Camilla's hair and eyes, the Count's erect figure and military bearing,—upon these time had had no power. Wherever they had met, each would have instantly acknowledged, " Yes, it is you !"

" Camilla !" the Count began, at last, as if testing by his voice her willingness to hear him, and then waiting for a reply.

" Count Gleichenau !" she said, in as low a tone, and yet trembling to hear herself speak, " I was not prepared 'for a meeting——"

" To which you would perhaps never have agreed," he gently interrupted her, " if you had been consulted. I could not trust it to that chance. But has not Xaver intimated——?"

" My son has indeed spoken of you," Camilla assented, to prevent his saying more than she thought she could bear at the moment. " My son is convinced that he has found a friend in you, Count Gleichenau, and I can but hope that he is not mistaken."

" He has found a friend," he replied, advancing a step and speaking warmly,—" a father. I thank him that he does not reject me as a father."

A pause ensued. The Count never averted his gaze from Camilla; and she, as if she knew it and feared his eyes, cast down her own upon her hands, that lay folded in her lap. She might have been praying for composure and submission, and perhaps, moved by Xaver's entreaties, she was praying, and the wayward quiver of her lips was due to the pride that would not yield the field.

" You have had cause for anger, Camilla," the Count began

P*

again, "and I may not judge you. I cannot even complain if you reject the hand held out to you in pledge of peace, for you are the injured one,—you alone have aught to forgive. I can but pray you to remember that we have one interest in common, and that its object suffers severely from our disunion,—our son——"

"Our son——" she repeated, in a faltering voice. "Oh, that is my bitterest wrong,—that for so many years he has not been *our* child!"

"I will not exculpate myself," the Count replied, "but he has forgiven me, and in all else I have sinned against you alone,—to you alone I owe reparation. You were ever a stern creditor,—no repentance, no entreaty, could move your indulgence. Well, Camilla, I cannot now undo what is done, but an accident enables me, at least, to avert the consequences of my injustice. An accident! But it is by my own choice that I make use of it. Listen."

He seated himself at the table before her sofa, and took out the papers which Xaver had given him. "These papers," he continued, "which have only been lent to me, and which I now place in your hands, afford the long-sought-for proof that your father, Carlo Bellarota, belonged to an ancient Florentine family of rank, which became impoverished in revolutionary times."

Camilla sat erect, and looked timidly and inquiringly from the yellow papers on the table to the Count's face. "These papers, Count Gleichenau, these papers,—and where were they discovered?"

"In the ancient palazzo of the Bellarotas, in Florence, in a secret repository behind the wainscot, that had to be broken open because the key could not be found. The key, Camilla, is in your possession."

"Mine?"

"You have your grandfather's missal,—we have often enough

turned over its leaves together. Upon the cover there is a medallion head of Christ. Have you the book here?"

She stretched out a trembling hand across the arm of the sofa to a little table whereon lay pictures, portfolios, and some books in rich bindings, and, taking up one of the smallest of the latter, she looked attentively for a moment at the head of Christ, still wearing the crown of thorns above its sorrowing brow, and then hesitatingly handed it to the Count, as if to ask, "Why do you want the book?"

The Count examined the cover closely, felt around the edge of the medallion, then suddenly turned and pressed it; it sprang open, and a key of curious shape fell out upon the table. "Right!" he exclaimed. "The description is correct. Who could suspect that the guardian of such important facts was concealed here? Too well concealed!'

Camilla had looked on in surprise, extending a warning hand when the head sprang open, as if she feared the ornamentation of the book were injured. She now picked up the little key, looking from it to its late hiding-place, and then at the Count. "But how did you learn——?" she asked, with an expression of the greatest surprise.

He told her of the discovery of the papers, and read to her some of the most important of them. "I begged Xaver to let me have them," he concluded, "because I wished to hand them to you myself. How priceless in value they would have been to us years ago!"

"Yes, yes, priceless in value!" she assented, looking over the manuscripts. "And now they are most important to me. They prove, beyond a doubt, that my father was no vain boaster, no liar,—that he really bequeathed to me an ancient name."

"I never doubted it," the Count observed.

"And yet——" she said, and paused. Her fine eyes, in which tears, a tribute to her father's memory, were glistening, grew dark and gloomy.

" My own belief, however, availed nothing," the Count went
on to say; "proof was necessary. The absence of this proof,
Camilla, was not the only reason why I separated myself from
wife and child to secure to my impoverished name the inheritance of a brilliant estate, although that it had weight with
me I do not deny. But of the other reasons I will not speak.
I cannot defend myself without accusing you, and I come here
now only as a suppliant. If the cause I have mentioned be
the sole or the decisive reason for my estrangement from you,
cannot your own pride in the name you inherited teach you
to deal leniently with me? Still, condemn me for my weakness, if you will; I cannot take advantage of yours. Only
believe the truth,—that I loved my wife and child even when
I consented to separation from them, and that what I now do
is in obedience, not to force, but to the joyful promptings of
my heart, although by my act one must suffer who is bound
to me by a near tie of blood."

Camilla listened with agitation. "I do not understand you,
Count Gleichenau," she said. " What do you propose to do,
and who will suffer by your act?"

" You understand me as little as Xaver understood me," he
replied. " Let me tell you how important these documents
are: they install your son—our son, Camilla—in all the rights
belonging to the eldest scion of the name of Gleichenau."

" Count Gleichenau," she exclaimed, "my son——?"

" Is the legal heir of all my estates of Gleichenau, since
my first marriage is now proved to have been a noble one.
Even if I would, I could not alter it now. I must have destroyed those papers, if I wished to secure the inheritance
to my second son. Kunibert knows what he must resign in
Xaver's favour, and does it most cheerfully."

With these words the Count arose. Camilla made a gesture
as if to detain him. " I cannot comprehend—I cannot——
Does Xaver know?" she asked, trembling with emotion.

" He does not know, because he has too little regard for worldly wealth to think of himself in this matter. He must learn his good fortune from the mother whom he loves so fondly. Tell him—no, he does not need the assurance—that his father rejoices in his joy."

Camilla arose, and held out her hand. " My son's rights are established," she said, with gentle dignity; " I can no longer frown upon his father."

He bowed over her hand, and pressed it to his lips. " Camilla, can you forgive?" he faltered.

" It was Xaver's entreaty," she replied, " and now—it is an easy task."

" Xaver's entreaty," he repeated, warmly; " yes, we should one day have been at peace through him, without these papers."

" Oh, if he were only here!" exclaimed Camilla. " If we could but tell him——"

The Count pressed the hand that he still held in his own. " I trust," he said, " that we three shall often be together in future. The spell that has parted us is broken,—we belong together. Will you exclude the fourth in our new alliance,—Kunibert?"

" Bring him to me," she said, hastily. " Xaver's brother shall be welcome, although I am not his mother."

The Count took his leave. " I must not beg for more for myself to-day," he said. " How much more calm and glad a heart I carry hence than I brought hither! But I shall come and go now every day, and every day will, I trust, bring me fresh hope for the future."

Camilla made no reply; but a gentle light in her eyes bade him take courage.

" Can this be I?" she asked herself, when she was left alone.

CHAPTER XXVII.

At an early hour the next morning Xaver presented himself at his father's.

It was a most unusual time for a visit from him; but the Count attributed it to a previous interview with Camilla, and went to meet him with a joyful face and open arms.

The Professor submitted to his cordiality, but hardly returned it, and there was so gloomy a frown upon his brow that his father feared some unforeseen misfortune had occurred. " Have you had bad news from Moritz Amberger ?" he asked, anxiously.

Xaver replied, No,—that Moritz had written that he had heard from Köstling's physician that the old man was ill, too ill to receive any one, and that therefore all further attempts to induce him to alter his decision were useless.

"That is to be regretted," said the Count; " but it does not explain to me your present mood. I thought you would be so light-hearted; or do you not know that my interview with Camilla yesterday paved the way for the happiest hopes for the future ?"

"I know it," Xaver replied. "I saw my mother last evening, and this morning again. I have just come from her. Certainly no one would more heartily rejoice at the happy issue of your interview than I, if——"

"If what ?"

"If a most annoying piece of intelligence had not spoiled my pleasure."

"What intelligence, Xaver ?"

"I have come to speak of it to you, father, before you take any measures which it might cause us all great inconvenience to annul. If you had told me what you meant, to do with those papers that have been found in Florence——"

" Oh, is that it?" exclaimed the Count.

" I was perfectly blind," Xaver continued, " or it never would have occurred to me to show those papers to you, to intrust them to you to give to my mother. If you could believe that I was actuated by a single thought of self-interest——"

" Make yourself quite easy on that score," the Count interrupted him, laying his hand upon his shoulder. " I assure you you have nothing of that sort to fear. I saw immediately that you had no suspicion of the importance of those papers to yourself, and I confess I saw it gladly. I should have thought you perfectly right had you come to me with the papers and demanded your rights; but I prized most highly, as a proof of your unworldliness, your want of all comprehension of their importance to yourself, and it enabled me to perform a duty as if I were bestowing a gift."

Xaver's face cleared up a little. " I thank you," he said; " but we have not done yet. You seem to be sure that you have only to give for me to take. No, father. I have been used, from my early youth, to depend upon my own resources, and I do not prize what I do not derive from them. Even my Freiherrship, to which I was born, is of little value in my eyes, and would be a great bore to me were I obliged to take it into the lecture-room with me. A man must grow up with such a title not to be oppressed by it. And now you would have me alter my whole plan of existence in consequence of a mere accident, while others whom I love are losers by it. It is asking too much, father. Because a young man called Philip Amberger entertains a silly enthusiasm for old curiosities, and carries it so far that he must tear down and transport over a hundred miles, to his own home, the entire wainscot of a room, and because, in doing so, a secret cupboard is discovered, where documents have been hidden, and might have

remained hidden to the end of time, if they had not been fer-
reted out by that mole, am I suddenly to be transformed into
another than the man that my education and inclination have
made me, and be transplanted like a tree or a flower? No!
Chance is an idol that I will not serve, and, so long as I am
free, will not worship."

"Chance!" the Count repeated, shaking his head. "Chance!
Do you not believe in a Providence that shapes our ends, and
brings about, all in good time, results scarcely to have been
hoped for, and never foreseen?"

Xaver smiled. "I will not make Providence responsible
for the short-sighted acts of mortals. What is neither reasonable nor necessary I prefer to attribute to chance, and neither
reason nor necessity has anything to do with the finding of
those papers."

"Then all laws of inheritance rest upon very insecure foundations," the Count interposed.

"You cannot force my privileges upon me," Xaver maintained; "least of all such entirely unjust privileges. I have
induced my mother to return those papers to me,—they really
are not safe in her hands,—and I shall take good care that no
one, even of those most dear to me, shall prevail upon me to
found any claim upon them whatsoever."

The Count looked grave. "This is like you, as I have
learned to know you," he said, after a pause; "but can you
expect that Kunibert will be behind you in magnanimity?
He has already been informed by me that yours is the elder
and the better right. Do you suppose that he will consent to
take advantage of your refusal to claim it?"

"He must!" Xaver replied. "There is no way of forcing
me to produce the proof of my capacity to inherit Gleichenau;
his mere affirmation has no legal weight. He might resign
also, but only in favour of some other branch of the family.
That would be folly. He must not forget that, to secure these

estates to his family, his father sacrificed, for many years, the repose of his conscience, and embittered his existence, while broken hearts——"

He paused, and the Count turned away.

" And it stands to reason, is not his right the elder and the better ?" Xaver continued, more earnestly. " He was bred to it from the cradle ; he has been conscious of it as long as he can remember thinking and feeling ; it is part of his life. If he is deprived of what is thus native to him, he will languish like a plant deprived of air. No ; I will not rob him !"

" Magnanimous as ever," the Count rejoined ; " but if Kunibert be what I think him——"

" Let me speak with him," Xaver begged. " He is reasonable, and will not refuse to listen to a sensible view of the matter. I have another reason for my conduct ; you shall admit that it is self-interested ; it has had some weight with my mother. I love Katrine Amberger, and desire to make her my own as speedily as possible. She gave her heart to Professor Schön-rade, and did not refuse to love the Freiherr von Höneburg, since her mother thought him a more suitable match. But the Majoratsherr Count von Gleichenau would be no mate for her, the daughter of a merchant, whose ancestors were of patrician but never of noble rank. My Katrine would be in constant dread of sharing my mother's fate. She could not enjoy her happiness for a single day."

The Count bit his lip, and looked down. " I never thought of that," he said, after awhile.

" But I have !" Xaver exclaimed. " As I feel to-day, the entire estates of Gleichenau do not weigh a feather against Katrine's love."

" You are not like your father," the Count observed, with a smile ; " you would always feel so."

" ' Lead us not into temptation,' " the Professor said, seri-ously. " No, no, we can none of us be sure of ourselves.

Could you have distrusted yourself when your whole heart was filled with the girl whom you loved? Time changes all that is mortal. It is well to think and hope the best of ourselves; but let us, at least, with the innocence of the dove, not forget so much of the wisdom of the serpent as shall teach us to avoid snares and pitfalls. And then, in sober earnest, for whose benefit should I force all my inclinations? I myself have more than enough for my wants, and my children could never inherit Gleichenau. Are the years of sorrow endured by my mother and yourself to bear, as their bitter fruit, only one more disappointed life? Do not ask me to support this burden. Let us have peace among ourselves at last; it can only be secured by ignoring these miserable papers."

The Count wrung his son's hand, and, without speaking, led him into Kunibert's room. "He is right," was all he said, as he left the brothers alone.

Of course, since Kunibert was sixteen, frank, generous, and excessively fond of Xaver, a very stormy scene ensued. There were asseverations, entreaties, and even tears upon his part; but Xaver maintained his composure, let the boy rave till he was tired, and came off conqueror at last, by consenting to receive, for a time at least, a certain portion of the revenue of the Gleichenau estates. The Count, who was called in as a witness to this final arrangement, declared, "If Camilla is only content, my happiness is now complete."

Camilla's pride had found it difficult to surrender the new-found documents to her son, with the distinct understanding that, in his possession, they were to be again consigned to obscurity. Her reconciliation with the Count had been effected through her joy at their discovery, and she was now called to rest content with being the mother of a son who might assume all his inheritance if he only would. She loved him too tenderly to acquiesce readily, and there was still too much irritation in her heart against the Count not to grudge to his son by his second marriage that which was not lawfully his. But Xaver was so resolute that she felt it would be useless to rebel; she must yield with the best grace that she could, and since she had braved so many sorrows in life with an undaunted front, it was hardly worth while to succumb now.

She did not at first attach as much importance as Xaver did to his view of Katrine's future. It is a weakness of human nature, from which she was not free, to forget to measure the sorrow of others by one's own in like circumstances, and to credit them with an immense power of endurance and self-sacrifice. There had been a discussion. almost amounting to a dispute, between mother and son. Xaver had not hesitated to say all that he could to make her look at the case from his point of view, and her passionate nature had been severely tried. When Xaver left her, peace had been but superficially restored between them; but when he came again in the evening, she had had full time to reflect and consider, and the result was entire acquiescence in her son's views.

Of course this was accompanied by a radical change of mood. As a violent storm passes and leaves the skies serene and blue, so all that was fiery in her nature seemed to have exhausted itself, and to have given place to gentleness and benignity. Xaver found her sitting at her piano, singing one of her favourite songs, with true artistic enjoyment of the music. He stood still at the door, which he had opened softly, and applauded when the song was ended. He saw how it was with her, and it only needed the gentlest touch upon his part to restore between them the old cheerful confidence. As a reward, and to dispose her favourably towards Kunibert, he told her of their interview of the morning, and this had the happiest effect.

Thus there was nothing to prevent the Count and his son from paying Camilla a visit on the following day. All tacitly agreed to let bygones be bygones, and to accord the present its entire rights. The Count treated Camilla with the most respectful attention, refraining, although his former feeling for her had returned in full force, from any confidential expressions that might seem to re-establish their former relations,— judging it best that her trust in him should have time for growth, and that she in the mean while should give the tone to their intercourse. Kunibert at first approached her shyly, fearing lest he should be in the way, but, as Camilla received him kindly and cordially, he soon became all admiration and devotion. It seemed as if she wished, through him, to testify to the Count that all anger had faded from her heart, and that the boy desired to prove to his father his filial love and reverence by his attentive consideration for her. As Xaver and Kunibert were upon thoroughly fraternal terms, it could not but be that their parents found themselves united in their children. The greater part of the day they spent together.

Thus everything would have been all that could be desired, had not Amberger's affairs assumed a menacing aspect. Moritz's letters grew gloomier every day. Feinberg, he informed the Professor, was exhausting every means in his power to ruin him,—stirring up his friends among the civil officers to make complaint because, in negotiating the purchase of the tile-kiln and the meadow on the other side of the bridge, the purpose for which they were bought, *i.e.*, the erection of a railway-depot, had not been made public. The former owners of the property on the streets leading to the green gate demanded immense securities for their payment, and the mortgage-holders desired to foreclose shortly. At Feinberg's instigation, a society was in process of formation for "the preservation of historically famous structures of the ancient Hanseatic town," and old Dr. Sperling, the Recorder,—of course without any sinister design,—was doing his best to induce every one to become a member of it. There was talk of having the green gate restored after a drawing of the sixteenth century. A letter to Köstling, signed by many of the towns-folk, had been written, thanking him for his "loyalty to his native town in preserving untouched by selfish rapacity one of her most valued memorials," and, in conclusion, entreating him to resist with firmness all future efforts to deprive their beloved town of any of its antiquarian glory. Furthermore, there was talk of a petition to the government to forbid, in the interest of the public weal, any destruction of the green gate, which petition would doubtless find in other quarters of the town many signers, who feared that the new railway-depot might interfere with their trade. The green gate, but lately considered a stumbling-block in the way of traffic, had suddenly become a celebrity, the loss of which would be very detrimental to the town. Thus obstacles upon obstacles were heaped in his path, and he should be unable to maintain his position if something decisive did not shortly occur in his favour.

In his last letter Moritz mentioned a new cause of alarm. Old Köstling was suffering from a disease of the heart, which might terminate his life at any moment. He was apparently aware of this, and had deposited his will with the authorities. Very probably he had decided the fate of the green gate in this document, and if, as seemed likely, the obstinate old man had bequeathed to the town a considerable sum for the future preservation of the old structure, there was an end to all their hopes.

Schönrade thought this fear by no means unreasonable, but he could not confer at present with his committee, since Councillor Wiesel had at last yielded to his wife's entreaties and departed for Wiesbaden, accompanied by Mr. Fairfax and Lilli. A letter written to Mr. Fairfax was answered most cautiously, the Englishman assuring him of his steadfast friendship, "if only for Lilli's sake,—she would allow no disloyalty," but proposing that the whole affair should be postponed until the

fall, when they might try what could be done by legal coercion. Legal coercion! Just what the Professor wished to
avoid. The Councillor's wife must have benefited by the use
of the Wiesbaden waters, since she sent her regards to the
Freiherr von Höneburg, and a remonstrance for not "discovering himself sooner to his best friends."

Thus, as matters stood, the Professor might have gone to
Florence to the wedding, and even have remained there several
weeks, but, great as was his desire to see Katrine, he was possessed by a spirit of unrest quite foreign to his nature, that
prevented him from coming to any decision upon this point.
He could not determine to refuse the invitation, but painted
in the warmest words his longing to be once more with her
whom he so loved; still, he hesitated to consent to go, and
even asked whether the marriage might not be postponed.
How the position of affairs might change within a week or
fourteen days he could not tell, but, as is often the case with
very resolute natures, after he had honestly done his best he
could not believe in failure, but looked for something "to turn
up" that should justify his confidence.

Had this "something" happened, when one morning he
received a letter, addressed in a strange handwriting, demanding his sympathy, from a quarter whence alone he could now
hope for succour? Dr. Kreutzer, a physician, wrote that he
felt it his duty to acquaint him with the fact that he was
attending Herr Köstling, but that he had very little hope of
his recovery from his present attack of heart-disease, since
the patient persisted in aggravating his symptoms by constant
agitation of mind. Spasms and fever were the consequence;
he raved for hours at a time, and, although in his delirium it
was easy to see what was occupying his mind, there seemed
but little connection in his thoughts. He talked continually
of a sister named Camilla, whom he had lost, described most
vividly the contests between his ancestors and the Freiherrs

von Höneburg, asserting, however, that all enmity should be buried in his grave, and appealing, when he was questioned at all, to the testimony of Professor Schönrade, who knew all he had suffered. He had so much still to say to him, but he could not send for him for fear of troubling his mother; and then he would repeat perpetually the words " his mother,— his mother," more and more softly, until he fell asleep. " I learn," the physician concluded, " that you, my dear sir, paid him a visit and had a long conversation with him just before his present seizure. His old housekeeper declares that from that time he never left his room. Her suspicion that your visit was the cause of his illness is entirely unfounded, since it is merely the development of a disease from which he has suffered for many years, and which now manifests itself in spite of the determination with which he has struggled against it. At the same time, your interview with him, that must have been occupied, in spite of what Herr Amberger says, with the discussion of other subjects besides the green gate, has much to do with his mental agitation; and, at all events, you seem to be the only one cognizant of what occasions his distress of mind, and you are perhaps possessed of the power to relieve it. Two days ago I found him, to my great surprise, out of bed and seated at his writing-table. He was, he said, writing his will, that his peace with God and man might be concluded. I was commissioned to see it deposited with the suitable legal authorities. Since then he has been much calmer, with a less frequent recurrence of the spasms; but his strength is failing, and I fear that he will not live long. In my opinion, a visit from you would not be attended with the slightest danger to my patient, but might, on the contrary, tend to alleviate his sufferings. At all events, since he is evidently very desirous of seeing you, I have judged it best to write to you, leaving it to yourself to act as you shall think best in the case.

" Your obedient servant, etc."

Xaver hastened with this letter to his mother, who was greatly affected by its contents, and strongly approved his determination to depart by the next train, that he might be with the old man in his last moments. She trembled with emotion, and could not restrain her tears. " Make haste! make haste!" she said, as if he could hurry the moment of leaving. " I will tell your father. Oh, how guilty are we if he dies with no word to us of forgiveness!"

CHAPTER XXVIII.

WHEN, two hours afterwards, Xaver was standing upon the railway platform, Camilla suddenly appeared. He thought she had some farewell message to give him, and had brought it herself, but, to his no small surprise, she announced her intention of accompanying him. Her luggage was already attended to. " For days," she said, " I have been contemplating a visit to the house where, as a friendless orphan, I was so kindly received, and upon which I brought such sorrow. When you first told me of Köstling, I longed to hasten to him and entreat his forgiveness, but I was withheld by the thought that he might believe me to be actuated by a desire to promote your interests. Perhaps even now he may think me prompted by selfish aims, but I cannot delay any longer; his hours seem numbered, and I must not lose the few that remain. It would be a life-long regret to me not to see him again."

Xaver pressed her hand warmly. " It is like your own dear self, mother," he replied. " Even if the physician should forbid you to see him, you will never repent doing all that you can to retrieve the past. Yes, we will go together."

The train was not very full, and mother and son had a carriage to themselves. Their talk was affectionate and confidential; there were no longer subjects that must be avoided between them, and if their discussion still gave pain, the pain was wholesome, and Camilla did not spare herself.

The Professor established his mother at the hotel, and then went to confer with the physician, to whom he explained the relations existing between his patient and the strangers. Dr. Kreutzer, though he hoped for a good result from their visit, thought some preparation of his patient was necessary to prevent a shock, and they drove together to the Köstling house, postponing until afterwards any thought of introducing Camilla to the sick-room.

Schönrade remained in the anteroom while the physician entered the sick man's chamber.

After a few minutes he returned, saying, "I was right; you are welcome. I asked him frankly whether he wished to see you, and there was no doubt of his ready assent. Go in immediately, that he may not become agitated in waiting. I will pay another visit, and then return to see how he is." He ushered him into the room, and left him.

The two cats were lying on the window-sill, purring loudly; at the writing-table sat a Sister of Mercy, the nurse, engaged with some sewing. The bed had been placed with the head against the wall, so that it could be approached from three sides. The old man lying in it raised his head a little, and stretched out his hand towards his visitor. "You are kind to come," he said,—"to come on my account, the doctor tells me. I should not have dared to ask it."

The Professor sat down at his bedside. "I could not wait," he said, "until you were recovered, to express my hope that there is no serious danger——"

The sick man smiled sadly. "There is no need to conceal my condition from me," he said; "I am prepared for every-

thing, and, now that I see you once more, I have hardly a wish
ungratified."

The Professor advised him not to look forward to a fatal
termination of his present attack. Painful as the disease of
the heart was from which he suffered, the subjects of it frequently lived to extreme old age.

"Could I think that desirable?" Köstling gently replied.
"Do not grudge me death, young friend. You know that I
have lived too long already, and am a burden to myself and
others. Do not gainsay me. A man who has lived as lonely
a life as mine must attain self-comprehension at last, or he is
an incorrigible fool. For years I have lived only because I
could not die. Is the continuance of such an aimless existence to be desired?"

"But could it not be so filled," Schönrade asked, "as to give
it value in your eyes?"

The old man shook his gray head. "How could that be?
There are men, unfortunately, so governed by a single idea
that upon it the whole interest of existence depends. How
many have gone through an experience like to mine, and yet
in time their sorrow has passed away, and they have addressed
themselves anew to the building up of their future. He who
cannot forget what is irretrievably lost, is lost himself,—a man
to whom the whole world is but a reflection of his own diseased
mind. Such men willingly lay the weight of their woes upon
those in health about them; as they cannot get away from
themselves, they seek to draw others into their companionship,
to infect them with their disease. Why, at our first meeting,
did I relate to you the whole history of my sorrow,—to you,
the son of the woman whom it was my misfortune to love,
and who herself loved so unhappily? Believe me, I have reproached myself bitterly for so doing. How hateful I must
have seemed to you! And yet at that very time I felt my
heart drawn towards you,—Camilla's son! I had long since

forgiven her, and it was against myself that I raged when I thus tore open the old wounds. There are strange contradictions in us, that no reason can explain, and a sick heart——"

His face worked painfully, and he clasped Xaver's hand to his breast. Xaver returned its pressure most warmly. "You do yourself injustice," he said. "I should have misjudged you if you had not spoken, and if you spoke at all you must have said what you did."

"No, no!" Köstling replied, with a grateful look; "I lost then all the self-control I had so hardly learned; and so I could not bear to die without seeing you once more. Now I —can die."

"And I may tell my mother that you forgive her?" asked Schönrade.

"Forgive!" the sick man exclaimed, raising his voice; "what have I to forgive? That she could not love me as I loved her? It is true there was a time when it angered me, but if you could think that all anger against her had not long since faded away, it must have been because my vivid memory of her gave to my words a cutting distinctness. No, tell her that those years of my youth brightened by her sisterly love have been a precious gift to me, a gift that I would not resign even if, in exchange, the sorrow that succeeded them could be blotted out; that they have been the main stay of my solitary life, and that I should most surely think of her in my last hour with the same affection, even although I knew her happy in another's love."

Xaver's eyes were moist. "I thank you," he said. "My mother will find the comfort that she needs in your magnanimity. You do not know how bitterly she reproaches herself, how grieved she is by your illness, how gladly she would hear from your own lips that you have forgiven the ingratitude that she has so sincerely repented. If she were not afraid——"

He paused. The sick man had closed his eyes, and was

gasping for breath; his hand had grown cold, and seemed scarcely able to press that of the Professor, which lay in it. Evidently great caution was necessary to prevent a return of the spasms. Xaver stood motionless by the bed for a long while, until the invalid's breath came more and more gently, and he fell asleep.

Dr. Kreutzer was quite content with the Professor's report, and afterwards with the condition of his patient. " He is apparently much relieved," he said, " and will no longer dwell upon what has been troubling him. His life must needs be short now; all that we can do is to make his few remaining days as comfortable and happy as possible. Let me arrange a plan." He told the sick man that he had engaged another nurse for him, and that he must be prepared for the sight of a new face.

" Will not my visitor of to-day remain beneath my roof?" asked Köstling, and fell asleep, with a happy smile, when he learned that it should be so.

The next morning Camilla sat at the writing-table, in the Sister of Mercy's accustomed place, and anxiously awaited the old man's awakening. By the advice of the physician, she had some sewing in her hands, and a book lay open upon the table before her, that she might seem to be occupied as was usual with the attendant. The two cats were lying on the floor at her feet. The watch above the head of the bed ticked audibly.

At length Köstling coughed slightly, turned his face towards the window, and opened his eyes. The strange nurse did not startle him; and yet there must have been something about her that attracted his attention, for he lay for awhile gazing fixedly at her. Seen from his bed, the beautiful profile was sharply defined against the light background of the window; and there was a bluish lustre upon the waving hair. The picture was one to demand admiration, but it stirred strange memories,—it was unknown and yet familiar. He gazed at it, closed his eyes to see if he were awake, and then looked again. His face glowed with pleasure; he breathed more quickly; his hand sought his heart. Did he know whom he saw before him? did he still doubt? could he venture to hope? was there no fear of dispelling a delightful dream? or did he feel that he owed it to himself and to her to maintain his self-control? What were the thoughts passing in the mind of that man, weary and worn with the sorrows of his life?

Camilla had heard the cough, and, by one hurried glance, satisfied herself that he was awake. Her eyes were now bent steadily upon her book, but her heart throbbed to her very temples. She had so often determined how she would approach him, and what she would say; but now she was conscious of nothing save a vague feeling of anxiety. Although her eyes were downcast, she distinctly felt that Köstling was gazing at her fixedly,—that he was, as it were, photographing her picture on his mind; and she grew giddy, as one does when the photographer removes the cover from the glass of his apparatus and says " now!" For some seconds she lost all sense of where she was, and of the meaning of the moment. Years vanished, and she was once more sitting with the playmate and friend of her youth in his pleasant room in the Köstling house. Yes, it was the same room that had always been his, because he so liked the outlook upon the garden. She was roused by the low call, " Camilla!" and, not knowing what she did, she answered the familiar voice as she had always done, so many many years ago, " Lorenz dear?" She looked, and saw the old man half sitting up in bed, his pale face flushing, his eyes sparkling with delight.

"It is you!" he exclaimed. " It is really you!" and sank back among the pillows.

Camilla was herself again in an instant. She saw that he

must not be left to himself, but that any display of emotion on her part would agitate him. She went to his bedside, and, kneeling down, put her hand upon his arm, and said, gently, "You must be calm, dear Lorenz,—quite calm,—or I cannot stay with you; and I should like so much to stay. Will you not be perfectly calm?"

"I will, Camilla," he answered, in a faltering voice; "only stay with me."

"We need say nothing more to each other, Lorenz," she continued, stroking his hand. "We have both consigned all that troubled us to my son's keeping; his love has purified it, and returned to each only what can bless. I know that I need not ask for forgiveness, and you know that I have never forgotten my dear brother. Let us not say another word about it. Dr. Kreutzer will let me stay and take care of you if he sees that it does you no harm, and that it gives you pleasure. So be calm, Lorenz dear."

He gently smiled. "I have you again, Camilla," he said, "and it is as if I never had lost you. Ah, I never lost you,— you have been with me always. But to behold you once more with mortal eyes before I died was more than I dared to hope, and it makes life dear to me again."

"Do not talk of dying," she entreated. "Let us hope you will soon be well again."

"I have been ill," he replied; "but that is all over now. Let the end come when it will; I can face death or life with equal courage."

Camilla seated herself beside him, and he took her hand. Thus they talked together, like friends who have long been separated, and who have much to ask and to learn. Thus Xaver found them.

"Why have we lived apart so long?" Köstling asked.

The physician himself was surprised to find the old man's pulse so calm. "Your mother has a soothing effect upon him," he observed to Schönrade. "We may leave them together without anxiety. But you must not entertain the idea that this improvement in his condition gives any hope of recovery. A heart so diseased as his often ceases to beat very suddenly."

Two days passed without any perceptible change. By degrees Köstling learned everything concerning Xaver's relations with his father, even to the latest occurrences that had led to the Count's reconciliation with Camilla. On the morning of the third day, after an excellent night, the sick man began to speak of this again. Camilla would have talked of other things, but Köstling said, "I can hear it all without jealousy. I am really your brother once more, Camilla. If I had the disposal of your hand, and the Count sued for it, I would gladly place it in his. From all that I hear, he is now worthy of you."

Camilla was silent.

"It is strange," he continued. "I imagined that I hated the Count as I could hate no other man, and certainly I was filled with hostility towards him. But now that I know you reconciled to him, it is as if I partook of your gentler disposition of mind. I cannot think unkindly of him any longer. And—shall I tell you all?—it seems to me that I must place the seal upon your forgiveness of him, that it may be full and complete, and no jot of rancour remain between you. Yes, yes! I should like to clasp his hand once more in this world, that the last spark of enmity between the two houses might be extinguished, and Xaver's inheritance be perfect peace. I should like it."

Camilla consulted with her son. It was agreed to telegraph for the Count. The next night he arrived, and the morning afterwards Xaver announced his arrival to his mother and his old friend. "We have been talking together in my dreams," the latter said. "Bring him to me, and tell him that I know all there is in his heart; he must trust me."

Half an hour afterwards Xaver led his father to the old man's bedside. The Count was much agitated, and could with difficulty suppress a passionate entreaty for forgiveness. Köstling's hand, too, trembled, and his voice faltered as he said, " Let us close the book whose pages are inscribed with the enmity of centuries. I wish to leave this world in peace, and I will take it with me to lay it down before the throne of God. And that the cause of the last conflict may be blotted out, and wrong be made right, receive Camilla from my hand, Count Gleichenau. For the first time, she will be truly yours." He beckoned Camilla, who stood, much agitated, at a little distance, to approach, drew her towards him, kissed her, and placed her hand in the Count's. " Be once more what you were," he said, gently, " when love united you. God bless you—as I do—from my heart—from my very heart——"

His words grew fainter and fainter ; at last his lips moved only in an indistinct murmur, and his head sank forward upon his breast. Xaver had thrown his arms around him to support him; he felt the old man's weight become heavier, and he laid him gently down upon the pillows. The dying gaze sought Camilla, the failing fingers clasped the hands that he had united in his own,—and the heart ceased to beat.

For some minutes profound silence reigned in the room, broken only by a sob from Camilla. Then the Count turned to her, put his arm around her, and said, " Will you understand his request to us? Camilla, will you honour his last words?"

She burst into tears, and threw herself upon his bosom. Xaver embraced both. " Mother ! Father ! Through conflict to peace !"

CHAPTER XXIX.

LORENZ KÖSTLING was gathered to his fathers in the family vault in the church-yard of the old Liebfrauen Church. His coffin was followed to the grave by half the town. Moritz and Lena appeared among the chief mourners; they walked side by side, and every one now knew that they were betrothed.

A few days later his will was opened. It consisted but of a few lines. Camilla was the heiress of his wealth; a handsome legacy was left to the town, and his old housekeeper was recommended to Camilla's care. The fear lest there might have been a clause directing the preservation of the old family structures was entirely unfounded.

" He had forgiven before we were aware of it," said Xaver; " this will, drawn up before my arrival, is an undeniable proof of his magnanimity. Thank God, no one can accuse us of influencing his testamentary dispositions !"

" And the green gate?" Moritz asked, who had been not a little anxious on that score, although from delicacy he had hitherto refrained from speaking of it.

" It now belongs to my mother," Xaver replied, "and she certainly will but carry out the wishes of the deceased if she removes from mortal eyes this memorial of ancient enmity."

" Let the inscriptions and carvings be first carefully preserved, to be placed beside our friend's coffin," said Camilla. " All that then remains of the old gate is yours, to do with as you think best."

This was the end of their troubles. The gate could be taken down, the street could be opened; the great railway-project was assured, and Moritz Amberger held his head high again on 'Change. Feinberg felt he was vanquished, and gave up

Q*

all opposition. There was a rumour that he intended leaving the town for a distant city, where his future son-in-law was to be his partner in business. It was thought that the latter needed to be closely watched. Frau Feinberg and Sidonie remained in Berlin, where a magnificent house was purchased, that the young couple were to take possession of upon their marriage.

Moritz Amberger undertook to conduct the affairs of the projected railway and put them all in working order. " Let me show now what I have learned, and of what I am capable," he said to Xaver. " You can go to Florence, where your heart already is, with perfect safety."

Old Vogelstein was induced to remove with his daughter and granddaughter to the Köstling house, as steward of Camilla's rich inheritance. Lena's outfit, also, could be much more easily provided in town. Camilla, the Count, and Xaver showered gifts upon her. " Do not make it too easy for my Moritz to marry a poor girl," she said, gaily. Her mother was in an ecstasy. " Dear child!" she exclaimed; " she deserves it all for her brave father's sake!"

" Pray make haste," Moritz begged, " that our marriage may not be long deferred. Of course we must wait for my mother, who has not yet even bestowed her maternal blessing upon our betrothal. But let the marriage take place as soon as possible after her arrival, and there shall be a merry winter in the old Amberger mansion! Philip and his young wife, and I and my young wife! If the Herr Freiherr von Höneburg-Schönrade and his young wife will but spend Christmas with us, there will be jolly times indeed!"

" Höneburg-Schönrade!" Xaver exclaimed, with a laugh. " I like the combination; it shall surely be engraved on my next visiting-cards. What do you think of the Countess Gleichenau-Bellarota?" he whispered in his mother's ear.

" For shame!" she whispered, in return. " As if I could be married from off the stage!"

Every day Xaver grew more impatient to be off for Florence, whither he would have departed already, had not Camilla expressed a wish to accompany him,—without, however, seeming in a great hurry to arrange the preliminaries. At last Xaver declared that Philip could wait no longer, and the time of his departure was fixed. That very day the Count and Camilla had a long *tête-à-tête* conversation, after which the Count took counsel with his son with regard to " a most important matter." Xaver left him with a cordial grasp of the hand and an assurance that all should be prepared.

The Count then returned to Berlin, to attend to various formal arrangements and to bring back Kunibert. In the mean while, Xaver announced that he wished to take actual possession of the Höneburg. He took a corps of workmen thither with him, and returned forty-eight hours afterwards, declaring that his castle was now ready for the reception of guests. " And I desire to invite you all," he said, " to spend to-morrow with me. My mother, my father, and my brother, who are to arrive to-night from Berlin, Moritz Amberger and his Lena, friend Vogelstein and his daughter, and, lastly, Dr. Sperling, who knows more about the old castle than all the rest of us together, with the pastor of the Liebfrauen Church, who spoke so touchingly at Herr Köstling's funeral. These last-named gentlemen I shall drive over myself; carriages will await the others at the Amberger and Köstling mansions. I pray you all to come in festal array."

It was a glorious morning; the sky down to the very horizon was as clear and blue as if no clouds could ever veil it ; the air warm, but not sultry. The occupants of the carriages rolling through the green gate and across the bridge looked down into the ditch where, on the gravel-paths, the lonely old man in the blue coat was no longer to be seen. Over the beds and through the bushes the two cats were scampering after the birds,—they were now Lena's especial care ; on the moor the larks were carolling gaily; on the tow-path some boatmen were dragging a skiff along the river by a long rope, its red pennon hanging limp at the mast-head. When the road near the ruins grew narrow and uneven, the guests descended from the carriages, and went the rest of the way on foot to the garden.

As they entered its precincts, a flag fluttered out from a flower-wreathed flagstaff, on the summit of the old watch-tower, and from the lofty platform around it floated down the notes of a hymn, played by a band of wind instruments. A triumphal arch of flowers was erected over the stone door-posts of the garden gate, and there was another inside the court-yard, while all the path to the house was strewn with roses and green boughs, and the windows were hung with wreaths and festoons of green. It was a beautiful sight.

Xaver received his guests at the old fountain, embracing most fondly his mother, who was greatly agitated, and then clasping his father's hand warmly, without speaking. He was almost overcome at the thought of all that had here transpired between these two, so dear to him.

He conducted them within the house, and when, after a quarter of an hour, they appeared again in the court-yard, a delicate wreath of flowers rested lightly upon Camilla's black hair. Xaver conducted them along the flower-strewn paths to the lindens by the old wall, beckoning to the rest of the guests to follow. There, above the old altar-stone, a mimic chapel of greenery had been erected, and within it stood the venerable clergyman in his surplice, waiting for the pair who now knelt before him. Xaver laid his hand upon Kunibert's shoulder, and Moritz and Lena stood arm-in-arm.

Again the notes of sacred music floated down from the high tower,—a most touching sound; and then the clergyman spoke, reminding those present how lately they had stood beside an open grave, to which had been consigned the mortal remains of a man who had suffered much during his life, but who had left the world at peace in his heart with those who had done him great wrong. " To-day," he continued, " we are about to fulfil his last and fondest wish, to obey his injunction, to forget as he forgot, and to remember only as he remembered. At this solemn moment let his spirit, the spirit of peace and love, hover about us and consecrate our thoughts. Through conflict and struggles you have attained peace ; he in whom your love was strong has reunited you,—the son to whom you gave life enriches your own fourfold. In memory and oblivion then let there be solemnized, not a new union, but the confirmation before these witnesses of the old one, and let it be so strong that an eternity shall not suffice to dissolve it. God grant that this may be !"

He then performed the marriage ceremony, and laid his hands in blessing on their heads. The music from the tower completed the solemnity.

No one liked the idea of going within-doors on such a glorious day. A table was spread beneath the old linden by the fountain, and here the guests enjoyed the marriage-feast which the lord of the castle had prepared for them. " We will return here in the autumn," said the Count, " when Xaver and Katrine, Moritz and Lena, celebrate their double marriage, and we will pass some quiet weeks here. Shall we not, Camilla ?"

She assented. " If Xaver does not need the house."

" Oh," he exclaimed, " there will always be room enough here for you."

" Then, Moritz," said Lena, with a pretty little pout, " what is to become of your promise to buy the castle ?"

" It is such a step from the town," Xaver rejoined ; " and a Professor, you must remember, does not have very many holidays."

The same evening the Count and his wife departed for Florence with their two sons; but they travelled too slowly for

Xaver's impatience, and he left them at Munich, to hurry on to his Katrine, from whom he had been separated for what seemed an interminable length of time.

Ah, what a meeting it was! Frau Amberger placed Katrine's hand in the Freiherr's, remarking, with a self-satisfied smile, that she had always thought the Professor was somebody. Philip presented his Lucia. " It was an exceedingly clever idea of ours," he said, shaking his friend's hand, " to leave the choice of a hotel-conveyance to chance !"

" But," the Professor replied, in a warning tone, " suppose you had said eleven instead of twelve ?"

" I cannot," said Philip, " suppose that I could possibly have been so stupid."

Not long afterwards, a happy party were sitting again around a table at a marriage-feast, this time not beneath the open sky, but in the spacious dining-hall of the Palazzo Bellarota. Signor Uccello did the honours with great dignity. When the champagne was sparkling in the glasses, Xaver called his Katrine's attention to the decorated ceiling. She looked up, her fair hair almost touching his black curls, and with his glass he described in the air the circlet in the decoration above them. " Look! Do you not see," he said, " that we have fortune's wheel in our escutcheon ?"

She laughed a low, happy laugh, and, looking across the table, he met Camilla's tender smile.

THE END.

Milton Keynes UK
Ingram Content Group UK Ltd.
UKHW010716280324
440307UK00004B/201

9 783385 387263